Carol Wensby-Scott was born and educated in Brighton, Sussex. She used to run an antiquarian bookshop before giving her full time to writing. Her first novel, PROUD CONQUEST, was published in 1979. She carried out much of the research for this novel about the Percy family in Northumberland.

Carol Wensby-Scott

Lion of Alnwick

Volume one of the Percy trilogy

Futura
Macdonald & Co
London & Sydney

A Futura Book

First published in Great Britain in 1980
by Michael Joseph Ltd

This edition published in 1983
by Futura Publications, a Division of
Macdonald & Co (Publishers) Ltd
London & Sydney

ISBN 0 7088 2339 4

Reproduced, printed and bound in Great Britain by
Hazell Watson & Viney Ltd, Aylesbury, Bucks

Futura Publications
A Division of
Macdonald & Co (Publishers) Ltd
Maxwell House
74 Worship Street
London EC2A 2EN

1357–1358

'*The royal egle . . . that with his sharpe look perceth the sonne*'
—Chaucer

It was not yet noon but already the sky was dark and the growl of thunder from beyond the Cheviots heralded the coming storm. The horsemen paused beneath the scatter of trees that would be their last shelter before Berwick. The man riding in the lead stood in his stirrups and squinted into the distance; a short squat ugly little man who looked as if he were carved from the granite hills that reared at his back. He twisted in his saddle and grinned ferociously at the man who rode in their midst.

'Berwick, Your Grace,' Lord Percy announced mockingly, 'and freedom.'

David Bruce, King of Scots, said nothing. Freedom? To do what? Return to the bleak poverty-stricken Scottish court and at a price that would cripple him for years? He glanced around him as they moved away. This was the threshold of his kingdom: a desolate tract of barren waste, a no-man's-land of burnt and arid soil where nothing lived or grew. The scars of the last devastation were barely healed, the scattered stones and charred stumps of levelled cots skinned over with peat moss and here and there, on the higher ground, a brave patch of green showed through the scorched and trampled earth. He had heard it said that once the valley had been lush and green, the river banks crowded with the huts of salmon fishers, the level meadows scattered with hamlets and farms. He could never remember it as anything more than it

5

was now, ugly and bleak with the blackened shapes of England's fortresses marching west along the Tweed. Yet perhaps if you looked closely you could see the ghosts of wasted fields, the sudden rise of ground that might have been a farmstead, the ridged shadows of a long-dead orchard. A long time ago, before his time, before Edward Longshanks had cast his greedy covetous eyes on Scotland. The Hammer of the Scots they had called him and in truth, he had ground Scotland into the very dust. A fair land had been turned into a black smoking desert overnight, burnt and stripped and plundered till Edward of England had sat at his ease in the palace at Scone.

Edward had bullied and bribed John Baliol out of his uneasy kingship and named himself Lord Paramount of Scotland. The Scots had had other names for him: tyrant, murderer, butcher, violator of the Holy Church. They had prayed for a miracle and found it in his father, Robert Bruce, Lord of Annandale, Earl of Carrick—also tyrant, murderer, butcher and violator of the Holy Church: a fitting match for Edward Longshanks. But he had dragged Scotland up off her knees, wresting her back inch by inch with an army of ragged kilted savages who could march thirty miles a day on a scoop of water and a handful of raw oats. They said that Fortune always favoured the underdog and in the year 1307 she had delivered an unlooked-for gift into Robert Bruce's bloodstained hands. The Hammer of the Scots had beat out his last stroke on a hot July day near Carlisle, and if the Bruce had shaped the old king's successor with his bare hands, Edward of Caernarvon could not have been more to his purpose. Lecher and pervert who whored himself to pretty boys and who was ready to plunge England into civil war for love of one. Every dog has its day and his father's had been Bannockburn. The glory of it lived with them still; thirty thousand Englishmen slaughtered like rats, cut down or drowned as they fled from a rabble army one third of their number. Roxburgh, Edinburgh and Stirling, the prize, had fallen like ripe apples into Robert Bruce's hands. And that had been just the beginning. England was turned inward upon itself on the verge of civil war and by the year 1330 mourned a murdered king. Another Edward, a boy of fourteen, had been the cipher by which the French murderess Isabella and her paramour

6

Mortimer had ruled. Queen Isabella had been eager to buy peace at any price, even to ceding all the disputed lands and Edward Longshanks's claim to the overlordship of Scotland. He himself had been part of that bargain, a husband for Isabella's seven-year-old daughter Joanna, a flesh and blood seal on his father's hard won peace. He had been four years old then.

He swayed drowsily in his saddle, his mind dulled and somnolent with memory. Twenty-nine years ago, thirty since his father had died and he had been crowned King of Scotland, more than forty since Bannockburn. He smiled wryly to himself. At least he was Scots enough to keep harking back to that. There had been other names since: Dupplin Moor, Halidon Hill, Neville's Cross where he had been captured eleven years ago; a long and shameful string of defeats and humiliations that had eaten away all that his father had achieved. The truce had barely outlived his father by six months. A boy-king of five years old and an inept Regency had been too much of a temptation for English and Scots alike. Edward III had grown into the mirror of his grandsire and it had not been hard to stir up old feuds. The son of old John Baliol had been the first to take the bait, reviving the old rivalry between Bruce and Baliol, all under Edward of England's approving eye. He had reminded those lords uneasy under the rule of a child that Robert Bruce had usurped the throne from King John. It had all begun again. Less than five years after his death, the divided loyalties that the Bruce had laboured so long and hard to weld into one strength were split asunder. Greed, envy, thwarted ambition, all the tried and tested weapons of the English king's armoury; it was these that had broken Scotland more surely than any army he could have raised.

David Bruce remembered the strange sense of relief that had swept over him when the news had come that Edward Baliol, with an English army at his back, had been crowned King of Scotland. So the wheel had come full circle. Edward of England had a Baliol under his thumb again, a puppet king to be jerked this way and that at his pleasure; a grateful king well aware that if it were not for Edward of England he would be no king at all.

And for David Bruce it might have ended there, living in comfortable exile in Paris, his bleak unwanted kingdom forgotten amid the beauty of the Ile de France. If Baliol had not shown himself so clearly the King of England's man; if Edward himself had not overplayed his hand and forced the surrender of Edinburgh and Dumfries; if his name had not been Bruce and carried with it all that lost splendour.

He had been seventeen when they had brought him home. His arrival had weaned away the last of Baliol's fairweather supporters and he had scuttled back across the Border into the arms of his mentor. He had been king again and with no more taste for it then than he had now. He had suffered five empty stilted years of petty skirmishes and broken treaties until he had led his army to that final crushing defeat at Neville's Cross eleven years ago, almost to the day. He'd acquired a taste for luxury since then; for the silks and tapestries that adorned the halls of even the minor English lords, for women that smelt of roses and lilies instead of sweat and woodsmoke, for good food and wine. In eleven years he'd become more of an Englishman than King Edward himself.

They were within sight of Berwick, a pyramid of roofs and spires crowded onto the long outflung arm of land above the shining width of Tweedsmouth. The key to Scotland and in English hands for the last five years. *Berwick and freedom.* His mouth twitched in sudden bitterness. He knew the freedom they offered him, the brief transient freedom of a hunted beast. Freedom, but on Edward of England's terms. It would need only one slip, one independent moment of thought and he'd be hauled back like an errant child. He shivered, suddenly cold with fear, not of his captors but of the freedom that would soon take the place of his comfortable captivity.

The rain came as they reached the town, blind heavy rain that rattled on their armour and swept the gutter filth down the steep narrow streets. David Bruce slowed his horse to Lord Percy's command as they reached the steep tortuous path that climbed the headland. He tilted his head back and peered through the rain. England's banner hung wetly from the keep: the leopards of England and the lilies of France. He smiled, a grudging envious smile that did not stretch his mouth out of line. Of course, Edward had other interests now, other crowns to cast his greedy English eyes upon. David Bruce had seen the booty that had come

8

back from the French defeat at Crécy, more jewels and plate and gold than could ever have been found in all of Scotland. He had heard of the slaughter and devastation too. It was strange that it pained him more to think of the quiet fields of Normandy ablaze than any of his own cities. He was fond of France. It was the only time in his life he could remember being happy.

They waited while a man lumbered from the gatehouse and raised the iron grille. He held his breath; an hour, less than that, and it would be done. He would be free.

He looked round at the faces of the men who closed him in, faces he knew even better than those of his own lords. Clifford of Westmorland; Umfraville, Lord of Redesdale and Earl of Angus. Lord Percy and his son he marked especially. Hereditary Lords of Northumberland, Lords Warden of the Marches, Keepers of Berwick Castle, Guardians of the Border—the ancient and bitter enemies of Scotland. He could not remember a time when there had not been a Percy on the Border. It was a Percy who had hounded his father to the Isles in the days of Edward Long-shanks; another who had led the slaughter at Halidon Hill and burned Annandale black for the sheer pleasure of hearing the screams of men being roasted alive. The man who stood beside him now had led him in chains from the defeat of Neville's Cross and had been his gaoler on that long humiliating ride to London, parading him like a trophy through the streets of Westminster. For eleven years Henry Percy had led him back and forth between Berwick and London when King Edward had deemed it politic to let him out of the Tower. Now he was to lead him home. He stared with burning dislike at the too familiar face: the coarse pitted skin, brown and hard as tanned leather, the fleshy nose and mouth seamed by a wound from a Scottish axe. He could not have been more than forty years old but the deep lines that clamped his eyes and mouth gave him another ten. There was nothing about the youth at his side to mark old Percy as his sire. He was tall, a full head and shoulders above the old man, a courtier by his clothes and the damascened breastplate that gleamed dully beneath his sodden cloak. His yellow hair was dark with rain and the arrogant jaw rough and golden with a night's growth of beard. A strong cruel face that bore the

9

unmistakably Plantagenet stamp of his mother; an English face, a Percy face.

David Bruce looked away as they rode through the dark tunnel of the gatehouse. Different men, different faces—but all English, all with the same look; the cold unquenchable hatred passed from father to son, hatred of him and his people and anything that smelt of Scotland.

In the Great Hall the bishops were already in their places. The Archbishop of Canterbury and the bishops of Carlisle and Durham for the English seated amid the sheen of damask copes and pearled mitres. The Scottish churchmen, plain and drab, sat in a wedge, and, across the hall, as separate and apart as if a wall stood between them, the Scottish and English lords faced each other.

Hal Percy took his seat behind his father's chair as John of Canterbury rose to his feet with an impatient shuffle of papers. His thin voice brought them all to silence, asking if all were present, all prepared to do their duty . . . 'on this solemn day, the third of October in the year 1357, and bear witness to the treaty made between the most high and puissant prince, Edward, King of England and France, Lord of Ireland. . . .'

The Archbishop's voice droned on, glossing the stark terms of David Bruce's release with ecclesiastical verbiage. A hundred thousand marks to be paid over ten years, twenty hostages of gentle birth to be held in England as surety for the payments, another three of the Scots nobility to be held as security for the keeping of the truce. The sudden angry murmur of the Scottish lords drew Hal's eyes toward them, yet for Edward this was generous and at this particular time he could afford to be magnanimous. France still trembled from the recent English victory of Poitiers and their king was an almost willing captive esconced in the luxury of the Savoy Palace as David Bruce had been in the Tower. That was always Edward's strategy, the softening of resolve with gifts and favours, shackling his enemies with English ties and loyalties till they were weaned from opposition by a life of ease. Hal looked along the ranks of Scottish knights and felt the tremble of outrage that ran through them. He picked out the

10

faces that he knew: Maxwell, Lindsay, Dunbar, and William Douglas, Lord of Annandale and Galloway, looking like a merchant who has paid too dearly for worthless goods. And one that held his eyes for a little longer than the rest, William Douglas's bastard brother, the man they called the Black Douglas. The name was apt, encompassing in a word the crow–black hair and the long angular face as dark and treacherous as a blackamoor's. His eyes were surprisingly blue and fixed with contempt on the Scottish king's back, remembering no doubt that his own father, James Douglas, had been led to London in chains rather than submit to an English king. Their eyes met briefly and the Scotsman inclined his head in stiff recognition. It was a hard bitter look that held a thousand unpaid debts and the promise of an early settlement. Hal smiled faintly. Here at least was a worthy adversary.

Then it was over. They were at peace and David Bruce was King of Scots in reality again. The parchment with its pendulous seals that curled under John of Canterbury's hand bore witness to it. Yet nothing had changed and the men who shuffled uneasily from their places had no illusions. This was for Edward of England's convenience; the ransom to fill his empty treasury, the truce to pursue the war with France without the fear of Scotland snapping at his heels. A breathing space for each to gather strength but no more than that.

Hal eased his damp cloak from his shoulders. The hall was hot and stifling now, thick with the dank smell of steaming cloth. His father would be another hour yet and he felt restless among the company of so many Scots.

Outside the rain had stopped and the cloud lifted enough to show a dim and grudging sun. Below the ramparts the cliff dropped sheer to the long fingers of piers and wharves prodding the soft mud of the estuary. The tide was out, ebbed to a thin silver foam around the narrow headland and the sand flats were crowded with wading birds that pecked and fought for lugworms among the marooned and heeling boats. He stared broodingly across the shining sands. He had no time for peace. Peace was a void into which frightened old men and cowards plunged themselves. He was seventeen and he'd already tasted the dreadful

11

fascination of war. The glory of Poitiers still clung to him. He could conjure it up as easily as the remembrance of a fair woman: the scream of horses, the hiss and whine of a flown shaft, that strange mingling scent of blood and sweat and earth, the potent taste of raw wine and dust in his mouth. It came so close to him again for a moment that he did not hear the soft footfall behind him till it was almost at his back.

He whirled and his hand went instinctively to the small jewelled dagger at his belt. The Black Douglas smiled at him mockingly.

'Gently, gently, young Percy,' he said. 'We are at peace now.'

Hal drew in his breath. 'For the moment, my lord. Only for the moment.'

'And you would not always have it so?'

Hal moved so that he could see the Douglas's face before he answered. 'No more than you,' he replied quietly.

'No, of course not.' Douglas leant his arms on the rough corroded stone of the ramparts and turned his dark face toward him. 'It would suit neither of us to have peace for long, would it? The power of the Percys depends on defence of the Border. If there were to be a lasting peace then there would be no need for you and your kind. You would be just another of the lordlings who scrabble for favour at Edward of England's feet.'

The calculated insult brought a flush of anger to Hal's face. 'Then I could take the place so recently vacated by your king,' he flung back hotly.

Douglas laughed, a soft musical sound from deep in his throat. 'You cannot insult me though David Bruce,' he said. 'You can say nothing of him that I have not already thought myself.'

Hal watched the long impassive face cautiously. He knew that Douglas was baiting him; the fledgling and the hawk. He would be hard put to match a man who could give him ten years and more in experience. He said slowly, 'In England we would call that treason, my lord. Whatever else he is, he is still your king.'

'Aye, if we can keep him. I will concede your King Edward the victory there, feeding the Bruce's weakness for ease till the thought of Scotland turns him sick. There'll be little to spare for plate and fine robes with a ransom of a hundred thousand marks to find.'

12

'Then why pay it?'

'Because better a weakling for king than your Edward.'

Hal smiled to himself in the growing darkness. He'd found the rhythm now, the steady beat of a ball being bounced from hand to hand. It was a game, a game of words and wit, question and answer. 'Would that be such a bad thing?' he asked. 'Any son of David Bruce would be more English than Scots in blood.'

'In blood perhaps. But not in thought and custom.' Douglas turned to face him. 'If there were ever an English king of Scotland then there would be no Scotland. And remember, my fledgling lord, if there is no Scotland then mayhap there'll be no Percys.'

'Oh, there will always be Percys, my lord Douglas,' Hal said maliciously. 'There were Percys when the Scots ran in bare feet and rags. And you're little better now; a ragged pack of savages who feed on raw flesh and oats and never know when you're beaten.'

Douglas smiled. So he had a tongue in his head, this Hal Percy. And remarkable eyes that seemed to take their colour from light and mood, like ice water running over mossed stone; now green, now blue, and when the light struck them the amber flecks in their depths turned them to gold. His father had kept a young eagle with eyes like that; a wild treacherous thing that would tear a strip of flesh from a man's cheek before it was tamed. He looked away. He was growing fanciful. This was just another Plantagenet whelp cast in the rigid Plantagenet mould. Yet there *was* something else, something that might have passed unnoticed beneath the courtly veneer. But Douglas had a trained eye, a sixth sense that had kept him alive against the odds these past ten years. His skin pricked with sudden premonition. This man was dangerous.

He said very quiety, 'Don't crow too soon, my little cockerel. This time it is you who are the stronger. Berwick is yours but your Edward is greedy. Soon he will be away to France again and he will sap the north of her strength to fight his useless battles across the water.' He smiled. 'Then perhaps it will be Scotland who is the stronger.'

'Is that a threat?' Hal said and added with a flash of irony,

'Shame on you, my lord. To speak of breaking a sworn truce before the ink is hardly dry.'

'Truces have little to do with peace,' Douglas answered him wearily. 'It's a written consent between both parties for respite, that is all. Do you really believe that a seal on the end of a parchment could wipe out the fifty-odd years of blood that's been shed between us?' He raised his fierce eyes to Hal's face. 'It's the scribblings of priests and clerks who know nothing of war. But you know and your father knows that as soon as one Scots cow strays onto English soil the Percys will cry violation.'

'So Scotland is always blameless,' Hal sneered. 'The deflowered maiden. The raped virgin. Could you give me your word to keep your moss troopers from ravaging English villages as soon as there is a bad harvest or their cattle take sick?'

'No,' Douglas answered levelly. 'No more than you could give me yours to keep your men at arms in their garrisons when they are bored for lack of a woman.'

The rhythm faltered and ground into silence, the barren empty silence of insoluble argument.

'So it will go on then?' Hal said at last.

'Yes. It will go on. You and I. Your sons and my sons and their sons after them. *A l'outrance*, my young cockerel. *A l'outrance* and without quarter.'

'Till one of us has the victory.'

Douglas smiled. 'You think there can be victory out of this?' He shook his head. 'There can only be losers. Always, there will only be losers. The English will come and burn my lands, kill my people, rape my women. And after a space, when I have licked my wounds clean, I shall come across the Border and do the same to you. If you killed my son I should kill yours. Which of us would have the victory out of that?'

'So we shall always be enemies?' Hal said. Why had he asked that? Because he wished it might not be so?

'What else could Percy and Douglas ever be? We were born enemies and shall die such.' He smiled faintly. 'It is what passes in between that counts. If it were between us two, man to man, enemy to enemy, yours wits against mine—' He laughed out loud. 'Perhaps we might see a victor then.'

'Is that a challenge, my lord?' Hal asked quietly.

The Douglas's smile faded. 'Yes. You may take it as such,' he answered gravely. 'When the time comes. When you are a man.'

'Then I accept,' Hal said, though he was not even sure what Douglas wanted of him. The old fight; Percy and Douglas. He could understand that. But this was more. This was to be shared by him and Douglas alone. 'You might have a long wait,' he said.

'I have time enough,' answered Douglas. 'You forget, we have a ransom to pay and a milksop king to put to rights first.'

Hal smiled. Yes, it would keep. It had kept for sixty years, it could wait a while longer.

Lady Mary Percy sat in the wide embrasure of her private solar. The view that stretched before her was familiar almost to the point of boredom; a stretch of yellow trampled grass turning black in the shadow of the high curtain wall. Beyond that the bright thread of the river was the only relief in the endless curve and dip of moorland. Always the same, unchanging except in winter when the deep snow swept down from the north and shut them in for months at a time. She hated the Border, hated the interminable bleak hills and the chill dampness of walls that never seemed to warm through even in summer, the endless talk and threat of war and the stench of garrison soldiers. Most of all she hated the loneliness and the eternal wind that chapped and blistered her fine skin. Her beauty had gone, dried and shrivelled by twenty years in the north; the soft girlish dreams of her youth swept away by the reality of marriage to Henry Percy. She would be forty-two next spring—and it showed, in the fine dry lines that meshed her eyes and seamed the well-shaped mouth. Her hands were small and displayed her jewels to advantage but the bright golden hair had faded and she kept it covered with a velvet cap. Her gown was velvet, a deep Burgundy that enhanced the whiteness of her skin. It was not quite of the quality she would have liked, though that was not for any lack of wealth but because the best silks and velvets were always slow to reach the merchants at York and Newcastle. Not that her husband Henry would have noticed. Henry disdained the pomp and show of London and preferred sensible fustian to keep the cold out. She smiled her condescending little smile. Poor Henry, without an ounce of grace—yet in her way she had grown fond of him; more so since the distasteful task of sharing her bed with him had ceased. It had been a long time since there had been anything but blind duty between her and Henry.

She shivered, suddenly chilled by a gust of wind through the open casement, yet she hesitated to close it and shut herself in the yellow gloom of the thick-horned panes. Gracefully she rose, smoothing her skirts with her fine white hands, breathing the air that carried the damp river smell and plagued her lungs. It was quiet here at this time of day and almost beautiful with the last of the grudging autumn sun warming the lofty towers of Henry's new gatehouse: the harsh forbidding beauty of space and silence and of a kind totally alien to her.

The faint hiss of movement behind her told her that Thomas had come into the room. Thomas, her youngest son who moved with the stealth of a fox and whose smile unnerved her so. She turned slowly. He was almost halfway across the room, his face still in shadow but she knew its look. Quietly resentful, the vulnerability of his sixteen years not quite disguised by the pose of manhood. She smiled into his eyes, blue like hers, the only thing apart from his height that he had taken from her. All else was his father's; the shock of dark unruly hair, the flat aggressive features. Sly Thomas, Henry called him and in a way he was, always first to see a slight to himself, to notice that his brother had a slice more meat on his plate or that his cup was fuller. The childish rage that had always followed when Hal had bested him at this or that had become the quiet smile that disturbed her so. In her heart she did not blame him for it. It was hard to compete against someone like Hal. Everything always came so easily to him.

The rattle of hoofbeats on the timber bridge drew her swiftly to the window. Her eyes scanned the wind-flung banners before they dipped beneath the dark hollow of the barbican: Percy, Gray, Umfraville and Clifford and, held slightly apart, the scarlet saltire of Neville. She frowned. So Ralph Neville was here. She might have known that he would not miss the chance of licking the boots of the Duke of Lancaster.

16

Thomas stood beside her, his quick eyes reproaching her. 'Your father is home,' she said quickly and saw him smile; that familiar sneering curve of his mouth like the threat of a storm on a summer's day. She resisted the temptation she always felt to strike it from his face. She would not let him spoil Hal's homecoming.

She sat poised and remote above the roar of noise, her lineage written in the proud and haughty lines of her face: the great–granddaughter of King Henry the Third, descended from the French kings Louis and Charlemagne; sister of Lancaster and cousin to the King. None watching her in the crowded and noisy hall could fail to be aware of it.

She wore all her jewels. The heavy collar of sapphires that had been part of her dowry, the pendant of rose gold set with a diamond star. There were pearls in her hair and on her gown and each of the long fastidious fingers was ringed and heavy with gems. This was as near as she ever came to happiness—the noise, the colour, the laughter that drowned the sweet subtle hum of minstrels, the smell of good food and wine and the rare and coveted presence of her beloved brother Lancaster.

It was almost two years since she had seen him yet he was unchanged and still looking half his fifty-eight years. He was that rare breed of man whose loyalty and honour had set him above all criticism. For years he had poured his wealth into the always impecunious King Edward's lap and his generalship had brought France to her knees, yet looking at him now it was not so hard to recall the handsome young man who had spoiled and teased her and who was still so deeply and possessively loved.

All this was for him: the extravagance of twelve tuns of best Burgundy wine; the precious and seldom-used candles of Paris wax that blazed unstintingly from their sconces and filled the hall with light; the profusion of game and venison and the best of her salted meats. For once Henry had noticed and his eyes accused her from his place beside Lancaster. But she smiled and dabbled her fingers in the rosewater bowl as the steward bore in a subtlety of quince and sugared violets. Tonight she was above reproach.

Then Henry leant toward her and she averted her nostrils

delicately. He had not cared to change and he smelt of sweat and horseflesh. Her eyes dwelt resentfully on the length of snagged silk that trailed from his sleeve. His robe was none too clean, the facings of sleek russet fur spotted with grease. Henry's clothes were always dull and unkempt save those few that she chose for him and even those he managed to wear like a scarecrow. Sometimes she still marvelled at the incongruity of it. What demon of fate had prompted her father Lancaster to sanction such a coupling? She had wept when she had first seen him, wept and railed and screamed till they had summoned a priest for fear her mind had gone. Then duty and the sharp stinging slap of her mother's hand had smothered all. It was the King's wish and therefore must be hers. She had never wept since, even when her adored father had died, but she still sometimes dreamt of the Savoy, the palace outside Westminster that her father had built from the ransoms of captured French knights, where she had laughed and danced with the handsomest men in England and her father had whirled her high above his head and called her his Belle Marie. In her mind she would always be Belle Marie—Marie Plantagenet, daughter of Lancaster, sister of Lancaster. . . .

Abruptly she snapped the thread of painful thought. There was no point in harking back. She was Mary Percy now, Lady Mary Percy, yet even that was lacking. It could have been more, so much more if Henry had had the ambition. Her dowry and influence had already placed them at the head of the northern hierarchy. Her brother could have eased the road for him, a Garter at least, an earldom would not have been impossible. But it *was* impossible for Henry. He was content; his world went no further than the bleak empty hills that edged them in. He was Lord of Northumberland and that was enough.

Hal was different. Hal was Lancaster bred, raised on the promise of wealth and high office. She glanced lovingly toward him, the one compensation for her soured wasted life. His chameleon eyes were bright with candlelight and his hair gleamed the dull tawny gold of a young eagle: the mirror of her brother Lancaster and the point at which the empty separate lives of herself and her husband touched and became something more than duty. Her mouth tightened imperceptibly as Roger Clifford

18

came and lounged against his chair. The old lord's widow, the dowager Idione, was a Clifford and had already laid a solid foundation for Mary Percy's dislike of all her house. Clifford grew above himself, bolstered by his recent betrothal to the Beauchamp girl. Like all the Cliffords he was glib and coarse and shallow, Warwick's man now and proud of it.

She pursed her small mouth, her eyes skimming thoughtfully over the assembled faces. They were all here, any man whose birth entitled him to a place at her table, come to parade themselves before the most powerful man in England after the King. It was almost a pleasure to watch: the bluff good humour, the hearty laughter, the smiles—still smiling as they stabbed each other in the back. She had grown used to it now, like the stink of sweat beneath winter velvet, but she was never off her guard. It would not be hard to shift the delicate balance of power that held them all in their place. There was no law here save that which they made themselves, the unwritten law of might is right, the man who wields the biggest stick wins the day. Today that man was Henry Percy, tomorrow it might be Clifford or Neville. You could hire a man for twopence a day and livery and the towns were full of drunken, brawling soldiery whiling away the time till the renewal of the French war. It was easy enough to pick a quarrel. They all lived cheek to jowl within the vague disputable borders of custom and usage where possession was all of the law. Raiding was not the sole prerogative of the Scots. The savage gangs of moss troopers who lived wild in Redesdale Forest could as likely turn on their own kind if the pickings across the Border became slim enough. No man rode out after dark with less than a hundred men at his back. Life was cheap and death sometimes cheaper if there was enough to be gained from it.

Her eyes, suddenly hostile, roamed the tables and saw the predominance of Clifford's livery. He was the Percys' greatest rival for dominance of the north. His Westmorland lands, already vast, seemed to multiply with an insidious thoroughness. He already had a sizeable foothold in Northumberland and who knew what he could wheedle from his prospective father-in-law, the Earl of Warwick.

Gilbert Umfraville was there, swilling her best Rhenish as if it

19

were common ale—Earl of Angus and Lord of Redesdale, that small but infinitely desirable tract of land that flanked their own from Kale Water down to Simonsburn. Beside him sat his newly wed Countess, the sole heiress to the Lucys: plain and thin as a broomstraw but, with eight thousand acres in Annandale and a score of fat manors in Cumberland and Lincoln, there was more than compensation.

Henry Scrope sat between his sons Stephen and Geoffrey. She liked Henry, though less since he had wed his son Geoffrey to Ralph Neville's daughter Eleanor. But then the Nevilles had the knack of fortuitous marriage, wheedling their way into the highest families with skimpy dowries and pretty faces. And always young too. Ralph Neville never kept a mouth that needed feeding in his hall any longer than he had to. She watched him talking in his loud rough voice to Tom Grey, wincing as he showered her pristine cloths with morsels of half eaten food. He and Henry were two of a kind, rough unpolished Border lords who cared for nothing else. The marriage of Henry's sister Maud to Neville's son had rubbed the edges from the hereditary rivalry of their houses, but the uneasy friendship of the fathers did not extend to the sons. John Neville made no secret of his dislike and resentment of Hal. That he was here at all tonight was surprising. It must be all of two years since he had set foot under a Percy roof and that last time they had almost come to blows. She remembers his face as Hal had teased and goaded him into stammering red-faced impotence. Hal had the gift of words and could charm and repel at will. For John Neville he had always reserved the sharp searing wit that could reduce better men to helpless rage. There were other hatreds too. Neville's wife was a Percy and he had never attempted to conceal his resentment at being wed to a women eight years older than himself, and no beauty at that, who had managed only to give him daughters instead of the sons he longed for. She glanced to where he sat. He was older than Hal, with a habitual belligerence that somehow reminded her of her own son Thomas: handsome in a dark aggressive way, though his face was a little too fleshy and his eyes too small. Too good for Maud though. She'd not wish Maud Percy on any man, even a Neville. She smiled at the thought, but beneath the smile there

20

was a flicker of unease. John Neville had a special kind of ambition. There was not much he would not do to get what he wanted, especially if it were at the expense of a Percy.

Then the smile became complacent. Hal was beyond his reach, safe in the cocoon of birth and heritage that she had spun for him. She could rely on her brother Lancaster for Hal's advancement. Cursed with daughters, he had raised Hal as his own son. A pity though that the King's son John of Gaunt was to have his daughter Blanche. She'd once had hopes of Blanche for Hal— foolish hopes, for they were too close in blood and the King would never have agreed to let the vast Lancastrian estates pass too far from the Crown. But there was time enough. De Bohun's daughters would soon be of marriageable age, less to look on than Blanche but that was more than compensated for by the earldom of Hereford.

The discreet murmur of the steward disturbed her thoughts and she frowned, glancing round the tables. Her best damask cloths were a ruin of spilt food and wine, especially near the door where the garrison soldiers fed. She eyed them disdainfully as they prodded about in the dishes for a last morsel of food and wiped their fingers on their tunics. The only good thing about war was that it kept them occupied; now they would spend half their time roaring drunk, the other half fathering bastards on any wench willing to accommodate them for a shilling or two.

Reluctantly she nodded assent for the tables to be cleared and scraps to be fed to the hounds crouched in slobbering expectation beneath the tables. It was almost over, another hour perhaps before the company would be drunk enough to want their beds. And then tomorrow they would be gone, her brother and Hal back to London taking Thomas with them. It could be months before she saw them again.

Thomas had drunk too much and sat grinning fatuously at the exposed square of Elizabeth Scrope's bosom. He would bring up his dinner before the night was over, as he always did. She would miss him in a perverse way, if only for the pleasure of keeping him in his place.

Hal felt his mother's possessive gaze upon him and turned away. John Neville was also watching him, either him or his

21

father or Tom, as if he searched for some weakness that he could turn to good use. Then suddenly Tom grabbed his arm. He was half on his feet, his throat working violently. Irritably Hal grabbed his arm and steered him through the buttery door at the back of the dais and out through the kitchen. They had gone no further than the stabling block when Tom fell on his knees and retched against the wall.

Hal grinned with a secret indulgence he reserved for Tom and hauled him to his feet, walking him up to the cool air of the battlements. Tom sank down on the narrow walk, his stomach heaving, tears of humiliation starting in his eyes. He stared down into the blackness of the moat. Dark still water mirrored the high walls and towers behind him; he saw the pale blur of his own face between the crenellated stones, like a head waiting on the block for the headsman's axe. He spat and fell back against the wall and glared defiantly into his brother's amused eyes.

'You should stick to ale, Tom, wine is a man's drink.'

It was said teasingly but Tom felt the old childish rage welling up inside him. Sometimes he almost hated Hal, perhaps because he had tried so hard to be like him and fell so far short. Hal always made him feel so graceless. He was court bred, and it showed in the quiet richness of his dress and the quick silver speech that could tie him in knots. That was their mother's doing: only Lancaster's household would do for Hal; Clifford's had been good enough for him. But it was Hal who had secured him a place at court and somehow that made it worse, that he should always have to be grateful to Hal. But it was what he longed for, escape from the cold critical eye of their mother and the dreary north. There was nothing for him here, except the vague affection of his father and the inevitability of second place. He wanted more than that out of life.

He struggled to his feet, his head still spinning, and wiped his mouth on his sleeve. Hal, by design, was not looking at him but staring out into the darkness. Through the trees he could see the gleam of the silent river, and the soft contours of the moor that stretched from sky to sky. All Percy land, as far as the eye could see and beyond that. It would all be his one day.

'When father dies, all this will be yours.' Thomas's slurred

22

voice echoed the half-formed thought at the back of his mind.

Hal glanced at him sharply. Did it show so much, that dreadful lust for possession? It would all be his some day. But not yet, though he itched to take the reins from his father's hands, seeing with younger eyes the small everyday things that his father through close association missed: the stewards at Warkworth were slovenly and kept poor accounts; Topcliffe needed money if it wasn't to fall about their ears; and half their Yorkshire manors were becoming damp and uninhabitable through neglect. His father was too set in his ways, refusing to accept change or the fact that half the villages between York and Alnwick had been deserted and crumbling since the plague. Too much work for too few men and they clamoured for something better now than the mere right to eat and stay alive. If it had been up to him—he let the thought remain unfinished. Not yet. He could wait. He loved Northumberland but he loved his father better.

He swung round and regarded his younger brother with a mingling of affection and impatience. Though there were only two years between them he had never been so aware of it until now. But Tom would learn; a few months at court would set him on his feet, give him something more to think about than the petty imaginary grievances of a younger son. He smiled into his face, still pale but with the old belligerence back. 'Father tells me you have a new hawk,' he said in his soft voice. 'Come, show it to me.'

He had hit the right note. The mention of his birds or a fine piece of horseflesh could always rouse Tom from his sulks. They walked together towards the stabling block, Tom talking quietly about his new acquisition. The horses stirred as they passed and set up a whinnying, and the hound tethered outside the mew sprang to the length of his chain until Tom's voice quietened him. He unhooked the lantern hung outside the faulkener's hut and held it to the meshed cage at the end of the mew. The hawk's yellow eyes blazed suddenly in the feeble light, the bells strapped to her legs jingling softly as she moved back on her perch. Hal ran his eyes over the sleek lines of the close folded wings and the sharp spread claws. Tom knew his birds, all right. He had known him sit for hours in the mew, talking, coaxing, stroking their throats and legs with a feather, whistling soft and deep in his throat till they knew his call. Hal squatted down on the damp grass, careless of his fine clothes. 'She's a beauty, Tom. Where did you find her?'

Tom smiled at the words, his face alight with pride. He sat crosslegged beside his brother, keeping his voice low so as not to disturb the hawk. It was like old times, before Hal had gone to court, when there had been nothing between them but shared secrets and dreams, before the two years between them had stretched to an unbridgeable gulf. Hal was a stranger to him now, who kept company with kings and princes, who had fought his first battle, whereas he . . . . But all that would be changing now; they would be together again. He leant his dark head close to Hal and smiled his childhood smile, full of quiet charm. Sometimes he found it hard to hate his brother.

1358–1376

'Ther was the douve, with hir eyen meke'

—Chaucer

Margaret Neville sat quietly on the hard wooden bench, her back against the cold bare walls of her father's hall. She could hear his strident voice quite clearly even though there was almost a foot of solid oak between them.

'Gowns—new gowns?' His voice rose to an outraged bellow as it always did when anything touched his pocket. 'The girl's in mourning. What does she want new gowns for?'

'Dear God, the child's in rags, Ralph.' Her mother's voice was almost as loud. 'Do you want the world to think we are beggars?'

Margaret stared down at the tips of her worn and faded shoes. Yes, that might sway him. Mean and pennypinching he was, but he cared what other people thought. She rose, nervously smoothing the meagre folds of the dusty black gown as the door was flung open.

Her father came out and glared at her, his mouth tight in his heavy beard. 'Have you naught to do, madam, but stand and stare?' he shouted. 'If you stay under this roof you'll earn your keep. There's no place for idlers at Raby.'

Margaret said nothing and watched him stride off down the hall. She was used to being bullied; her dead husband William Ros had taken a particular pleasure in it.

She turned at the sound of her mother's heavy step. Alice Neville walked with the long purposeful stride of a man and the

25

added spring of a battle won. She had first claim on any luxuries that were to be squeezed from her husband, and her gown was of rich blue sendal edged with pearls. More pearls collared her thick neck and every finger of her large ungainly hands blazed with a jewel. She stared at her youngest daughter with vague irritation. Margaret looked like a nun with the white starched coif framing her face. Her gaze became critical: too thin, too meek and those great staring eyes.

'For God's sake, daughter,' she snapped. 'Must you look so martyred? You cannot go on grieving for ever.'

Margaret smiled suddenly, amused by the thought that any should think she had cared for William Ros. The drab widow's weeds were her only concession to mourning.

Alice Neville pursed her full mouth in surprise and approval. The smile was a revelation, warming Margaret's thin face and lifting the shadows from her soft grey eyes. She had forgotten what a pretty child Margaret had been. Her eyes measured her like a pig for market. If she was fattened up and decently gowned she might be quite a beauty. Her teeth were still good and at least she had not brought a pack of brats with her.

She laid her heavy hand on Margaret's narrow shoulder and smiled. 'All's well,' she said. 'You can leave your father to me.' Then her smile became a little strained as she met her daughter's unresponsive gaze. 'Will you not take a little air, child,' she said in her firm brisk voice. They would not find her another husband while she looked like that.

Margaret went eagerly, glad to escape that cold appraising look. She knew what her mother was thinking, what her father was thinking. She was an encumbrance, another unwelcome mouth to feed. They'd not keep her at Raby any longer than they had to.

It was almost seven years since she had been home. Nothing had changed, there was still the same remembered warmth of golden stone, the shining lake, the sprawling endless green of the deer park, the secureness of high walls ringed with water. The little bower down by the water's edge was still there, the cascade of moss roses in tight pink buds; once a place of dreams and secret thoughts. It was here that they had come to tell her that

26

she was to marry William Ros. She had been eleven years old then.

The stone seat was damp and filmed with yellow moss. A family of thrushes had usurped the corner where her brother John had once sat; the birds had long flown, only the ragged cocoon of their nest remained. All the Neville birds had flown: Margaret's brothers, William and Robert, to the free companies in France, Alexander into the Church. Her sister Katherine was Lady Dacre, Eleanor a nun at the Minories. Poor Euphemia was wed for the third time, to Sir Walter Heslarton. Only John had stayed and then only because he had to. But she had come back, the little sparrow with bruised and broken wings.

She stared out across the lake, watching the silver shadows of trout gliding beneath the surface dark with tangled weed. The old boat was drawn up on the far bank, it's hull rotten and crumbling. She smiled, remembering when she and John and haughty Katherine had rowed across. John had been red as a turkey cock, his miscast strokes showering them with water. Katherine had shrieked that her gown was wet, and from the bank Euphemia had howled in derision as they had spun in helpless circles. That had been her last summer at Raby. She had married William Ros in the following spring. She had wept all that day and for months afterwards. No more Raby, no more John—only the pimply faced boy of twelve that was her husband. She stumbled abruptly to her feet. She did not want to think of William. He was dead and she was glad of it.

She walked beneath the trees at the water's edge, stepping between the tall stems of loosestrife that grew along the path. A fish leapt from the lake in a shower of silver water. In the tall spiked reeds a heron screeched and beat the air with long white wings. A shadow darkened the surface of the lake. A young osprey circled above her, gliding on the wind, swooping so low that the still water mirrored its golden image. She watched it rise, beating the air with its strong wings to gain height. It circled once then dropped like a stone, the long pointed wings folded high on its back. The great curving talons skimmed the water and threw up a jewelled mist, then it rose, the struggling fish clamped tight between its claws, climbing in wide circles till it reached the

27

height of the trees. Then it was gone. The rippling lake was still again.

She stared at the empty sky as if to will the bird back into her vision. Would there ever be such freedom for her? To come and go at will, to take what she wanted with such ease? A dream, like the childish dreams of the rose bower. There were no more dreams now, no refuge from hurt, no freedom. Even the bird was not truly free. There were other, stronger birds—and men. Even now it might be falling with an arrow in its breast.

She did not hear the soft footfall behind her or see the tall shadow that fell across the path. Even when the loved and teasing voice fell upon her ears it came as an echo of her thoughts.

'Still dreaming, Meg? Did you wish that you could fly with him?'

She turned, her face alight with joy. 'John! Oh, John!' She flung herself into his arms and he whirled her round, knocking the severe little mourning cap awry. He set her down and pulled at the laces beneath her chin.

'Jesu, Meg. Take that hideous thing off. It makes you look a hundred.'

Laughing, she shook her hair free. It was long and thick and only barely escaped being black. Her brother smoothed it with his hand. 'You look thin, Meg,' he said gently. 'Did they not feed you at Hemlake?'

She smiled and covered his hand with her own. 'It's my spirit that's starved, John.'

He smiled back and drew her hand through his arm. 'Then we must feed it. Father will approve of that,' he added drily. 'Love costs nothing.'

They walked in silence for a while along the little sheltered path, thick with budding sorrel. She glanced up into his face and saw the discontent around his mouth. So nothing had changed for John either. He had breathed and eaten frustration for as long as she could remember. Their father was as grudging with his power as he was with his money. Even at twenty, John was kept well to heel, his youth and promise turning sour. They sat beneath the willow tree that trailed gnarled roots in the lake. John picked up a pebble and skimmed it across the water.

'What will you do now?' he asked.

She smiled wistfully. 'You speak as if I have a choice, John. What else can I do but stay here till father finds me another husband?' And that would not be long, she thought despairingly.

'You could take the veil, like Eleanor.'

He was teasing her but she answered him gravely enough. 'I think I'd rather do that than be married again to a man I did not love.' She raised her large grey eyes to his face. 'Is there no other way, John? Nothing else . . . ?'

Her voice tailed off into tears and he caught her hand, pressing it to his cheek. 'Don't cry, Meg,' he said desperately. 'We'll think of something.'

Irrationally she laughed. 'Oh, John. You sound just as you did when we were children.' She touched his cheek lovingly. He had always been her protector, finding words for her when her tongue had stuck to the roof of her mouth in shyness, adding his tears and pleadings to her own when they had married her to William Ros. He had not been able to save her from that, but his rare and precious visits had been her only joy in those long six years.

Her brother smiled ruefully. It was so easy to forget with Meg. In her heart she was still a child; tears to laughter, laughter to joy, following so swiftly one upon the other that he had never been able to keep pace. Perhaps that was why he cared for her so much. She had so little defence against the world.

He said thoughtfully, 'Old Umfraville's taken a new wife.' He paused before he committed himself too far. Meg would only be confused by uncertainties and then there was their father to think of, though it might even please the old skinflint. It would mean that he could be rid of her and still have the benefit of her dowry lands. He looked up into her expectant face. 'If I spoke to the Countess, if I told her, she might find a place for you in her household.'

'Oh, yes, John. Anything, anything.' She turned her lovely shining face toward him and he felt a sudden ridiculous unease. He had always thought of her as a child, the sad unhappy child he had always loved and comforted. Looking at her now he realized with a sense of shock that she had been a woman for a long time.

John rode with her as far as Durham. From there she and her small borrowed escort would go on to Harbottle alone. She had wanted it that way: an affirmation of her new freedom. She felt no regret about leaving John or Raby. They were part of the old memories, the old pain. Almost eagerly she led the old white palfrey to the brow of the hill. Below her the city sat like a jewel in the ring of hills, the facets of roof and tower gleaming in the morning sun, the needle spires of churches pricking an aquamarine sky, all dwarfed by the soaring beauty of the cathedral.

In the far distance she could see the haze of hills and bleak empty moorland that was Northumberland. She could feel the sting of the north wind upon her face. She thought of the young osprey circling above the lake, the sun upon its wings. Perhaps she might fly with him yet.

There was a rowan tree down by the river, old and gnarled, its branches twisted to serpent shapes, its slender leaves scorched to a premature gold by the wind. Margaret had watched it bloom from hard green shoots, she had seen the tender white blossom fall and drift downstream to Holystone; now the first of the berries showed raw and green. It was September.

A raven watched her from the topmost branch, its glossy wings half spread for balance as a gust of wind tossed its slender perch. There was always wind in Northumberland, howling down from the Cheviots with rain and thunder at its back; sometimes gentler, laden with the smell of peat and heathered moss, but always there, a dull accepted roaring in her ears.

She curled herself on the damp river grass and looked out onto the jewelled landscape: the amber glow of moorland, the emerald and amethyst of purpling heather, the topaz of gorse and the diamond thread of streams and burns. To the north the dark granite hills soared into opaline cloud: The Cheviot, Hedgehope, Comb Fell and Bloodybush Edge veined with the drove roads into Scotland, falling westward to Auchope Cairn, the Schil and Windy Gyle where the Wardens met on truce days. At their feet the sombre green slopes of Redesdale Forest were flecked red like a bloodstone. Serene, sparkling, almost peaceful in the autumn sun. Deceptive as a sleeping child, for the grim black fortress behind her was the last before Scotland, the monstrous sire that had spawned the tall peel towers that crowned every knoll from Harbottle to Rothbury. She had counted sixteen in all, each with its own alarm bell and a fire pan in the roof. Umfraville's steward had told her that it was a rare sight in winter to see the flames leap from tower to tower. She had heard all the old tales, sitting in that great comfortless hall with its draughts and pervading smell of dogs and horseflesh. October was the prime month for raiding, when the cattle were sleek from summer pasture and still loose on the hills. Then they would come, savage bare-legged hordes mounted on shaggy unshod hill ponies, come to fill their empty bellies; brutal and well-drilled bands of moss troopers come to loot and kill, and once the Bruce's army had burnt a path through Redesdale as far as Newcastle. But only once, Umfraville had been quick to remind them. The Lord of Redesdale was very conscious of his charge.

That she disliked him was more for her mistress's sake than her own. He was graceless, a destroyer of beauty, a sot who could drink himself into a stupor and still be found with his head on the board in the morning. There was an essence of William Ros in him that filled her with fear and disgust.

She turned at the plaintive call of her name. Dame Isobel leant from the terrace walls bleating like a sheep. It must be late. She was always late. It had earned more than one reprimand from Dame Isobel.

She was waiting, plump arms folded beneath her ample breasts. 'In heaven's name, Lady Ros! What have you discovered at the bottom of the river that you can stare into it for hours on end? If you wish to contemplate, then the proper place is in the chapel.' Her small eyes dropped in heavy censure to the damp hem of Margaret's skirt. 'Come,' she said stiffly, 'the Countess is waiting for you to put up her hair.'

Margaret looked as chastened as the grimace of the postern guard behind Dame Isobel's back would allow. Isobel, if haughty and unforgiving of the fact that Margaret outmatched her both in rank and looks, was harmless. She bullied everyone, even the Countess.

31

Margaret followed her beneath the low arch and up the twist of worn stairs where the cressets' flame laid black spears of soot on the walls. The long tunnelled passage at their head was cold and bare; plain slabbed granite oily with damp, the grudging light of arrow slits filtered through eight feet of stone. She thought suddenly of Raby and the glow of golden stone. There were no graceful archways here, no smiling heads leaning down from the corbelled roof, all was plain, serviceable and ugly; like the man who was its lord.

Countess Maud was sitting with her eyes closed, listening to the twelve–year–old Elizabeth Seaton reading from *The Romaunt of the Rose*. She opened her eyes and smiled as Margaret came to stand behind her and whispered her apology.

'No matter, I have been well entertained,' the Countess said, and her smile widened to include the little Elizabeth Seaton. 'An old song, but given a certain freshness by our Master Chaucer, would you not say?'

Her voice was Maud Umfraville's one beauty. It had the liquidity of music, a resonance that brought each cadence to a soft and perfect pitch of sound and feeling. She used it as most women used their eyes. She turned back to the mirror, lifting her hair free from the nape of her neck. The dark eyes beneath the plucked slanting brows were dispassionate and looked back at her without criticism or interest. Her pale skin needed colour and her mouth was a little too wide. It was a sharp clever face that looked older than her eighteen years.

> 'For this trowe I, and say for me,
> That dremes signifiaunce be
> Of good and harme to many wightes,
> That dremen in her slepe a-nightes
> Ful many thinges covertly,
> That fallen after al openly.
> Within my twenty yere of age,
> Whan that Love taketh his corage
> Of yonge folke . . . .'

She sang the words softly to an old courtly tune, glancing up as Margaret scooped the glossy hair back from her face. 'Do you dream Margaret?' She laughed and answered her own question, 'But yes, of course you do. Of love and fair knights in shining armour . . . .'

'I dream of contentment, my lady,' Margaret answered with a little smile. She was past all other dreams now.

The Countess shuddered. 'One man's dream is another's nightmare,' she said. 'Contentment would be death for me. Nothing to strive for, all ambition gone.'

Margaret threaded a silver pin through a coil of hair. 'And when all your ambitions are fulfilled, what then?'

The Countess's mouth softened. 'Then I shall strive for my sons and their sons. If a woman has children then there is no end to ambition.'

Margaret smiled uncomprehendingly. Her only ambition was to be safe and loved. She knew and wanted no other. What else was there of any worth except love?

The hall at Harbottle was a man's hall, as its lord was a man's man. The Countess had done her best to transform it; the hangings were from her castle at Cockermouth, the plate and silver from Langley, and the set of carved oak chairs her brother Anthony had brought back from Italy. But Umfraville preferred his comfortable squalor and there were still piles of harness and rusty mail on a bench by the door. The hounds still fought among the rushes for greasy bones and her husband's prized gyrfalcons maintained their lofty perch behind the dais and showered the wall with their droppings. But tonight he had conceded a little ground and exchanged the greasy leather jerkin he had worn for a month for a tunic of red velvet. It did little to enhance his mottled skin and unkempt beard but at least it was clean.

The company was large and in high spirits: the visiting Marcher lords replete and pleasantly mellow, the rowdy garrison in the first flush of a noisy drunkenness that would rise to its ultimate crescendo in an hour or so and fade by degrees to a slurred mumbling and final oblivion. The meal had been long and quite sumptous for Harbottle: fifteen courses and the best Rhenish any man had ever tasted. But then Umfraville could always be relied upon for his wine. The fish might be badly

33

cooked, the mutton a little ripe, but the wine was always good and there was always plenty of it.

The talk was of war or lack of it. Scotland lay impotent as a gelded bull and France held back while her king—addressed by Edward as 'our dear cousin of Valois', but stripped of his title and liberty—got drunk daily at the Savoy.

Umfraville took a mouthful of the spiced malmsey he preferred and sucked it appreciatively through his teeth. 'What news from court, then? I hear the Frenchman drinks his ransom money daily.'

Hal Percy smiled. 'He was sober enough when I saw him last, and green with fright. The King presses him heavily.'

'You think he'll sign this treaty then?'

'Oh, he'll sign right enough,' Hal said. 'In the end.'

'And then we shall all be at peace,' Roger Clifford said with his handsome mouth full of raisins. 'With nothing better to do but tend our manors.'

'And pray for another war,' Hal added drily.

They all laughed, the warm conspiratorial laugh of a secret shared. All bred and raised for nothing else, war was life's blood to them, a necessity. The identity of the enemy was of little consequence.

'I doubt if the Scots will last the course,' Clifford said. 'Robert the Steward is none too pleased with the restoration of the Bruce.'

'Why should he be?' Lord Percy picked at a rough nail. 'He's been king in all but name for the last eleven years while David Bruce sat on his arse at our expense. Robert the Bruce was the Steward's grandfather. He's almost as good a right as David Bruce—some might say better, if it were ability not blood that counted.'

Hal for once was silent, letting the discourse flow around him. He thought suddenly of the Douglas. He had seen or heard nothing of him since that day at Berwick. He wondered if he still remembered his promise. Then Clifford touched his arm.

'And will France capitulate as easily to Edward's demands?'

'Lancaster says not. Even if his father signs the treaty there is not much chance that the Dauphin Charles or his counsel will agree.'

'He'd be a bloody fool if he did,' Lord Percy grunted. 'Half of France given up without a blow being struck and for a halfwit king that they would be better off without.'

They all agreed on that. Edward's price as always was high, a ransom of three million gold crowns and a third of western France from Calais to Gascony to be held by Edward free of all ties and fealty. And in exchange Edward would cede his empty title of King of France. No wonder the Frenchman baulked at it.

'Then what's the point?' Umfraville demanded bluntly. 'If the French won't agree to it, what's the point of the treaty?'

'If the Frenchman signs and the Dauphin and his ministers refuse to keep the terms, then King Edward can claim violation. We'll have right on our side and that French Pope sitting at Avignon can no longer whine about persecution. Edward will cry forsworn and be fully justified in pressing his claim again with the added security of King John as hostage.'

'It's a pity that the King cannot make up his mind whether he'd be king of Scotland first, or of France,' Lord Percy observed. 'If we'd kept hold of David Bruce we'd have Scotland well under our heel by now.'

Umfraville scowled, thinking of his lost earldom. Scotland should have been their first priority. Under the first King Edward the border had stretched as far north as Edinburgh. All that was gone now because the King could fill his pockets better in France. He nodded drunkenly into his wine. France was all right for boys like Hal Percy looking for glory. But land was the real treasure, good solid land that could hold its own against ransoms and booty any day. He squinted down to the far end of the dais. His Maud had brought him a fair parcel of it, enough for him to suffer the evil tongue that could flay a man clean to the bone when she had a mind for it. He watched her rise, thin as a broomstick and twice as hard. Praise God, he thought, she was going to her bed and taking her mealy–mouthed clutch of women with her. He took a long draught deep into his throat. Christ, but that old hag Isobel had enormous breasts. His first wife had been like that, big breasts and thighs, a breeder too. Three sons and a daughter had slid from those broad hips with the ease of a bitch in whelp. And he'd outlived them all. He stared mournfully into his wine. A man had to have sons. What was the point of it all if a man didn't have sons? But he had Maud now; she'd give him sons, though God knew she had little pleasure to give him.

Beside him Hal toyed with the stem of the gilded cup, turning it idly in his hand. Silver fish plashed in a blue enamel sea, their fins pricked out with gold. Strung out around the rim there was the word *Souvenance*. He set the cup aright and allowed the slovenly page to fill it but he did not drink. He was bored and hot and sick of the stench of Umfraville's pig-swill knights. He watched them staggering in one another's arms, singing, swearing, rolling beneath the tables with the dogs. Then he smiled ruefully, remembering that there had been times when he had been little better himself; the nights when he and his cousin John of Gaunt had slipped across the river to Southwark and fallen out of the Tabard hardly able to stand, or had greeted the dawn from the warmth of a whore's bed. Those times were gone now. They had both outgrown the pleasure of whoring and John had become suddenly chaste since his betrothal to Blanche of Lancaster. But there were always women, virgin and chaste, lusty and wanton and sometimes a delicious combination of both. There was a little maid in Arundel's household, soft and golden as a ripe peach; Hal smiled at the thought of her, and the tawny flecks in his eyes grew imperceptibly larger remembering the soft insistent pressure of her body against his in the dance at Windsor.

He glanced to where his father dozed over his wine. The old man missed Thomas more than he would admit though he doubted if he would have recognized his youngest son now. Tom had changed since he had left the north. He was taller, his eyes quieter, and he wore Lancaster's livery as if it were cloth of gold. He had found his own friends, men of war, hard-bitten soldiers who were more at home in the mud of a battlefield than the king's court. Tom thought and talked of nothing else. It was in his eyes, the longing for the dreadful savage joy of battle, the certain release of all his frustration in one swift deadly blow to an enemy skull. Tom would make a fine soldier one day.

Then a voice like a silver play of chords arrested Hal's thoughts. He turned his head. The voice always left him unprepared for the disappointment of the Countess's face but he smiled

36

and carried her hand to his mouth. Crone or maid, he treated them all the same. His eyes drifted on past her face to the women who trailed behind her, the old dame plump and red as a turkey cock with a skin of wine inside her, a child who all but slept on her feet—and there his gaze stopped and held. Her face was half turned away from him, her eyes unknown shadows, but he could see the soft hollow beneath the pearled bone of her cheek, the full mouth drooping with tiredness into a wanton curve. Then she turned and looked full at him. The sad grey eyes engulfed him and he saw the flattering colour stain her cheeks; a child's face, innocent as the white marble virgins that gazed down from the niches of a church. He smiled, the slow tender smile of possession and saw the answering curve of her mouth before she turned away.

Umfraville followed his gaze and grinned. 'So you've taken a fancy to the little widow, have you?'

Hal smiled thinly and steeled his ribs against the sharp invasion of his host's elbow. 'Who is she?' he asked.

Umfraville leant close and favoured him with a blast of his rank breath. 'Margaret Ros, the widow of that snot–nosed Yorkshire knight who got himself killed on some fool crusade or other.'

'*Marguerite*.' Hal spoke her name in the French manner. 'Like the flower.'

Umfraville leered at him with the long ridged teeth of a dog. 'Widow or not,' he said, 'I can't see John Neville letting you bed his sister.'

Hal smiled his slow lazy smile. So this was Neville's daughter. It was an obstacle, but not insurmountable. For him it was the chase, not the kill, that mattered.

In the large and airy bedchamber, Margaret unlaced the Countess's gown and let down her hair. The wine and the heat of the hall below had made her head spin and the room seemed bathed in its own jewelled light. Her cheeks were touched with rare colour and her eyes had a brightness that had not been there before. She stroked the tangles from the Countess's hair and stared at their joint reflections in the sheet of polished silver. The Countess was smiling.

'Still no dreams of love and fair knights?' she asked teasingly. Her lovely voice recalled and held the moment. Margaret remembered the sweet honeyed taste of wine in her mouth; the blur of azure velvet, the linked serpents of Lancaster, the gleam of tawny hair and eyes. Ridiculously she thought of the young osprey she had seen above Raby. But eagles did not stoop to sparrows. She knew who he was, Northumberland's heir and Lancaster's indulged nephew. He would have his sights set on sleeker prey than her.

'I doubt if he even saw me,' she said wistfully.

The Countess's voice sharpened. 'Jesu, do you always have to be so humble? I saw the way he looked at you.' She laughed suddenly, seeing Margaret's stricken face in the glass. She was quite lovely in a sad, fragile way, she thought. Like brittle glass, ready to shatter at the first unkind blow. 'I'm jealous, *doucette*,' she said gently. 'I wish he had looked at me like that.'

Then they both spun round as the door crashed open. Umfraville lolled against the wall and Margaret swallowed in disgust at the look of him. He was drunk and his beard was stiff with spilt wine and food. Her jerked his thumb at her.

'Out, wench,' he shouted. 'Get to your bed and let me get to mine.' He grinned and spat onto the pale silk rug. 'Let's see if my lady can give me a son.'

Margaret glanced at the Countess but she had averted her face. She raised her hand in a faint gesture of dismissal, 'Yes, go,' she said. 'I shall have no more need of you tonight.'

Margaret ran. As she passed Umfraville she could smell the sweat and the sour wine on him. She felt tears burn her eyes. The world was full of Umfravilles. Men like Hal Percy were only a dream.

The fair at Elson was a noisy reeking labyrinth of tents and booths sprawled in a noxious haze by the river. Merchants bawled from rickety canvas stalls crowded back to back along the meadow; cordwainers selling long-snouted shoes of Spanish leather, poulterers with attendant flies, a draper's stall stacked head high with bales of Holland cloth and green Lincoln wool. There was a spice booth, a scented cave hung with cinquefoil, where pepper and raw ginger merged with ambergris and myrrh into a throat-burning pungency; stalls that sold ribbon and lace and yellow brass pots; steaming trestles piled high with hot sheeps' feet and slabs of gingerbread; a gaudy tent that housed a man with two heads and seven fingers to each hand.

Margaret abandoned a string of amber beads reluctantly. Ahead of her Dame Isobel and the Countess elbowed their way from stall to stall, expounding on the rarity of sugar, haggling over an odd length of tarse silk, chivying the grooms who trudged behind them already laden to the eyes with twelve pounds of tallow wax, a brass pestle, a bolt of purple Lenten cloth, three ivory combs, a pair of silver gilt buckles and a sticky parcel of dates and figs.

She moved on through the glare of garish colour with the wide excited eyes of a child. There were acrobats, wrestlers and tumblers, ballad-mongers with reeds of parchment sticking from their sacks like quivers full of arrows; cheapjacks and pedlars, a quack hawking bull's blood and urine as a cure for flux, and a pardoner with enough fragments of the True Cross to re-roof Westminster Hall. The noise was deafening—barking dogs, the drowned desperate wail of pipe and tabor, the shrill jackdaw cries of the hucksters who thrust hot crumbling pies beneath her nose. She pulled up doubtfully before a curtained booth lurid with stars and grotesque signs, and a voice close to her ear whispered, 'Save your penny. I can tell your fortune for nothing.'

She knew him even though she had never heard his voice before. She turned and looked up into his eyes. They were green as jade without the light on them, solemn, staring, at odds with the smile that curved his mouth. And she could think of nothing to say, even though in her mind she had danced with him, held him, kissed him every night since she had first seen him.

He took her arm. 'May I walk with you?' He led her down to the river's edge. It was quieter here with the bass drone of cattle and the soft cacophony of caged birds. She watched as an oriole dashed its yellow wings against the bars of its cage. There were so many; drab, silent little nightingales, tiny gold crests with their breasts dyed scarlet, cushat doves with sleek grey plumage and flushed pink throats. On impulse Hal bought one, laughing at her solemn face as he put the little cage in her hand. 'For the colour of your eyes,' he said softly.

They were selling horses from a wattle enclosure and he lifted her onto bales of warm hay so she could see. He leant beside her; their faces were close, his hand brushed her arm. She made a pretence of watching the horses. A soft-gaited palfrey with a hung belly that had seen better days. . . . Sweet Mother, say something! He must think you a halfwit. A shaggy Welsh cob with velvet eyes. . . . Ask him how the Grace of Lancaster does—no, how the Queen does. Oh God, ask him anything!

Then he said, 'Are you cold? Your hands are trembling.'

'Yes, a little.' Fool—with the September sun burning your back?

'Then I must warm you.' He lifted her hand slowly to his mouth, kissing her palm, her fingers, the throbbing little pulse at her wrist.

She could not move or speak and her heart had slowed to such a sluggish beat that she thought it might stop. He raised his head and the sun stripped the colour from his eyes and left its image.

'*Marguerite*,' he whispered. '*Comme la fleur, ma fleur Marguerite*.' He kissed her, a kiss of slow expert passion that had her lifting her arms to his neck before she knew it.

'Forgive me,' he whispered. 'I should never have done that, not when there are eyes to see.'

She slid her arms from his neck and smiled. She would not have cared if the whole world had seen.

He leant back against the pillar of hay. It was just as well that there were eyes to see or he could never have held himself. It usually took more than a kiss, but this kiss had been laced with all the visions he had had of her: naked in wet moonlit grass; between perfumed sheets, her hair spread on silken pillows. He closed his eyes on the agony of frustration. He *had* to have her—but when? How? Tomorrow he would be eighty miles away in Leicester. He turned his head and watched her. Her eyes were closed, her mouth turned in a faint secret smile. A tendril of dark hair spiralled against her neck. He felt almost a sense of shock that it had come this far: one kiss yet they were already lovers. And he had not even had to woo her. Quietly he said, 'I have to leave for Leicester in the morning.'

She opened eyes dark with disappointment. 'Till when?'

She's like a child, he thought. Every feeling reflected clear as glass in her eyes. 'Christmas,' he answered and felt his own heart lurch. Three months. Sweet Christ! He could not wait three months. He took her hand and laid it against his mouth. There was only tonight. He could ride to Harbottle after dark. They could meet by the river, beneath the trees where the grass was long and slicked with wind. Oh God, the breath was tearing at his throat as if the thought was already the deed.

Her voice quietened him. 'The Countess Maud said that the King is to keep Christmas with the Duke of Lancaster. I know that she intends to spend a week at Leicester.' She smiled hesitantly. 'She is bound to take me with her.'

He smiled into her eyes. Three months, three months was not so long and the pleasure would be all the sweeter for waiting. He knew Leicester like the back of his hand. There were bowers and walks and shadowed galleries and such a throng of people that they would not be missed for hours. He lifted her down and held her deliberately against him for a moment. 'Till Leicester then,' he whispered and kissed her again.

Away from him the magic faded. The breathless joy was gone, the dream diminished and tainted by the thought that it would all pass and she would be left as dry and empty as before. The old self-doubt assailed her. He must have thought her raw and graceless—and so she was. She had never been to court; she had never even seen the King, and all she knew of men and love were the times when she had lain passive and disgusted beneath the weight of William Ros.

There had been others for him, she had known that from the practised touch of his mouth. Had they succumbed so easily and gladly? She remembered the kiss with shame. She had been so eager, greedy and hungry for more. Jesu, but he must have thought her an easy kill! She thought of his eyes: the lake, the sun upon the water and then only the sun. He had wanted her then. She had breathed it, tasted it until the need had become her own.

41

And that was the worst of it—for her the need was still there, unsatisfied, growing, as fast as the hope of its fulfilment faded. It could all have been a dream but for the cushat dove.

It watched her now with its round black stare. She had never set it free as she had meant to. Perhaps when she knew, when she came back. . . . She smiled as it cooed at her. She had set the cage by the open casement and the wind ruffled its feathers into snowy peaks. 'When I come back,' she promised, 'I'll set you free then.'

She laid the last of the Countess's gowns reverently in the sandalwood chest. In two days they would leave for Leicester. In two days she would see him again. The beading on the velvet surcoat rattled in her hands. He might not even acknowledge her—or worse, there would be the tight strained embarrassment of a moment best forgotten. For her it had been everything, for him it might only have been the passing of a bored hour.

She went quickly through into the small chamber she shared with Bess Seaton. She looked around at the two narrow virginal beds, the carved box that held her combs and trinkets; her three gowns hung on their poles, two of sensible Lincoln wool that she had brought from Raby, the other a rubbed, cut-down velvet that had been her mother's. She saw the pattern of her life stretching before her as clear as the road that dropped down to Holystone. This, or living at Raby on her father's grudging charity, till he found her a husband who was not too demanding over the matter of dowry. Another William Ros? A man like Umfraville?

She heard the sound of footsteps and hastily wiped her tears. Little Bess Seaton burst through the door in an abandoned whirl of skirts. Her face was pink and bursting with excitement.

'There's a messenger come with a package for you.' She giggled, choked, wiped her chin and drew a deep tantalizing breath. 'From Leicester.'

Margaret stared at her. 'Where is it? Give it to me. Oh, for heavens sake, give it to me!' She snatched it from behind Bess's back. It bore his seal, a lion rampant gorged with a crescent and the silver label of the eldest son. Her hands were trembling, fumbling, tearing at the canvas wrapping like a thing demented. Oh, Jesu, she was going to cry again.

42

It lay glistening in her palm; a marguerite, the petals pale slivers of opal, the golden heart clustering topaz. She could hardly read the little strip of parchment for tears.

Marguerite. Comme la fleur. Mais plus belle que la fleur.

She was laughing, weeping, whirling poor Bess around the room till they were both sick and dizzy. It had all been for nothing; the tears and uncertainty, the shame and reproach, all vanished now, dissolved in the brightness of a jewel. He loved her. He was waiting for her. There was no more fear now.

When Bess had gone she lay on the low bed, the jewelled flower pressed so hard against her that it pricked blood. She closed her eyes and listened to the soft thudding of her heart. Soon it would beat with his stroke for stroke, mouth to mouth.

She heard the mournful call of the dove from the next room. It wanted its freedom too.

She slid the latch of the cage, cupping its wings in her hands. It lay still with fear as she held it up to the watery sun. She felt the frantic pounding of its heart, the struggle of its wings for flight. She loosed it and watched it soar straight toward the sun. 'Go, my little dove,' she whispered. 'Go and fly with the eagles.'

The hall at Leicester was green as a forest, the dark cavernous roof hung with sharp spiked evergreen that drifted a carpet of fine needles beneath their feet. A Lord of Misrule capered in scarlet and green and minstrels in blue and white doublets played fragile virelays and lusty rondos. The pageants were ended; a pious depiction of the Nativity to please the Queen, the Adoration of the Magi in honour of the King and his royal guests John of France and David Bruce, who as all had predicted had taken the first opportunity to scuttle back into England. Now the dancers spun and dipped and swayed like a flight of gaudy birds.

Margaret looked on bemused, drunk with noise and colour. The furs, the gowns, the jewels—and above it all, the glittering apex, Edward Plantagenet and his golden brood of sons. She knew their faces now. The King himself, tall and voracious; his eldest son Edward, Prince of Wales and the acclaimed victor of Poitiers; Lionel the blond giant with his bland and easy smile;

43

Edmund of Langley, his fair good looks spoilt by a weak mouth and a vague eye that roamed emptily around the hall. And John of Gaunt, always smiling, a secret introspective smile not meant to be shared.

There were women too. Philippa the Queen, dark and heavy as a Flemish mare. Beside her her daughters Isobel and Mary; Joanna, Countess of Kent, a bejewelled silken vision with the eternal smile of a courtesan; Elizabeth de Burgh, Prince Lionel's wife, and the lovely ethereal creature that was Lancaster's daughter Blanche. Hal moved among them, he was one of them, laughing with the King, talking with quiet affection to his uncle of Lancaster, his cousin of Gaunt's arm flung conspiratorially around his shoulder. Joanna of Kent smiled and raised her lovely painted face to him. The doubts came back then. Jesu, what did he want with her when he could have had his pick from women like that?

For the past three days she had moved in an alternating world of joy and despair. Joy when he was near her and his eyes caressed her face; despair when he raised another woman's hand to his mouth or led her into the dance. She tore herself apart with imaginings. Did he look at them as he had looked at her? Did he hold them as close? She remembered that first night. Leicester had been full to the walls, every house and hospice crammed with lords and knights, clerks, butlers, stewards, grooms, chaplains and the rest of the King's vast household that could not find lodging within the castle. They had reached Leicester at dusk, and though the town gates were a bare stone's throw from the castle, it had taken a full agonizing hour to struggle through the press of laden horses and crawling carts that had blocked the streets. She had sat her little palfrey stiff with dread—dread that he would not be there, that a nail from a passing cart would tear the precious gown of Italian silk that the Countess had given her, that she would die from the waiting. But she had not died or torn her gown, and he was there, tall and golden, the reality of the dream.

They had danced together once, a chaste courtly dance where only their hands had touched, but his eyes had stroked her skin to fire and his mouth provoked her to a vivid remembrance of his

44

kiss. *The lake, the sun upon the water, and then only the sun.* She had bathed naked in the lake and warmed herself in the sun. And that was all she'd had for three days; the soft secret exchange of eyes, a few snatched encounters and the memory of his body, close and hot as a kitchen fire. Never once had they been alone. He was bound by constant duty to Lancaster, she to the Countess. And then there was John.

He was watching her now with that vague disturbed look he had worn ever since he had arrived at Leicester and his eyes would often stray to the jewelled flower she wore upon her gown. It was the first time in her life that she had greeted John with anything but absolute joy. She found his protectiveness irksome now; he was always watching her, insistent on accompanying her on the few precious occasions she had been free from duty. Perhaps he knew. She betrayed herself every time she looked at Hal. John would hate that. He hated Hal—because he was a Percy? Or because he had everything that John longed for so much? She flushed at the disloyal thought. She had been glad enough of John once when there had been no one else. She could not push him aside now. Covertly she glanced to where his wife sat, timid and dowdy as a mouse just emerged from the wainscot. Maud was a Percy, the runt of the litter, John called her. She smiled at him. Poor John, all his bright ambition shackled by such a dimming presence. No wonder he had no love for Hal Percy. But all that would change. She would see that he was better advanced; Alexander too, though he had less need of it. He was already a deacon at York and the Archbishop's most esteemed pupil. All said that Alexander was destined for great things.

A fleet of pages entered with a fresh supply of wine. She sighed. Jesu, would they never have had enough? Her hands strayed to the little scrap of parchment tucked inside her gown. Two hours, perhaps less, and they would be together. She smiled and the knight sitting opposite her blinked as if he were blinded by the sun.

The round silver eye of a full moon looked in through the high window and filled the room with shadows. At first she thought it

45

was empty, till one of the shadows moved and she saw the gleam of yellow hair. 'Oh Hal, I thought I should never find it.'

He drew her quickly into the room and closed the door. 'I'm sorry. I forgot you didn't know Leicester.' He smiled wryly. 'Not very elegant, is it? But with half of England bedded down here, it was the best I could do.'

She giggled and looked round the walls. There were bales of tight-packed hay bristling with sword hilts, a pile of rusty mail in a bath of vinegar. In the corner, pieces of scoured armour hung on a crossbar like a disjointed scarecrow.

'It's the armourers' room,' he said, 'where they clean the armour.' In heaven's name, what was he saying? He'd sweated and schemed for this moment for the last month and, now it was here, they were standing as far apart as the room would allow and he was babbling about cleaning armour. 'Oh Christ,' he said aloud. 'I thought I should die from waiting.'

Suddenly all the laughter had gone between them. He stared at her with bleak and hungry eyes. She was even lovelier than he remembered. The musk rose of her gown made ivory of her skin and her hair gleamed like satin through the web of her caul.

'Let down your hair,' he whispered. He watched it fall, soft and dark as the night outside. He lifted a handful of its shining warmth to his mouth. It tasted of honey and flowers and summer rain. He touched her cheeks with his long sensitive hands, running them gently down the curve of her neck to the soft shadow between her breasts. He saw her eyelids droop and felt the pulse beneath his hand begin to quicken. He drew her against him. It would be so easy to take her. She gave so much, so eagerly that it almost frightened him. He kissed her, the soft skilled pressure of his mouth opening hers, holding her between agony and pure delight. His hands touched her, brushing the hard tips of her breasts, caressing her till she trembled and strained against him in ecstasy.

He pushed her down gently among some loose straw. His heart was pounding like a drum and he could hardly see for tears. 'Oh, I want you,' he whispered. 'Dear God, how I want you.' The heat in him was a burning angry pain, the thin desperate thread of

46

control strained by her hands in his hair. Then she was beneath him, soft and pliant, the well of all pleasure.

The thread snapped and he almost cried out with the relief. 'Don't stop me now,' he moaned. 'For pity's sake, don't stop me now.'

She cried out beneath the sudden violence of his mouth. His hands were hurting her, bruising her, pushing her down till she could feel the cold dampness of the floor beneath the straw. She opened her eyes and saw the hard red line of his mouth. He drew up her skirts. His hands touched her thighs—hard, bruising hands, like William's hands. She could smell the animal smell of lust again, ugly, violent, pounding against her till she had wept in pain. She screamed and struck out at him. 'No, no, don't touch me, don't touch me!'

He lay on his back, his arm flung up over his face. His breath came in great painful sobs. He felt sick and his cheek throbbed where her nails had scored his flesh.

She began to weep. 'Oh Hal, I'm sorry. I'm sorry. I thought. . . . It was something I remembered. Oh Jesu, I'm sorry. I love you Hal. I love you so much.'

It was a long time before the agony left him and he could speak. He lifted his arm from his face and felt blindly for her hand. 'It's all right,' he said so quietly she could hardly hear him. 'It's all right. I frightened you.' He had frightened himself too. He had never felt like that in all his life—but then he had never wanted a woman so badly before.

He turned to look at her. Her hair was tangled. Her face looked so pale and sad. The lovely gown was crumpled and there was an inch-long tear in the skirt. 'I'm sorry too,' he said softly. 'It's only that I've never wanted anyone as much as I wanted you tonight.'

She began to cry again and he held her in his arms, stroking her hair until she was quiet. She sat up and looked at him, touching the anguished line of his mouth.

He rose to his feet and held out his hand to her. He began to laugh softly as he picked the wisp of straw from her hair. 'You're laughing at me', she accused him, on the verge of tears again.

'No.' He dropped a soft kiss on her brow. 'I'm laughing at myself.'

He walked with her as far as the little stone gallery. He held her face in his hands. 'I'm sorry,' he said again. 'I wanted it to be so beautiful.' He kissed her and she clung to him desperately.

'Do you love me, Hal?' she whispered.

The age-old question. How many times had he heard it and answered it with soft evasions?

He stared at her for a long time. 'Yes,' he answered at last. 'Yes, I think perhaps I do.'

'I saw you. Hanging round his neck like a panting whore.'

Pale and stunned, Margaret stared into her brother's face, that beloved face, alien now and ugly with hatred.

'How could you shame yourself—shame *me*?' He was almost weeping, banging his fists against the walls of the small antechamber. 'Has he had you yet?' He lunged towards her and grabbed her arm. 'Has he?'

She felt sick at the look in his eyes, sick and dirty and ashamed. She shook her head blindly. 'I love him, John,' she whispered. 'I love him.'

'And that makes it all right to lay on your back for him, does it?'

She struggled to stay upright on her feet. 'No—I haven't . . . I—Oh John. It isn't like that.'

'Then what is it like?' His fingers tightened on her arm till she cried out with pain. 'Tell me what it is like. Tell me how you are different from all the others.'

'Others?' she stared at him blankly. He had released her arm and she backed away from him and leant against the wall for support.

'My God, Meg. Are you really such an innocent? He's had more women than you have years. Him and that royal fornicating bastard Gaunt. They used to go whoring in Southwark.'

The words hammered against her ears. She felt so cold, so tired. She must say something. She must stop him destroying the dream.

John struck his clenched fist against his own palm. 'Christ, I should have killed him last night when I saw you.'

'Then why didn't you John? Why did you stay safely in the shadows?' Was that cold little voice hers? Had she said it or only thought it? She saw the surprise widen his eyes.

'I did not want to cause you any more shame than you had already brought upon yourself,' he said pompously.

She smiled faintly. It would be all right. She was warmer now. 'You hate him, don't you John? Just because he is a Percy.'

'*No!*' He was shouting with rage. 'I hate him because he is a destroyer. He tears people's hearts out for the love of it, Meg.' His voice dropped to a gentler note. 'He'll tear yours out if you let him.'

She was steady enough to take a pace toward him. She was free now. Free of John and Raby, free of the cage of her own mind. Like the cushat she could fly among the eagles. 'I don't believe you,' she said calmly. 'I love Hal Percy and he loves me. You'll have to get used to it, John.'

Why was he staring at her like that?

'My God, Meg—you don't think he's going to marry you?'

'Why not?' Sharp and angry, she stared at the once loved face.

'You bloody little fool, Meg. He's Lancaster's man and he'll marry the rich little heiress that's picked out for him.' His voice was gentle, coaxing. It tore the dream into small velvet pieces. 'You're such a child sometimes, Meg. A man doesn't take the woman he's going to marry into dark corners.'

'I don't believe you,' she said again.

'You'll bloody well believe it when you've got his bastard in your belly!' John shouted. 'That all he wants from you. To get you on your back in the grass like some tavern whore.'

She could have killed him. His smug face was so close she could easily have torn it with her nails. Instead she said wildly, 'That's what *I* want. To be on my back in the grass with him. If that's all I can have of him then I'll take it and gladly. I did it often enough without love. I deserve something—'

He struck her so hard that she screamed aloud. '*You slut!*' he yelled. 'You dirty disgusting little slut.' He stared down at her

49

where she lay sobbing on the floor. 'I'll see you in a convent first. I'll see you dead before you become Hal Percy's whore.'

She lay for a long time after he had gone, rocking back and forth, staring round the room at the truckle-beds strewn with discarded gowns. A piece of tawdry veiling had caught on a splinter of wood and floated out like a scarlet banner. Then little Bess Seaton crept in from the next room.

'Oh Margaret, I heard. Oh don't cry, please don't cry.' She sat on the bed and drew Margaret's head into her lap. 'It will be all right, Meg. He doesn't mean it, he's just angry. He'll forget.'

Margaret raised her head. 'I don't care about John,' she cried. 'I don't care if I never see him again.' But Hal, she cared about Hal. She must see him, she must talk to him, have him soothe this dreadful agony. 'Find him, Bess,' she pleaded as she struggled to her feet. 'Find Hal for me. Tell him I'll wait for him where we met before. Oh please Bess, if you love me, find him.'

The room looked even worse in daylight: the dusty chest, the raw damp smell of neglected steel, dull and tarnished like the dream. No one had been here since. The scattered straw still held the hollow where they had lain, where the ugly memories from another world had come crowding back. That world was never far behind her. Demons with the sharp little teeth of uncertainty dragged her back to the pit of misery from which she had climbed and into which, their whispering voices reminded her, she could so easily fall again. The demons all had John's face now. *Whore ... slut ... he'll never marry you ... a destroyer ... he tears hearts out for the love of it.*

Then she heard his step upon the stair. The long stride of a tall man, the infinitesimal pause outside the door. The demons retreated back into their dark corner as he stood in the doorway.

She flung herself into his arms, pressing herself against him, desperate to share his warmth. 'It's John. He knows. He saw us together in the gallery.'

He held her away from him and touched the red angry weal on her cheek. She saw how pale his face was. 'Did he do this?'

'It doesn't matter.' She looked up into the lambent green eyes. 'He called me a whore. He said that you would never marry me.'

He pulled her to him and caressed her hair. She felt the softness

50

of velvet against her cheek, the sharp prick of the gold work on his collar. Suddenly there was no warmth, even in the circle of his arm. She pulled back sharply. It was true. Oh dear God, it was true! John had been right—smug, sanctimonious John had been right after all.

'You said you loved me.' She heard her own voice like the plaintive cry of a child.

'Oh my sweet—if love were all that was needed between us!' He felt sick at the look in her eyes. He loved her and wanted her—but badly enough to marry her? That was the stumbling block, the sharp prick of the thorn beneath the rose. For him and his kind, love and marriage came by pure chance after duty and dynasty had been served, the dictates of wealth and policy satisfied. Margaret met none of these needs; her family were his ancient enemies and she had neither wealth nor influence. He thought of Lancaster and the ambitious future he had planned for him. There would be no place for Margaret in that future and though he loved her there were others he loved and to whom he owed duty and obedience. 'Our lives are not our own,' he said softly. 'For us to wed would not be easy. There would be some who would speak against it. Your brother for one.'

She looked up into his face. 'And you would give me up because my brother spoke against it?' The corroding pain inside her turned to anger. 'When have you ever cared for the word of a Neville? John spoke the truth when he said you were ruled by Lancaster. You'll sell yourself to some fat heiress for her dowry because Lancaster decrees it.' She backed away from the comfort of his outstretched arms, weeping tears of anger and shame. 'Well, I wish you joy of it,' she sobbed. 'I'll not trouble you again.'

She turned and ran and left him with the echo of her weeping. He stood for a long time, staring at the bed of straw where they had lain the previous night. Then his mouth set in a stubborn line. The Devil could have her. He would not think of her again.

He paced the limits of the narrow room he shared with Warwick's son, Tom Beauchamp, pausing at each turn before the tall lancet windows that Henry of Lancaster had set into his father's

51

palace of the Savoy. He shut his eyes to the gentle slope of green that ran to the river's edge and the tall elms that hid all but the misty roofs of Westminster. He closed his ears to the roar of Beauchamp's voice as he roamed the courtyard searching for him. He saw and heard nothing but her face and the soft remembered anguish of her voice. He had seen her but twice after that night and never once alone. So small and pale, and still that subtle blend of child and woman that had first enchanted him. He swore softly beneath his breath and aimed a vicious kick at the chair beside his bed. He was behaving like a love-sick boy, like the pimply youths who mooned at the feet of Joanna of Kent and poured out their hearts in sickly sweet verse.

Beauchamp's voice grew louder and more plaintive. Lancaster would be waiting for him, impatience drawing his brows together, his temper fraying at the delay. Not the best time to ask an indulgence—and that was what marriage to Margaret Neville would be; a favour, a release from duty that Lancaster would find despicable. He smiled wryly to himself. So great a sacrifice for possession of that slim white body. . . .

The chill of the marble stairs struck him like a blow. Cool in summer, cold as a grave in winter, the staircase of Italian marble was only one of the wonders that the Savoy boasted and that had swallowed twice the fifty thousand marks Lancaster had received in ransoms during the French war of 1345. It was his uncle's jest that the French had rebuilt the Savoy. He took the steps two at a time, negotiating with ease the unexpected sharp curve that had cracked many a page's head. He knew and loved every stone of this place, for it had been his home since he was ten. Against the Savoy, Westminster and Windsor seemed like tawdry shadows and it was a sharp and bitter source of envy to some. If any man but Henry of Lancaster had held it he would not have held it long, but Lancaster cupped England in the palm of his hand. There was no man in England who spoke his name with anything but respect.

But Lancaster was not above anger, and he was out of his chair and pacing when Hal entered the hall. He said nothing as Hal murmured his apology and bowed low before the French king, but his eyes were quick to notice the shadows beneath Hal's. So the rumours were not so wild then. It was true that Hal was making a fool of himself over Neville's daughter. He frowned in concern and watched Hal come toward him. It was the only tragedy of his life that he had no sons, and Hal had become the next best thing. He studied the product of his loving stewardship. The fair Plantagenet beauty was sharpened by Percy blood. The mouth was strong and the eyes were proud and held a hint of ruthlessness. All this he approved, but he also knew the flaw: the rash, unpredictable streak that lay beneath the gilded surface, the hot churning northern blood that would sacrifice all for a moment's gratification of the senses.

Then the frown lifted indulgently. The lad was young yet. He would come to his senses. He'd been raised too well for him to baulk at his duty, though it might not be a bad idea to get him wed. He laid his well-shaped and jewelled hand on Hal's shoulder and smiled. Yes, he must speak to de Bohun about his wench.

Outside a watery sun struggled from behind a grey drift of cloud and struck gold from Lancaster's livery. Hal mounted the fine grey stallion that had been Lancaster's gift to him and steadied the head of the French king's white gelding; that had been Edward's gift, a subtle pun on John's royal impotence.

The Frenchman flashed him a brief smile of thanks. His dark eyes were steady but at the back of them Hal thought he saw fear and uncertainty. He knew the negotiations for the French king's release were not going well; that much he had gleaned from the gossip of the court. What he knew with more certainty was that 'our dear cousin of Valois' was not proving so pliant as the King had hoped. He was still treated as a valued and honoured guest but there were always two men at his back now, who were there for less honourable reasons than to see to John's comfort. His first refusal of Edward's demands had been followed by evasion and hesitation and now the French king was visibly weakening. His kingdom was ground into the dust, threatened from its heart by Charles of Burgundy, stripped of its strength and beauty by the free companies who harried and plundered in peace and war alike. It needed only the barest turn of the screw; hence their visit to the Tower today, ostensibly to inspect the King's armoury but in reality for John to catch a glimpse of the strength that England could turn against him if he did not yield.

Hal rode close by him as they turned into the Strand and the white pious faces of the Bishop's Inns. The air was crisp and smelt of spring. A little way ahead, past Temple Bar and the sluggish trickle of the Fleet, a grey pall of smoke heralded the City. Hal had no love for London, especially the City, where the narrow unhealthy streets with their stinking gutters concealed rank poverty beneath the glitter of trade. Trade was the new symbol of power that enabled upstart merchants to buy their way to court. Edward needed the vast sums that only the rich merchant guilds could provide; the loans became gifts and were rewarded with knighthoods and land. So fishmongers and fleshers stood alongside the highest in the land.

They entered through Ludgate in the dark shadow of the convent of the Black Friars. The streets were already swarming with people and carts coming from outside the city to Newgate Market. When they reached St Paul's, the French king held his cloak fastidiously over his nostrils against the stink of rotting entrails that rose from the Shambles and blew down to the Butcher's Bridge.

Tom Beauchamp, riding his flank, pulled a sneering face and said, 'I suppose they have no such stink in France.'

Beauchamp's jibe reflected the mood of the city. The merchants came to their doors to stare and hungry-eyed 'prentices watched from dim interiors. The guards riding ahead cleared a way through the standing crowds, pushing them back against the tall narrow houses. Silence rolled before them like a great wave and closed in at their backs with a few belated cheers of 'Lancaster!' A few spat noisily in the French king's path but his face remained composed, except for a twitch of muscle at the corner of his mouth. His eyes stared straight ahead to where the Tower loomed over the sloping roofs of Thames Street. He had greater things on his mind than the insults of a few Englishmen.

Edward received them warmly in the royal apartments, kissing his royal kinsman and calling him *'mon cousin'* as if there were nothing between them but affection and shared blood.

Hal's eyes went to the tall lounging figure that stood behind the

King and he raised his hand in answer to John of Gaunt's smile. John was the nearest he had to a close friend. They were alike in age and temperament, linked by blood and the affectionate domination of Lancaster. They had been brought up together, and now that John was to wed their cousin Blanche the circle drew closer. Yet even that tenuous bond was under a strain. It was a lesson he had learnt early in life: friendship was an indulgence of childhood, to be cast aside as one grew to manhood and discovered that ambition and power were held dearer. On the surface all was as it had always been, but John's motives had changed subtly. His friends were chosen now with policy in mind, men who could serve him well and unquestioningly, the younger sons of younger sons, men who had little to lose and everything to gain by throwing in their lot with him. Men like Hal's own brother Thomas.

Edward himself led them down to the armoury, talking in his quick voluble French and smiling the wide devouring smile that left his eyes quite cold. The long vaulted chamber in the Wardrobe Tower was cold and silent; it was like a graveyard, row upon row of empty disembodied breastplates and faceless helms burnished to a brilliance that hurt the eyes. Some were stacked flat like corpses in a plague pit, dulled with goose grease to keep away the rust.

John paused to admire a particularly fine piece, the King's own, damascened in gold and chased with the royal arms of England and France. His hands smoothed the mirror sheen while his eyes swept round the room. He saw the stacks of lances and pikes, the iron grilles that ran the length of the chamber bristling with swords and axes, and all this just for the King's retainers alone.

They moved on, down to the yards and the tall wooden sheds where the siege engines worked by torsion and counterpoise, were housed. And last, with subtle irony, to the low huts full of the scent of cut wood. Six-foot lengths of seasoned ash and yew lined the walls as thick as a forest, and a hundred fletchers, almost hidden behind the great barrels of steel-tipped willow shafts, worked with flying fingers setting the goose feathers to their tails. Edward's eyes were bright with mockery for this was England's strength, the strength that had decimated France's chivalry at Crécy and Poitiers and made their king Edward's captive; a simple weapon wielded by simple men and far beneath France's dignity.

A small bitter smile curved the length of the French king's mouth. Edward's message was clear. *Yield now and save what you have.* The alternative was all around him, intensified by the threat of Edward's eyes. Still smiling, he nodded and lowered desperate eyes. He had seen enough.

They took wine on the close-cropped lawn of the Queen's Garden and Hal climbed the wall that ran between the Salt and Lantern Towers. The sun had melted into a white opaque sky and the wind that blew in his face carried the smell of the river and the wharf rats who gorged themselves on city leavings. He stared round at the wide sprawl of walls that encircled the turreted keep of the Conqueror. Prisoners were housed there who did not succumb to Edward's charm. It was a natural progression, the velvet glove of Westminster to the iron gauntlet of the Tower. John of France would feel its grip soon if he did not lay his mark on Edward's treaty.

A light step behind him jerked him round. John of Gaunt was watching him, his handsome mouth turned in his inevitable smile. 'What ails you, Hal? Are you sick or, like me, just bored?'

Hal grinned. 'Both.'

John came and leant against the wall beside him, staring down to where the two kings walked, trailing their gaudy retinues like a stream of butterflies. 'Do you think he'll sign?' he asked broodingly.

'Does it matter? Either way there will be war,' Hal said 'Your father is set on being crowned King of France, treaty or no treaty.'

'And praise God for it,' John said. 'I'm sick to death of peace.' He was silent for a moment, then he nudged Hal gently in the ribs. 'And what's this I hear about *la belle Marguerite*?'

'Well, what did you hear?' Hal demanded irritably.

'That you are smitten and are like to ruin yourself by marrying her.' He stretched out his hand and gripped Hal's arm. 'It's not true, is it? You'd not be such a bloody fool as that.

The question touched Hal on the raw. 'For Christ's sake, John. I'm not offering for some kitchen wench. She's a Neville. Her blood is as good as mine.'

John raised his brows. 'But not as good as your lady mother's. And anyway, that's not the point. It is what she can bring to the marriage that counts, and from what I hear that isn't much.'

'Is that all that matters?' Hall cried. 'Dowry?'

'Yes. It is,' John answered him bluntly. 'To you and me it is. You should know better than to ask that.'

'Is that why you are marrying Blanche?'

'Yes,' John admitted. 'I love Blanche. You could not help but love Blanche, but I would marry her even if I didn't.' He turned and stared hard into Hal's face. 'Power is everything, Hal,' he said urgently. 'Wealth and land and power. One begets the other. Without them you will be nothing.'

'To the exclusion of all else?'

'If need be,' John answered slowly. He looked down into the well of the gardens. He watched his father strutting like an arrogant peacock; his brothers Lionel and Edmund, both fools. All he grudged Lionel was his advantage of birth. It was his elder brother Edward whom he really envied. Edward had everything that he would have given half of his life to possess.

Hal watched him and saw how his mouth hardened slightly, how the cold blue eyes became ruthless as they passed from face to face. He was staring at Lancaster now as he bent his head to catch something the king had said. Hal's own mouth tightened in disgust. John's eyes measured Lancaster like an embalmer measured a corpse.

'You can't wait for him to die, can you,' he said abruptly.

John's head came up sharply as if he had been struck. Anger flared briefly in his eyes, then quietened. 'And what of it?' he said defensively. 'We are all waiting. My brother Edward waits for our father to die so that he can be king. You wait for yours to die so that you can have Northumberland.'

'But not so eagerly, John,' Hal said derisively. 'Not counting the days left to him and hoping that each will be his last.'

'You should have gone into the Church, Hal,' John snapped. 'Only priests should be so selfless.'

'I think I'd rather do that than do what you are doing,' Hal said. 'You say power is everything, but not to the exclusion of all honour and loyalty.' His eyes became scornful. 'I shall make my own power, not wait for a woman to lay it in my lap. There is more in me than to have to wait for dead men's shoes.' He met the sudden animosity in John's eyes steadily. There was warning in their depths, a reminder of who he was. Cousins they might be, but they would never be equals. Royal blood was measured in quantity not quality and John was still the King's son.

John turned away from him. 'You'll regret that you ever said that, Hal,' he said quietly and went down to the garden below.

Hal looked down to where the King's barges dragged on their chains by the Water Gate. All this for a woman he had seen but a dozen times? The choice was his. The road forked here and he must choose the path: power, and his future ordered by Lancaster's influence and continued affection; or Margaret Neville. His heart had leapt toward the thought before his mind had even formed her name. There was no choice. He must have her. Whatever it cost, he must have her.

They crept down to the meadow where the river narrowed and trickled through long reeded grass, running like errant children in the shadow of the tall beeches till they were out of sight of Harbottle.

Hal pulled her down beside him, the pale colourless grass snapping beneath her skirts. Deliberately she did not look at him and held her eyes closed while he loosed her hair from the stiff little cap. He gathered the shining fall in his hands, watching the sun lift it from darkness to a soft amber gleam. Softly he laid his mouth on hers, a gentle kiss without passion or force, a mere touching of their flesh.

It had taken him three weeks to reach the north and every mile he had had her face before him. There had been other faces; his brother Tom's, amused and incredulous and more than a little pleased at his impending fall from grace. And Lancaster's, cold and chill with disapproval. It was the first time in his life that Lancaster had ever looked at him with anything but affection. The worst was to come, and the vision of his mother's cold rage had begun to take on the dimensions of nightmare in his mind. Abruptly he flung himself on his back.

Margaret watched him through half closed eyes. She did not speak and knew from the tense angry lines of his body that he did not want her to. She struggled against the tears that had burned her eyes ever since she had seen him ride into Harbottle. After that first wild clamouring of hope had come the thought that perhaps he had only come to use her again. She knew the full measure of love now, the joy of his physical presence, the soaring delight of his touch. She also knew the emptiness of days without him, without hope or love. She expected nothing now. If that was all there could be between them then she would take it; an hour of joy in exchange for the six ugly years with William. She deserved at least that.

She opened her eyes as he rolled over and lay staring at her. The sun was at his back and put his face in shadow.

'*Marguerite*,' he whispered. 'As fair as the flower. Too fair to stay unpicked in the field for long.' His mouth dropped to the curve of her neck. 'Will you still have me, sweet *Marguerite*?'

She felt the anguish of his voice and touched his mouth with her fingertips. There was no need to answer. He knew it each time he looked into her eyes.

'Neville's daughter?' The roar of Lord Percy's voice resounded through the narrow vaulted passages of Alnwick. 'Neville's daughter?'

'Yes, Neville's daughter,' Hal snapped back. He was sick to the stomach of hearing that, as if he had offered for some nameless maid. 'And before you ask, she has nothing,' he added defiantly.

His father's thick brows shot beneath his dark unruly fringe of hair. 'Are you mad, boy? Your mother will never allow it.'

Hal's voice was unusually cold. 'It is not my lady mother's consent that I need. Only yours.'

'And Neville's.' His father glared at him. 'Have you sought his consent yet? Not that he'd refuse it, with two widowed daughters on his hands. He'll think himself lucky to be rid of one—and to a Percy at that.' He sat heavily and stood again. 'Does Lancaster know?'

Hal nodded and sat on the hard unyielding edge of the bed they were to share.

'And?'

'He does not approve, if that is what you mean,' Hal replied stiffly. 'Did you expect him to?'

'No.' Lord Percy could not resist a little smirk. This would not accord with Lancaster's high and mighty plans. Yet for different reasons he did not approve either. He paced a few steps toward the door and groaned inwardly. This would set the fat in the fire; bad enough for Hal to offer for a penniless nobody, but a Neville into the bargain. The thought of Mary's fury set his teeth on edge. Marriage for love did not come within her orderly compass of things. Yet he did not grudge the boy that; he knew the misery that the other could bring. Virgin by name and virgin by nature, there had been times when all Mary's beauty and Plantagenet name had not compensated for the frozen disgust with which she allowed him into her bed, as if he were some errant hound come in from the yard to paw at her skirts. He laid his hand gently on Hal's shoulder.

'Have you thought lad,' he said gruffly, 'have you thought deeply on this? No, hear me—' He held up his hand against the protest he saw in Hal's eyes. 'I'm not speaking of dowry, though that, of course, is important. But love, Hal. It dulls the mind, slows the intellect.' His eyes clouded. So long ago, yet he could still remember that first ecstasy of feeling when they had given him Mary Plantagenet to wife. A reward for services rendered. Yet there had been love there once, on his part anyway, till her cold haughtiness had driven it out.

'The girl's a Neville,' he went on gruffly. 'No matter how much she cares for you, her thoughts will be Neville thoughts. She'll not willingly see harm come to her family at the cost of Percy advancement. She'll plead for them and always have her eye on their welfare, and because you love her you'll give in. And do not deceive yourself that there will ever be anything but enmity between the Nevilles and us. Oh, I agree, old Neville and I jog along well enough together now. We've had to, for the sake of the Border. But his sons are of a different colour altogether, especially John Neville. He wants our land and influence. He wants supremacy in the north and he'll not hesitate to slit your throat to get it. You'll not be able to fight back so easily with your hands tied by a Neville wife.' He ruffled the bowed golden head affectionately. 'That's the way of it, lad. The one virtue of not marrying for love is that you are still your own man, not swayed by tears and tantrums.'

Hal stared into the meagre fire that flared in the hearth. It was the longest speech he had ever heard his father make, and the cold hard core of his mind knew he spoke the truth. But he was ruled by Mars, and beneath the polished malleable surface they had imposed on him was a spirit as obdurate as freshly struck steel. He shook his head. 'I'll not change my mind,' he said and met his father's eyes.

Lord Percy sighed. He knew that look, the look that a hundred childhood beatings had not managed to break. For all his mother's high-flown plans there would be no ordering of his life. He'd always follow his own road, for good or ill, and none would ever keep him from it.

Lady Mary Percy stared stonily at her eldest son. Her chair was set against the light, her narrow back hard against its cushioned spine. Her skirts were arranged in precise folds and each small hand clasped the grizzled head of a Percy lion that sprang from the dark grained oak. The queenly pose was not lost on Hal. This was the second crossing of swords; the first time—yesterday, when he had first broached the matter—had resulted in wordless white-faced fury that had left him trembling as if he were a boy of ten. Today she was calmer, but the sure and aggressive set of her mouth left no doubt in his mind that she meant to have her way. 'So you have a mind to wed then, Henry?'

The formal use of his name set the tone for the meeting. She rarely called him that unless she was vastly displeased.

'And this person, this Margaret Ros. . . . She is your choice?' Her voice, high with incredulous disdain, touched him on the raw.

'Yes, she is my choice,' he declared stubbornly and saw spots of colour burn her cheeks.

'She'll bring you nothing; you know that, I suppose. She has

61

nothing from her former husband, and Neville offers a pittance as always. Nothing at all, not even purity.'

His face flamed with anger but he kept his voice steady. From the corner of his eye he could see his father's grim and uneasy face. 'I care nothing for that,' he said. 'I have offered for her and she has accepted, and Father has given consent.'

'Then he is a bigger fool than you are, Hal,' she cried furiously. 'You could have a splendid match, a bride who brought you wealth and position—'

'Like you did to Father,' Hal broke in angrily. 'And spent the rest of your life regretting it.'

Fury drove the blood from her face. 'What does that matter to a man? Once he's wed he can rid himself of his lust in a whore house—' The blue burning gaze left his face for an instant and stabbed at his father. 'Also as your father does.'

'*Enough*, madam.' His father lumbered forward, his face an ugly red with suppressed anger. 'As far as I am concerned Hal can marry where he pleases. The girl may have nothing but she's of good blood and I've enough faith in Hal to think that he'll get what he wants out of life without the prop of you and your brother Lancaster.' He thrust his forefinger towards the white incredulous face. 'I want no interference, either from you or Lancaster.' He turned and stamped out of the room. He would pay dearly for that later. But it did not seem to matter now. His life was almost finished. Hal's was just beginning.

They were married at Brancepath in the soft seductive warmth of July; quietly and almost furtively with none of the high nobility that Mary Percy had once envisaged. She let it be known, especially to Alice Neville, that her presence here was enforced, because her husband had insisted.

Lancaster had not come but then none had expected him to. Hal's defiance had hit him hard and since his return to court he had treated his former protegé with cool indifference. Thomas was the man of the day now, eagerly filling the place in Lancaster's affection that his brother had so rashly vacated. Thomas was Gaunt's man too, one of the new ambitious breed that had sprung up like weeds around the future Duke of Lancaster.

Today he had come to gloat on his mother's outraged pride and his sharp mocking gaze reminded her of it frequently.

John Neville had stayed away. His resentment towards Hal was undiminished, growing stronger at a pace that filled Margaret with dread. Maud had borne another daughter and the very name of Percy was anathema to him now. Secretly Margaret grieved for him, knowing that he was as lost to her now as were all the golden days of their childhood.

Margaret glanced around the faces gathered in the flower-hung hall and saw the transient smiles that concealed old hostilities. Her father moved among his guests, his stiff unsmiling mien thawed by a tun of Rhenish. Her mother sat beside Matilda Clifford, smugly calculating the worth of the wedding gifts; the castle and manor of Tughall from Lord Percy, a pair of silver chalices from the Countess, a generous purse from the King and Queen besides all the plate and silver. On her left the Bishop of Durham strained his eloquence over the small stiff figure of Lady Percy. Her face, framed in goffered silk, was cold as winter ice and never once during the long day had she acknowledged Margaret by word or glance.

She shivered and stole a glance to where her husband towered over her brother Alexander with his golden height. Their eyes met and his mouth curved in its warm lazy smile. She felt the glow of pure happiness. What need had she of any but him now?

They stood facing each other, their hands linked loosely at their sides. The room was warm and soft with candlelight; he breathed deeply, spinning out each perfect moment. It would never be like this again, for as long as he lived they would never be able to recapture this first time.

He loosed his hands and lifted her face toward him. He kissed her slowly, hardly touching her; the damp clinging warmth of her mouth clouded his mind with a mist of pleasure and he released her, pulling at the ribbon that held the thin silk gown.

She closed her eyes, shutting out everything but the exquisite pleasure of his hands on her bare flesh. Wine and passion had heightened her senses: the fire of his mouth upon her breasts, the velvet of his hands against her thighs. She felt the beginning of a soft throbbing heat in the pit of her stomach. She moved against him. He was naked beneath the long robe, his body taut and hard as a drawn bow. She stroked the soft golden hair that grew at his throat and heard the soft quickening of his breath. She opened her eyes: his were fever-bright and the colour of a topaz.

He lifted her gently onto the bed and lay beside her. He kissed her eyes, her throat, her eager mouth, the soft rosy mound of her breast. Her hands moved lightly against him, soft, uncertain, like the brushing of a bird's wing, stroking his neck, his heart, down to the hard ridged muscles of his belly. He pulled her roughly against him. She felt the hot anguish of his breath on her mouth, the iron hardness of him against her. He turned her onto her back. His own hands were trembling, his heart beating in hard painful strokes. He raised his head to look at her. Her eyes were wide and vulnerable, grey as a summer storm, sea mist clouding the sun, the dark swirling depths of a river in full flood.

Then he was drowning in the deep shining water of her eyes, in the warm clinging darkness of her body. The blood pounded hard and painful in his loins. He closed his eyes. Sweet Christ. Not yet, not yet, he prayed. He bit hard at his lip till he drew blood. The pain was sharp enough to pull him back and he slowed his pace, gently, leisurely, stroking her hair, whispering against her mouth.

'*Marguerite*, my flower, my dove, my gentle frightened little dove. Come and fly with me, *Marguerite*, fly the summit with me, my dearest love.' He kissed her fiercely, salt sweat and honey, the taste of his own blood. She sobbed and strained against him. Her hands were in his hair, holding his mouth hard against her.

He felt the darkness rise and engulf him, throbbing against him, drawing him down. He plunged deeper, harder. There was fire now, on his back and thighs where her hands tore at him. Fire deep in his belly, burning, bursting, roaring, a river of flame rending its banks. 'Oh, I love you. Christ, I love you.' He felt blindly for her mouth. 'Kiss me. Hold me, oh, hold me.' Then the river was loosed, draining him, flooding him with an ecstasy he had never dreamt existed. His mind and body were numb and he could feel the warmth of his own tears upon his face. He closed his eyes. He had no regrets. Whatever he had lost it had been worth it. She would be all of his life now.

———

London
Margaret lay curled in the dim rustling arbour of trees, screened from the house by trellised vines. White stars of campion opened to the summer dusk and spread a soft carpet of furred leaves beneath her. Above her head a lark sang and from the cote by the stableyard came the warm throaty call of a dove overlaid by the creak and rumble of carts going home from Cheapside. She stroked the head of the wolfhound pup that lolled against her skirts. The dog was Hal's, a bitch called Bebba after the Saxon queen of Bamburgh. When Hal was away she was her constant companion. Sometimes it was the nearest she could get to him.

Through the lattice of branches she watched the pigeons wheel above the steep gabled roof. This was her refuge, her sanctuary from the noisy household and the sharp disparaging glances of Lady Percy which even after a year had not diminished. There was no refuge from the demon thoughts. They were still there, still breathing life into that old fear of abandonment which had never quite left her even when she was with Hal.

Without him, the demons haunted her; the face of her brother John, the cold aloofness of Lancaster intensified by the scorn in Mary Percy's eyes.

Margaret's new mother-in-law had made herself quite clear from the first. A month after they had been married Hal had taken Margaret back to Alnwick. She disliked Alnwick; the harsh imposing grandeur that suited Mary Percy so well had seemed to reduce her to insignificance. It was cold and forbidding, the setting for a brighter jewel than she. Mary Percy had come to her chamber on the day that Hal had left her to return to court. She had circled her like a skirmishing enemy, her stiff embroidered skirts hissing as she walked.

'Well then, daughter—' her smile had the bite of a sliver of glass, 'I must congratulate you, if nothing else. You trapped my son with the skill of a courtesan.'

65

Margaret stared at her mutely, the square of embroidery limp in her hands. Lady Percy came and stood over her. She could smell the pungent scent of lavender that clung to her gown.

'You'll not keep him, you know,' she said softly. 'A man's appetite is soon jaded. He'll tire of you as he did of the others. The lure of your body will not be enough to keep him. Hal is destined for power, I raised him for it. I mean to see that he has it.'

Margaret said nothing. She sat numb with shock, staring at the thread of red silk that spiralled like a trickle of blood across the linen square in her lap.

'You can't keep a hawk caged for ever.' Each soft malicious word was like a hammer blow. 'Sooner or later you will have to loose it. For a while it will be content with the lure, then one day it will fly too high. It will feel the strength of its wings beneath it. It will see the space and freedom and feel the pull of its own true nature, the lust to hunt its own prey. The lure will be no more than an insignificant speck on the ground. That is how it will be with my son,' she added cruelly. 'Once he has seen the world spread out beneath him he'll leave you far behind. You'll just be someone to bear his children and order his household; an insignificant little speck on the ground beneath him.'

Margaret could still feel the cold horror of it. The words had been meant to frighten her and they had. There was another demon now—with the cruel sharp face of Mary Percy. And she was beginning to believe it. Already she sensed a restlessness in Hal, a need for something more than she could give. Her eyes clouded as she remembered the eagerness with which he had grasped at the rumour of war with France again. Edward's patience had been exhausted by the New Year and only after a month of close confinement in the Tower and Edward's warm reception of envoys from his rival and cousin, the King of Navarre, had John of France been ready to sign. Yet the arduously wrought treaty had proved worthless. The Dauphin Charles had refused Edward's demands, despite the harassment of Burgundy and the chaos of his own government. And Edward for his part had not been slow to cry French perfidy. There would be war—and such a war. Already the King's Commissioners of

66

Array led their newly recruited hordes into London. The whole city sweated with labour, assembling the multitude of carts and waggons that would carry anything from the King's plate to the forges for shoeing his horses, and all along the waterfront blunt-nosed warships rode heavily at anchor.

She shivered, suddenly cold, and called the pup back from where it nosed inquisitively in the undergrowth. The sun had slid behind the tall towers of St Martin le Grand, and the wide pleasaunce that stretched down to the Grey Friars' church where they had buried the Dowager Queen Isabella a month ago was half in shadow. It was growing late. Hal would be back soon and, as if in answer to the thought, she heard the slow leisurely pacing of horses in the yard. The strident voice of Lord Percy floated over the high yew hedge and was answered by the soft infectious laughter she knew so well. She scrambled to her feet and stooped beneath the blossom—laden branches, running across the clipped lawn till she reached the cobbled yard that brought her in sight of the house.

On the threshold of the small sunlit chamber she paused. Lord Percy stood in the oriel with his back to the light. Hal was bending to his mother's cheek, laughing, touching, the small intimate tableau reminding her again that she was the outsider. Then Mary Percy's chill glance travelled the length of the room, encompassing the wisps of grass that clung to her skirts, the scuffed velvet of her shoes, the dusty imprint of a dog's paw on her bodice. Margaret flinched beneath the wordless scrutiny and looked for the reassurance of Hal's smile before she advanced into the room.

He kissed her and tickled the dog beneath its velvet chin. His mother's voice cut between them like the stroke of an axe. 'Good news, daughter.' She rose and came toward them, her hands clasped across her small waist. 'Hal has been chosen to lead troops under my brother of Lancaster.' She laid a small jewelled hand on his arm. 'It is a great honour. A chance to prove his worth to the doubters.' Her voice rose softly with innuendo. 'We had hoped to see him well advanced before now.' She was mistress of the insult, the soft courteous words shaped by her malefic tongue to sharp and deadly effect like the blade of a misericord.

Margaret held her look, fighting down the sick little feeling that this woman's eyes always gave her. It was as good as a slap in the face, a glimpse of things to come.

In their chamber she waited till the door had closed behind the page who had brought water and fresh linen. 'When shall you leave?' she asked quietly.

Hal dropped a kiss on her brow. 'Not yet awhile. A month at least.'

'How long? How long will you be gone?' She heard her voice like the petulant wail of a child.

Hal shrugged himself out of his tunic and pulled the fine linen shirt over his head. 'Six months, perhaps more. King Edward is set on being crowned at Rheims by Christmas.' He sluiced his face and neck with cool water, keeping his voice deliberately casual. Margaret was like a young faun and frightened easily.

Margaret sat heavily on the wide bed and plucked at the gilded marguerites scattered on the coverlet. Six months meant a year at least; a year without him, a year at the mercy of his mother's poisonous tongue. Sudden panic filled her: suppose he didn't come back! William hadn't come back. He could be maimed. She had seen the poor creatures who hung around the garrisons: eyeless, limbless, stumps for arms.

'Don't go,' she said suddenly. 'Don't leave me, Hal.'

He raised his head slowly. Water dripped from his honey-wet hair and streamed in rivulets down his back. She felt her danger in his very stillness. Fool, she thought. All men went to war, all men wanted to go to war; especially Hal wanted it. Against all her instinct she persisted; fear drove her on, even when she saw the reluctance in his eyes. Shamelessly she used the unfailing weapon of her body and flung herself against him. She felt the warm damp strength of his arms, his mouth tasting of wine and rosewater. 'Don't go Hal. For pity's sake, don't go.'

He eased her from him gently, drawing a deep breath against the sudden pounding of his blood. She could rouse him so easily. 'I must,' he said huskily, kissing the tears from her eyes. 'You know I must.'

68

'Why must you?' she pleaded. 'Your father is always complaining that the king leaves the Border at risk. Could he not persuade Edward to appoint you his deputy in his absence?'

He said nothing and stared down into the lovely face that still enslaved him. He remembered his father's words: *love dulls the mind and slows the intellect.* And it was true; he was not his own man any longer. He could be swayed by her tears and, more, by the insatiable demands of his own body. He moved his hands to the warm swell of her breasts. 'I'll try,' he murmured and pulled roughly at the lacing of her gown. The lie fell too easily from his tongue.

'So there's to be war again.' Euphemia, Lady Heslarton, echoed the same trite remark that Margaret had already heard a thousand times. 'They say the King has asked the Commons to vote him another subsidy.' Her eyes dropped covetously to the clasp at Margaret's throat, costing her gown and the gem-starred caul that held her hair. 'My God, if Walter and I had even a thousandth of his revenues we could live like kings for the rest of our lives. Half a mark duty on every sack of wool sent abroad, besides his other income—and still it's not enough.'

Margaret attempted to put a little warmth into the smile she gave her sister. Euphemia had cause to feel resentful. Three husbands and not yet twenty-five, and this last even less to her taste than the others had been. Walter Heslarton was not the catch that Reginald Lucy or Robert Clifford had been; a humble knight with empty pockets whose only worth had been to free Euphemia from the charity of their father and find her a place at court. Her sister talked of little else but the paucity of her wardrobe and her husband's lack of wealth. These latter complaints she directed solely at Margaret. A true Neville, she saw no reason not to profit from her sister's good fortune.

Her voice dropped to the wheedling note that had already deprived Margaret of two of her best winter gowns. 'Walter says that Hal is to command troops under Lancaster. Walter's always had a mind to serve under Lancaster. Not that Oxford's not an able commander but Lancaster always has the pick of the troops, the pick of the prisoners. Perhaps if Hal were to speak for him, take Walter under his wing so to speak?' The broad hint hung in the air and strained Margaret's smile. Sometimes her family sickened her. Greedy and favour-seeking, where there was no opportunity for advancement they would make one.

Her brother Alexander was no better, his brilliant scholarship overwhelmed by ambition. He clawed his way up in the Church and cloaked hypocrisy with holiness. And John? She'd had nothing from him save the barest acknowledgement on the few occasions they had met. John would not come to her for favours but she knew that he would not hesitate to sacrifice her if she stood in his way.

Abruptly, she turned her head and met the cold lambent stare of Lady Percy. Enthroned on a gilded chair, her feet upon piled cushions, she laid an affectionate hand on the shoulder of Elizabeth Mowbray, the heiress to the Segrave estates and recently wed to Hal's cousin John. The gesture spoke worlds: Elizabeth Mowbray would have been a bride worthy of her son.

Margaret hid her trembling hands in the folds of her skirts. Jesu, was she never to be forgiven? Even when she was the mother of Hal's sons would she still be treated as the intruder, the Neville upstart who dared to cast her eyes on Mary Plantagenet's son?

Close at her elbow a voice echoed her thoughts. 'She'll not forgive you, you know.' Startled, she looked up into the smiling malicious eyes of Hal's brother Tom. His sharp face was softened by the sparse precocious beard that thinned to reddish down upon his cheeks. She forced a smile. She liked Tom in a strange uneasy way. He reminded her of John, aggressive yet unsure of himself. He was one of the few who had showed her any kindness since she had married Hal.

Politely she said, 'I hear that you are to fight in France.' War and the ascendancy of Gaunt were the only subjects that interested Thomas.

The frightening brilliance that leapt into his eyes was answer enough; the same look, less controlled, that she had seen in Hal's.

'The King is to address the council tomorrow at Westminster.' Tom settled by her side in eager animation. 'Though nothing has

70

been formally announced, I have it from Chandos that the advance guard under Lancaster will leave at the end of the month.' He laid special emphasis on the name of Edward's greatest general, converting a nodding aquaintanceship into that of a close counsellor. 'Naturally, the Percy contingent will fight under Lancaster.'

At the end of the month. Less than two weeks. Hal had not told her that and she wondered what else he had not told her. She glanced across the hall to where he sat in avid discourse with Salisbury. She could guess the subject and knew with sudden cold certainty that Hal would not give up his place in the King's army any more than Tom would. She would have to let him go. She remembered Mary Percy's sneer. *You can't keep a hawk caged for ever.* She swallowed hard to ease the dry feeling from her mouth. No, but they always came back to the lure. Hal would come back. He'd feel his wings in France and then come back. She would wait for him at Tughall. There was warmth and peace at Tughall. Old Sim the steward, grumbling and slovenly but kind in his abrupt way. His wife was a silly little Gascon woman like a plump hen, but she made Margaret laugh, even if she did steal the wine. And then there was the babe to think of; a son—would it be a son? She balanced the safe comforting thoughts against the weight of unease, and glanced round the hall. Tom had drifted off, bored with her lack of enthusiasm for the war. Euphemia had abandoned her for the more lucrative pursuit of Oxford's wife. From the corner of her eye she caught a glimpse of a short stocky young man in the bright saffron livery of Clarence. She smiled and beckoned as his eye fell upon her. He bowed courteously over her hand, his long sensitive mouth turned in a smile.

'You are welcome, Master Chaucer,' she said and bade him be seated. 'I trust that you do not wish to speak of the war?'

He smiled. His eyes were dark, the raw anguish of genius softened by humour. 'War distresses you then, my lady?'

'A little. There is talk of nothing else of late.'

'I fear that war is a necessary evil. Even I must serve my Lord of Clarence though I have little heart for it.'

'I have read some of your work,' Margaret said, remembering

71

how the Countess Maud had loved his poems. 'I thought them quite beautiful.'

Pleasure lifted the sadness from Geoffrey Chaucer's eyes. Praise was a rare commodity to him, like wealth. He was the son of a vintner who would never aspire to anything greater than a simple esquire. He had neither the gift for arms nor the inclination, and his only claim to riches was the few pence he earned scribbling love verses for the knights of Clarence's household. But he had the gift of insight. He could see the flaws and defects beneath a perfect countenance. He had an eye for beauty, an instinct for the purity of a soul and in his mind there was a wealth of feeling, as yet unformed. He smiled his thanks for her words and watched her face as she spoke of his verse. He saw the frightened shadow of a child behind the lovely eyes, the haunting fear of a grief yet to come. In his mind he laid her soul bare and captured its essence in a dozen words.

The next day they went by barge to Westminster, beneath the bridge hung with gawping Londoners, past the cranes that dipped and swung great vats of Gascony wine onto the quay at Queenhithe. Margaret sat straight-backed beneath an awning of azure silk and watched the watermen plunge matched white oars into the steely water, speeding them past Baynards Castle and the pungent trickle of the Fleet. The barge rose and fell sharply over slapping waves; the Percy crescent flashed on sleeve and cap and from the stern the Lion of Louvain trailed its angry tail upon the water. Lord Percy gave her a reassuring smile, dwarfed and dowdy beside the tall regality of his wife, who sat robed in faultless green samite, her frigid gaze turned up to where the scavenging gulls wheeled over Southwark. Margaret's hand slid to the comforting swell beneath her gown, smiling at the sudden overwhelming joy. Such bliss tempted providence; the greater the joy the greater the fear of its loss. Instinctively her eyes went to her husband's face, the face that calmed all fear and drove out the demons. He was her rock, her refuge against the consuming fear, the altar at which she worshipped. She drew his image round her like the warmth of fur.

After the daylight, Westminster Hall was dark despite the high windows and the cressets that flamed every yard's length. Mammoth tapestries graced every wall, giant figures glowing with the muted warmth of Arras silk looked down on a glittering company that seethed like shining beetles at their feet. At the end of the hall sat the King, his sons at his elbow, his ministers at his back; Lancaster, de Bohun, de Vere and Warwick, the closed and fast circle of nobility that radiated from the King like the spokes of a wheel. To his left Queen Philippa sat in drab splendour, her fine dark eyes glazed with pain and want of sleep, and beneath the thick sallow skin the blood flamed at furnace heat.

Then the roar of Windsor Herald turned all heads. The King had risen to address them and he waited till the last whisper had died. He had aged this past year, as if time had held back her hand then come upon him suddenly with a vengeance. His yellow hair was streaked with grey and crescents of unhealthy flesh pouched his eyes. Yet he could still command them; his voice could raise them to undreamt of heights, lifting each man from the dirt and squalor of the battlefield, cloaking Death with the brightness of chivalry. Margaret looked around her at the spellbound faces and saw greed and hatred and the bright avidity of chivalry. The King's strong voice filled the hall and touched the dark corners that lay in all of them: the inbred hatred of the French, the barbaric lust for blood that lay beneath the thin veneer of courtliness—Edward called them all out, inspected and approved them. England's cause was blessed by God. Had not Crécy and Poitiers proven where His favour lay? His voice bound them into one spirit: King's men, all of them, from the lords at the high table to the meanest scullion by the door.

'My lords, we are weary of French perfidy, of our trust and grace finding only treachery its reward. In all good faith we set the terms of the treaty and John of Valois has set his seal to them; yet his ministers are content to see his word dishonoured, to see us cheated of the lands won and held by our forefathers for six generations. They demand fealty of us when in truth, the fealty is owed by them.' He rose from the chair of estate and came to stand before them. His eyes blazed fiercely in the high colour of his face, the thrall of his voice inciting them to passion. 'For the sake of peace we were willing to cede our right to the Crown of

73

France, but that peace has been spurned, my lords, thrown back in our faces by French scum.' The hypnotic cadence of his voice rose above the angry growl. 'Are we to let them conquer without a blow? Shall we forever let them harry our trade and drain England's wealth?'—this to the merchants whose grudging loans paid for the King's ships. 'Or do we fight and grind these insolent French dogs into dust? Will you array yourselves, my lords, and attend us to our glorious crowning at Rheims?'

Margaret swayed against the bulk of an unknown knight. The fevered roar of voices drummed in her ears and she felt the crushing weight of the crowd at her back. All around her, ravening mouths chanted Edward's name till the hall resounded like a drum. She looked at Hal and saw his face transformed by subtle cruelty, his eyes hard and brilliant, full of the faceless enemy conjured by the King's invective. She touched his arm and he turned, as if surprised by her presence. The look in his eyes turned her sick.

Calais, the brightest jewel in Edward's crown, trembled to its foundations with the pounding feet of his soldiery. They crammed the narrow streets, spreading beyond the walls into the wide fields where the banners of the free companies bloomed like gaudy flowers. In the town the very air quivered with discontent. Victuals were scarce, fresh meat was a dream and a loaf cost a fortune; only in the brothels and ale houses that stood cheek to jowl in the grimy quayside streets was trade brisk.

Hal edged his horse through the labyrinth of sloping streets. He was bored and slightly drunk and sick of the strench of rancid meat that wafted from the cookshops plying on every corner. For a month the advance guard under Lancaster had striven to control the drunken rabble of mercenaries that had flocked to Calais to join the English. Then Edward had arrived, tardily and out of humour and with such a vast following that half the waiting companies had been turned away. Only Englishmen and a few Germans had been retained; the rest were turned loose to vent their spleen on an already stricken countryside. It was October now and the cold crisp air held the threat of winter. The King's commanders muttered darkly on the scarcity of food and foretold a bad winter. But the King was deaf to hints of postponement; he would be crowned at Rheims before Christmas. He would settle for nothing less.

Unchallenged, Hal rode into the outer bailey, weaving his way through the streams of wagons and plodding oxen that edged their way to the King's bulging warehouses. The tall salt-encrusted towers of the keep rose white and clean from the sweat and dung of the bailey but inside the air was heavy and malodorous, the wide passages crammed with knights who had nothing better to do than check and polish weapons that had been checked and polished a hundred times before.

In the high-roofed hall fires roared at either end and the crushed stems of lavender rose in scented dust beneath his feet. The courtiers were a mass of jostling colour: the arrogant red and gold of the nobility, the warm amber of furs, and here and there the dusty black of the clerks of Edward's chancery.

Henry of Lancaster was seated on the dais between the grim dourness of the de Bohun brothers. He held Hal's eye in stiff formal acknowledgement, the barest of greetings, as if he were the lowliest knight in his retinue. Hal turned away, anger and grief hardening his mouth. That it could come to this, when Lancaster had been father to him in all but name. . . . Pride rose and quickly covered the hurt. He had no need of Lancaster, his affection or influence; he had no need of any but himself.

Across the room the sound of a woman's laughter floated, distinct against the deep rumble of so many men. Significantly, in the place reserved for the Queen, Joanna of Kent sat robed in costly velvet wrought with a fine silver thread that traced the heavy swell of her breasts. Her silk-shod feet were warmed by a page and, beside her, Prince Edward curled his great length and fed her fat Burgundy grapes. She must have been past thirty but she was still lovely. Her rich russet hair gleamed from beneath gossamer veiling and the heavy emeralds that clasped her neck were the exact colour of her eyes. Salisbury's widow and Holland's mistress before she became his wife, she warmed the Prince of Wales's bed now. She had that quality of making any man feel infinitely desirable and, though Hal knew she had cut her teeth on men like him, he could still feel a quickening of his blood at that smile. He bowed and brushed the long jewelled fingers with his respectful kiss. The green eyes caressed and promised but he knew the measure of that look now. Any man under fifty was eligible for it, but no more than that. Joanna had her sights set on higher peaks and though Thomas Holland's timely grant of the Governorship of Normandy had given credence to her presence in France, all knew except poor cuckolded Holland himself that she came less to serve her husband and more the Prince of Wales. But Hal smiled and his eyes paid her dutiful homage; it was expected of him and he was not fool enough to offend the woman who might be the next Queen of England.

He found himself a quiet corner screened by a knot of clerks. The hall was hot and stinking with humanity. Men sat back to back, knee to knee, laughing, swearing, quarrelling, tense with uncertainty. His lungs ached for a clean breath and he thought of Margaret and the strong sharp air of the north. Frowningly, he remembered the manner of his departure; the tears and her stubborn refusal to bear the child in the safety of Alnwick. He thought of Tughall and the walls that sweated with damp, of the steward and his wife who took full advantage of Margaret's gentleness. She had seemed so frail and helpless when he left her. Half child, half woman, with a child's wild excess of emotion that swung from joy to groundless despair in the space of a breath. It was that which he had once found so intoxicating, the pure and joyful innocence of youth clothed in the delight of a woman's body. Now the child dominated and robbed the woman of her charm.

A voice at his elbow made him glance up irritably; Roger Mortimer clambered over the priestly skirts of the chancery clerks, clutching a brimming hanap in each hand. Hal smiled and squeezed along the narrow bench. He could suffer Mortimer, as clean and open as the Welsh marches he ruled so ably, one of the few men in whose company he could speak freely without fear of his words being used against him. It was the nearest he ever came to friendship now. He drank deeply; the wine was old and turning sour but it helped to blunt the edge of his ill humour.

'What news then?' he asked.

Mortimer licked pungent droplets from his yellow beard. 'We march in two days. A straight orderly march to Rheims where it seems that the French Archbishop has been persuaded to set the crown on Edward's head—for a consideration.'

Hal's mouth turned in a wry smile. All men had their price, even archbishops. He looked round the assembled faces and saw the quick ready smiles, the assiduous attendance that parodied friendship; all anxious to please, anxious to catch the regal eye. There were a few exceptions, his father perhaps, sitting cheek to jowl with Salisbury, as out of place as a crow among peacocks in his plain serviceable fustian. There would be no earldoms or Garter robes for him; those were reserved for the ambitious few skilled in policy and blandishments, the time-servers and favour-seekers who scrabbled for patronage among the lords who held the grip on land and power. Like his brother Tom, trailing after Gaunt and his lickspittle crew. Hal's cold contemptuous glance sought Tom out among the knot of courtiers who clustered round Gaunt; John Neville, his hand set lightly on Gaunt's arm; Richard Lyons and Stafford, all but fawning at his feet. And Tom, his face wreathed in eager smiles, hovering like a hound scenting blood. Whatever his own price was, it was higher than Tom's; Tom had always sold himself too cheap. As if he felt the pressure of his eyes, Tom turned and advanced toward him, resplendent in new velvet, quilted and bordered in vair.

Hal's brows lifted in faint mockery. 'Your master pays fine wages, Tom,' he observed acidly.

His brother's face flushed an angry red. 'And what is that supposed to mean?'

'It means whatever you take it to mean, Tom.' Hal smiled maliciously. 'Whatever your conscience and pride allow it to mean.'

Tom's cheeks burnt crimson beneath his scrawny beard and he was agonizingly aware of Mortimer's amused stare and that of the clerks who had abandoned logic and grammar in favour of eavesdropping. 'You're jealous,' he said tightly.

'Jealous?' the malicious voice rose on a note of feigned amazement, 'Of what, pray? Of the fact that your garb is reminiscent of a popinjay in malt or of how you acquired it?'

'You're jealous because I have Prince John's favour,' Tom retorted with an unsuccessful sneer.

'An honour you share with any man prepared to sell himself body and soul to our royal cousin,' Hal said dryly. 'That I do not number among them is by choice, not necessity. One Percy at his heels is quite enough.'

Tom smothered the yelling rage that boiled in his throat. The cruel mouth that housed the venomous tongue that he could have gladly torn out was smiling, goading him to the sheer delight of lashing out with his itching fists. He swallowed hard, smiling faintly at the triumph of self-control. He'd learnt that much at least. He'd not give Hal or their grinning audience the satisfaction of a rough-house.

'Well, Tom—lost your tongue or merely worn it out licking His Grace's boots?' Hal's eyes gleamed with sadistic pleasure, aware that Tom carried tales to Gaunt and through him to Lancaster, damning him even further in the old man's eyes. Then Mortimer's discreet cough warned him. He looked up and saw Gaunt at his brother's back, his hand upon his shoulder. 'There, Tom,' Hal said with deliberate contempt. 'Here's my lord come to rescue you.'

He rose unhurriedly and bowed. 'Your Grace,' he said with heavy courtesy.

Gaunt caught the infinitesimal slurring of his speech and sneered. 'Looking for courage in a wine cup, Percy?' he said. 'Afraid that some Frenchman will slit your throat?'

Hal gave his slow unnerving smile. 'Drunk, I grant you, my lord, but afraid, no. Death is something I have never feared. It comes to us all. We all wait for it.' His eyes left Gaunt's face for a moment and sought out Lancaster in the throng. 'Only some of us wait more eagerly than others, my lord,' he added quietly.

The skin around Gaunt's mouth grew pale and tight, and in the silence that fell the men around them quickly veiled their eyes and set their countenances lest a careless look should betray them. The silence grew and ran the length of the hall then burst into a furtive whispering. Neither man spoke; both rode out the uneasy quiet with faint surprise that they had come so near open hatred almost without being aware of it. Then Gaunt turned away and the ranks of courtiers closed in at his back but his eyes left Hal with the promise that his words would be remembered and repaid with interest.

Mortimer's face was anxious. 'Have a care, Hal. You'll do yourself no good to make an open enemy of Gaunt.'

Hal shrugged and called for more wine. It was too late for that. Each knew the other too well for empty gesture and compromise.

'He's a powerful man, Hal,' Mortimer went on. 'When Lancaster dies—'

'When Lancaster dies then *he* will be Lancaster,' Hall interrupted savagely. 'Believe me, Roger, our princely cousin dreamt all of this before you or I ever thought it. He waits for dead men's shoes and rewards his premature court with promised glory. Well, I'll not be one of them, Roger. My brother toadies enough for both of us.'

Mortimer stared at his boots. He was wary of power. His own grandfather had been hung like a common felon for love of power and this misfortune had dogged his father's short life. It had taken twenty years to win back his lands and the King's trust. To many the name of Mortimer was still sullied with a King's blood. He glanced at the still, brooding figure beside him. It was easy enough to make enemies, harder to lose them; Hal Percy would make them deliberately, out of pride and temperament, because he would not bend or yield. John of Gaunt would fear a man like that, who could not be bought or bribed and knew no master but his own stubborn will. Mortimer gave a wry little smile. Hal was the kind of man he would like to have been if fate had not decreed otherwise.

Two days later the royal army had left Calais, split into a deadly glittering triumvirate that kept the French pinned within their walls and allowed the English to pillage unhindered. In Artois the English reaped the harvest they had sown two summers before. The stricken countryside yielded nothing; the fields were a bare wilderness of crows and ragged children digging with bare hands for worms and beatles. The women came by night, thin dirty skeletons willing to lie with a dozen men at a time for a crust or a handful of grain. By day, children crept from ditches as they passed, braving the hooves and cartwheels to run alongside with outstretched hands and pitiful little cries of '*Ayez pitié.*' By the second week in December they had reached the outskirts of Rheims and even as the King planned his triumphal entry, the news came: the turncoat Archbishop had turned his coat yet again and refused them entry to the city. Edward had raged for a day, then calmly deployed his forces round the impregnable walls and all had sat down to keep a cheerless Christmas before Rheims.

A group of fifty horsemen sat motionless in the shadow of the trees, listening to the ceaseless drip of water from branch to branch. Hal glanced at the set faces of the men beside him, dirty, hungry and dishevelled, with their bones shining through unshaven cheeks. He looked back to the wet glistening roofs of the town. It was no more than a single street flanked by tall houses opening out into a market square and a little way apart, ringed by a hedge, the shadow of a church. All virgin and untouched, a prize that the scavenging mercenaries had missed.

He forced his mind away from the grinding ache of his belly. It was almost two days since he had eaten and he had fared better than most. Twenty miles away England's vast army lay sprawled round the walls of Rheims, verging on starvation. This was the fifth week of the King's fruitless siege; five weeks of freezing wind and rain that had all but broken their spirit. Food was scarce and what little the land could have yielded had been taken behind the city walls, but stubbornly Edward refused to withdraw while his army wallowed in mud and water and fed on turnips and the flesh of horses that had died for lack of fodder. No man thought of glory now. Food and shelter commanded a higher price than gold.

They slid out of the darkness almost furtively, their hooves muffled by mud and soft turf. They slowed to a walk as they entered the dark narrow funnel of shuttered houses. A painted sign above a cordwainer's shop flapped and creaked unnervingly on its pole. They crowded close, nervously fingering their swords, aware that once in the bottleneck of the street they were trapped.

In the market place a corpse in the rags of English livery dangled from a gibbet and flung the stench of rotting flesh into their faces. It was deathly quiet, no sound except their own, no sign of a watch. Then suddenly a dog leapt snarling on a length of rusty chain. Hal saw the glow of red eyes, the gleam of white fangs in slavering jaws. Then it yelped once and dropped like a stone, the blade of an axe buried in its skull. But it had served its purpose. The town erupted into sudden terrified life. Cressets flickered at hastily opened windows; faces appeared and quickly withdrew, voices pitched in terror at the thud and rip of axes against their doors.

Hal kicked in the last splinters of the tailor's door. At the back of the shop two skinny 'prentices crouched in a corner. There were bales of cloth stacked shoulder high; linen and silks, a bolt of murrey velvet spread out and pinned on a trestle. In the small upper room a woman sat screaming on a truckle bed, clutching a sheet over huge white breasts. A man, the tailor, as sharp and pointed as his own needle, struggled into shirt and hose. He stared and swallowed then fell on his knees.

'Mercy, lord. For pity's sake spare us.' He shuffled forward on his knees, frantically stripping the rings from his hands. 'Take what we have; a few jewels. A purse of fifty crowns.' He garbled through a froth of spittle, one terrified eye on Hal's face, the other on the men who moved round the room, stripping walls, hacking the locks off chests and presses, heaving anything of value through the window into the street below. They found a cupboard fastened like an armoury. The woman shrieked like a mad thing as the door splintered and gave.

They stood staring like children at the contents: two loaves of trencher bread, a moon of cheese, a plate of salted herrings and a half-eaten ham—a treasure house of smell and taste that flooded their mouths with saliva. Hal stuffed his mouth with the soft fragrant cheese and tore a hunk of bread from the loaf. It was stale and dry as sawdust but to his empty roaring belly it was nectar.

They herded the tailor and his wife out into the street. Clifford had already fired some of the houses and the gush and roar of flame was loud in his ears.

81

Soldiers crowded in doorways and darted past, laden with plate and ornament; a woman ran naked from a burning house her body glowing in the scorching light. He turned away in pity as the dark shadowy figures of the mercenaries surrounded her.

The rain had eased to a fine insidious mist that spat and hissed on the flaming houses. Clifford rode toward him, dragging two Frenchmen by their hair. He dropped them casually at Hal's feet and kicked the older of the two to his knees as he attempted to rise.

'The bastard had food, Hal. Sacks of it, hidden away, this man says.' He jerked his thumb at the bruised and terrified face of his informer.

Hal looked at the older of the two Frenchmen. Fat and prosperous, a merchant by his dress, he turned a white humble face up toward him.

'He speaks false, my liege,' the merchant gabbled. 'There is no food, only what you see in my humble kitchen, nothing more.' He shuffled forward on his knees, his bonnet clamped to his brow with a ring of sweat. 'We are a poor town, my lord. You see—' he flung out his hand toward a group of shivering children, 'Even our young ones starve.'

'But *you* do not starve, monsieur.' Hal sneered as he eyed the merchant's quivering jowls. 'Such a mountain of flesh needs more than a diet of turnips to sustain it. Come—' he prodded his sword into the Frenchman's paunch, 'tell us where your food is and we will leave you in peace.'

The Frenchman's eyes narrowed craftily. Gold they could do without, food was a different matter. 'I tell you my lord, there is none,' he whined. 'It's not to be had even for gold.' His eyes darted from side to side like a frightened rabbit. 'Perhaps if you would allow me to confer with the elders of the town,' he said, 'a sum might be raised. . . .'

Hal leant down from his horse, leaning close so their faces almost touched. He grabbed his hair and turned the Frenchman's head to where the gibbet thrust out its short ungainly arm. 'The food, you dog, or I shall hang you in chains and let my archers use you as a target.'

The Frenchman's tongue darted fearfully over his lips and Hal saw the thoughts that passed across his sweating countenance; hope of a miracle, hope that the enemy would settle for a little wanton destruction and plunder. That last hope fled as the man looked into the cold empty eyes of his captor.

Grudgingly he led them to the hiding place beneath the dirt floor of an outhouse. Hal counted the sacks of grain and flour, the salted meat and fish carefully wrapped in greased cloths, enough to feed his men for a week. While the food was being loaded he went back out into the dark street. Fire still gnawed sullenly at the corner of a barn and the doorways heaved with the ugly coupled shadows of soldiers and sobbing women. He rode in among them, shouting at them to disperse till he saw the riderless horse blazoned with his own arms—Tom's horse. He rode toward it, his heart thumping in sudden alarm, then he heard his brother's voice followed by the sharp painful wail of a child.

A boy cowered in the corner of the hut, his mouth a yawning cavern of hunger. His left cheek was ridged by angry fingermarks and his eyes were wide and staring, fixed on the filthy loaf in his brother's hands. Tom turned and flushed at the look in Hal's eyes.

'French scum do not eat while Englishmen starve,' he shouted challengingly.

His eyes cold, Hal plucked the bread from his brother's grasp and thrust it at the child who snatched it without a word and ran out into the night. He smiled at his brother's fiery cheeks. 'Such lack of foresight, Tom,' he mocked. 'We must feed the little knaves or there'll be no Frenchmen left for you to kill next year.'

They rode easily in the lengthening shadows, the hounds panting noisily in their wake. A freshly caught buck swung weightily on its poles and trailed blood onto the white chalk road. Roger Mortimer eased his mount alongside Hal's.

'Christ's Blood, I never thought I should taste venison again.'

Hal grinned and glanced along the line of men: well fed, well heeled, their pockets lined with Burgundy's wealth—a transformation from the half starved crew that had limped into Chalon a month ago. At the end of January, the King had admitted defeat and withdrawn from Rheims, turning south–east into Burgundy. Their luck had changed with the weather and they had taken Tonnerre as the first spring sunlight struck a steaming warmth from the ground. Then on to Guillon where their sprawling camp had threatened the budding vines that were Burgundy's life. It was a land of plenty, only lightly touched by war, and therefore had the more to lose. The King's price, as always, had been high: two thousand gold moutons in exchange for a three–years' truce. Duke Philip had paid it and gladly, like a man pays to rid his fields of vermin.

Strung out in single file, they passed through the straggle of dwellings that had once been a thriving village. In the distance the solemn note of the curfew bell of Rouvray echoed back from the vine-clad hills and Clifford, riding in the lead, held up his hand to slow the pace. He turned his head slowly to the blank doorways and his mouth flew open in alarm. It was all the warning they had before the rustling shadows shaped themselves into men and horses.

Hal's horse wheeled and plunged in the sudden circle of attack. Shock had slowed his reactions and almost too late he saw the upraised sword and felt the stinging bite of steel opening his cheek. He flung himself flat across his horse's neck, spitting blood. He could hardly hold the beast as it screamed and lashed out with its hooves while the yelping dogs bit and tore at its belly in their own panic. He jabbed his bloody spurs hard into its flanks, dragging grimly at the bit to turn it back into the chaos of men and dogs and horses. Then the weight of steel-encased flesh struck him full in the back. He hit the ground with a force that knocked all the breath from him and only blind instinct saved him from the trampling hooves. He crawled into the shelter of a doorway. Blood pumped from the gash in his cheek and trickled into his mouth. He could hardly see for the stinging tears of pain.

He was almost on his feet when the flail wrapped itself around him. The five spiked heads anchored themselves in his back and raked his flesh to an agonizing fire. He lashed out blindly with his sword and met nothing but shadows. The flail snaked out toward him again and he leapt back out of its reach into the darkness of a derelict house. He leant against the crumbling wall and saw the dark shape of the Frenchman fill the doorway. He was swinging the flail in a figure of eight and Hal could see that he held a sword in his other hand. He ducked as the flail hissed toward him and hit the wall behind his head, spitting a hail of broken stones and mortar into his face. He made two lightning thrusts but his blade slid harmlessly off the Frenchman's heavy armour and he had laid himself open to attack from the swinging flail again. He screamed as it bit and gouged his chest but he managed to grab one of the chains and wound it round his wrist, jerking the Frenchman slightly off balance. He dropped his sword and drew the little dagger from his belt, still jerking the Frenchman round so that his sword-thrusts fell short. Using all his height and weight he pulled the man hard against him. The thin blade slid easily between the join of the visor and the mail gorget. The Frenchman made no sound as Hal severed the vein at the base of his jaw. Hal felt the body arch and stretch away from him and the warm blood rush over his body. He withdrew the blade and the Frenchman fell quietly to the floor.

He leant in the doorway, choking on blood and dust. His back was torn and bleeding from the flail and the left side of his face was a burning focus of pain. Outside the light had almost gone. There were only a score of men left in the clearing, a few shadows indistinguishable as friend or enemy. He saw one of the huntsmen moving deftly among the wounded dogs that writhed in agony. One thrust, quick and clean, and it was done.

Clifford sat cradling his head in his hands. He looked up and squinted at Hal with one bright eye, the other closed and purpled from the cut on his brow.

'We did it, Hal,' he grinned and showed startlingly white teeth. 'Armed to the teeth and nearly twice our number but we sent them packing, didn't we? Routed them to a man.'

Hal nodded and wiped the blood and sweat from his face. He saw one of Mortimer's knights picking his way through the slain. At the edge of the clearing the rest of the dogs fed happily on the forgotten buck. Hal smiled. Mortimer would not have venison after all. He scanned the faces crowding together beneath the trees.

'Where's Mortimer?' he asked Clifford.

'Not seen him.' Clifford stripped the tattered blood–stained doublet from his back. 'Not since the attack.'

Hal looked toward the dark squat shapes of the houses. There was a body slumped against a wall, its head lolling grotesquely sideways. It was not Mortimer. He found another two in a narrow alleyway, both French, both dead. The body of the Frenchman he had killed was still there, his blood drained into a dark wet pool around his head. In the last house he found Mortimer. He lay where he had fallen, his belly slit from breast-bone to thigh. His entrails bubbled obscenely from the wound and oozed onto the dirty floor. A rat sat crouched upon his chest, its long whiskers dabbled in blood. It raised bright red eyes and stared at Hal.

Hal leant against the crumbling wall and shook the stinging heat from his eyes. Then slowly he turned and retched onto the floor.

He lay in the warm scented sweetness of the hay, his eyes closed against the shaft of sunlight that pierced the barn's ill-kept roof. He was drunk, gloriously and magnificently drunk, and had been to a greater or lesser degree since they left Rouvray. He had been knighted by Prince Edward that same day yet the joy of it had been dimmed by Mortimer's death: gutted and packed in salt, his corpse marched with them, and the remembrance of his friend's hideous death still woke Hal, sweating in the night.

He turned on his back, his body slack and drowsy with wine. In the corner Tom Beauchamp droned a tavern song and three of Clifford's knights played drunkenly at dice, making the most of this brief respite before they marched in the morning and ploughed their furrow of destruction up to the walls of Paris. A week after Mortimer's death, news had come that had stopped them in their tracks. The French had attacked the English coast and burnt Winchelsea, massacring the inhabitants whilst they knelt at mass. Edward, in his fury, had turned back the way he had come and loosed his bestial troops on fair unspoilt Burgundy. None was spared and now the screams of tortured flesh and ravaged women were the daily accompaniment to their progress.

He turned his head as Clifford's voice sounded outside. He straddled the doorway, his teeth white in his dark greasy beard. Half a dozen women crowded before him, submissive as sheep, the terror of rape dulled by repetition. They began to yelp in fear as he herded them forward and his laughter shook the timbers as his knights came and tore at their clothing.

A vicious shove sent a girl sprawling in Hal's lap. He stared at her through a haze of intoxication. She was barely pretty, the fine eyes and the soft roundness of youth marred by fear. Strangely, he felt no desire, though it was six months since he had touched a woman. His memories of Margaret that roused him to agony in his dreams were quenched like ice water when it came to the reality of another woman.

He stretched out a hand in reassurance as the sound of Clifford's noisy lust floated between them. The girl drew back on her haunches, her eyes narrow with hatred and suspicion, then slowly she leant toward him and spat full in his face. The spittle frothed and bloomed upon his cheek and filled him with sharp anger. He caught at her wrist and pulled her roughly toward him; she spat and hissed like a cat and sank sharp teeth into the soft vulnerable flesh of his neck. The sharp agonizing pain transfixed him for a moment then he wrenched at her hair and flung her brutally on her back. His hands shook with sudden inexplicable rage; he thought of Mortimer, dishonoured and slaughtered like a pig by French scum, French scum that cowered behind their castle walls and refused battle.

She screamed and clawed at his face, opening the barely healed wound on his cheek. Beneath his imprisoning weight she fought and writhed against him and the sheer violence of her movements sent hot needles of lust through his body. He breathed curses in her ear as he tore her gown, bruising the soft white flesh that sprang into his hands. Margaret's face rose and burned briefly in his consciousness but in that moment he was lost to all but the raging anger of his mind and body.

It was brief, the swift waves of ecstasy mingled with pain as she bit and clawed at his skin. The girl lay quiet now, so quiet that his heart leapt in fear till he saw the tears slide from beneath her trembling lids. Gently, he covered her with the warm hay and turned away, looking straight into the grinning sneer of Clifford's squire. Hal smiled and walked toward him. Still smiling, he drove his fists with all his force into the fat lecherous face.

Tughall

Maud Neville dipped her fingers for the third time into the comfit dish at her elbow. She was with child again and her high round belly thrust from crimson sarcenet like a ripe damson. Her hair was coiled in thick braids and surmounted by a high-horned cap that gave her face a faintly bovine look.

She bit into a sugared voilet. 'You must try to cheer yourself, Margaret. Hal will not fret overmuch for the loss of a daughter,' she said in the forthright blundering manner she shared with her brother, Lord Percy.

'Sons are the thing as far as men are concerned—as I know to my cost,' she added bitterly. She rose, oblivious to the look of pain that swept Margaret's face, still talking in her high complaining voice of the grievances that she would never have dared utter before her husband John. Maud was afraid of John, afraid of his almost fanatical need for a son and his inevitable disgust when she bore yet another daughter. Her passionate desire to please him remained unfulfilled. She knew that John did not care for her in a fleshly way. He came to her bed reluctantly and only to get her with child again.

Margaret stared from the casement, watching the winding thread of the road till it dipped and was lost in the sweep of moorland and clustering forest. Maud's voice rattled in her ears, the clumsy ill-chosen words opening up the barely healed wound. Hal would not mourn for the loss of a daughter, but she did, mourned with all her heart and mind for the frail thing that had been born, struggled briefly and died all within the space of a breath. A day and night of grinding pain and blood and, at the end of it, a small shrouded bundle no bigger than the span of her two hands. And the fault was hers. Her thoughts scourged her like a penitent's lash. She had defied Hal and remained at Tughall

88

in spite of the threat of a harsh winter. Christmas had come and brought the cold crushing snow down from the north, freezing man and beast alike beneath its white innocent face. Somehow she had survived the killing cold that crept beneath the doors and glassed the flagstones of the hall.

Fires roared at every hearth and forced the snow that capped the roof into a grudging thaw, but outside the drifts still climbed the walls and imprisoned them in a twilight world. Then the day had come when she had awoken to the relentless drip of melting snow. Spears of ice had snapped and plunged from the eaves and the fields were patched with the blackening thaw. Gaily she had ordered the steward and his men to dig a path from the door and had taken her first clean breath in months, smiling up at the pale sun struggling from behind leaden clouds. Then the world had tilted and spun crazily; the sun had slid behind the grinning gargoyle's head that surmounted the roof. All through the long dark hours, that hideous face pinnacled with sun and snow had stayed in her mind.

She turned, dimly aware that Maud was still speaking, and stared at her plump, stupid face, as she picked the last of the fragrant crumbs from the bottom of the empty dish. ' 'Tis something you grow used to,' Maud went on. 'No woman expects to rear more than half the children she bears. The Queen's grace has lost three and I myself two, and one a son at that.' She smiled her fatuous, empty smile. 'And Hal will be home soon. There will be more babies within a month and you'll be letting out your gowns again.'

Margaret rose and stretched her cold lips in a smile. She did not expect Maud to understand the pounding grief of her loss. Maud bred like a sow, fat, healthy infants that slid from her wide hips with ease. Envy soured her tongue. 'Then we must pray that if you bear a son, it will live,' she said with rare spite. 'As you say, Maud, none of us expects to raise all the children we bear.'

Maud blinked foolishly, sharp enough to sense attack but unsure of its direction. Suddenly Margaret pitied her brother. It was a long time since she had thought of John, a long time since she had thought of anything except her own crushing loneliness which the rare furtive visits of her sister-in-law did nothing to relieve. John had his coveted knighthood now, bestowed by the King himself, outside the walls of Paris. She was glad for him, but nothing more. Even her beloved brother had faded from her world now.

'Will you tell John that you have visited Tughall?' she asked suddenly, and saw the guilty colour creep into Maud's face.

'I think not,' Maud said. 'He would not care for it with my time so near.'

Margaret allowed the clumsy excuse to pass. How like John—stubborn, unforgiving John, and cowardly too in his way, venting his anger against her on poor defenceless Maud. 'Well then,' she said, 'we shall agree to say nothing.'

She watched Maud's departure with relief and stood by the window till her litter had swayed from sight. She closed the shutters against the piercing daylight and moved softly into the small windowless room that adjoined her chamber. Candles gleamed in the velvet-hung gloom and the Virgin's face shone in the white translucent flame; a woman's face, compassionate and understanding. She knelt before the prie-dieu and closed her eyes against the scalding tears. 'Sweet Mother of Christ, give me strength,' she whispered. Self-pity rose inside her. Jesu, how she had suffered with none but a witless crone for comfort. She had come so close to death and had prayed for it in those last hours. Instead, death had taken the babe she had longed for. She had even failed Hal in that and she could imagine the spiteful satisfied curve of Mary Percy's mouth when they returned to Alnwick. But it was over. She must find her strength in that. The war was over; Hal was safe, landed at Dover a week since. A week, perhaps less, and he would be home. She closed her eyes and held the thought close like a talisman.

The rumble of men's voices so long unheard filled her ears like a joyous song. Their spurred feet trampled the wax sheen of the boards and scuffed the rushes into dusty heaps; the servants, stung into sudden life, scurried back and forth with wine.

Margaret stood at the foot of the stairs, her hands trembling in the wide belled sleeves of her gown as he came toward her. He was subtly aged by the short golden beard and thinner, the leanness adding to his height. The scar on his face had barely healed and added a new ruthlessness to his expression. She saw by his face that he had heard about the child and leant close against him, feeling the warm strength of his arms around her. The halting, loving words whispered against her cheek brought soft tears to her eyes; his arms closed tighter around her and she was filled with pounding life. She was whole again and for the first time since his going was rid of the chill of fear. She turned to the company that sought lodging for the night before riding further north and smiled her hospitality, though she grudged them every minute that they kept her from Hal. But she had waited this long, a few hours more would only make the joy of it all the sweeter.

She marvelled at her own transformation and saw herself mirrored in his eyes; the bloom of sudden colour lifting her face from the whiteness of grief, her body melting from its perpetual cold in the warmth of his presence. Their hands touched furtively beneath the cloths at the high table and she was reminded of the lovers who had strained to each other in the dance at Leicester. With an effort she kept her thoughts anchored to the little company who sat and feasted at her table. She smiled at old Lord Percy's strident bellow and suffered Clifford's lecherous wink and heard again the glorious conclusion of the war that had been snatched from near defeat.

After Burgundy the royal army had turned toward Paris and camped on the heights overlooking the city. The Regent Charles had still defied them and even after a month of English brutality had refused to meet Edward's terms. The King had turned south again, towards Chartres and the unravaged valley of the Loire, camping outside Brétigny at the end of September. The sky at their back had been banked with black-bellied clouds and they had pitched their tents in the uneasy silence of a coming storm. Then suddenly the world was dark. A wind, sprung suddenly from nowhere, surged and roared in their ears. Lightning tore at the darkness and turned it into fearful day, stabbing earthwards, turning their armour into sizzling shells of death. Then the rain came; ice cold, driven in wild forking gusts by the wind, freezing into pebbles of ice that felled men and horses where they stood. Men ran wildly without direction or purpose, rushing blindly into the paths of demented horses, shedding their lethal armour as they stumbled through a sea of mud. From the shelter of the town, the King had watched and wept as he saw his army vanquished before his eyes.

Yet out of this had come triumph. In the morning, beneath a sky of smiling innocence, they had counted their dead and hacked their graves from frozen mud before moving on to Chartres. While the King lay prostrate with grief on the cold stone of the cathedral floor, the French bishops had come and sued for peace.

'All that the King had asked for and more.' Lord Percy thumped the table with his fist and looked triumphantly round the gathering as if he himself had wrought all this.

'*And* three million crowns ransom for that idiot king of theirs.' Clifford picked his large white teeth with his forefinger.

Margaret said softly, 'Then we are at peace? The war is over?'

Clifford looked at her as if she were a simpleton. 'Peace!' he shouted derisively. 'Only for as long as it suits us, my lady. This fine treaty is only paper and so full of holes that I could ride my horse through them.' He tapped his stubby forefinger on the cloth. 'Let us see if they keep the terms before we speak of peace. I've never met a Frenchman you could trust yet, and there's Mortimer's death to avenge.' He crossed himself hastily. 'Gutted like a rotten herring in some filthy villein's hut—'

'His son Edmund is to become the King's ward, I believe,' Hal interrupted swiftly, seeing Margaret's colour fade.

His father nodded, picking the soft kernel from a walnut. 'It seems to be the curse of the Mortimers,' he observed, 'The father never lives to see the son in manhood. There's not one of them lived beyond thirty for three generations.'

Margaret looked away. She did not want to think of Mortimer and his fatherless son or the dreadful implication of Clifford's words: endless war, endless separation from Hal. Covertly she feasted her eyes on his golden height and the lithe formidable grace of his body. She saw where the shadows dwelt in the hollows of his face and where amber demons lurked in ambush in his eyes. The face of angel and devil combined and all she ever wanted to look upon.

Hal rode down alone through the field of seeding poppies, the dust of newly threshed corn dry in his mouth. The sun was hard and bright in his eyes and for mile after mile the sun-bleached moorland glared with flowering gorse. He turned his horse along the course of the river where fish dreamt in summer warmth, spurring to a gallop along the flat tussocky meadow. The ground blurred beneath the pounding hooves and spat soft mud into his face. A heron shrieked and rose from the water with a flap of silver wings. He felt the rushing air burn his face and snatch the breath out of him as he plunged into the dark thicket. Crouching low over the flying mane he jerked his mount between the shadowy boles and leaf-laden boughs that slapped and raked his skin; then out again into the sunlight where his horse checked, blinded by the sudden light, then thundered obediently on. The ground dropped away below him, humped with purpling heather, and slicks of brown peat. He slackened his pace, leaning his weight away from the rushing slope. The hedge loomed up, a tangle of blackthorn splashed with nodding heads of meadow-sweet. He pulled at the reins till the horse's head was up and he could feel its haunches quivering with power. It rose effortlessly, stretched in an arc of gleaming bronze amid the sight and whisper of rushing air, and landed faultlessly in the tree-ringed clearing.

Hal dismounted and flung himself down in the cool shadows. His legs still trembled from the force of his ride and his breath was dry as sand in his throat. He lay back in the warm scented grass and watched the sun tip the height of the tall oaks, remembering when he and Tom had ridden this same ground with their first fledgling hawks and shared foolish boyhood dreams. A long time ago. He and Tom were strangers now, gone their own separate ways; but he still remembered the dreams. Tom was to have been the invincible warrior, carving fame and fortune from the wars. And he, already cast in his uncle of Lancaster's image, had dreamt of power; lord of the north, the scourge of the Scots, the intimate of kings and princes. Perhaps in his heart the dream was still there, but not the way it had been then, all bought and paid for by Lancaster. He was his own man now and at the beck and call of none. He smiled ruefully; perhaps not entirely his own man. He was bound with chains of a different kind now, chains of his own making. Margaret was with child again and lost in a world of shadows that had no place for him. She woke sometimes in the night, screaming with fear and imaginary pain, and of late the chains had drawn tighter. She resented his absence, even for a few hours, and his only relief was to ride every day, out onto the wild ungovernable moorland whose spirit he shared, riding till his face was chafed and raw with the wind, and the day had burned into the brilliance of noon. Once it had seemed enough, Margaret and his beloved Northumberland. Now his brain was addled with husbandry and he longed for the sharp discourse of men like Salisbury and Mowbray. Peace and the brilliance of Edward's court weaned all but the very old from their lands and drew them south to an endless round of feast and tournament. News and rumour came to him, brought by a smug and malicious Thomas. Tom rode high on royal favour and had all but filled the place in Lancaster's affection that had once been his. Out of stubborn pride, Hal refused to compete and kept to the north like a sick hound to its kennel.

Restlessly he rose and mounted his horse, riding back the way he had come. He turned into the narrow track that led to the ramp of Warkworth. The broken outline of a half finished tower thrust above the curtain wall and the muted tap of mallets and the whine of pulleys carried clearly on the warm air. He paused as the squat towers of the gatehouse came into sight. Above the sheer unscalable walls the Percy lion floated against an unblemished sky; on the dark silent surface of the moat dragonflies danced in a mist and slept beneath the lichened ribs of the bridge. Of all his father's manors he loved Warkworth the best, and in his mind it was already his because he willed it so. His father had lost tenure by neglect, preferring the harsh grandeur of Alnwick. Hal had grasped eagerly at its stewardship, mending the breaches in the battered walls, tearing down the crumbling towers and building anew. The masons who worked on the new tower worked by his command; the high tracery windows that flooded the old hall with light, the lofty columns that stretched and lost themselves in the dark beamed roof, all were his doing, all his restless bursting energy transformed into the still beauty of stone.

He walked his horse through the dank void of the gateway, raising his hand in greeting to the guard who looked down from the tower. Across the green sward of the bailey his warden ran, darting through the labyrinth of white marker cords and piles of dressed stone.

'My Lord,' the warden panted up to his stirrup. 'A visitor, my lord. Sir Archibald Douglas. I bade him wait in the hall. I hope I did right.'

Hal threw the reins of his horse to a groom. So, Douglas had not forgotten, even after all this time. He had not seen him since that day at Berwick, and what news had filtered across the Border had told him nothing save that Douglas held a high place in David Bruce's council. He smiled at the warden's grim face. It went hard for him to think of the Douglas as anything but the enemy.

The hall seemed dark after the sunlight. Douglas stood, a small shadowy figure against the tall pillars that marched the length of the hall. He turned slowly, his mouth already curved in mockery, and swept his hand around the room, indicating the tapestries of the English victories at Crécy, Poitiers and Halidon Hill.

'You have a taste for magnificence, my lord,' he observed drily. 'I wonder what you English will do when there is no more gold to be squeezed out of France. How will you buy such luxury then?'

'We shall look north again. To the Scots, my lord. Those who cannot match us in the field must be prepared to pay for failure.'

The first exchange was like the slither of unsheathed swords and Douglas came toward him stiff with outrage.

'True, my lord,' he snapped, 'If you will concede the same privilege should you ever fail.'

Hal smiled. Douglas had not changed. His dark skin was burnt almost black by the sun and showed his eyes a vivid, almost unnatural blue; the flagrant challenge was still there, the private war they had begun at Berwick four years ago. Hal said, 'It is the rule of war. To the victor go the spoils.'

The shadow of a smile flared in Douglas's eyes for a moment.

'Then perhaps I will not strain your purse if I beg hospitality for myself and my men. We have been on the road since dawn and are as dry as dust. My men are penned in your gatehouse at the mercy of your belligerent guard and are likely planning an assault this very minute.'

Hal laughed and called to the squire who had stood reluctant guard upon their visitor, bidding him see to the needs of Douglas's men. Casually he asked, 'How far are you come?'

'From Newcastle this morning, from Greenwich two weeks since.' Douglas sipped his wine appreciatively. 'King Edward passes the summer there; but then I expect you know that.'

Hal smiled above a flicker of the old excitement. So that was the bait; the Black Douglas had business with the King at Greenwich. He would not ask. If he waited long enough Douglas would tell him. It was why he had come.

He turned his head at the steward's dry announcement. Douglas's men advanced slowly, uncertain of their welcome, uneasy with their feet on Percy soil. Hal turned to Douglas, his eyes bright with secret amusement. 'Will you take a night's lodging, my lord? Or was your business at Greenwich so urgent that you cannot spare a day?'

'I have leave of absence without limit, my lord.' Douglas smiled provokingly. 'His Grace of Scotland remains at Greenwich for a while. I'll stay gladly—if I am truly welcome,' he added with a lift of his heavy brows.

'You are welcome, my lord,' Hal answered lightly. He doubted if Douglas would ever know just how welcome.

The meal that night was long and as lavish as such haste allowed. Hal treated Douglas royally, setting him on his right hand, and took a savage delight in the discomfort of the English knights who had scrounged a place at his board. Douglas's sharp wit was balm to his starved spirit and afterwards they sat late into the night while the men who slept in the hall snored and grunted and eased themselves from the draught that whined under the doors. Then Douglas said bluntly, 'My business at Greenwich. You are not curious to know of it?'

'Perhaps I already do,' Hal countered, his eyes steady and measuring on Douglas's face.

'Not this time; though you'll know of it soon enough, I dare say. King Edward is not renowned for keeping close counsel.'

'I know that His Grace of Scotland has empty pockets and cannot pay his ransom instalment,' Hal said.

'Aye, all England knows that,' Douglas said bitterly. 'But what you'll not know is what he offers in its place. Like Esau he sells his birthright for a mess of potage. If King Edward will waive the ransom, the Bruce will declare Lionel of Clarence his heir. After the Bruce, Lionel Plantagenet will be King of Scots.'

Hal was silent and for a moment had a glimpse of the man behind the mockery. He knew the dream, the old worn-out dream of Robert the Bruce—of a Scotland, free from English mastery, with a king who did not shame them with every breath he took. 'Then why so loyal,' he asked quietly, 'to a man who betrays Scotland at every turn? Robert the Steward is King David's rightful heir and half of Scotland would crown him tomorrow if they had the chance.'

'Yes—and give your armies the excuse to cross the Border in defence of the Bruce,' Douglas said with a sneer. 'The Bruce is King of Scots, crowned and anointed. I'll not go against that.'

'Then you will accept Clarence as King?'

'David Bruce is not dead yet,' Douglas answered. 'And when he is I'll not be bound by his oaths and promises.' He smiled at the sardonic lift of Hal's brows. 'Ah, yes. I know that King Edward will bring his army in and attempt to force his authority on us again. But he'll not succeed this time. We'll not rest while an Englishman holds a foot of Scottish land,'

'Then why are you here, my lord?' Hal asked coldly. 'If my hatred burned as hot as yours, I'd not sleep easy under an Englishman's roof.'

Douglas gave a crow of laughter. 'You'll not know then that the Bruce is to grant me the lordship of Galloway. Our lands will march together with only the thread of the river between us.' His thin mouth tilted into a smile. 'Know thine enemy, my lord. Know him as well as you know yourself and the battle is half won.'

'And I am your enemy?'

'You asked me that four years ago at Berwick, and my answer

is the same. What else could you be? What else could Percy and Douglas ever be?' He paused and stared into his wine. The logs slipped with a sudden flare of dormant flame and a shower of fine ash. Then Douglas said, 'King Edward keeps great state at Greenwich. I counted his retinue at a thousand, every man in England with a name to make. I had thought to see you there, yet I find you hiding away in the north.'

'Not hiding, my lord,' Hal retorted sharply. 'My duties keep me here of late. You once said that if I were not a Percy I should be no more than the lordlings who scrabble for Edward's favour; well, I am a Percy and my place is here.' It was a clumsy answer and not worthy of him.

'And this contents you? Tending your manors like a shepherd while the game is played out behind your back? For it is a game, you know, a game of chance. Land, power, influence—won or lost on the throw of a dice or at the caprice of a king. A pity to lose without ever having taken part, would you not say?'

Douglas's voice goaded him like a hot iron and the thrust was truth enough to hurt. He *was* hiding. There was nothing to keep him here, nothing except the plea of Margaret's eyes. If it had not been for Margaret. . . . He smothered the disloyal thought and said nothing, though inwardly he squirmed beneath Douglas's look.

The older man stared at his face, remembering its bright malicious beauty that day at Berwick and his own inexplicable fear of the man he had seen shaping behind that face. He did not misjudge a man often. He knew the reasoning that shaped most men's lives; land and high office, wealth and power. All these, by right of birth, could have been Percy's for the taking, yet he shunned them. Douglas could guess at the reason; he had seen it in the frail defenceless beauty of Percy's wife and the way her eyes rarely strayed from Hal's face. He had been in error. A woman had turned Percy soft and taken the sting out of him. Douglas rose softly to his feet.

'Forgive me, my lord,' he said. 'I was mistaken. I had once thought you a dangerous man.'

Their child was born a week before Christmas; a daughter, small and frail and hastily named for her mother since the physician pronounced her unlikely to live. Yet she did live and her tiny feeble cries reached Margaret through a haze of exhaustion. The sharp convulsive pain that had racked her narrow body for ten long hours had gone and was replaced by the ache of torn and bruised flesh. She opened painfully swollen eyes and felt the ice of fresh linen at her back. The room was dim and heavy with the stench of childbed; she called sharply, blinking as the bed curtains were thrust aside and the pale winter light flooded her eyes. The old crone who had delivered her thrust a head and ample breasts pouched in soiled linen through the opening. Sweat clung on the hair that clothed her upper lip and gleamed on her plump cheeks.

'A daughter, my lady,' she pronounced. 'Small but well formed.'

She laid the child against Margaret's slack outflung arm. The tiny face was turned toward her, its eyes shut fast against the light, the soft mouth nuzzling her flesh. She drew it to her breast and felt the soft enveloping warmth of the questing mouth. The baby sucked with greedy and tenacious strength. Margaret closed her eyes and knew the fierce delight of possession; this small defenceless creature was hers, to love and cherish without reserve. With infinite tenderness she traced the shape of the tiny perfect face and touched the small clenched fists. Through the curtains she saw the pursed doubtful mouth of her physician; he thought the child to frail to live, just as he had thought her too frail to bear it. But they would both live. There was no fear now, only the certainty of joy. From the door she heard Hal's voice, quick and eager and edged with uncertainty; suddenly she realized that for the first time in years her waking thoughts had not been of him.

Spring came with bursting warmth and a wealth of blossom that turned the meadows around York as white as snow. On the shining Ouse, swans preened and nested in the tall rushed islands and swept low over the water in joyous flight. In his father's house by Walmgate, Hal lazed in the luminous green of the pleasaunce and watched the lofty elms tap their sheathed buds against the walls. They had come to York for the babe's christening, performed with all due splendour by Margaret's brother Alexander. Margaret was changed. The child had wrought a curious magic in her. There was no fear in her now, only fears of draughts and humours that might harm the babe.

For Hal it had meant freedom, now that her every thought was not of him. But freedom to do what? When the thaw had come, he had ridden with his father on his customary progress through his lands; long wearying days in the saddle, and when the distance was too far to be covered in a day, the grudging and sparse hospitality of a monastery at night. The weeks had run into a blur of duty, the close scrutiny of bailiff's accounts, the yearly manorial courts where his father dispensed swift and harsh justice. He saw too the filth and squalor of the common people counting their winter dead; the silent bitterness and hopeless discontent of the villeins bound to the land, as much the chattel of their lord as the horse he rode. He learnt at first hand the meaning of true power; he knew now whence came the respectful fear of greater lords; beyond the Tyne it was another world, where the edicts of the King were delivered through the mouth of a Percy, and Edward himself was as remote and intangible as God in His Heaven. In the north they knew no king but a Percy.

There was still war in France but not his kind of war. John of France had been released last October but the bickering over the flimsy treaty that had been signed at Brétigny still went on. On the surface there was peace but the fighting continued under cover of the disputed claim to Brittany. The English fought for John de Montfort, the French for the rival claimant, Charles of Blois.

The peace with Scotland remained unbroken. The Scots had too many troubles of their own to look south. David Bruce had proved to be all that Archie Douglas had said he was, and what little strength Scotland might have had after Berwick had been decimated by factions and growing support for Robert Stewart. The yearly border raids still went on but they were only crofters and outlaws come to fill empty winter bellies. They did little damage and their prime target was English cattle. Hal thought of the Black Douglas. His brother William was Earl of Douglas now, the bribe that had weaned him from adherence to Robert

100

Stewart. It was typical of Archie Douglas that, despite his contempt for the Bruce, he had still remained loyal.

Hal closed his eyes, his thoughts mulling over the sounds that reached him on the soft air; the raucous twittering of nesting birds, the covert laughter of the pages who idled at dice behind the stabling block—the sigh of a hem upon the short, cropped grass. He kept his eyes closed till the light kiss fell upon his cheek; then, laughing, he pulled her down beside him. She was more beautiful than she had ever been, her dove–like eyes sparkling with life, her skin glowing against the gown of merging green and gold. He put up a hand to loose her lustrous hair and laughed as she glanced blushingly about her.

'There's none to see, sweeting,' he whispered, 'save the birds and they have no time for us.'

He bent to kiss her and paused at the sudden shout from the courtyard. A clerk ran across the green sward, his gown hitched up to reveal spare white calves and dusty sandals. His father's steward came hard on his heels.

Hal rose slowly to his feet, pulling Margaret with him. What news would bring Alexander Neville's clerk in such an abandonment of dignity? The worst of reasons had flashed through his mind and been dismissed when the clerk came panting up. He felt the hot laboured breath upon his cheek as the man leant close.

'There is plague at Leicester, my lord. The Duke of Lancaster is stricken.' The words fell into a cold empty silence. Only the birds, oblivious, kept up their song.

Hal grabbed the clerk's arm. 'You are sure? Who says this?'

The man licked parched lips. 'The Sheriff of Lincoln has come with a warning to close the gates. His Grace the Duke ordered Leicester to be sealed when it became known there was pestilence within, but when he himself was stricken the people ran riot and broke down the gates. There is rumour that it has reached Derby already.'

'And the Duke? Who attends him?'

The clerk crossed himself. 'Only God in his mercy as far as I know, my lord.'

Hal turned away, sudden tears stinging his eyes. Proud

101

Lancaster, left to die like a rat in a drain without friend or confessor by him. He ran suddenly, past the startled faces of his steward and the serving men who clustered curiously on the threshold. He heard Margaret calling him and closed his ears. All he could think of was Lancaster and the thousand memories that crowded his mind.

In his chamber he snatched a cloak. He heard the sobbing gasp of Margaret's breath upon the stairs and glanced back into the icy coldness of her face.

'I need not ask where you are bound,' she said.

Hal stamped his feet into soft leather boots. 'I cannot leave him to die like a dog.'

Margaret leant her back against the door and clenched her hands upon its iron latch. 'In God's name, why? Would he do as much for you? He spurned you easily enough when you wed me.' She moved swiftly toward him. Imploringly she said, 'You cannot save him, Hal. He might even be dead before you reach him.'

'Then my conscience will be easy. I will have tried.'

He took her hands. 'I loved him well enough once,' he said softly. 'If it were you, would you think well of me if I kept away merely because I could not save you?'

'But it's *not* me,' Margaret shouted. 'It's the man who cut you out of his life because you married me. You owe him nothing.' She pulled her hands from his clasp and looked hard into his face, seeing certain defeat in the hard inflexible line of his mouth. She had never crossed him before in his purpose; it was the first time his stubborn will had been turned against herself. A year ago she might have yielded amid soft tears and recriminations, but not now, not when she had something to fight for other than herself. She moved to where their daughter slept and laid her hand on the edge of the cradle. 'Do you think so little of the child that you would bring the risk of pestilence into this house?'

He stared at her with suddenly cold eyes. 'Then I'll keep away, lady,' he said stonily. 'I sacrificed Lancaster for you once. I'll not do it again.'

He rode all through the night, reaching Doncaster in the flooding dawn, begging a fresh horse from nervous aldermen who promptly closed the gates to all comers at his departure. At Nottingham they refused him entry and he rode on, his pace slowed by his flagging horse, following the line of Trent and Soar, through towns and hamlets hugging their banks and where the red rose of Lancaster bloomed from every street and tavern sign.

It was dusk when he rode into Leicester, across the splintered planks of the gate and down the darkening street. The gateward's hut was empty, his mastiff dead on its chain. The tall houses stood eyeless and deserted. There was no sound, no movement save for the slither of rats in the gutter. Yet there was life somewhere; it roared and shrieked and sobbed and wailed, strident as a new born babe, full of the agony of death.

Through the quickening twilight he rode on. There was light ahead, the luminous yellow glow of sulphur, the vermilion stain of burning thatch. A bale of damask from a looted tailor's shop spilled a carpet along the street and wrapped itself like a winding sheet around a corpse. There were shouts of drunken laughter from an alleyway, a muttered prayer, the repeated unanswered call for a priest. A man lay spreadeagled in his path, his nose and mouth clogged with buzzing flies. Beside him lay the torn and dirty banner of Lancaster.

Hal went on, his stomach heaving at the stench, his mouth dry with fear. The light grew stronger, the voices louder. He turned into the market square and found himself in Hell. A plague fire burned, red flames and swirling yellow smoke. An old man sat perched drunkenly on a roof and scraped at a broken viol. Beneath him men and women leapt in a mad, half naked dance; screaming, singing, staggering in one another's arms, lying where they fell in an obscene tangle of bare breasts and legs. A man in Lancaster's livery lay open-mouthed beneath the streaming cock of a wine butt; others too drunk to stand crawled on their hands and knees, retching into the clogged runnels. A woman in velvet skirts crouched on all fours like a dog, flopping back and fourth in the grip of a garrison soldier. Hall called to him and the man ran off into the shadows, dragging the woman with him.

The others advanced toward him like demons, unreal and wraithlike in the distorting smoke. For a moment he could not move, then a hand reached out for his bridle. He saw the yellow running sore that wept on her cheek, the mottled pustulous hand. He jabbed his spurs viciously into his horse's flanks. The beast leapt, then checked and almost stumbled as the woman fell beneath its hooves. He heard their screams of abuse, the foul obscene torrent that spilled from their lips. He rode on like a madman. If the woman was dead he was glad. There could be no worse death than this.

In the castle ward the sulphur fires bathed the keep in an unearthly yellow light. Silence greeted his shouts but he knew that there were men within the gatehouse, watching him with furtive eyes. He hammered on the postern door till his hands bled. He heard the muted whisper of voices, the indecisive tread of feet advancing and retreating then coming on again. There was a rattling of chains and a groaning of bolts. An eye appeared in the knife edge of the opening.

'There is plague within, my lord.'

'I know it.' Hal thrust at the door and all but knocked the man off his feet. He was a priest, his face like a wedge of yellow cheese, his robes soiled and stinking. He turned and set the bolts to the door again. 'His Grace the Duke?' Hal demanded urgently and felt the breath stick in his throat as he awaited the answer.

'He is alive, my lord—barely.'

'Then take me to him.'

The priest hesitated, then said, 'There is naught to be done, my son. His Grace has been shriven and now awaits death like a true son of Christ.'

'Nevertheless, I wish to see him.'

The priest dropped his gaze and led him back through the dark passage. The doors of the Great Hall stood open and Hal turned his head from the shadowy figures that groaned and retched into rotten straw. He had a sudden vision of Lancaster and himself seated by the warm comfort of the fire; the man and the boy, bound close by pride and affection. Sweet Jesu: who would ever have thought that it would have come down to this? Biting back tears he moved in the priest's shuffling wake and saw the high doors of the Duke's chamber loom like the gates of Hell. How many times had he passed through them at Lancaster's side, attending him to Mass, to bed, to all the hundred duties it had

104

been joy to perform? Now he trembled before them like a child.

Inside the door his courage almost failed him. The stench that came from the man on the bed burned Hal's lungs and turned him sick. Death crept out from the dark corners of the room and manifest itself so clearly that it took all his will to stand his ground. He was not afraid of death but he was afraid of this suppurating evil that left a man to rot and die in his own bloody vomit.

The monk who knelt beside the bed rose uncertainly, glancing from the shadowy intruder to the man in the bed. The Duke moved his head slightly.

'What is it?'

The voice gave Hal courage, as strong and resonant as ever. He signed to the monk to move away and walked slowly toward the bed. Lancaster's eyes dwelt on him for a moment, then he turned his head so that his foul and tainted breath should not touch him.

'So you came then, Hal.' There was no question in his words. It was merely the affirmation of a hope. He had hoped he would come.

'Aye, I came, my lord.' Hal forced the gentle words from shocked lips. Fever had stripped the flesh from the long bones and thrust them agonizingly from the mottled flesh. Revulsion rose in his throat as he saw the sores that wept darkly onto the linen sheets.

'Out of pity, Hal?'

'Out of love, my lord.' Hal saw the slow tears slide from beneath the red tortured lids.

'I knew that you would come; I hoped for it and dreaded it.' Lancaster's voice broke with unaccustomed speech. 'I should send you away, back to that gentle wife that you defied me to wed, but I'll not send you to her this time. I'm a selfish old man who craves a kind voice in his last hours. You'll not blame me for it, Hal? My conscience is heavy enough.'

Hal sat on the soiled splendour of the great bed. 'I came of my own will and will stay of it,' he said simply.

Lancaster nodded and sighed. He seemed to drift into an uneasy sleep, muttering softly to himself, shaping past glories, remembering old forgotten deeds. He would lie quiet for a space then break into thick and heavy speech, his voice discordant against the whispered prayers of the monk. He woke suddenly, as if startled by some uneasy thought.

'Blanche,' he whispered hoarsely. 'Look to her for me, Hal. If she bears a son, Lancaster must come to him after Gaunt. Swear you'll look to his right, Hal—see that he comes to his inheritance without scathe.'

'I swear it, my lord,' Hal said gently and blinked back the warm tears of pity.

Lancaster nodded, satisfied, and unthinkingly held out his hand before realization came and he snatched it back, plunging it beneath the coverlet.

Hal stared at the well-shaped hand that sickness had pared to a skeletal width. It twitched among the folds of royal velvet; the hand that had once lain with affectionate lightness on his shoulder, that had pulled him from the mud of a fall and slapped him to silence when his hot temper had got the better of him, and that now lay empty and needful, barred from the touch of human comfort by hideous death. God shaped men's lives and their deaths. What did it matter now? The touch of Lancaster's hand could bring him no nearer death than the hour he had sat and breathed the tainted air of the room. Trembling, he stretched out his own hand and lifted Lancaster's from its hiding. It struggled briefly then lay still, the fingers curling into the warmth of his palm.

The Duke turned his head. 'So you'll even challenge death, Hal?' He essayed a laugh. 'I tried to shape you, mould you into the son I never had. But then if I had succeeded you would not be here with me now, bringing me my last comfort.' He smiled painfully. 'What fools we are to think we can shape other men's lives.'

For the last hour he lay quietly, each breath drawn agonizingly through his tortured lungs, then his hand stiffened in a spasm of pain. His chest rose and fell as the breath was squeezed from his throat. The monk crept out from his corner and dipped trembling fingers in the oil, signing the cross on his brow, touching his eyes and mouth, whispering the words of exhortation. Then the hand that gripped Hal's till the bones cracked went suddenly limp. Hal

106

heard the monk's cracked voice whisper round the room: 'And may God in his mercy forgive thee all thy sins.'

Lancaster was dead. The words beat from the drumming hooves and dulled the roaring of the night wind in his ears. His spurs struck blood as he pushed his horse to a frenzied gallop and the harsh bitter tears of grief dried like ice upon his cheeks. Henry of Lancaster was dead and John of Gaunt was Lancaster now.

It was July before Margaret saw him again; two months since Henry of Lancaster's death, two months of agony and bitter tears for her. He had not even sent word to her. Only his steward had come to York a week later with a terse little message that she was to return to Tughall. She knew that after Lancaster's death he had gone to Alnwick. How Mary Percy must have rejoiced in that. They could grieve for their beloved Lancaster together.

She looked up into his eyes: *the lake, the sun upon the water and then only the sun.* There was no sun now, only deep unfathomable shadows that she could not read. He touched her cheek and she turned her mouth against his hand. She should have been angry, she should have screamed and berated him for staying away so long, for all those sleepless lonely nights when the demons danced upon her heart. She might have done so if he had come sooner, but the fear that he might not come back at all had taken too great a hold on her. He was here now, touching her, wanting her, still loving her. She would be content with that.

'Forgive me,' he said against her hair.

She laid her hand swiftly against his mouth. She did not want to hear the reasons. His hands moved softly against her full breasts and she closed her eyes. She had not told him that she was expecting another child. Yet when he kissed her nothing had changed. That thread remained unbroken. He eased the gown from her shoulders and kissed the warm curve of her neck. She felt his need for her, strong, undiminished. It was as if he had never been away from her, till she saw his eyes. She knew then that she had lost some essential part of him. She served his body but not his mind. He was in need of something more than she could ever give him. Mary Percy had been right. He had flown

107

too high and glimpsed his freedom. He was not entirely hers any more.

The lusty peal of York Minster's bell rang out over the clamorous city. In the streets and narrow alleyways, the citizens fought and kicked for a view, climbing to the rooftops and balancing precariously on the narrow walk that topped the city walls. The royal procession moved slowly down from Castlegate; the mayor and aldermen proud in their scarlet tippets, the King's heralds with yard–long silver trumpets, and between them the knights on gently prancing coursers, the glowing colours of their tabards hiding the mirror sheen of armour. Then came the King, regal in the splendour of velvet and cloth of gold, a sight that struck the citizens with silent awe and left them gaping, caps in hand as they knelt to his passing.

At the far end of the procession a litter swayed and lurched over the rough cobbles, the curtains drawn up to allow the crowds to gaze their fill. Margaret kept her eyes fixed on the veiled pinnacle of the Countess of Arundel's headdress. Beside her, Elizabeth Mowbray raised a muskball to her delicate nostrils, complaining of the stench in her high lisping voice. Another voice, well remembered, brought a faint smile to Margaret's lips.

'If my lady finds the stink of York so appalling, it might be wiser to go mounted next time. It gives one a small advantage, to be that much higher above the dung.'

It was a long time since Margaret had seen Maud Umfraville. For years now the Countess had kept herself to her Cumberland estates—hard years, by the look of them. It was difficult, seeing her face now, to remember that she had ever been young. She was thinner than Margaret remembered, her eyes harder beneath the dark slanting brows and the mouth that housed the infamous silver tongue was drawn tight in discontent. Her gown was plain, almost to the point of being dowdy and she wore no jewels though she could have bought and sold most of the women there a dozen times. It was little enough compensation for being married to a man like Umfraville and being childless into the bargain. That the Countess was barren Umfraville bemoaned the

108

length and breadth of England and he had enough bastards to his credit to prove it. It had turned the Countess into a bitter, unlikeable woman whose presence made all feel ill at ease, yet for Margaret there were little remembered kindnesses to soften the image: the present of a silk gown, the generous marriage gifts, the unstinting sympathy when she had crept back, rejected, from Leicester. There were so many things that could have been said and never had been. For that she would always be grateful.

Margaret shivered and counted herself fortunate. She had her sons now, three-year-old Harry and Thomas born last spring and, though Hal had only recently arrived home from Spain, she was with child again. She smiled in secret contentment. It was five years since Lancaster's death and it seemed that his passing had banished the shadows from her life. Lady Mary Percy had followed her brother within the year and, strangely, Margaret had been the only one to weep, out of pity that a soul could carry its bitterness to the grave.

The steward had woken her at dawn and even before she had stumbled from the bed her ears had been filled with Mary Percy's screams of pain. The chaplain was already in the room and for one wild moment she had thought the great bed empty, so indistinguishable had the white face been from the pillows. But the eyes still burned with the same cold flame, undiminished by pain or fear. In her extremity Lady Mary had called for her lord, for her sons, for her brother Lancaster—and only Margaret had been there, the despised and hated intruder. Out of pity, Margaret had taken the frail hands that clawed the coverlet and had seen them snatched away: even in death Mary Percy would not accept her.

Lord Percy had wed again. Plump and round as a ripe apple, Joan d'Orreby was all that Mary Percy could never have been. Neither Margaret nor Hal had grudged the old man a last happiness. Joan loved him and mothered him and saw to his needs, and Margaret had lost her dislike of Alnwick now that the grim walls resounded with her easy infectious laughter.

Margaret's first son had been born that year and had made Hal's absences less painful. She had grown used now to the inevitability of war. The peace with France lay heavy on English hands and King Edward had diverted his unemployed soldiery in a subtle pursuance of the war by interfering in the disputed succession of Castille. French support for the bastard Trastamere against his brother King Pedro had resulted in eager English aid for the deposed and exiled Pedro. She knew the way of things now. War was a necessity of life and if the real thing were not to be had then men played at war, like today in the great tournament devised to honour the Prince of Wales's Castilian victory at Najera.

The litter came to an unsteady halt. Margaret gave her hand to the waiting page. The crowds that had followed the procession surged against the restraining fence, hoarse from cheering and light-headed from the free wine. On the flat meadows beside the river the lists had been set up and the flicker of flame and drifting smoke came from the travelling forges set up beneath the trees. The greensward was a blaze of blinding sun and colour, the flash and dazzle of polished steel, the myriad colours of the pennons that floated above the pavilions, the bright beribboned sleeves of coxcomb knights at their first joust. In the royal lodge the King and Queen sat beneath purple awning. Philippa looked pale and dowdy beside the radiance of Joanna of Kent, the Princess of Wales since Thomas Holland's timely death two years ago. She bloomed with rosy health despite the fact that she was heavy with her second child. The first, named Edward for his father, was barely two years old and all England prayed for another son to ensure the succession.

Margaret seated herself beneath the coolness of the canopy. Elizabeth Mowbray fussed with her skirts and dabbed her moist cheeks ineffectually with a kerchief.

'Save your preening, my lady.' The soft malicious voice of the Countess Maud cut through the maidenly whisperings in the lodge. 'This day the King's harlot outshines us all.'

In the shocked silence none could resist a covert glance to where the King's latest mistress flaunted herself in scarlet sendal. Edward had been unfaithful before; it was to be expected, but discreetly, without offence to the Queen and the matrons of the Court. Alice Perrers was different, and the King paraded her like a triumphant banner. Her bright acquisitive eyes missed nothing, each slight and favour stored in her agile mind for retribution or reward. Already her influence was being felt at Court.

Margaret turned away. She cared nothing for the doings of the Court. She had her own world and was content with it, especially now that it contained Hal again. She scanned the scarlet-roofed pavilions for a glimpse of him. It seemed that the whole world was here: faces and names long forgotten; a red-headed child who had been her maidservant at Raby now plump and smug in the royal train; her sister Katherine, Lady Dacre, bestowed a watery smile on her from her place in the Countess of Warwick's lodge; and then of course there was Euphemia, all but smirking beside the Queen.

She saw Hal on the margin of the lists astride the tall high-mettled stallion he had brought from Castile. Its skin gleamed with ebony sweat as it wheeled within its tight-reined circle, kicking at its skirts of emerald silk. Hal cantered easily across the sward, two squires running alongside ready to haul at the reins. He dismounted at a distance and came toward her, his helm with its nodding plume tucked beneath his arm. He smiled and kissed his hand to her, his teeth white against a skin bronzed by the Spanish sun. The sight of him still melted her and, ridiculously, she felt her heart beat faster as he bowed before the royal lodge. The handsomest man in England and hers even now, still hers. She knew instinctively that she had no rival.

Beside her, the Countess Maud watched him too and for a moment her hard eyes were softened by the echo of some long forgotten dream. Then they turned bright and clear again to the scarlet-clad figure of the marshal. His white wand was raised aloft and the cry came: 'Laisez aller!' The tournament had commenced.

The screech of trumpets and the roar of the crowd drowned the first frantic thundering of hooves. Arundel and Salisbury ran the first course and at impact both lances snapped like twigs. Then Arundel was down, floundering on his back like a great shining beetle. The crowd roared gleeful approval. Arundel was never popular.

Then from the corner of her eye, Margaret caught a familiar blazon: the bull's head of Neville. Her heart leapt and she almost

111

rose from her seat and called to him. It was her brother John, but not the John she remembered. Dour and unsmiling, he advanced toward the lists, passing her by without a glance though she knew he was aware of her presence.

Neville bowed low before the royal presence, smiling briefly as he was acknowledged. He moved on and paused among the crowd, scanning the pennons that lifted sluggishly in the summer breeze. With sudden dread, Margaret knew the device he looked for.

Hal waited at the entrance of the lists for his combat to be called. He turned, half smiling as the light touch fell on his shoulder, then looked from John Neville's dark face to the gauntlet that lay at his feet.

He prodded it gently with the toe of his mailed shoe. 'Do I take this for a challenge, Neville?' he murmured with the mocking smile that verged on the insulting.

'Aye, Percy,' Neville snapped. 'You may take it so.' He beckoned to the hovering steward to enter his name in the lists. 'Sir John Neville, Lord of Raby,' he said loudly. He smiled as he saw Hal's lifted brow. 'Yes, you heard aright. Lord of Raby, since yesterday. I promised myself years ago that my first deed as soon as I was my own master would be to lay you flat on your back, Percy.'

Hal smiled and wondered uneasily if Margaret knew. 'Brave words, my lord of Raby,' he said drily. 'I only hope that you can match them with the deed.

'*A challenge, a challenge!*' The whisper ran round the enclosure and brought all eyes to the lists. Margaret edged forward onto the hard rim of her bench, her eyes shining with tears. She had heard the whispers that swarmed and hummed around her. '*Old Neville is dead . . . Neville is dead of the flux at Raby . . . Old Neville of Raby is dead.*'

Her father was dead, and her brother had thought so little of her that he had not even cared to tell her himself. If she had wanted proof that John cared for none but himself, she had it now. And he had come here to do what he would never have dared do while their father was alive. She saw the future all too clearly; with her father gone the frail bond that had held Neville

112

and Percy together had gone too. There would only be hatred between them now; her sons would be bred on it.

She dragged her unwilling gaze back to the lists. Hal sat his restless horse and waited, a bright faceless figure in his damascened helm. At the end of the palisade John seemed small and insignificant, prancing and cavorting to the sporadic cheering of the crowd. The marshals and heralds scurried between them to the safety of the stockades, waving their batons and shouting warnings to the eager crowds who pressed dangerously close.

Close by him, Hal heard the long rasping intake of the marshal's breath that broke in a scream of *'Laisez aller!'* His horse leapt forward at the first touch of his spurs, thundering down the line of the palisade at a speed that merged the earth and sky into a dizzying blur. He raised his lance, slanting it across his chest, the foiled tip aimed for the four rivets of Neville's shield fastening. The impact came, sooner than he had expected, and all but knocked the breath from his body. The last few seconds had been a blur of flashing steel and deafening noise; only the pain of his wrenched shoulder told him that his lance had found its mark. His horse plunged on and wheeled at the edge of the field. He looked back and saw Neville struggling to keep his seat and turn his horse. Again they charged; this time it seemed only seconds before they met and his muscles screamed with the shock of his splintering lance. Neville leapt and twisted in the saddle, fighting vainly against the plunging of his terrified horse. Then he was down, his helm rolling free in the trampled grass.

Hal leapt from his horse, his heart hammering with powerful excitement. Neville was on his feet, his sword drawn, and the crowd had fallen silent, catching something of the deadly intent of their combat. They moved in slow cautious circles, matching each other's movements like courtiers in a dance. Neville opened clumsily; their blades met with the dull clang of blunted steel and slid harmlessly away, only to come together a second later with deadly intent. They were well matched, too well matched, parrying the other's brilliant thrusts with an equal skill that made the crowd roar and gasp in turns as each won and lost a precarious advantage. Then a quick flurry of blows with the flat of Neville's sword almost knocked Hal senseless. The blood roared in his ears and the stinging heat of pain blurred his vision.

Neville pressed his advantage and raised his sword in a full swinging stroke to the head. Struggling for balance Hal met the blow and slid it down from his head, then hilt to hilt they turned together, the blurred contortion of Neville's face so close that he could see the froth of spittle that slicked his beard. The sky and earth swung with them, merged into a sickening streak of colour. But Neville was tiring. When they closed, Hal could hear the breath rasping in his throat and when they sprang apart his shoulders heaved like an old man's. He stepped back a pace to recover his reach; Hal followed his circling movement, though his muscles were agony beneath the leaden weight of his armour and the cords of his wrist were numb as he parried Neville's renewed thrust. Back and forth they moved, each the other's shadow, neither yielding an inch of ground save the backward pace it took to regain arm's length and stand the other off. Neville beat off a fresh attack, his sword lifted in defensive recovery. Hal set his teeth against the grinding pain of his limbs and darted beneath the sluggish blade, blocking the counter-stroke. Startled, Neville backed off to regain his own reach and Hal saw his chance. Pace by pace Neville retreated before the furious onslaught of blows that gave him neither time nor space to regain his ground. Hal swung his blade in a last measured stroke, directing all his force and strength into the length of steel; a slow, almost leisurely blow that struck the blade from Neville's hand and sent it singing into the earth.

The huge tremulous sigh that shuddered the crowd swelled into a roar of approval. Hal dragged off his helm and shook the blinding sweat from his eyes, looking for Neville among the figures that ran between them. The bright virulent face of hatred that was turned toward him shocked him more than any of Neville's blows had done. His eyes drove home the threat; Hal would never be forgiven for this.

The marshal bustled between them, his directions drowned by the avid screams of the crowd. Wearily Hal followed in his scarlet wake; his breath quivered and sobbed in his throat and the strength of his legs threatened to desert him. Neville was beside

114

him as they knelt before the King. Edward's praise was balm for his tortured limbs but beneath the bland smile there was a warning: no more; whatever is between you, let it rest here. Hal glanced at the man kneeling beside him, his cousin by blood, his uncle and brother-in-law by marriage and now his open enemy. Neither had had the true mastery yet. This was just the beginning.

That evening Margaret sat before her glass inspecting the sudden blemish upon her cheek, a minute reddening of the skin brought on by excess temperament. She calmed her thoughts and applied the cooled distillation of camomile, yet it was hard to dismiss the remembrance of John's face today, even harder to forget its implication and the fact that she too was a Neville. No. She pushed away the thought fiercely. She was a Percy now. Lady Margaret Percy; her sons were Percys and therefore her loyalty must lie with them. There had never been any doubt of it in her mind. She had chosen her own path when she had married Hal and never once had she wished to turn from it. John was her flesh and blood but he must look to himself now. The path he had taken today was of his own choosing also. Calming, sensible thought . . . yet still the uneasiness and the blemish remained to plague her.

With unaccustomed sharpness she called her tiring woman from where she fussed among her gowns. Ellen's hands were soothing as they moved against her neck, dividing the dark fall of hair in two and then again, twisting a thread of gold into each thick braid and coiling them on each side of her face. The fillet of gold she placed herself so that it rested an inch above her finely plucked brows. She stood and breathed against the discomfort of her tightening gown, turning once to free her skirts and see that they hung correctly, then softly she went through into the small chamber where her children slept.

Meg was still awake, her brother curled in the crook of her arm, his dark curls tangled against the glowing fairness of her skin. The babe Thomas slept apart in his cot, his fat round cheeks flushed with sleep. Silently she kissed them, lingering a moment to watch them. Only John's face rose to cloud the perfect picture.

He had determined their heritage this day. Half Neville, half Percy, John would care nothing for the Neville half of their blood. Their sire was a Percy and that was enough to condemn them. For the first time she mourned her father. She had never loved him. There had been nothing to love in that hard capable man who had used his children as assets to increase his bargaining power. Yet he had kept the peace and laid restraint on John's vindictive spirit. There was nothing to hold him back now except that hard streak of commonsense and ambition. John would do nothing rash. Today had been his one indulgence but from now on he would use cunning and guile to achieve his ends, as he had done when they had been children. John had infinite patience in that respect and it made him the more dangerous.

In the hall below the air was stifling hot and sickly from the jasmine that grew in profusion along the walls of the pleasaunce. As with every house in York it was crammed to the roof with the King's retinue and the lords that had come for the joust. They slept on and beneath tables, in barns and outhouses, some even beneath the open sky in the gardens. Between them, they had consumed in a week enough food to have lasted her household for a month.

From the doorway she signalled to the steward, whose duty it was to maintain a watchful eye over the thirty pages in his charge who kept the company plentifully supplied with wine while they marked time before leaving for the King's tournament feast. Before he reached her she felt a soft hand upon her arm and turned to meet the sharp clever eyes of her brother Alexander. Dark and sombre in his rich clothes, he drew her smilingly from the throng. He studied her face for a moment, then said, 'You know of our father's death, then.'

She nodded and, glad as she was to see him, she wished he had not come now, when she was trying to put all thoughts of John from her mind. 'Did you know also that John challenged Hal in the joust today?' she asked.

'And lost,' Alexander observed significantly. 'It would have been better for all of us if he had won.'

'What will come of it, Alexander? What good will it do to start a feud between us?'

'Come, sweet sister, wipe the scales from your eyes.' Alexander smiled his devious smile. 'There has always been a feud between the Nevilles and the Percys—save that our father, God rest his soul, saw fit to bury it for his own ends.' His quick mobile face wore the mask of sympathy, though inwardly he was unmoved by his sister's distress. He saw things only as they touched him, weighing the possibilities carefully before he committed himself. Whatever his private feelings, he himself was not yet ready to come down on his elder brother's side. Any public betrayal of emotion was total folly and in this John had erred and earned his censure. He laid his white priestly hand on Margaret's arm. 'John has begun nothing new, Margaret. He has merely brought it to life again.'

'And what of me, Alexander?' Margaret demanded, loud enough for her brother to glance nervously around him. 'What of myself and my sons? Must they be cut off from all their Neville kin because of John? Has he not thought where my loyalty must lie?'

Alexander stared at his sister uncomprehendingly. He only had one loyalty, to himself, and he could envisage no other. His dislike of the Percys came from nothing deeper than that they hampered his family's power. He felt nothing stronger than that and even that small spark was tempered by caution. Old Lord Percy had run his course. It was his son who should be marked and studied, an unknown quantity still, and one that he did not entirely dismiss as being without usefulness to himself. Margaret had disappointed him in that respect. Her marriage had not brought the hoped-for influence but there was still time. He had done well enough without her; he had the prebend of York, and the archdeaconship of Durham was surely his, but he had his sights set higher than that and the higher he climbed the fewer enemies he could afford to make. He was certainly not ready to make them just to please his brother.

He patted Margaret's hand and broadened his smile. 'It may come to naught, sister. You know our brother, always blowing hot and cold. When the King confirms him in possession of his lands he'll have more to fill his time than the settling of old grudges.'

'And if he does not,' Margaret said slowly, 'where will you stand, Alexander?'

He smiled his bland and inexpressive smile. 'I am a churchman, a man of God,' he said with light reproof. 'I can take no part in private quarrels.'

Margaret turned her cheek for his cool parting kiss and walked with him to the outer door. From the shadow of the wide porch she watched him mount the powerful grey gelding housed in crimson and gold. She saw the richness of its trappings, the wide embroidered reins, the saddle of costly Spanish leather—the horse of a tourney knight rather than a priest. But then Alexander was a priest only in name. In his heart he was like all the Nevilles, and she had been a fool to expect anything but self-interest from him.

It seemed that half of England was crammed into York's vast hall. Lords of rank stood cheek to jowl with importune knights; merchants in sober Holland cloth gathered in uneasy knots and gaped at the women; all moved under Edward's benign and still potent gaze. The ladies covertly preened themselves and strove to catch his restless eyes; the courtiers, ever watchful, stood ready to anticipate the King's slightest whim. Yet there was an air of change; the Court sensed it, like hounds sniffing the wind. Edward was ageing fast and his grip had slackened. The path to his influence lay through the mistress he flaunted convention to please, and had made queen in all but name. She sat close beside him, her high round breasts thrusting from dull crimson satin and within reach of his exploratory hand. Her shrill laughter rose and mingled with the shriek of the viols, and many of the ladies of high rank had retired early in deference to the Queen.

Margaret watched the dancing, tapping her foot to the lilting rhythm as knights clapped the measures and called the changes. Once she had loved to dance, but tonight her feet were as heavy as lead.

The stiff rustling of skirts at her elbow caused her to look up. The Countess Maud stood beside her, the sharp sallow features framed in a severe and nunly coif. She had made a small concession to gaiety in the colour of her gown, a Burgundy satin that lent the barest colour to her skin. 'You do not dance, Margaret?' she asked.

Margaret rose as etiquette demanded and sat again with the Countess. 'Nor you?' she enquired politely.

The Countess smiled. 'No, nor I. My feet lost their joy years ago.'

Margaret looked back to the dancers, searching for something to say. The Countess roused too many memories and, though outwardly she defied pity, Margaret did pity her. For all her wealth and position she lacked all the things that she herself held most dear. She felt the Countess stiffen. Umfraville was lurching toward them, shaking off the well-meaning support of Hal's arm. He was drunk, his great fist clamped hard round a brimming cup that slopped redly over his tunic. He bowed low before Margaret, planting a wet reeking kiss upon her cheek. Swallowing her revulsion she smiled politely into his red raddled face.

'You're a lucky devil, Percy.' Umfraville grinned and slobbered over the back of her hand till he felt the cold gaze of his wife upon him. He straightened and slewed round to stare at her in open dislike. 'You had more sense, Percy,' he muttered insultingly. 'You picked a wife that could give you something more than a sour tongue.' He lurched against her and the Countess's nostrils dilated against the blast of his breath. 'Too skinny, Maud, that's your trouble. Too skinny and dry and empty as a pea pod.'

Hal caught Umfraville sharply by the arm but the Countess was smiling, her lips parted to reveal startlingly white teeth. 'Indeed, my lord,' she said softly, 'I would have thought that you carried enough fat for the two of us.' Her cold eyes travelled insultingly to the gross belly that burst from his doublet. 'In fact, my lord, we might all be forgiven for supposing that you yourself carry the child whose lack you never cease to prate upon.'

There was a silence and then Hal laughed, a deep merry laugh that brought the blood flooding into Umfraville's face. The Countess sat and arranged her skirts coolly as her husband staggered back across the hall. She glanced up into Hal's eyes and smiled. It was the first time in years a man had looked at her with anything near admiration.

By the end of the week, York lay silent and empty as a grave. Like vultures, the Court had picked the city clean, paying for nothing and leaving nothing but bare bones and the burgesses bewailing their empty pockets. It was September and the first chill of autumn had crept into the long summer's warmth. In Walmgate, the household groaned and stirred itself for the journey back to Alnwick.

Hal rode out for a last day's hunting, alone except for his father's surly old falconer. He turned east to where the gentle slumbrous line of the hills ran unbroken down to the sea and the moors were threaded with tiny becks that trickled into the Ouse.

The dogs ran on before him, splashing through the streams and yelping with delight at this rare freedom; the falconer rode at his flank as silent as the hooded bird he carried on his wrist.

He rode at a leisurely pace, through the dark leafy forest where the sun struck spears of light into the gloom and touched the fading leaves to amber, across the wild moorland purpled with heather and the grey shapes of grazing sheep. On the last rise of hills before they sloped down to the Derwent, he reined in his horse. Beyond the sparkling width of the river he could see the road that ran to Beverley and the gaping mouth of Humber: the southern border of his father's lands. It was a fair inheritance; from Berwick to Hull his family were undisputed masters. Only the Crown lands of Durham and York and the thin wedge of Neville lands that intruded between the Tyne and Richmond broke the thread—the Neville thorn in Percy flesh. And John Neville was Lord of Raby now, ambitious and unscrupulous and burning with such a hatred that Hal's blood ran cold at the thought of it. He was not so foolish as to think that such a force could not touch him but he was not ready to come to terms with John Neville yet. He was still his father's apprentice. While Lord Percy lived, Hal had nothing of his own save the few manors that had been granted him. He had no choice yet but to bide his time and let Neville make the running. He turned his horse and smiled quietly to himself. From sky to sky all that he could see was Percy land. He would be a dead man before Neville took one acre of it from him.

Lord Percy pulled the furred mantle a little closer. He was cold, always cold as if the north wind that howled outside the walls of Alnwick had invaded his bones and settled there. Yet there was more warmth in his life than there had ever been. Joan was the fire that warmed his starved heart with the glow of her smile and the soft comfort of her willing body at night. It was more than he deserved, more than he had ever hoped for—and come so late that he had forgotten that such warmth existed. He sighed and twisted his scarred mouth in a smile. Perhaps too late; he was old and tired, though he had never felt it till this last year. Now all the familiar pattern of his life was changing: Mary, and Henry of Lancaster, were gone and England still mourned the good Queen. England was ruled by a harlot and the realm suffered through bad governance. It had been a bad year for the north, a bad year for England. Death, flood and famine were the order of things now. There was plague in London and in the north the harvest had been a disaster, the ripening corn flattened by endless rain or lost completely beneath the floods. In August the Tweed had burst its banks and swept away a dozen villages; nearer home, the Aln was still a swollen flood, the surrounding meadows pooled with stagnant lakes. What little grain that had been salvaged was wet and swollen and had rotted in the barns before the month was out. It was still to be had—at a price; two shillings a bushel in York and more, they said, in London.

Old Neville was dead and his death most of all had sounded the knell of the passing years. He had grown to manhood with Ralph Neville and had fought his first battle alongside him. Neville's Cross, Halidon Hill—victories that were past glories now and only remembered by the old men. But Neville had always been there; their differences set aside for the weal of England and the Border. He could not remember a time when Ralph Neville had not been part of his life.

He stretched his stiffening limbs out to the fire and heard his bones crack, old man's bones swollen to a painful tenderness that set his teeth on edge. Yet he was well content. He had his sons and was now the somewhat foolish father of a two–year–old daughter. His line was well assured by Hal's little knaves and the new babe, another son, named Ralph for his grandsire. Thomas had yet to be wed and he had no hopes of that yet awhile. Tom would sooner pay his price in a whore house than saddle himself with a wife and when he did it would be for gain, a plump heiress with a dowry to match. But the lad had exceeded all his hopes. Commander of Lancaster's troops in France and, lately, seneschal of La Rochelle. He had no fears for Tom. Tom was destined for great things. But Hal?

A frown drew his thick brows together and shadowed his eyes. Hal was an unknown quantity, even to him. Unpredictable and proud as Lucifer, yet these last few months he had broken his back over the comfort of villeins, setting his men to felling trees to rebuild their hovels, riding home with starved children to be fed and warmed in the kitchens. The bailey was full of them and the stench of their poverty pervaded the air. He gave a dry chuckle. Mary would not have approved of that, the halls of Alnwick soiled by the bare dirty feet of villeinry. He smiled at the irony of it. Neither of his sons wore the coats that had been made for them. Thomas was the courtier fired by the high ambition that should have been his brother's, while Hal soiled his fine court-bred hands with the dirt of common people. That part of Hal came from him, an obsessive love of the north and all that was in it. Northumberland had received all his life and love; its soil was watered with his sweat and its fine towns prospered by his vigilance. He stared into the lambent fire and his shrivelled lids drooped over his eyes, narrowing his vision to flickering yellow flame. He dreamed in their warmth, harking back, remembering his own father and the time, almost beyond remembrance, when he had been young.

Faintly he heard Joan's light step upon the stair bringing his warmed posset. A dry cackle of laughter escaped his throat. Ralph Neville would have seen the humour in that; old Percy swaddled in furs and coddled like a babe. But Ralph was dead, lying cold beneath the flags of Durham's nave. He closed his eyes and his gnarled and calloused hands slid beneath the furs. The fire was burning low, the flames diminishing into tiny points of light behind his eyes. He would sleep, just for a while, just until Hal came home.

Eight miles away Hal sat his horse in driving rain. The mud churned thick as quagmire beneath the horses' hooves. Ahead a cart was stuck fast and Hal watched with brooding eyes as the men waded ankle-deep with armfuls of faggots. The wheels gripped, then spun wetly free only to stick again at the next turn.

He turned to the reeve who dripped miserably beside him. 'How many more?' he questioned sharply.

The reeve shook the trickle of rain from his chin. 'Three, my lord.' He beckoned to the shadows who stood huddled in the porch of the church. They came forward uncertainly, lifting their feet in ungainly strides over the clinging mud. The man dragged the sodden cap from his head and stood twisting it between his large hands. The woman and the child hung back, treading mud and water, their eyes fixed firmly on the ground.

'Gilbert of Amble, his wife and child,' the reeve announced dispassionately.

'Free or bond?' Hal asked and glanced at the woman trying vainly to shield the child from the wind with her threadbare cloak.

'Free,' the man answered swiftly and raised his eyes for the first time to Hal's face.

'Then you must look to yourself,' the reeve said sharply. 'You are free to go and find work and lodging where you can. Only bondsmen can look for my lord's protection.'

The man turned dull eyes to Hal. His skin was stretched over famished cheeks and his eyes had the hopeless look of a beaten dog. If he'd had the courage he might have asked where he was to go, where there would be work for a man who knew nothing but the land and who had never worked anything but the soil of his own village in his life. The flood had taken all that he owned, his house and few pigs, the strip of crops that eked out his bare existence. Instead he looked down at the squelching rags that bound his feet. 'My wife and child,' he muttered, wringing his cap between his hands till the water splashed his feet. The woman and the boy moved forward and looked at Hal with ancient eyes. The boy's teeth were chattering with cold and his clothes were no more than a covering of rags.

Dear God, Hal thought, surely death would be better than this.

123

He said abruptly, 'Set them in the cart with the others.' Then to the man, 'The abbot at Hulne will give you food and shelter for the moment. Take what wood you need from the forest and rebuild your house. There will be work for you in the spring.'

The man's eyes sprang into a brief flaring warmth. He knelt in the mud, pushing the woman and the boy down beside him, mumbling his thanks to the reeve's haughty retreating back.

'The young lord,' he told his wife. He shook his wide-eyed son by the shoulder, 'The young lord. Remember that, Will.'

The boy stared after the horseman disappearing into the mist of rain. A magical figure, a golden giant like those he had seen painted on the hangings of the church. He looked back to his father. 'The young lord,' he repeated obediently. He would not forget.

Hal rode on through the straggling village, past the laden carts and the trudging villeins sifting through what was left of their homes. He had done what he could, if indeed it was anything at all. Life was cheap and easily replaceable. His mother had said that villeins were like weeds and grew thicker for being cut down. Death and hunger were commonplace and no man who worked the land expected to live beyond forty, especially in the north. Yet these were the men who had won England's battles, the common pikemen and the archers who had mown down French chivalry with simple weapons fashioned with their own hands. They were the men that England needed. He would not see them starve for want of effort on his part.

In Alnwick the streets were deserted, submerged beneath floating islands of refuse. A broken shutter crashed monotonously against a wall. Its fellow lay across the street where the wind had flung it. The bridge was down and as Hal rode across the rumbling boards a figure came from the gatehouse and saw him, turned and ran back into the bailey.

His father's seneschal was already on the steps. He ran toward Hal, his wet cloak flapping round his legs. He hauled at Hal's bridle, blinking as the rain fell full into his eyes.

'Come quick, my lord,' he gasped. 'Your father is dying.'

Hal stood in the doorway of the chamber and wiped the rain from his eyes. He was aware of the faint staccato sound of weeping; the steady beat of driven rain on the exposed tower wall. Margaret stood close to the bed, her arm around Joan's trembling shoulders. Their son, Harry, hid himself in her skirts, wailing with a child's instinct for disaster.

He stared in silence at the still shrouded figure, a stranger to him now with all the fire and strident life drained out of him: the wry smiling mouth was a thin sunken line in his beard; the bright, intense eyes blank and shuttered beneath the weight of death pennies. The dog, Siward, still kept vigil by his side, growling softly at the smell of death. He raised his head and stared at Hal, pawing at the silk pall which covered the old man. Then he padded slowly over and leant his great head on Hal's hand.

Hal stroked the velvet ears and struggled against the mingling of grief and exaltation. The old Lord was dead. Hal was Lord of Northumberland now.

———

Alnwick

Hal stared at his brother in mild surprise. It was three years since he had seen him and the gangling aggressive youth had become a man. He had broadened and settled into the stocky lines of their father yet he carried himself with grace and height. His rich beard and well-made clothes sat easily upon him and self assurance reposed in every line of his face. Only his eyes were unchanged, quick and hot and ever watchful.

'Quite the courtier, Tom,' Hal mocked him gently. 'It must be the exalted company you keep.'

Tom grinned. Once a remark like that would have brought the blood rushing into his face but now he could take it as it was meant, in good part.

'And how does our royal duke and cousin?' Hal enquired.

'Well enough,' Tom answered. 'Aquitaine suits him, though less so now that the Prince of Wales has returned. I fear His Grace and his brother do not always see eye to eye.' He rose and strode the length of the chamber that had been their father's. 'There is bound to be war. Prince Edward's taxes fall heavily on the Gascons, and Charles of France is willing to support any trivial cause that could force us out of Aquitaine. And then there are still the points of the last treaty that he refuses to ratify. It would need only one small spark to fire a rebellion in Aquitaine. And you Hal?' Tom came and stood beside him. 'Still content with your frozen north?'

Hal smiled and pushed the flagon of wine toward his brother. 'For the moment, Tom,' he answered softly. 'Only for the moment.'

Tom looked down into his wine. He still hadn't lost that habit of chewing his lip when he was uneasy. 'What's past is past, Hal, between you and me and between you and Lancaster.' He glanced up and met his brother's eyes. 'We have need of a man like you. His Grace would let it lie if you would.'

Hal raised his brows. Yet another facet of Thomas revealed: soldier, courtier, statesman—and now peacemaker? 'Did Lancaster say so?' he asked.

The faintest touch of colour showed beneath his brother's bronzed skin. 'Not in so many words, Hal, but he often asks after you. You were close to him once. There's no reason why you should not be so again.'

Hal said nothing. He did not trust his brother any more than he did his master. There was the affection of blood but Tom had his own interest too close to his heart to warrant any measure of trust. Could it be that this time their interest ran together? He probed a little deeper. 'Why so solicitous for my welfare, Tom?'

Tom met his look with open mockery. 'Why not, if it serves us both? We share a common enemy now, Hal. John Neville is high in Lancaster's council and loses few opportunities to work against us.'

So that was it. Thomas the favourite had been ousted by Neville and he needed an ally. 'Oh, Thomas, Thomas, my fickle one,' he said with a flash of his old mockery. 'I never thought to see you tremble in Neville's shadow.' Then sharply he added, 'What can Neville do to us that he has not tried and failed at already? His influence with Lancaster is nothing to me. I hold no high office that he can deprive me of. My lands are mine by inheritance, confirmed by the King. Lancaster is not the King, Tom, and the King is the only man I have a duty to.'

'Christ, Hal, you're so bloody sure of yourself.' Thomas jerked violently to his feet. 'Edward is finished, Hal, he's become almost senile, dominated by that Perrers woman. She flaunts herself in the Queen's jewels and the Court does not take petitions to the King now, they take them to her. The Court is a shambles, ruled by a whore. Prince Edward is preoccupied with war and Aquitaine and neither Lionel nor Edmund have the wit to keep order in a convent. Who else but Lancaster, Hal?' He did not wait for an answer but went on in his quick persuasive voice. 'You've not forgotten the way of it, Hal? Quarrels are easily picked. Better men than you have lost all that they had on the whim of a king. Whose influence will you have if it came to it?'

'My own, Tom, and I need no other,' Hal flung back angrily. 'As you say, quarrels are easily picked. If I stay in the north and mind my own affairs, who can quarrel with that?'

'No man is inviolate, Hal. Not even a Percy. Remember that all is held by the King's grace and what has been given can just as easily be taken away. There are always new faces at Court, new men hungry for land and power—John Neville for one would give ten years of his life to possess a quarter of what you hold.'

Hal turned away from his brother's urgent face, reluctant to admit that he needed favour, especially Lancaster's favour.

'What are you afraid of, Hal?'

The question turned his head violently as if he had been struck. Thomas with his strange perception had homed straight to the mark as unerringly as one of his beloved hawks. He was afraid, but only of himself and the violent, unpredictable temperament that he forced into constant subjugation—and something else that even he did not fully understand, a lust and craving for power that, once given its head, would carry him to destruction.

He turned and met his brother's critical eyes. 'I'm afraid of nothing that either Neville or Lancaster can bring against me, Tom,' he said steadily. He smiled. 'And if His Grace wants peace then let him say so. I'll not settle for anything less from Lancaster.'

War came with the inevitability of the seasons and in the spring Hal returned to Court on the summons of the King. Margaret saw Edward for the first time since the death of the Queen and saw an old man, his flesh the colour of tallow wax, his fierce eyes drained by grief. The Court lived in perpetual mourning, for no sooner had they shed it for the Queen than they donned it again for the King's second son, Lionel. Lionel's untimely death in Italy had struck Edward a hard blow. In a year he had aged ten, and the white-haired dotard who walked with an old man's gait was a mere shadow of the man who had filled them with terror in Westminster Hall all those years ago.

By his side strutted the smug arrogance of Alice Perrers. Her mourning gown of black silk was powdered with tiny pearls and at her throat a cabochon diamond gleamed with dull fire. She made no secret of her power now. Any who wanted to please the King had to please Alice Perrers first.

'She'll bleed the King and England dry,' Euphemia said furiously. 'Last week the manor of Wendover. Fifteen hundred livres for jewels at Christmas and not content with that, she demanded that I give up the Queen's jewels that had been entrusted to my care.'

Margaret watched the peacocks bickering on the pleasaunce below. The spread of an angry tail caught the light and flung a hundred colours into the sun. 'Have you had word of John lately?' she asked abruptly.

Euphemia paused. 'He awaits Lancaster in France, the last I heard,' she said with scant interest, and returned with fresh malevolence to the subject of Mistress Perrers.

So Hal and John would be together in France, Margaret thought. And Lancaster too, though she had less fear of him. Lancaster was a prince of the blood and above petty revenges. John was not. Already there was dispute over a strip of Percy land that marched with his; useless and valueless, the dry arid soil unfit even for sheep, yet John would have it, because it was Hal's. Behind her Euphemia's voice clacked on the score of grievances that had festered for lack of a willing ear. She and John had much in common, both vindictive, both full of self-interest. Yet

128

Euphemia was harmless and shallow; it was John that she feared. It was John who would cloud every day of her life till Hal came home again.

In the White Chamber, Hal bowed low and respectful before the King's paramour. Her crisp black hair was cauled in pearls and her small jewelled hand rested proprietorially on the King's sleeve. She turned her thin red mouth in a smile, the dark shrewd eyes assessing at a glance what she might expect from him. His own were amused and faintly admiring, for Alice Perrers made no secret of what she was. He did not blame her for that. The reign of the King's mistresses was usually brief; it took a clever woman to come out of it with anything more than a ruined reputation.

Lancaster watched him from the dias, a blank staring look that told him nothing. He would have passed on but for the beckoning smile of the Duchess Blanche. He kissed his cousin with affection. Pale and fragile as a wind-blown flower, her eyes evoked a painful memory of her father Lancaster.

'You are a welcome sight, cousin,' she said in her gentle voice. 'We had thought to see you long before now. You must come to Bolingbroke when you return. Our sons would do well together.'

Hal's eyes dropped to the infant clad in stiff brocade who stood unsteadily beside his father. His eyes were blue and grave and beneath his velvet bonnet his hair was the colour of tawny wine. He smiled and bowed. 'My Lord of Bolingbroke,' he said with mock gravity. 'I am pleased to do you duty, cousin.'

The boy's vague answering smile struck a chord of memory. Hal remembered his promise to Lancaster, a promise made to a dying man for an unborn child to sooth his fear of the approaching darkness. '*Look to his right, Hal. See that he comes to his inheritance without scathe.*' But what need .was there of that when his sire was the most powerful man in England?

'A fine boy, cousin,' he said to Blanche's proud face. 'A pity that his grandsire did not live to see him. He would have been proud of him.'

He saw the involuntary tightening of the Duke's hand on the boy's shoulder. He glanced up into his face, careful to keep his eyes empty of all but formal courtesy. 'My duty to your grace,' he said lightly.

Lancaster inclined his head. 'My lord of Northumberland,' he said, and there was the ghost of a smile in his eyes. 'It grieved me to hear of your father's sudden death. I had not expected to see you raised so high, so soon, my lord.'

Hal swallowed on a sudden burst of laughter. Behind the dry mockery there was an echo of that time when the bantered insults had been tempered by affection. So Tom had been right; Lancaster wanted peace. Yet he could not resist a last thrust. 'Nor I, your grace,' he said pleasantly. 'Death has been bountiful to us both, has it not?'

Bordeaux blazed like a jewel in the high summer heat. Above the red sloping roofs of the town the gilded domes of St André dominated a cloudless sky and threw a dark engulfing shadow across the Prince's palace of the Ombrière. Beneath the white marbled walls the Garonne flowed silently and cooled the burning day.

The hall was long and pillared like a church, and dusty filtered light hung like clouds in the vaulted roof. From beneath the shadow of watered silk John of Lancaster watched the assembly with cold blue eyes and this night the blandishments of his courtiers fell upon deaf ears. Beside him his brother Edward attempted a pitiful gaiety, though his skin still burned with fever and his trembling hands could not be still long enough to raise his cup to his lips. Edward was dying. The thought overwhelmed him and filled him with a strange shameful exaltation. He glanced beneath carefully lowered lids and saw how the Princess Joanna guided his hand to his food. Yes, Edward was dying; this year, next year, two years at the most would see both him and their father in their graves. Lionel was dead and the succession rested in a frail boy and a newborn babe. He dropped his eyes to the ruby depths of his wine. That left himself and young Thomas as guardians of the kingdom till Edward's sons came of age, if they ever did. The prospect set his own hands trembling and he thrust them out of sight beneath the damascened cloth, forcing his thoughts back into cold precise order. It would need care and caution, the right moment, the right men around him. He knew his own weakness. He lacked the vital spark that drew men to him, or that could turn a rout into a victory. He needed men at his back who carried the people with them, men like de Bohun and Salisbury but not cast in his father's mould as they were. He needed his own men, men of power and influence who could court the popularity that he lacked; men like Hal Percy, perhaps him most of all because he already knew the thing that others merely guessed at. They were two of a kind, ambitious, eager for power at any price. Hal knew it, the knowledge recognized but never acknowledged. He still fought against it, fought against Lancaster because he saw himself too clearly in Lancaster's image.

Lancaster sipped his wine thoughtfully and rolled its bitter sweetness across his tongue. Hal would come round, he was almost halfway there, and once across the line he would be the more prized for having stood out against him. Covertly, his eyes slid across the wide expanse of jasper tiles and sought him out beside the slight boyish figure of young Mortimer. He frowned. The fifteen-year-old Earl of March was an even greater danger to his plans. His marriage to his brother Lionel's daughter had placed his interest close to the throne and he was full of the hot arrogance of the Marcher lords. Lancaster suspected that the treasonable slur on his own birth that named him changeling had come by way of Mortimer. He had been William of Wykeham's ward, well placed for the hearing of it, even better placed for the spreading of it. Then and now Lancaster gave no credence to the rumour: that his mother the Queen had confessed to the prelate Wykeham on her deathbed that at his birth she had exchanged her own stillborn child for the son of a Flemish porter. The tale had run its course, dying a natural death among the court gossips, yet it still unnerved him and once or twice he had been tempted to ask Wykeham the truth of it. Not that he would have had it. Wykeham was too mindful of his position to admit to the betraying of a sacred confidence and now Lancaster's own pride had smothered the doubt. It still rankled, the fact that men like Mortimer had a ready-made insult to use against him, with or without foundation. As if to taunt him, Mortimer's boyish laugh rang out across the hall. His pale cheeks were flushed with wine and laughter, his arm flung round Hal Percy's shoulder, their heads close as if they conspired together. Lancaster smothered the hot flame of dislike that threatened to burn its way into his eyes and schooled his face into rigid lines of composure. But the thought remained; after his brother Edward's sons the Crown could come to Mortimer's brats. A dangerous bait to dangle before a boy like Mortimer. His eyes shifted to the man beside him: perhaps tempting enough for a man like Hal Percy.

Hal checked his step as the gilded ball rolled beneath his foot. A child's plaything, the silver bell within tinkling softly as he picked it up. He glanced up at the casement thrown wide to the sun and met the smiling eyes of the Princess Joanna.

She sat in the deep embrasure, her face lifted to the streaming sun that turned the hair of the child on her lap to molten gold.

The boy scrambled down and ran toward Hal on unsteady legs as he saw the ball in his hand. His small silk-shod feet slithered on the smooth tiles, his slender body jerked back and forth struggling for balance then he slid to a tearful halt at Hal's feet. Hal scooped him up, laughing as the small petulant mouth quivered in indecision between tears and a brave smile. Then he smiled and snatched the ball, waving it aloft in triumph as Hal carried him to the Princess. Gently, Hal set him down and knelt before the imperious gaze. The boy's face was small and delicate as a flower, the wide blue eyes fringed with silver lashes. His mouth was shapely as a woman's and only the beginnings of a long Plantagenet nose saved his face from utter femininity. The child plucked at his sleeve.

'I am the Lord Richard,' he said in his piping voice. 'Who are you?'

Hal took the boy's fat little hand and held it to his lips. 'Henry Percy, Lord of Northumberland. My homage and duty, your grace.'

Richard crowed with delight. 'Northumberland,' he lisped, 'Northumberland,' repeating it till it flowed easily from his tongue.

Joanna smiled proudly and swept him up, bestowing a soft kiss

132

on his brow. 'Your cousin, sweeting,' she said and beckoned to the hovering nursemaid.

'My cousin of Northumberland,' Richard repeated triumphantly and smiled up into Hal's face as the nurse lifted him from his mother's arms.

Hal watched him led away, still repeating his name in his childish sing-song voice. 'A handsome child,' he said and saw Joanna's proud smile fade in subtle discontent.

'Yet frail, my lord, as is his brother Edward.' She motioned him to sit beside her and turned her face back to the sun she loved. Below her in the sunlit courtyard, her two Holland sons sparred playfully. They were little credit to her; John was a bully with a streak of cruelty that sickened her and Thomas was little better. Yet they were strong and bursting with health, a parody of her royal sons' frailty.

It was for the eldest that she feared most. Edward was always sickly, shivering with chills even in the height of summer, a mockery of his father's great strength. And even that was fading now. She shivered, though the sun burned her skin, remembering Edward's sweating countenance and his eyes perpetually dulled with valerian. Canker, the leeches called it, and though she had little faith in the bungling fools who called themselves physicians, she knew with cold certainty that he would die from it. All her hopes were pinned now in her royal sons, but she would need allies if Edward died before they came to manhood. She was safe as long as the old King lived but for how long could she depend on him? She needed men to work her bidding now, while Edward and his father still lived.

She glanced at the man beside her, his eyes courteously averted as he waited for her to speak. The sun touched and fired his hair and she smiled softly. A handsome man, as fair as Edward had been once, and fairer now, for Northumberland had the beauty of health and strength. It burned behind the golden skin and in the long taut lines of his body; a pleasing ally whose company she would not find irksome. Abruptly she said, 'Prince Edward is grievously sick.'

Hal raised his eyes slowly, 'Not sick enough to die though, my lady.'

133

'Sickness is merely a prelude to death, my lord. The Prince suffers constant pain and I have seen him almost swoon with weakness. Perhaps not this year or the next, but he will not live to be king.' She leant closer and he breathed the scented warmth of her skin. 'My sons will need good lordship. Men who are free from the dominance of Lancaster.'

He looked at her sharply. 'And you think I am one?'

Her smile was tinged with mockery. 'For the moment, my lord.'

Hal glanced away from the bright perceptive gaze. Yes, only for the moment. Since the beginning of the campaign he and Lancaster had maintained an uneasy peace. Neither had made an open bid to renew their old friendship but each day they were thrown closer together, each day it became harder for him to deny his allegiance to Lancaster. The blood and loyalty of his house were Lancaster; beside the Percy crescent he had once worn Lancaster's cognizance of the red rose, yet still he held back, his foot trembling on the brink, unable to take that final step that would bring him irrevocably into Lancaster's camp.

Joanna was still watching him, her eyes narrowed against a shaft of sunlight. She was running to fat and her skin had lost the wondrous glow that had once made a man's fingers itch to touch it. But she was still fair, fair enough to tempt a man. It was hard not to satisfy the question he saw in her eyes, harder still to admit to himself that once where he had been so sure, now he doubted. There were other forces come to cloud his judgement; Mortimer and his crowd of henchmen jostling for their share of power. And now Joanna, all seeing shadows where perhaps there were none. Did he really rate Lancaster's ambition so high?

'Why should you fear His Grace?' He asked the question that he had asked himself a hundred times. 'If Prince Edward should die before the King, what could be more fitting than that his brothers would have charge of the princes?'

Joanna's voluptuous mouth narrowed spitefully. 'For his own ends, my lord, not theirs. You see how he usurps Prince Edward's power now. What more will he do when he is dead?' She touched his hand outspread on the bench between them and her voice was slow and deliberate as if she spoke to a child. 'The King is old and

134

Prince Edward sick unto death. Lionel of Clarence is already dead. Who will there be to stand against Lancaster's domination of my sons? Gentle Edmund or young Thomas? Who will there be to prevent him taking the Crown from a weak boy?'

Hal came abruptly to his feet. It would not come to that. Lancaster wanted power but not at any price. He felt the cold disappointment of Joanna's eyes upon his back but no more than he could speak for Lancaster, would he speak against him. He turned slowly, 'Your Grace, you have my loyalty and that of all my house. When the time comes I shall acknowledge none but your son as king.'

He saw her mouth curve in amusement. 'You disappoint me, my lord,' she said coolly. 'I had thought you the one man at Court free from taint. I can see now that I was mistaken.'

He walked out into the sultry dusk. The air had cooled, and westward the sun drifted in vermilion cloud, gilding the river with streaks of golden light. Joanna's words gnawed at his pride, words that conjured thoughts he had considered a long time ago and that had lost their sting with familiarity. It was nigh on ten years since he had seen Lancaster's intent written plain upon his face. He had not been Lancaster then; death had brought him that and could bring him all England soon. Even the men of Prince Edward's allegiance were casting speculative eyes on Lancaster's rise, easing their coats upon their shoulders, ready to change them. And he still stood apart, his allegiance to none but himself and Northumberland, or so he had thought. But for how long now, how much longer could he hold out—and did he even want to? Had he a choice left, with all the cards fallen so neatly into Lancaster's well-kept hands? And then there was Neville, always at Lancaster's side, assiduous and attentive, poised to scale the ladder of high office. One thing was sure among all the indecision; he could not let John Neville rise unchecked.

The hall was already full and the air redolent with the aroma of spiced meats. He took his seat below the dais and saw the predominant blue and white of Lancaster's livery throughout the hall and the faces of the men who proclaimed their allegiance less boldly: smug and smiling but the smiles edged with caution, careful not to advance too far and leave themselves no avenue of retreat.

Across the table Edmund Mortimer sat between the Holland brothers and stared at Lancaster's unoccupied chair in mute discontent.

Hal looked past the pale vindictiveness of their faces.

Lancaster, Lancaster, always Lancaster, dogging his footsteps like an ill-omened bird. Hate and affection had mingled and he had named the resultant feeling indifference, yet he had never been indifferent to John of Lancaster. And now there was no middle road left to tread. Black or white, for or against, no comforting shades of grey to hide his indecision.

He turned at the first note of the trumpet. Lancaster entered with the Princess Joanna upon his arm. Every eye turned to them and looked away in significant silence: so the Prince was too sick to leave his bed. The knowing whispers sped round the hall as Lancaster advanced. Joanna's plump white hand rested on his velvet sleeve and her skirts of green samite rustled in indignation. Lancaster was smiling, the quiet exultant smile that he always wore when he had won a point.

John Holland pulled a face. 'Jesu, you'd think him the King already.'

Mortimer slewed in his seat, his eyes glittering with dislike. 'He bears himself well enough,' he said loudly, 'for the son of a Flemish butcher.'

In the appalled and sudden silence only the whiteness of Lancaster's face showed that he had heard. He turned slowly, almost reluctantly to meet Mortimer's insolent stare.

'You spoke, my lord of March?' he said quietly. 'I did not catch your words clearly. Perhaps you will repeat them.'

Mortimer rose, tardily and with ill grace. 'With pleasure, Your Grace,' he said smoothly. 'I merely remarked how like your sire you had grown, Your Grace.'

At the back of the dais a page gave a nervous titter. Then Lancaster smiled coldly. 'You are gracious as always, my lord of March. I wish that I could pay you the same compliment.'

He sat amid an astounded hush, for every man within a yard of the dais knew that he had heard, yet he had let Mortimer escape unscathed. So Lancaster was vulnerable and to such a baseless taunt. Hal looked at Mortimer, nodding and smiling at his pretty triumph.

'Clever, my lord,' he said as he caught his smirking glance. 'But hardly worthy of you. Such remarks would be better kept in a ladies' solar, where they belong.'

Mortimer flushed angrily but it was John Holland who spoke. 'And how long will it be before you declare yourself, my lord? You have the court on tenterhooks, wondering which way you will jump when you come down from your fence.'

'Perhaps he already has,' Mortimer snapped. 'After all, the Percys are Lancastrian bred.'

Hal raised his eyes slowly. 'I loved your father, Mortimer,' he whispered, 'and for his sake I'll pretend I did not hear that, but keep the smell of your petty intriguing from my nose. The stench offends me, Mortimer.'

Mortimer half rose from the table, his face contorted in purple rage yet confronted by Hal's pale colourless gaze and the utter stillness of him, his courage failed him at the last moment and he sank back, the blustering threats dying in his throat.

Then all heads swung towards the doors. A man thrust his way through the tangle of guards. Hal saw the familiar span of broad shoulders, the dark hair and rich curling beard. It was Tom. He stood and watched him stumble toward the dais. His hose were torn and his fine doublet powdered with dust. Hal called his name sharply and Tom sent him one uneasy glance before he knelt before Lancaster and whispered close in his ear.

He saw Lancaster rise and lurch from his chair, saw him fall against the laden table as he stumbled and felt his way like a blind man from the dias. Tom pushed his way through the uproar toward Hal, flinging off the restraining hands, shaking his head at the barrage of questions. Hal hauled him the last few feet.

'In God's name, what is it, Tom?'

His brother fell against him wearily. 'There's plague again in England,' he said hoarsely. 'The Duchess Blanche is dead of it at Bolingbroke.'

The November wind keened round the soaring spire of St Paul's and chilled the waiting crowds to frozen silence. As far as

Ludgate and along the tortuous black–bannered length of the Vintry, they stood mute and cold. For the third time in as many years, London was plunged into mourning.

Swathed in miniver, Margaret emerged into the grudging daylight, a drab colourless day where tall skeletal trees showed against an empty sky. The bright gaudiness of the city was masked in black, no vestige of colour showed and everywhere the black of mourning and priestly robes. She walked at crawling pace to the Bishop's Palace. Her limbs were cramped and cold from the long tedious mass and the wind was ice against her cheek. Ahead of her the King walked among his sons and chief ministers, his grey unhealthy cheeks streaked with tears. He was an old man now, dogged by misfortune as once he had been by success. But Mistress Perrers had not lost her hold upon him. She walked behind him, brittle as glass and twice as sharp, her restless eye wandering over the assembled faces. Those who caught it were careful to see that theirs showed nothing but respect. Anything less would have seen the loss of a manor or a privilege by the morning. Even the greatest lords were forced to acknowledge her influence now and if the King baulked, as sometimes he did, the unfailing weapon of her body would soon bring him to heel.

Inside the Bishop's Hall it was dim and oppressive, the bright costly hangings draped in the ubiquitous black. A page brought Margaret mulled wine and she sipped it gratefully, warming her hands on the steaming cup. She moved a little way apart from the ladies of her own rank who talked together in respectful whispers. She knew their subject; John of Lancaster was a widower now and royal dukes did not remain unattached for long. There was not one among them who did not preen herself in foolish expectation.

She stole a glance at Hal among the grave and sombre following of the King. Lancaster was there, his face pale and sweating with strain, his eyes still red from weeping. She noticed too that Hal's eyes were often upon him, questioning and doubtful and sometimes softened by pity.

She turned as a respectful cough sounded beside her and smiled in recognition. 'Master Chaucer,' she said with delight.

'The same, my lady,' he said with his wry, humorous smile. 'Much changed, but the same nevertheless.'

He had indeed changed; the fire dimmed and only the unquenchable ember left burning in his eyes. 'How goes it with you since last we met?' she asked gently.

He spread his long expressive hands. 'The war, my lady, as with all of us. Since the Duke of Clarence's death I have taken service with the King. A humble esquire, nothing more, but it suits me well enough, especially now that His Grace of Lancaster has afforded me his patronage.' He turned his bright gaze upon her. 'And you, my lady, all goes well with you? I hear that you have a brood of fine sons since last we met.'

Margaret laughed. 'Only three, Master Chaucer, and a daughter. But your work?' She turned the subject adroitly from herself. 'I have read nothing of late.'

The poet smile his soft dreamy smile. 'I have had little time and less inspiration of late, my lady. But you shall soon have something to read. Very soon.' His eyes sparkled with the look she remembered seeing the first time they had met. 'In memory of the Duchess Blanche'. He smiled almost apologetically. 'The Duke has graciously given his permission. It shall be named the Book of the Duchess, in memory of a perfect lady.'

Margaret looked past him, suddenly discomforted by the unseemly passion of his voice. She stared pointedly at the two women who hovered close at his back.

Chaucer followed her glance. 'Forgive me, my lady.' He drew a plain smiling woman forward. 'My wife, Philippa, lately of the Queen's household and her sister, the Lady Katherine Swynford.'

Margaret inclined her head and gave the elder woman no more than a cursory glance as she came into the light. It was the sister who held the eyes. Even the black of mourning could not dim her rich colouring and her eyes had a sensual beauty all of their own; a dangerous beauty that filled Margaret with ridiculous unease. Politely she enquired as to their health and children, leading up to the moment when she could graciously withdraw. She glanced down the hall looking for Hal and found Lancaster instead. He sat still as an effigy among the moving courtiers and his eyes were fixed steadfastly on the lovely face of Katherine Swynford.

The minstrel plucked a desultory tune, the notes at first slow and mournful then quickening to a gayer theme as the sound of voices and laughter filled the hall.

Beneath the dais where her lord sat, pouring Northumberland's best claret down his throat as fast as the page could fill his cup, the Countess Maud sat alone at a chess board. She eyed the pieces, moving them idly across the square; jasper and tourmaline, the king crowned in gold and emeralds. Fit for a king—like all else in the room. This would be her last night in the city. Tomorrow they would leave for the north, and the thought of the long comfortless journey filled her with dread. And at the end of it, bleak empty days, bleaker still when Umfraville left for France again, for he would take with him the bustling household that gave their vast sprawling estates a semblance of life.

She drank the last of the spiced hippocras and turned the goblet lightly between her hands. It was of silver, chased with the Percy lion; around the rim, damascened in gold, was the single word: *Esperance*. She murmured it softly to herself. Yet who did she trust? None here. Umfraville grudged her every breath she drew and she had never acquired the habit of friendship. *Esperance, Esperance en Dieu*. Trust in God? She smiled grimly. It could have been her own motto for there was none else for her to trust.

She set the goblet down so sharply that the chessmen knocked together. Across the room her host made his way towards the dias, tactfully disengaging himself from the voluble Bishop Courtney. She might have named Hal Percy friend if she had not been aware that the charm of his manner was not reserved solely for her. Old or young, he treated all women with the same flattering courtesy; but no more than that. Even she could see that he still had eyes for none but his wife. She eyed Margaret Percy with ill-concealed dislike, remembering the shy frail creature that had come to Harbottle. She had not changed; douce almost to the point of subservience and still timid as a rabbit, yet she envied her and grudged her the frail beauty that had brought

140

her Hal Percy though she had next to nothing. She could have matched that dowry a thousand times and still had land to spare yet she, with all her wealth, had once thought herself fortunate to wed Umfraville.

Deliberately she caught Hal's eye and held it, though he would have turned aside with a courteous acknowledgement. She felt the colour creep into her cheeks as he came dutifully toward her and the wild thought crossed her mind— perhaps, in the beginning, if there had been no Umfraville or Margaret Percy. . . . The thought died a cold little death at the look in his eyes: cool dispassionate courtesy, the deference due to her rank.

'My lady.' He bridged the awkward silence with a smile and nodded toward the chessmen. 'Do you play, Countess?'

'Better than you might think, my lord,' she answered drily and felt a strange unaccustomed warmth at the sound of his laughter.

'If that is a challenge, Countess, then I accept.'

She waited while he set the pieces in order, watching his long well-shaped hands move across the board, seeing the short golden hair that gleamed on his wrists and the groove where his betrothal ring cut too deeply into his flesh. From a distance she heard the familiar bellow of her husband's coarse laughter and glanced up to see him plant a wet kiss on Margaret Percy's cheek. A grim little smile curved her mouth as she saw Margaret flinch from his fleshy embrace. She would do more than flinch if she had to suffer him in her bed at night as she did.

Maud became aware of Hal's eyes upon her face and opened the play clumsily, advancing her pawn recklessly. It was a bad move and not worthy of her. Usually she played well, aggressively, each move calculated well ahead. But tonight her thoughts strayed to the man who sat across from her, seeing the way his hair curled over the high velvet collar and the thoughtful frown between his changeable brilliant eyes. Then he raised his head and smiled like a schoolboy in triumph as he put her king in check.

She smiled ruefully. 'I fear I gave you a poor game, my lord.'

He laughed. 'It is never a poor game if I am the victor, Countess.'

Yes, she thought, he liked to win and was used to victory, perhaps too used to it. She smiled and thought desperately of something to detain him, something to disturb the polite unruffled surface that he always showed.

'They say the Prince of Wales is like to die,' she blurted out.

He paused, slightly disconcerted. 'It might be so, Countess. Let us pray that it is not.'

'Then His Grace of Lancaster will be the power behind the throne, with the King in his dotage and Prince Edward's two little knaves hardly out of leading strings.'

He had half risen from his chair and she saw his mouth tighten as she forced him to resume his seat. She wearied him; she could see it from the strained smile that barely touched his mouth, yet she persisted. 'Then Lancaster's patience will be well rewarded. He has waited long for this I think, my lord.'

Hal fiddled with the chessman under his hand. He was sick to death of Lancaster, sick of policy and of the persistent attempts to draw him into the sticky web of intrigue. 'Forgive me, Countess,' he said coldly, 'I did not know that policy interested you.'

'I have little else to interest me, my lord,' she flung back. 'Perhaps like my husband you think a grasp of such matters is beyond a woman.'

'I did not say that.' For some foolish reason Hal felt himself at a disadvantage under the sharp biting gaze of this woman. 'But I think that perhaps a woman is sometimes too swift in her judgement, without full knowledge of the facts.'

She leant forward, her eyes bright. Excitement brought a rare colour to her sallow cheeks and stripped at least five years from her. 'What more do I need to know then, my lord? Lancaster has the King's ear in all things now, even above Prince Edward, and though all England knows that the failure of the last campaign can be laid at his door he is still Captain of Calais and likely to be Regent of Aquitaine. The King hears no voice but his—save that of his harlot, and she works now at Lancaster's bidding.' She smiled unpleasantly. 'How much clearer can he make himself, my lord?' She saw the lines deepen around his mouth and that he kept his eyes averted from her face. 'They say that you will soon be of his party, my lord. You see how he gathers the lords under his banner—for what purpose unless he means to take the Crown for himself?'

He rose abruptly. His voice was still icily polite but his eyes blazed with anger. 'You will excuse me, my lady,' he said unsteadily. 'I have matters to attend to.'

She held his gaze for a brief moment and smiled in pure triumph. She had touched him on the raw and had glimpsed the man that lay beneath the façade. The feeling ran in her veins like wine and for the first time in years she felt alive. 'Run then, my lord,' she hissed. 'Go and bury your head in delusion.' She laughed her soft insulting laugh. 'How Lancaster must rejoice to have men like you at his back.'

Abruptly he left her alone and smilingly she returned the curious stares of the company with her bright unassailable glance. She did not care. She had roused him and even if it was only to dislike, it was better than nothing.

The night sounds floated softly up from the city: the tramping feet and hourly call of the watch, the muffled chime of St Botolph's and, close by, the rattle and growl of hounds on their chains. The Countess Maud crept quietly from the bed and pulled a cloak around her bare shoulders. Umfraville still slept, his mouth open and the breath whistling through his rotten teeth. He would not stir till morning even if London fell about his ears. She crouched, shivering, before the dressing chest and moved the candle close. The small oval glass shimmered with light and she stretched out a hand to clear the mist of heat from the surface. Her face leapt into disturbing clarity; the eyes too small, the mouth too large, her only redeeming feature the luxuriant fall of hair that was never seen, fine and straight as gossamer thread. She pulled it tentatively round her face and saw it soften the high intelligent brow and the too sharp line of her chin. She eased the cloak back on her shoulders. Her breasts were still firm as a maid's, her waist as trim as a boy's, but still no beauty. There was nothing there for a man to lust after.

She closed her eyes and dragged the cloak around her nakedness. Past thirty and love had never touched her. Never once had a man looked at her with love or desire, never once touched her with real passion or laughed into her face with joy at her presence. Not that she had ever hoped for that from Umfraville. She

143

had married him because her brother Anthony had wished it. She had been young then and full of life. There would be children, sons to plan and scheme for, daughters to dress in silks and velvets. But there had been no children, nothing of warmth or beauty to call her own, only years of alternating hope and disappointment and then the final despair of her loneliness.

In the darkness her fingers traced the silver fish blazoned upon her cloak; the three luces, the emblem of the Lucys since the day of the Conqueror. Now Anthony was dead and she was the last. When she died it would all be finished, all her proud lineage come to nothing, all her lands dispersed to greedy strangers. Angrily she brushed at the cold tears that ran down her cheeks. She thought of Margaret Percy, her body thickening with yet another child, and wept out of pure despair.

'So, Lancaster is the man of the day now. It's almost certain now that the King intends to recall the Prince of Wales and appoint His Grace Regent of Aquitaine.' Euphemia pulled the stopper from a vial of jasmine and sniffed the contents. 'Thank God that Walter has taken service under Lancaster. Perhaps we shall see a change in our fortunes now.'

Margaret said nothing and watched critically as her tiring women laid her best gowns in sandalwood chests. Euphemia's hand strayed among the folds of dull silk, flaunting the large beryl that covered her finger to the knuckle. 'A gift from Lady Perrers,' she said smugly, 'A reward for good service.'

Margaret grimaced. 'Last time you spoke of her I do not remember you so kind, Euphemia,' she observed drily.

Her sister had the grace to blush. 'That was then,' she countered defensively. 'Things are different now. Lady Perrers has the King's favour and while he lives Walter and I are needful of it. Not all of us have great estates to retire to when matters at Court do not please us,' she added with a flash of spite.

Euphemia was right, Margaret thought with a sigh. She was more than fortunate. She had warmth and love and three boisterous sons to fill her days, and perhaps soon a fourth. Her sister only had that oaf of a husband who had to be driven like a packhorse to keep his hold on the few cramped manors

Euphemia had managed to gain for them. And things were changing, everything except the war that deprived her of Hal for months at a time. That seemed to go on for ever.

'Will you not come to Alnwick with us then, Euphemia?' She managed to put a warmth she did not feel into her voice. 'Walter is in France and there is nothing to keep you.'

Her sister hesitated, tempted by the thought of free lodging and her sister's renowned largesse. But places at Court were hard to come by and even harder to keep. An absence of even a month could see her place usurped in Alice Perrers's vacillating favour. Reluctantly she shook her head, then unwilling to close the door too firmly she added, 'Perhaps later, when Lady Perrers can spare me.'

Margaret left it at that, ashamed of her own relief and paying for it dearly by allowing Euphemia to cadge a pearl ring from her chest. Then Euphemia said, 'Will you go to Raby?'

Margaret paused. Raby. A magical word that conjured up a world of childhood memories. It was years since she had been to Raby, years since she had seen her sister-in-law Maud and never once her two young nephews. John had seen to that and his enmity had kept her away on the one or two occasions she had been tempted to go. But John was in France. She smiled happily at the thought. Yes, she would go to Raby, despite John.

The laburnam that had once bloomed in a yellow haze along the east wall was no longer there, nor the arbour of wild roses where she had dreamed as a child. The herb garden where she had once helped her mother pick and dry the pungent herbs had gone to seed; mandragora for easement, hoarhound for the fever and verbena for its bitter–sweet perfume, all lost among a tangle of weeds and seeding poppies. Raby had changed and burgeoned into new strident life under John's hand. Pale new stonework patched the mellow walls and sharp new turrets intruded above the weathered smoothness of the curtain wall. Only the view was unchanged, the sleepy curve of moorland and, in the distance, the shining spires of Durham.

She sank down among the long grass that edged the pleasaunce, almost wishing that she had not come. Yet Maud's pathetic joy at her presence made it hard to leave. Poor Maud had not improved with age. She was as foolish as ever and her plump vacuous face had a grey unhealthy tinge that was more a result of John's neglect than sickness. She lived in mortal terror for her two sons. A flock of nursemaids surrounded them day and night like an armed guard and a physician slept in their chamber lest some malady should seek them out at night. Ashamedly Margaret bit her lip as she thought of the elder of her two nephews. She had conceived an unreasonable dislike for Ralph and, though there were two full years between him and her own son Harry, it was Ralph who seemed the elder; a dark swarthy child who rarely smiled and who had inherited his father's contempt for poor Maud.

She turned her head lazily as a voice called her. Thin and querulous, she recognized it for Maud's and scrambled to her feet, brushing the clinging grass from her skirts. Closing her ears to the persistent cry she turned down the path that led to the lake. With the turrets of Raby behind her, it was almost as it had been when she was a child. The crook-backed willow still brushed the lake and the same white lilies starred the dappled water. Sadness shadowed her eyes. She had loved John so well yet now his enmity made her feel an intruder in her old home.

The trees rustled at her back and she turned half expecting to see Maud. Her prepared smile froze on her lips and she stared at her brother in disbelief as if she herself had conjured him up. Yet this John was real enough, flesh and blood, from the dark cropped hair to the cold tight line of his mouth. 'John,' she said with a brittle laugh. 'I had thought you in France.'

He regarded her dispassionately. They might have been strangers for all the recognition he gave her. At last he said, 'So I see. You would not have come otherwise, would you, Meg?'

Her heart lurched in painful memory. None but John had ever called her that. 'Would you have wanted me to, John?' she asked quietly.

He shrugged and walked slowly down the incline toward her. 'I was detained on His Grace of Lancaster's business. It is only by chance that I stopped here on my way to the coast. I came to see

146

my sons, yet I find you, Meg. You must forgive my surprise but I had never thought to see you at Raby again.'

'They are fine boys,' Margaret said evasively. 'Both you and Maud can be proud of them.'

John thrust his toe beneath a clump of weeds and lifted them clean into the air. Maud was like a millstone round his neck and he grudged her every breath she drew. Lord Latimer had more than hinted that when his daughter came of age he would not be averse to a match between them. Elizabeth Latimer was young and comely, and more to the point, she was Latimer's sole heiress.

'She took long enough to do her duty,' he snapped. 'I'll be an old man before my sons reach manhood.'

Margaret looked down at the bruised flower-head that peeped from beneath her shoe. 'For pity's sake, John,' she whispered. 'Must you always be so bitter?'

He laughed, a harsh grating sound that echoed across the lake and disturbed the flock of moorhens nesting in the reeds. 'You ask me that? Wed to my bitterest enemy?'

'By your choice, John,' she retorted, stung to self-defence. 'Hal has never harmed you deliberately nor means to. The hate is all of your own making.'

He gave her a wide incredulous stare. 'Can you lie with a man so long and yet know him so little? You haven't changed, Meg. You still only see what you choose to see. But I promise you that I know your lord better.' He looked out over the shadowed water, speaking almost to himself. 'As long as thing go his way you are safe. But once he loses, once he is beaten, then he's as dangerous as a cornered beast.' He kicked a stone from the dust at his feet and stooped to pick it up. 'He's never been beaten yet, Meg, not hard enough to hurt. Never once in his life has he faced defeat.' He threw the stone and watched it skin the water. 'He wanted you and he had you. He defied the old Duke to wed you and in the end it cost him nothing because even then the old man could not cast him off completely.'

'That's a lie, John,' Margaret broke in hotly. 'He could have been well advanced if he had not wed me.' Had not Lady Percy told her so often enough?

'By his own choice, Meg. Percy has never done aught that was not by his own choice. If he holds no high office it is by his own decision.'

He turned back to the lake. 'He is waiting, yet I do not know for what,' he said softly. 'Lancaster would have him tomorrow, yet he holds back.' He swung round sharply, his grey eyes intent upon her face. 'Why does a man disdain high office when he has been bred for it, when his whole life has been shaped to it? He wanted it once, Meg. I know he did. I knew him when he was a raw boy and he was as arrogant and ambitious as that cold, stiff-necked mother of his could make him. Then why when it was within his reach did he run from it?'

Margaret shook her head despairingly. 'You're wrong, John, so terribly wrong.'

The fleeting smile of pity he gave her was galling comfort. 'For years the Nevilles have waited on the heels of the Percys. Our own father was sworn to serve the old lord with twenty men at arms in peace or war. Well, I am not sworn, Meg. He'll not beat me and it's best that you should know it. When the time comes I'll give no quarter for all that you and I are kin. And what I cannot finish my sons will.' He came toward her in one bounding leap and clutched at her with angry hands. 'We are like two men who lust after the same maid. There can only be one victor and I mean it to be me. Tell him that, Meg. When he comes home tell him all that I have said. Leave nothing out, every word. And also this. One day there will not be a corner of England where a Neville does not hold some high office, no place where their power is not felt. Tell him, sweet sister, tell him of my dream and let it be his nightmare.'

Margaret strained her eyes to the fading colours of the tapestry and called to the page to bring another candle. It was barely three o'clock but the hall was full of shadows that defied the cressets' smoky glare. At her feet, wrapped in fur against the constant draught, her daughter Meg read from a manuscript of verse.

'*I was war of a man in blak,*
That sat and had y-turned his bak

148

> To an oke, an huge tree.
> "Lord," thoghte I, "who may that be?"
> And ther I stood as stille as ought,
> That, sooth to saye, he saw me nought.'

Margaret smiled softly as she listened. Master Chaucer had been as good as his word and she had had one of the first manuscripts, fresh from the copyist.

> 'I have of sorwe so gret woon,
> That joye gete I never noon,
> Now that I see my lady bright,
> Which I have loved with al my might,
> Is fro me deed, and is a-goon.
> Allas, o deeth! what ayleth thee,
> That thou noldest have taken me,
> Whan that thou toke my lady swete?
> That was so fayr, so fresh, so free,
> So good, that men may wel y-see
> Of al goodnesse she had no mete!'

She flexed chilled fingers grown stiff with cold. The poet's words lost their poignancy in the knowledge that Lancaster had taken Katherine Swynford for his mistress as soon as decency allowed. Men were weak, she thought sadly, driven by lust and greed. It was the women who had the strength, always douce, taking without complaint all that their lords chose to put upon them. She glanced around the half empty hall; old men and boys sat huddled in thick winter cloaks, all that could be spared from the war. Her eldest son Harry sat with the warden, his pale handsome face alight as the old man regaled him with tales of war. He grew more difficult each day, his fierce temper worsened by the cold and boredom, and she, fool that she was, could still deny him nothing. She sighed and threaded her needle with a length of purple silk, then laid it down again as Ralph and Thomas began to bicker over a plaything. Meg rose to quieten them and Margaret's mouth curved in rare pride as she watched her. Meg would be a beauty one day, fairer than she had ever been. She was blessed with handsome children. Harry, even at

149

ten, could charm the birds from the trees and Ralph and Thomas shared their father's radiant fairness. And now there was the new babe, another son, Alain, named for the ancient Percys of Louvain. She had more than enough to occupy her time. She kept Hal's seal and held daily council with the veteran knights who were her advisers. She kept the tally of rents brought in by the bailiffs of their numerous manors and gave tentative judgment in the squabbles of their tenants; but time still hung heavy on her hands. It always did when Hal was away at the war.

Christmas had come and gone, the merrymaking and the taste of rich food forgotten. Now all they waited for was spring, release from the cold and premature darkness of winter days that kept them penned within Warkworth's chill walls. And she, as always, waited for Hal.

It was two years since he had left for France, a year since she had seen him and then only briefly when he had brought Prince Edward home, stricken with grief at the death of his eldest son, his reputation stained with the horror of Limoges. It had been the shame of every Englishman and she remembered Hal's face the last time she had seen him, white and strained with shock as he had told her of the last months of the war. The tide had turned against them at the beginning of the year. The King of France had crossed into Aquitaine, and Limoges and its unscrupulous Bishop had capitulated within the month. The retaking of Limoges was burned into every Englishman's heart; three thousand innocent souls put to the sword at Prince Edward's command. No quarter had been given, women and children burnt alive in the funeral pyres of their own homes, babes piked and born aloft as screaming trophies. She had wept for their poor innocent souls, but more for Hal. She had never seen him so weary and sick at heart.

Angrily she snapped the thread and picked at the miscast stitch. It was always war; it had kept Hal from her for almost half of their life together, she saw its reward all around her, men maimed and useless, living like beggars. And in Jesu's name, who cared now for the King's pretension to the Crown of France? Not Edward, living at Shene in doting senility with his rapacious mistress. It was like a pestilence, spreading its contagion from generation to generation. Harry had caught the taint. He thought of nothing else, talked of nothing else and spent every moment out of her sight hanging round the guardhouse, letting his ears be filled with romances. Now she only lived in dread for Hal. Soon she would live in dread for both of them.

Meg tugged at her sleeve. She heard the grating of shod hooves on the icy stones of the bailey. She could never hear the sound of horsemen without thinking of Hal, but this was the gently ambling trot of a packhorse slowed by a cart. But still she turned her head sharply as her steward entered. Not bad news then, for his dour face was lightened by a smile.

'My lady, there are players without, my lady. They crave lodging in exchange for a night's entertainment.' His voice was almost merry and for the first time she realized how heavy the boredom of winter lay upon them all.

That night she dressed with almost foolish care, choosing the azure silk threaded with gold that Hal had brought her from France; the Percy colours that recalled his eyes and coin-bright hair. She hummed an old song remembered from her Court days as Ellen swept her hair into the tight fitting caul, noting with a little frown that she had lost flesh and that the gown was slack around her waist. The warm colour crept into her cheeks remembering the last time she had worn it. Hal had been home then and that first night had stripped it from her with expert passion. It was a long time since she had slept with any but Meg and the babe, long enough for the thought of Hal to turn her weak with love.

In the outer chamber the children sat, pink and bursting with excitement. Meg, serene and lovely in white tarse silk, strove to keep the peace between the younger boys. Harry sat on their shared bed, his eager face framed by the dark unruly curls that no amount of careful brushing could keep from falling across his brow. She plucked a stray hair from the shoulder of his crimson doublet and chivvied the boys into order, stooping to the cradle to see that the babe slept easy. She smiled lovingly at them all. 'Come,' she said in her gentle voice. 'Let us go down to the hall.'

The hall blazed with a rosy warmth, the great hearths banked with applewood. The tables were swathed in damask and set for a feast, for she had wildly ordered the steward to broach the last cask of malvoisie.

The strong spicy vintage burnt her throat and made her head as light as down. She laughed like a child at the jester in his cap and bells. The players in their gaudy ill-fitting costumes strutted through a pageant of St George; then came one of their own contriving, in honour to their hostess: a Percy lion in yellow hose and mane of saffron rags danced with a Neville bull clad in a bearskin with horns of curled parchment. Margaret laughed with the others and shrugged off the chill that the thought of John gave her. She had never told Hal of her meeting with John. Instead of his nightmare it had become hers.

Then an old woman darted from the players and knelt on the steps of the dais. Dark eyes blazed from a small wizened face and her long greying hair was bound with small silver bells that tinkled softly as she spoke. 'Your fortune, ladies, for a silver penny.'

Margaret hesitated, then as Meg pleaded and the boys shrieked she nodded to the steward to pay her. Ellen blushed and giggled at a prediction of a handsome husband; the steward's lady was entranced by a glimpse of lush manors and a titled husband for their daughter. The crone passed on and paused before Harry who regarded her with a mixture of curiosity and disdain.

'I have no need to see your hand, young lord. Your future is written clear on your face. A warrior's face, young sir, whose name shall be renowned throughout all England.' Harry grinned and looked sheepishly around him. If he had told the old hag what to say it could not have been more to his liking. Then the gypsy came and knelt before Margaret and stared at her with fearless knowing eyes. Her hand lay small and white in the crone's leathery palm.

'Well, then,' she said with good humour as Ellen giggled and Meg pressed an inquisitive face over her shoulder. 'What does the future hold for me?'

The crone raised blank eyes. 'Naught, lady, for there is none.' She closed Margaret's spread fingers quickly and smiled into the sudden awed silence. 'Naught save all that you have ever yearned for. Peace and tranquillity and easement of the soul.'

The steward's wife gave a shrill nervous laugh and Margaret forced a smile against the cold chill that gripped her heart. It was all nonsense, foolish glib predictions that always came to naught, yet she snatched Meg's hand away when the gypsy would have taken it. 'Our thanks, old woman,' she was surprised at how steady her own voice was. 'We have seen enough of the future for one night.'

The old woman said nothing and backed away clutching her silver. Meg's warm little hand slid comfortingly into her own and the moment passed, covered over with renewed laughter. It was nothing, a play on words to give credence to the hag's flimsy powers. She stretched her cold lips in a semblance of a smile. It would soon be spring and Hal would be home in the spring.

She woke shivering, to the fretful wail of the babe. In the dark silence of the chamber it sounded loud as a clarion but Meg still slept beside her, moaning softly as Margaret slipped from the bed. She knelt beside the dark humped shape at the foot of the bed and roused Ellen from her loud slumber before she crept toward the cradle. Her mouth dried in panic as she laid her hand upon his brow. His skin burned with fever and the linen of his bed was drenched with sweat.

She called sharply for light and Ellen fumbled sleepily with flint and tinder. In the wavering ring of the candle flame the babe's face burned a fiery red and his limbs pounded fretfully at the air. Margaret gathered him up and held him against her. 'Fetch the chaplain,' she snapped.

Ellen's broad face crumpled in fear and she crossed herself before Margaret's look sent her scurrying to the door. Meg had woken and came to place a cloak round her frozen shoulders. 'What ails him?' she whispered and smoothed her small brother's damp brow.

Margaret shook her head and laid trembling lips against her son's damp cheek. A chill, the fever, any of a dozen ailments that could strike at his precarious young life.

The chaplain came, amid complaints and the flap of hastily

donned robes. His knowledge of leechcraft was scant but better than nothing and, while Ellen feverishly pounded herbs, Margaret rolled the child in ice-cold cloths and spooned the warm posset between his parched lips. Then there was nothing to do but wait and watch the grey dawn light fill the room. The babe had quietened, its lusty screams diminished to a feeble whimper. Meg tossed restlessly on the high bed and Ellen snored gently on her pallet. Only Margaret remained sleepless, her eyes wide as the darkness lifted from the familiar shapes in the room and the candles turned pale in the light.

Her steps slowed by exhaustion, she paced out the limits of her chamber, averting her eyes from the still figure on the bed. Her lips moved in endless prayer, echoing the frenzied exhortations of the priest. Sweet Jesu, let her have Meg. She could bear to lose the babe but not Meg, her only daughter.

She glanced toward the bed and set her teeth as she saw the leeches swollen and black upon her daughter's white skin. They had tried all else, every herb and recipe she knew, till all of Warkworth reeked with their smell. It had been so swift. That very morning as she had nursed the sick babe, Meg had been unable to rise from her bed. She had thought the worst, but only for the brief dreadful moment that it had burned into her mind. This time her childhood habit of seeing only that which she wished to had stood her in good stead and kept her sane. She chewed her lip and waved away the cup of wine that Ellen brought her. The steward had ridden to the Abbey for a physician an hour since. All would be well when he returned. It was merely a lack of skill that defeated them. Whereas the monks at Alnwick were renowned for their leechcraft.

The distant grind of the portcullis gate sent Margaret flying to the door. She ran along the ill lit passage and down the narrow privy stair, past the mute reproachful faces of her sons who had been confined to their chamber all day. Today she had no thought for them, nothing mattered but Meg and that she should live.

She ran ahead of the black-robed monk, back the way she had come, fretting with impatience at his slow unhurried gait. She banished all but Ellen from the room, waiting with her back against the door while the monk bent over the bed. It seemed a long time before he straightened and moved across to the silent cradle. She saw his long hands delve among the fresh linen and the babe set up his whimpering again as he probed beneath his arms.

He beckoned her, his face impassive and set in cold harsh lines. 'I fear it is the pestilence, my lady.'

The whispered words drove all the breath from her body. She stared at him with wide bloodshot eyes. His grey face filled all her vision, the pits in his skin as large as a fist, the yellow jaundiced eyes averted and swiftly hooded by wizened lids. She drew the breath loudly through her nose.

'*You lie!*' she screamed. '*You lie!*'

He laid hold of her arm, his thin bony fingers searing her tender flesh. Over his shoulder he called to a trembling Ellen. 'A cup of wine for your mistress.'

Green with fear, Ellen slopped wine into a cup and brought it reluctantly. The monk forced the hard silver rim against Margaret's teeth and tilted the cup. She swallowed a mouthful before her throat closed up in fear.

'It cannot be,' she sobbed. 'Not plague! Oh, Jesu have mercy—not plague!'

Against the shrill wail of Ellen's voice the monk spoke softly. 'I have seen it often enough, my lady. The breath is tainted, and pustules forming in the groin.'

Margaret clutched at his coarse robe. 'But the plague is swift,' she babbled. 'The babe has been sick almost three days.'

The monk shrugged. He had seen men perish in less than an hour, sometimes they lasted for as long as a week, but always in the end they died. 'Nevertheless, my lady. It is the pestilence.'

Margaret wiped the trickle of wine from her chin. She wanted to scream, to weep and rail and vent her agony on this cold shrivelled little man who had shattered her world. Instead she heard her own voice, calm as a summer sea. 'Is there nothing to be done then, father?'

'Only pray, my daughter. It is in God's hands. We are all at his mercy.'

155

Little comfort for the dreadful agony of her heart. Stiffly she rose. Ellen was weeping, crouched in a corner like a beast. Sharply Margaret called to her. 'Send the steward to me, and Harry's tutor.'

In the small presence chamber, the fire burned cheerfully, sending darting warmth into the chill corners of the room. She sat in the carved, high-backed chair and surveyed the anxious faces of her henchmen. Strange that she should feel so calm when all the time the ground heaved and shuddered beneath her feet. She spoke calmly, without a trace of the mounting hysteria that threatened to choke her. To the steward she said, 'I have no need to tell you that there is pestilence at Warkworth. Take my sons and their household to Alnwick and keep them there till you have word from me. And tell the rest that I will keep none here who wish to leave.'

The steward shook his head, his rheumy eyes blurred with tears. 'My lady, I cannot leave you without protection.'

Margaret smiled thinly. 'What protection can you give me against plague?' she murmured. 'Give it to my sons who have more need of it. Brother William from Hulne will stay by me. We shall do very well together until it is over.'

She watched them go, her sons and all her household to the meanest scullion from her kitchen. She did not blame them, she did not expect loyalty in the face of such a death. Ralph and Thomas were weeping and from a distance she saw Harry's pale mutinous face turned back toward her. Though her arms had ached to hold them she had bid them farewell from a distance lest she carried the pestilence with her. She dared not acknowledge the thought that it might be the last time she would ever see them.

Tears ran slowly down her thin ravaged cheeks as she saw the black ugly pustules that marred Meg's pale skin. She slept quietly for though the old monk had no cure he had opiates for easement. Alain still fretted and set up a wailing that set her teeth on edge, yet she wiped her cheeks and went to him. The plague boils had burst and gave off a stench that turned her sick. He screamed as she lifted the soiled dressing from his groin and thrashed his legs feebly against the quilt. She closed her eyes and swallowed on the bitter fluid that gushed into her mouth. Cool gentle hands turned her away from the cradle.

'I will see to the child, my lady,' the monk said. 'Will you not take a little air? You will feel the better for it.'

She walked out into the deserted bailey that had once bustled with life and colour. Now it was as quiet as the grave, the only sound in all that emptiness the feeble slap of the pennon that flew from the keep. She breathed the mild clear air and felt it cool her throat burned dry by the stench of sulphur. It was almost spring; the birch trees were budding yellow and on the hills the grey winter grass was turning green. Hal would be home soon; a month, perhaps less, and he would be riding through the barbican gate, bringing the sun with him. She bit hard upon her lip to stem the tears that came all too easily now, and ran down the wide steps, letting her eyes wander round the quiet mossed walls. She loved this place. Warkworth was hers as Alnwick could never be, hers and Hal's, carrying his indelible stamp in the sharp cleanness of the new Lion Tower and the broken line of the new church. The grass was still white with powdered stone, the raw blocks stacked like giant effigies where the masons had left them. Gently she rubbed at the fine down of winter moss and saw the stone beneath gleaming with golden warmth. It would be a fine church, built to last long past the day when they would be dust beneath it. Then memory came, cold and sharp as hoar frost. The old crone's face the night of the revel: '*What does the future hold for me?*' and the answer, '*Naught, for there is none.*' She fell against the damp stone. Meg was going to die, they were all going to die. She would not see the church or Hal again.

She turned and ran, stumbling over her skirts and bruising her cheek on the sharp cornice of the doorway. Her dew-wet skirts dragged on the stairway, darkening the worn hollows of the stone, and in the empty hall the sharp incisive rasp of her breath echoed like the roar of the wind. Cold and empty as a tomb, her tomb, with walls ten feet thick.

She leant panting against the outer door of her chamber and heard nothing for a while except the sound of her own panic. Then as her breathing quietened she caught the soft drone of Brother William's voice. The high oak doors yielded reluctantly

157

to her touch and the wind rushed in before her, scattering the dead ashes of the fire in her path. The words came clearer now, mingled with the feeble cries of the babe, harsh and low and trembling with fatigue: 'The Lord gave and the Lord taketh away; blessed be the name of the Lord.'

She closed her eyes on blinding tears. Meg was dead, her lovely golden child was dead.

Between them they carried her to the old chapel and laid her before the altar, pillowed on soft velvet. Margaret knelt beside her, the whimpering babe clutched in her arms. Beneath the golden tissue that covered her she could discern the small and lovely bones, the quiet head that spilled its flood of silver hair onto the cold stones. But for the utter stillness of her, Meg might have been sleeping.

Brother William touched her arm. 'Come away, my lady. Return to your chamber, you have need of care yourself.'

She looked up into the colourless blur of his face; grey cheeks darkened with two days' growth of beard, grey tufts of hair spread like a dim halo round his tonsure, all grey, like the walls of the chapel around them. She shook her head, half in denial and half to clear the burning pain from her eyes. 'There is no need, father,' she whispered. 'I'll stay here, within God's sight.'

The monk's cool and fleshless hand brushed her brow. 'Then I'll stay also, my child.'

The babe died that night, quietly, almost without her noticing. She did not move from the hard bench where she lay and held it fiercely when the monk would have taken it, shivering though her flesh boiled beneath her gown. Her throat burned with thirst, but she could suffer no more than a mouthful of the watered wine that Brother William brought her; yet the worst was eased by the bitter draught he spooned into the corner of her mouth. She could no longer see his face clearly but she knew his kindness from the gentle touch of his hands and the softness of his voice. Wide eyed, she stared up into the soft golden gloom of the vaulting, listening to the creak of the breathing oak. If she closed her eyes the world lurched into fearful blackness and, like a child, she was still afraid of the dark. She tried to pray but memory came and snatched the halting words from her lips. Faces trembled on the edge of her vision; her sons, blessedly safe at Alnwick, and Hal, her beloved Hal. The darkness took his image from her as she closed her eyes. There would be no more Hal, no more waiting, counting the days for a sight of him. There was nothing now, except death. Tears spilled from her eyes and dried upon her steaming flesh. Perhaps this was the thing she had always seen in the shadows, yet now it was come she was not afraid. Death stood so close that she could feel its cold breath upon her cheek, she embraced it in the stiff slumbering bundle she held in her arms. She had nothing to fear. The gypsy's dark face rose before her: the future held nothing, save peace and tranquillity and easement of her soul.

In the empty chapel Hal's breath whispered like an alien wind. He lay face down upon the cold grey slab, his arms thrown wide as if he embraced them still. His eyes were dry and burning with unshed tears, yet he could not weep; even that small weakness he denied himself lest he should never be whole again.

The grey walls closed him in like the tomb he covered. A hundred candles burnt, their smoke hanging like clouds in the arched roof, yet they could not banish the shadows that clung to every pillar, that lurked in the hollows of the carved saintly faces and coaxed them fleetingly to life. Everywhere he looked he saw her face, laughing, weeping, lightened by that sad little smile that he had loved. His hands clenched on the sharp chiselled edge of the grave. She lay so close, only the thickness of the stone between them. If he had had the strength he would have torn it up and brought them out from the cold. He pressed his mouth against the slab, straining his body into the hard unyielding stone. He could not leave her here in the darkness with the stink of her own death around her. There was a place down by the river that she had loved where the water lapped softly against the rock and swans nested in the reeds in spring. He would lay her there. He would carve a shrine for her out of the rock below Warkworth. There would be candles burning day and night. She would never be in the dark again.

Stiffly, like an old man he rose to his feet and drew the flower from his sleeve. The marguerite, her emblem, its petals soft and white as she had been. He laid it gently on the cold stone and watched its petals curl against the sudden chill. 'Marguerite,' he whispered, 'too fair a flower to remain in the field for long.'

In the solar his youngest son Ralph snivelled into his nurse's skirts, hiding his face from the tall unsmiling gaze of his father. Thomas watched him with fearful eyes and only Harry seemed unperturbed, turning a disinterested shoulder while his father issued his final instructions for their care. He stared down into the yard where the horse pawed restlessly at the ground; his father's horse, waiting to take him to York and thence to Westminster. The groom that held its head bent to check the girth, soothing the beast's restlessness with meaningless clicks and muttered endearments. The wind lifted the black saddle cloth incised with silver crescent and the horse danced sideways in impatience. It was anxious to be gone as his father was.

Harry turned a blank expressionless face over his shoulder at the stilted farewell. For a moment he met his father's eyes, strange cold eyes, empty of feeling, that recalled nothing of the laughing man who had once whirled him aloft at each homecoming, who had set him on his first horse and softened each fall with gentle teasing. Then swiftly he turned back to the window so that Hal should not see his own eyes with their tell-tale misting of tears.

Outside the door Hal closed his eyes in sudden pain and fought against the urge to run back and gather them all in his arms. They were all he had left of Margaret now, all he had left to love. He moved quickly to the head of the stairs. Not yet, not while his grief was still raw and unhealed. It would not heal here in the north. He needed to be free and to fill his own empty life with the lives of others.

The groom doffed his cap and knelt to his stirrup, waiting till the horse had settled beneath its master's weight before he gave the wide reins into his elegant gloved hands.

Hal turned its head toward the gate, setting it to a walk while his men ran to winch down the bridge. He had not advanced more than a dozen paces when he heard Harry's shout. The boy was running toward him, the steward panting at his heels. He flung himself against the horse so that it swerved in fright and he almost fell beneath its hooves.

'Father, take me with you, take me with you!' He lifted his face, pale as chalk, his grey luminous eyes brimming with tears; his mother's eyes, as if she herself looked out from the child's face.

Without a word Hal leant down and lifted the boy onto his saddle. Together they rode out through the gate and took the road south to York.

It was less than a mile from Thames Street to his father's house at Aldersgate yet it took Harry the best part of an hour to find his way back from Lord Salisbury's house. He dawdled the length of Thames Street, wide-eyed at the splendour of the merchants' houses, peering nervously down the narrow alleyways that led down to the wharves. From Old Fish Street to Bread Street was a maze of tantilizing colour and smell. Poulterers and fishmongers yelled themselves hoarse behind piled trestles, scarecrow 'prentices emerged from dingy shops and weaved nimbly through the crowds, bare feet slapping uncaringly in the ordure that clogged the runnels. He turned up by Paul's Gate toward the Cheap and stood a moment to get his bearings in the milling crowds.

It was the first time he had ventured out alone in the city since his father had brought him a month before and his bravado was waning as the crowds pushed and shoved against him, carrying him away from where he wanted to go. A hundred faces loomed over him, the broad red faces of countrymen come for Newgate Market, the sly cajoling cheapjacks who plucked at his sleeve and waved ribbons and gewgaws in his face. Panic gripped him as he was thrust into a doorway to make way for a cart that filled the whole street with hardly a foot to spare. He struggled against the broadcloth back that penned him in. He could smell the sweat and the reek of tallow. He shoved against soft flesh and a woman turned, a hand raised to cuff him. She smiled in toothless pleasure as she saw him and pinched his cheek, shrieking with delight as he squirmed against her. Then he ran, fighting and kicking his way through the jumble of carts and barrows that rumbled towards Newgate, stopping only when he reached the familiar landmark of the great conduit in the Cheap.

He leant panting against the wall. He had lost his cap and his bright new livery was torn and splashed with mud but he knew his way now, past Goldsmith's Hall and Martin le Grand to where Northumberland Inn stood in the shadow of the city wall. He brushed ruefully at his stained hose, already feeling the sting of the seneschal's hand. For all he was the lord's son he received no favours. He shared the cramped quarters of the other pages, ate the same food which was always cold by the time they had served the others. He performed the same duties and, because he was the youngest, bore the brunt of their bullying. The work was hard and sometimes menial, rising at dawn to Mass, then a stringent hour of Latin and grammar before they were let out to the tilting yard and the iron discipline of the master-at-arms. For the rest of the time he was no more than a servant, always at the beck and call of the steward's roar. It had taken all of that month to subdue his unruly tongue. Now he was as douce as a maid, outwardly at least. For all the steward's bullying he would not risk being parted from his father. Not that he saw much of him. Each day Hal attended Parliament, each night supped with one or other of the lords who had houses in the city, and this last week he had seen nothing of him at all. Since the beginning of August Hal had attended the King at Shene.

Defiantly Harry walked past the chamberlain's amused stare and tramped into the hall. They were setting up the long tables for supper, the best cloths and best plate. With a leap of his heart he knew that his father would be home that night. The thought was a bulwark against the steward's acid stare and the muffled laughter of the pages. The steward came toward him, his brows drawn together in anger.

'You look like a scullion, Percy,' he shouted. He held up a hand to stem the sniggers then looked back to Harry's defiant face. 'We must find you work to suit,' he snapped. 'Get to the kitchen where it seems you belong.'

Harry's face flushed with temper and for a moment he stood his ground, biting hard on the furious retort. Yet it was within the steward's power to forbid him the hall and he'd suffer any humiliation for a sight of his father, however distant.

For an hour he ran back and forth to the bellow of the Flemish

162

cook's voice. The sweat ran in rivulets beneath his shirt as he strained to lift the great tuns of wine. Grease from the dripping banks of spitted meats filmed his skin and stained his tunic. The burning fragrance of cinnamon clogged his throat and pricked at his eyes, yet nothing was worse than the smug grins of the spit boys as they piled his dish heavier than the rest, smirking behind their hands when his feet slithered on the greasy rushes. He set his teeth hard together and met their looks with a blank expressionless gaze. He had no need to feel shame before scum. One day they would kneel at his passing and run like frightened rabbits to do his bidding. He could afford to indulge them this once.

But the steward was a different matter, and when he came for him the look that Harry gave him checked the scathing words upon his lips. The man watched him go to his quarters and tugged thoughtfully at his beard. He had his orders, yet sometimes he wondered at his lord's wisdom. The boy was untried metal, vulnerable with grief; to push him too far now might break him. He shrugged and cuffed an idling page from his warm corner. It was none of his affair, yet still he wondered why the boy's eyes gave him such a feeling of disquiet.

Harry moved among the laden tables, the heavy silver pitcher steady in his hands. Tall and slim as whipcord, the black unruly curls that sprang from beneath his cap gave him the look of an imp and his smile as he poured the wine was quick and courteous without servility.

Hal watched him mount the steps of the dais but turned away before their eyes should meet. He could not bear that starved hungry look that crept into Harry's eyes whenever they dwelt upon him. He had nothing to give the boy except his pain and grief. Any love that was left in him was sealed up within him. He did not dare let it out yet. Even when Harry stood beside him he did not look up and the moment of anguished hesitation before he passed on seemed like an hour, yet ridiculously, though he could not meet his look, Hal could not keep his eyes from him. Covertly, he had marked Harry's progress since he had brought him from the north. He had seen the back-breaking effort that had gone into the mastery of the high-mettled war horses and he

163

knew from the master-at-arms about the long gruelling hours Harry spent perfecting his swordsmanship. He had driven the boy hard, twice as hard as he would another man's son. And Harry had met the challenge. He would achieve perfection because his father wished it. Even Hal, from his distant vantage point, knew that the boy would work his fingers to the bone rather than fail him.

He drained his cup, a rich claret spiked with cloves that dried the palate and increased the thirst, listening with half an ear to Prince Edmund's mumbled opinion of his brother Lancaster's strategy. His steward bent close to beg leave to broach another tun of wine—the fifth that night, and it was barely dusk. He glanced round at the crowded tables; twenty peacocks and four hundred fowl picked as clean as corpses and every dish scraped clean to the silver. He'd watched them gorge themselves till his own rose, but he welcomed them; down to the last hanger-on, he welcomed them. He did not care to be alone these days.

A small jewelled hand slid onto his sleeve. 'Will there be dancing, my lord?' The voice, soft and sleek as silken thread, always left him unprepared for the hard brilliance of Alice Perrers's eyes. She smiled and leant against him so that the musk at her throat drifted into his nostrils. 'I should like to dance,' she murmured. 'My limbs feel the need for exercise now that the King has deserted me for the war.'

Hal laughed at the sheer brazenness of the woman. She was a whore and made no bones about it. But she was a king's whore, and that made all the difference. The hand that moved against his sleeve still kept the King enthralled and the soft eloquent voice still shaped his will. That the King had deserted her was an exaggeration. Only the capture of Poitou and Saintonge by the French had dragged Edward from her bed and forced him to wheedle yet another loan from the Londoners. Four hundred Englishmen rotted in French dungeons, his own brother Tom among them, and now La Rochelle and Thouars were threatened. Edward had no choice but to stir himself if all Aquitaine were not to disappear beneath the Frenchman's heel. And Hal for one welcomed it. He was tired of London, tired of Parliament and its petty squabbles and the need to drink himself to a near stupor before he could sleep at night. His body was still too numb to feel the need for a woman but it took a good malmsey to dull the ache of longing for Margaret and to kill the vision of her and his little ones beneath that cold slab. He stared down into his empty goblet; empty and useless till it was filled with wine, as he was. He called for more and drank till it burned his throat to numbness.

The laughter around him grew louder, white teeth in mouths stained red with wine, the shrill empty rattle of drunkards. Tom Beauchamp capered in motley hose with Prince Edmund's Spanish bride—another whore, though she looked as virtuous as a nun, a strange contrast to her sister Constanza, who was plain as a pikestaff and burning with religious zeal. But Constanza had other charms; she was heiress to the dispossessed King of Castile, bait enough to tempt Lancaster from his widowhood and the arms of his mistress Katherine Swynford. Already he had named himself King of Castile. Hal smiled grimly to himself. So Lancaster would have his Crown after all, albeit Spanish and yet to be fought for. It seemed that Lancaster's star could not be dimmed despite the disaster of their last campaign. He had no rivals. Who was there to stand against him now? The old King and his sickly heir? Gentle obliging Edmund who deemed it an honour to do his brother's bidding? Young Thomas was Lancaster's only threat, quarrelsome and vindictive and barely out of tutelage, too young as yet to question Lancaster's overbearing will. Hal smiled in quiet speculation. When he was of age the sparks would fly.

Since Hal had arrived in London he had seen Lancaster almost daily, though nothing had passed between them but courtly pleasantries. Their conflict still lay between them like a sleeping dog that neither would unleash nor call to heel. A page bent to fill his cup. He turned unthinkingly to smile his thanks and looked full into his son's eyes. Dark and grey as winter cloud; her eyes, as she had looked on the first night he had seen her. Memory engulfed him and he turned away, almost overturning his cup. He was a fool to have kept the boy with him but he hadn't the strength to send him back, any more than he'd had the strength to refuse to bring him. He could have laughed at the irony of it. He thought he'd left his grief in the north, yet he carried it with him, clear and bright in the mirror of a child's eyes.

The warships rode low in the turbulent water and dragged like leashed hounds on their anchor chains; four hundred of England's finest ships, chained and impotent in the tiny bay off La Rochelle. The French coast showed a thin grey line through the mist of rain—so near, yet it might have been a thousand leagues while the wind held them, tossing them like leaves on a pond, always blowing them back toward England. For a month now they had ridden out the gusting winds and driving rain, forty thousand men crammed into ships meant for half that number. Below the sea-washed decks, the King's army shivered and retched, helpless as children while a few miles away the French ravaged La Rochelle. From the prow of his ship Hal watched the French coast heave and fade from sight as the black racing clouds drove the last of the daylight from the sky. Another day wasted and lost, another night in the stinking bowels of the ship.

Lanterns flared at the mastheads as darkness shrouded the fleet; the horns sounded warning like the bleating of feeble sheep. Hal drew the sodden cloak closer round him and turned at the sound of feet slapping the streaming decks.

Bent double against the wind Edmund Mortimer squinted up at him, his sharp face a pale blur in the void of his hood. 'We're turning back,' he yelled and spat out the water that filled his mouth.

Hal came down and stood with him in the shelter of the castle deck. 'Turning back? On whose word?'

'The King's, and through him, Lancaster.' Mortimer sucked the water from the yellow hair that hung from his narrow lip. 'It seems that to the shame of defeat is to be added the shame of ridicule,' he sneered. 'We are turning back without a blow being struck, without even touching land. And all this we owe to Lancaster's bungling.'

Hal smiled bitterly. 'A harsh judgment, Mortimer. We might think him God but even he cannot control the elements.'

Mortimer drew closer. 'Always so quick to Lancaster's

166

defence, my lord. For all the rumour I had not thought you one of his party.'

'Would you rather I was one of yours then, my lord?' Hal enquired softly. 'I have never thought you without self-interest but lately you have exceeded all my expectations. The joy of fatherhood seems to have lifted your sights as high as Lancaster's and with less cause.' He smiled with grim satisfaction as he saw the flush burn Mortimer's cheek. It was joy to bait him, he rose so easily. 'A daughter was it not, my lord?' He pursed his mouth in mock sympathy. 'Well, all is not lost yet. I hear your Countess is with child again already. We must pray for a son this time, must we not?' His eyes played for a moment on Mortimer's face then he leant close, still smiling, as if he would whisper a confidence. 'Well, hear this, my lord of March, and hear it well. England is my party and if there's to be a choice then I'll choose who comes closest to her need. It will not be you, Mortimer, I promise you that.' He straightened and turned back into the wind. 'Go home to your Countess, my lord, and see if you can sire yourself a king.'

Mortimer lurched round to face him, his cloak puffed up by the wind. 'I'll not forget this, Percy,' he screamed.

Hal turned his cold empty gaze upon him. 'I trust not, my lord. I should hate to have to repeat myself.'

He stayed for another hour after Mortimer had gone. His hands were numb with burning cold, his feet unsure upon the slippery deck, yet the thought of the fetid airless quarters below kept him where he was. Out here was the only refuge, however comfortless. He could have wept with sheer frustration. They were turning back, with nothing accomplished except the squandering of the King's hard—won loan. The Commons would scream for a head and that head would be Lancaster's—for who could blame an old man and another who was kept alive by the sheer strength of his own will?

The wind had dropped but still blew persistently in his face. Darkness covered them like a shroud and only the yellow stars of the lanterns reflected in the oily water showed where the sea ended and the sky began. The sound of singing came from the King's ship, an old tavern song, the words blurred and disjointed by the slap of the sea.

'I had a maiden sweet and fair
That promised me my life to share.
She gave me sons and a daughter sweet,
And danced for me on nimble feet.'

'God saw her too and thought like I,
That she was too good for with me to lie.
Now I've naught save sons and a daughter sweet,
To dance for me on nimble feet.'

He shut his eyes against the sudden closing of his throat. Dear God! Grief must have turned his mind that he could be moved by those hackneyed words more than all the hours by her grave. He breathed against the weight of tears, and leant his cheek against the sodden bulwark of the deck.

'Sweet Jesu, let me weep,' he whispered. 'For pity's sake, let me weep.'

He whirled in sharp anger at the slither of footsteps along the deck. Harry edged toward him, his hair plastered to his cheeks.

'My lord,' he said against the chattering of his teeth. 'Will you not come below? I have mulled some wine.'

Hal looked away. 'Later, Harry. I'll come later,' he said, more harshly than he had meant.

Harry turned and felt his way back, his legs straddled to the roll of the deck. The ship lifted to a sudden gust and Harry lurched against the planking, his hands flung out to save himself. Hal turned at his cry as the ship rolled back against the swell and saw the boy flung like a doll against the gunwale. He heard the crack of Harry's head against the side yet he could not move. Stricken with fear he watched Harry push himself to his knees. Blood stained his cheek and paled into the stream of water that ran from his hair. He would have gone forward then but the boy's eyes stopped him. Dark with pain and anger they held him back till the boy turned and limped into the shadows.

Hal leant against the side of the ship, sick with shame. Harry was only a child yet he treated him with less thought than the lowest of his scullions. He did not even know why he had brought him; to torture himself or the boy? He had succeeded in both. He could not let him go yet neither could he bear him so close.

168

He looked down into the black heaving water cleaved by the green-slimed anchor chain. Tomorrow they would turn for home. He thought of Northumberland and the moorland that would be grey and still, waiting for the first snow. And Warkworth, desolate and empty, the tall new towers filled with corroding wind. He turned and walked unsteadily across the heaving deck. It was time to go home.

Beneath the sodden planking the stench of stale vomit devoured what little air there was. A lantern swung and grated on its hook and threw wild lurching shadows over the men who slept on the damp fetid straw. Carefully Hal picked his way to his canvas bed and would have thrown himself down, wet cloak and all, till he saw the boy. Harry lay crushed against the wall, the sharp knee of a knight in his back. His hand still clutched protectively at the now cold jug of wine.

Hal knelt and rolled the snoring knight onto his back and eased Harry away from the wall. His face beneath the grime and crust of tears was as pale as death, the cut on his cheek swollen and bruised. Gently Hal lifted him from the floor. His hose were wet and his shoes no more than bags of squelching leather. He laid him among the furs of his bed and eased himself alongside. With trembling fingers he stroked back the damp springing curls as Harry stirred and stared drowsily into his face.

'I'm cold, Father,' Harry whispered, 'I'm so very cold.'

Hal drew the boy against him and felt the warm dampness of his cheek against his throat. A small slender arm crept out to encircle him and he held him tighter, whispering brokenly into his hair.

'We'll be home soon, Harry. After Christmas we'll be back in the north. We'll see your brothers, ride and hunt together every day.'

Harry lifted his face and smiled tremulously. 'It doesn't matter, Father. I don't care where I am as long as it is with you.'

The tears came then, slow and painful, coursing unashamedly down his cheeks. While his son stroked his hair Hal wept like a child.

Crammed behind the solid wall of courtiers, Harry could see nothing but the top of the King's head as he passed. He knew the man who walked beside him, so tall and regal that he might have been the King himself rather than the bowed old man. John of Gaunt—King of Castile, Duke of Lancaster, Earl of Derby, Lincoln and Leicester, Lord of Beaufort and Bergerac, Roche sur Yon and Noyen, Seneschal of England and Constable of Chester—so many titles that he had walked the length of the hall before the herald had done.

He squeezed round the fat brocaded paunch of a royal knight and peered through a gap in the sleek doublets ranked the length of the aisle. Leaning heavily against his son the King mounted the wide steps to the high table. Solicitously Lancaster led him to his place, tucking fur round the spindly knees. He smiled gently, even meekly, turning pale benign eyes on the company as Lancaster sat alongside him. Another, whom Harry had barely noticed beside the dazzle of Lancaster, mounted unsteadily to the King's side. Harry had only seen the Prince of Wales once before and then he had been mounted and in full harness. Now, stripped of his armour, he was a mere travesty of the man who glowed in vibrant life from the tapestry at Alnwick. Could this be the victor of Crécy and Poitiers, this pale wraithlike creature who moved with the slow stumbling movement of a sleepwalker? Close by, Harry saw the furtive nudge of an elbow and the sly knowing winks. He knew what they said. It was common knowledge now that the Prince of Wales was dying.

He edged further forward and was shoved unceremoniously back by the greasy palm of a household knight. Undaunted, he writhed through the press of people toward the door, treading on hems and earning himself a blow from an irate gentleman usher. There was a space here, where the hangers-on and the uninvited waited hopefully for a place at the lower tables.

The herald gabbled names, Warwick, March, Norfolk, the lords Ros and Latimer. He craned above the Lancaster herald's shoulders; he could see his father, bent to the earnest mournful countenance of the Archbishop of York. He almost cried out with disappointment as Hal drew level and seemed likely to pass him by. Then he looked up and smiled, beckoning him out of the crowd. They did not speak but walked together to his father's place below the royal dais. Precedence forbade that he sit with

Hal but he stood proudly behind his chair, though he knew that his legs would ache with standing before the night was out. He needed no better reward than the quick loving smile of his father.

Like a vigilant hound he watched and saw those who Hal smiled at, those who he looked at coldly or with indifference. He saw those who kept their faces turned to their plates whenever his father's eyes rested upon them and sent him quick hostile looks when his back was turned. Sometimes his eyes strayed to the royal table: sickly Edward and his brother Edmund who giggled like a maid. At the end of the table the King's youngest son Thomas glowered into his wine and held tight-lipped conversation with Lancaster's Duchess. The Duke himself sat serene and unassailable, helping his father to a pap of pheasant, his ready smile concealing his boredom with his plain Spanish wife. Occasionally, his lambent eyes would seek out the young fair-haired boy who sat quietly between his tutors: the Lord Richard, younger even than Harry himself.

Then suddenly Lancaster's eyes fastened sharply on Harry's face, narrowed, with a look he could not recognize. Harry looked away in confusion, seeking refuge for his eyes in the hangings on the far wall. Gradually he summoned up enough courage to look back—and saw his mistake. It was not *his* face that the blue eyes sought but his father's. He glanced down and saw him, smiling, unaware, his golden head bent to catch the whispered jest of John Mowbray. Harry strained his body close to his chair as if the very nearness of him could cry warning. Wildly he looked back to the dais. Lancaster's eyes were still locked fast on his father's face and he knew the look now: the bright unguarded look of hatred.

1376–1381

'The false lapwing, ful of trecherye'

—Chaucer

It was the last day of April, 1376; four years and two months since Margaret had died, four useless, drifting years when time had been stagnant and each day as empty as the next. He had achieved nothing, attempted nothing, content to drift on the tide of war and ambition. But now the tide had turned; he had a purpose again, albeit only one of hatred. It let him know he was still alive.

For the second day running Parliament had crammed itself into the faded splendour of the Painted Chamber. Gold angels soared in the mazarine blue of the roof and from every wall the mild blue eyes of the Confessor looked benignly from the flaking lime. On either side of the dais men crowded together like opposing armies, crushed cheek to jowl on long hard benches or pressed against the muted gaudiness of the walls. Their voices had long been stilled with waiting; every face was tense and wary, as if they sensed the storm to come.

Across the empty aisle the lords sat in close array, the cautious and uncommitted to the rear, those of Lancaster's following to the fore. His eyes travelled slowly along the packed ranks: Richard Stury, lean and predatory; Richard Lyons, the fat London merchant between his henchmen, Peachy and Bury. And Lord Latimer, the King's chamberlain, bent close to his new son-in-law John Neville. Hal watched him with pleasurable speculation. Neville was the reason he was here, the reason that he had swallowed his dislike of Mortimer and ranged himself with the Commons. He glanced around him at the lords and bishops, who sat among the rowdy shire knights in quiet unease. Suffolk, Warwick, Stafford and March, the bishops Courteney and Spencer, all stiff with malice, all panting for Lancaster's blood like starved hounds. But *his* prey was not so exalted. He would be content with Neville, plucked and trussed and down from his dunghill. He smiled quietly to himself. The burgeoning warmth of hatred was pleasurable after the emptiness of grief. For the last three years he had watched Neville climb to power on the broken backs of others; steward of the royal household, leader of the King's corrupt privy council and, since Maud's death, Latimer's heir. And now he had struck at his only weakness, the Neville lands crept out from Durham and encircled Northumberland like a hostile army. His brother Alexander was York's Archbishop and his church lands blocked the Humber. The cold thought persisted in Hal's mind; when Latimer died, Neville's power in the north would be even greater.

He saw the darting unease of Neville's eyes, the cold thoughtful mien of Mortimer and the veiled impatience of the bishops. They were all waiting, some with dread, some with malice, but all waiting for one man.

He came, for once, with no other herald than the chime of Westminster clock. Within the dark doorway he paused, smiling apology and craving mocking indulgence for his lateness. The Chancellor Knyvet stood and fumbled through his parchments while Lancaster took his place. Hal kept his eyes on Neville's face as the Chancellor blustered through his preamble, his cracked voice rising with strain as he came to the painful business of the day: the Treasury showed a deficit; reluctantly the King was obliged to ask the Commons for another grant of taxes.

'The last campaign,' he continued nervously, 'though it brought England much glory was costly.' His voice tailed off at the angry rumbling from the Commons and even Hal raised his brows at the blatant lie. He had fought in that campaign and it had brought England naught but shame. Almost a year spent wandering the length of France like nomads only to be caught like rats in a trap in the wintry mountains of the Auvergne. A third of their army had perished from starvation and dysentery, thanks to Lancaster's bungling, and nothing to show for it save a few French prisoners whose ransoms had not even covered the cost of horse fodder.

There was a whisper of eager movement behind him as the Speaker rose; Peter de la Mare, Mortimer's seneschal and primed to their purpose down to the last word. He stepped out onto the polished tiles of the chamber and moved to face the Chancellor.

'With respect, my lord,' he said loudly. 'I fear that we are unable to grant your request at this time.' He paused as Knyvet threw a wild look at Lancaster. 'Perhaps it might be more profitable to all to seek the cause of the King's penury,' he continued. 'His Grace is old, he rarely leaves his palace at Shene. His needs should be few, yet once again we hear that the Treasury is empty. The populace will bear no heavier taxes, my lords. There is no remedy there. More, I think, it lies in prevention rather than cure. I think that perhaps the King has those about him who need a lesson in thrift.'

'More a lesson in honesty,' Bishop Wykeham shouted. 'It is not the King who is in need of revenue but those about him who constantly defraud him of it.'

Latimer leapt out onto the floor. 'The Church is the last to talk of fraud,' he yelled. 'Let he who is without sin cast the first stone!'

Then Lancaster rose. 'Well, my lord bishop,' he said. 'Is the Church without sin in this? What of your pardoners, hawking forgiveness and relics like cheapjacks? I have seen them, my lord. Pigs' bones for the feet of St Thomas, filthy rags for Our Lady's veil. And you do not call this fraud, my lord? The Church should rid itself of the stench of its own wealth before it sniffs at that of others.'

'*Blasphemer!*' Wykeham screeched, his face purple with rage. 'All of you, blasphemers and liars who dare to condemn Holy Church when your own pockets are filled with gold filched from a helpless old man!'

A few of the knights had risen to their feet and the howl of angry voices filled the hall. Mortimer signalled frenziedly to de la

174

Mare to restore order but the moment was lost as Lancaster's men rose shouting from their benches. His face grim with anguish, Hal shouldered his way through the disorderly knights. He knew Lancaster's strategy, to foster disorder till the Parliament came to riot, their purpose against him forgotten.

'Latimer!' The roar of Hal's voice brought slow and grudging silence. 'Yes, you, Latimer.' He waited till Lancaster's eyes were upon him, then said: 'Before Parliament I accuse you of consorting with the enemy in time of war, of selling the castle of St Sauveur for personal gain, of taking bribes for the release of captured ships, and that you retained for your own use fines that were payable to the King. And you, my Lord of Raby—' He turned slowly and in the moment that their eyes met, the force of his hatred was so great that his voice trembled as he listed the charges. Before the half of it was out, Neville was leaping from his seat, his face congested and ugly with fury.

'And furthermore, that together with the merchant Richard Lyons, you have permitted the woman Alice Perrers to gain ascendancy over His Grace, King Edward, and to gain grants of land and money to which she had no right.'

A great sigh shuddered through the chamber. It was done. What none of them could have done alone they had done together.

Throughout, Lancaster had sat silent. Now he rose, his face pale and twitching. 'You have proof of this?'

Hal smiled with joyful malice. 'We *have*, Your Grace—signed, irrefutable proof and the testimony of a dozen witnesses.'

Lancaster did not even glance at the white strained faces of his henchmen. His own face was drawn in shock and outrage. 'If this then is true. . . .' He shook his head in disbelief as he talked himself from blame. Hal glanced at Neville and saw him grow pale as Lancaster glibly extricated himself from their fall. Only Latimer's steadying hand kept him in his place. None dared turn against Lancaster; the Commons had dared it because they were many, and he. . . . He turned and met the cold virulent gaze of John Neville. He had dared it for the joy of seeing such a look on Neville's face.

In Richard Lyons's house in the Vintry, four men and a woman stood in deathly quiet, their eyes fixed on the shadowy figure of Lancaster.

'Will they do it?' Lyons whispered. 'Can they do it?'

'Of course they can bloody well do it,' Latimer snapped. 'With Prince Edward and the whole bloody Commons behind them of course they can do it.'

'Your Grace.' Lyons turned a pale sickly face toward the Duke. 'Is all lost? Perhaps,' he licked nervous lips and glanced around him, 'perhaps a sum could be raised. . . .' His voice tailed off and was lost beneath Latimer's shout of laughter.

'Christ!' he shouted. 'The man offers a bribe when it is the very thing we are charged with!'

'They're out for blood.' Neville plucked nervously at his full underlip. 'Mortimer and that bastard Percy. God knows what they'll dig up when they start sniffing into our affairs.'

Lancaster glanced up, his brows crooked in mockery. It was the first time he had seen fear in Neville's eyes, the kind of fear that could set his tongue wagging if he thought it would save him. He glanced down at his hands and smoothed a wrinkle from his faultless hose. Neville was useful but not indispensable. There were a hundred Nevilles to come running at the crook of his finger, but only one Hal Percy. He looked back to Neville's sullen face. Perhaps, even yet, the one would catch him the other.

Lyons was speaking, wringing his hands like an usurer. He of all of them had most to fear, with no birth or rank to protect him. 'The King,' he said, 'the King will surely speak for us. We have done him no harm. It was what he wanted, to be left in peace with Lady Perrers.'

'And who do you think will countenance the mumblings of an old dotard?' Latimer said scathingly. 'The King has no power left.' He turned and smiled archly. 'His Grace has seen to that well enough.'

Then Lancaster spoke. 'Gently, my lords, or your own panic will defeat you.'

'Easily said, Your Grace, but it will not be you who sits in the Tower if the Commons have their way,' Neville reminded him.

'But then it was not I who left a trail behind me that even a

176

lackwit could have sniffed out,' the Duke snapped. 'Bribery, misappropriation, treason even—and you think I can protect you from that?' He let his gaze fall to the gilded cup that turned restlessly between his fingers. 'You will have to be patient, my lords. The Commons and Mortimer are propped up by my brother Prince Edward. When he falls, so will they.'

'With respect, Your Grace,' Latimer said heavily. 'The Prince has been a long time dying. I would not wait so long for my liberty.'

'You will not have to. The King will not easily see his household dismissed and I still have his ear.' Lancaster smiled grimly. 'Whatever else they can do they cannot keep me from the King. Parliament cannot sit forever; when it disperses their power will be gone. All will be as it was before.'

'And what of me?' For the first time Alice Perrers spoke. 'Am I to be packed off like some errant kitchen wench?' She glared furiously at the wooden faces of the men. 'Edward will not allow it,' she shouted. 'He has more need of me than all of you put together.'

Lancaster smiled thinly. 'Let us hope so, madam, for all our sakes. In the meantime, I think it would serve all our interests if you were to retire from Court gracefully. As I have already said, till Parliament disperses we can do nothing.'

'And what of Mortimer and Suffolk and Warwick and Percy? They stand with the Commons and you cannot send them back to their manors like shire knights. What of them, Your Grace?'

Lancaster said nothing and moved with stealthy grace to the window. Suffolk and Warwick he dismissed out of hand but there was no easy solution to Mortimer. The same prize dangled before both their eyes; like two men lusting after a virgin, only one could be the victor. And Percy? He smiled in quiet triumph. The Nevilles were the key to Hal Percy's adherence, the spark that would fire the flame he knew was there. And the time was now. He was ripe and ready for picking.

The deep sombre tolling of St Paul's continued far into the night; long mournful notes that hung heavily in the June air and rolled out over the river to the far reaches of Southwark. Prince

Edward was dead and, even before his body was cold, Lancaster was supreme again. It had been so brief, the triumph come and gone before he had tasted its sweetness to the full. Latimer and Neville were recalled and restored to office and Alice Perrers sent to warm the King's bed again; the new council formed by Parliament had been dismissed by the King on Lancaster's word. The last six weeks might never have been. Now there was only Lancaster.

Hal looked from the scrap of parchment beneath his hand to the blank face of the messenger. The letter was written in the Duke's own hand. '*John, by the Grace of God, Duke of Lancaster*—' he had spared him the King of Castile— '*sends greetings to his cousin Henry Percy, Lord of Northumberland, and begs that he attend him at his palace of the Savoy.*'

Hal frowned. Should he read 'commands' for 'begs'? It was Lancaster's way to cloak up his intentions in fine words. Yet why should he now? Since Parliament had risen there was none to stand against him. Warwick and Stafford had already been bought off and the others except Mortimer and Wykeham were weakening. Only he remained, solitary and uncommitted, unable to throw in his lot with Mortimer yet still the niggling affront to Lancaster's supremacy.

All the same, Lancaster had let him alone while he had wreaked his vengeance elsewhere. Mortimer could not be touched but his spokesman and seneschal, de la Mare, had been arraigned and thrown into Nottingham gaol. But Lancaster had not harmed him or even tried to—until now.

He folded the parchment and tucked it thoughtfully in his tunic. To the messenger he said, 'Will His Grace have me come now?'

There was nothing to be read in the knight's bland stare. 'If it please my lord,' he answered civilly.

Hal gave a dry smile. 'Then let it be now. We must not keep His Grace waiting.'

Lancaster received him alone, his brow banded in gold, his jewelled hand resting lightly on a sheaf of parchments. The court had dubbed him 'Monsieur d'Espagne' and it suited him; a king yet not a king, a king who only lacked a crown.

He rose and came to meet him, his mouth set in his ready smile. 'My lord.' His voice was soft and courteous. 'I did not expect you so soon.'

Hal met his bland gaze with secret amusement. 'Did you not, Your Grace?'

Lancaster moved to the blazing hearth, his feet silent on the rich silk rug that left the mark of his heel in the velvet pile. 'There was a time, my lord, when I would not have had to choose my words with you,' he said slowly. 'There was a time when we understood each other very well.'

'Perhaps we still do, Your Grace. Too well for each other's comfort.'

Lancaster smiled faintly. 'Yes, that must be it Hal.' He leant against the tall marble mantel and folded his arms across his chest. 'But times change, Hal; people change. Disappointment shapes us more than we know.'

Hal said nothing but he moved to where the pale latticed light could search out every line and hollow of Lancaster's face. But the blue eyes followed his steadily and there was no tremor of uneasiness or deceit in the firm smiling mouth. 'You do not trust me, Hal, but then why should you.'

For the first time Hal smiled. 'No, I do not trust you, my lord, in common with the rest of England.' He saw that Lancaster's smile grew strained. 'Now perhaps we can speak plainly. Why did you send for me?'

The Duke spread his hands in a little gesture of resignation. 'I shall not win you with fair words, shall I Hal?' He laughed and sat in the high gilded chair that faced the fire. Then he said bluntly, 'You know that now my brother Edward is dead, the succession rests in his son, the Lord Richard?'

'I know it.' It was come; the bribe, the soft wooing that would bring him to heel. If he had expected Lancaster to declare himself he was not disappointed.

'He will need men of good council about him; one man in particular to hold the reins of government till he comes of age. I mean to be that man, Hal.'

'I never doubted it, my lord,' Hal said mockingly. 'Not for a moment.'

'I shall be the first man in the kingdom after the King.' He leapt suddenly from his chair and gripped Hal's arm. 'You hear me, my lord? *After* the King.'

Hal flung the restraining hand from his sleeve. 'And what will keep you from the Crown when you stand so close that you could reach out your hand and take it?' he cried. 'What will keep you from it then, Your Grace?'

Lancaster's mouth twitched with anger. 'You speak as if I am not worthy of it.'

'You are not,' Hal snapped. 'Not above Richard.'

'You think a boy of eight or nine could rule better than I?'

'No, Your Grace, and no better than your brothers Edmund and Thomas. That, at least, is what they will think.'

'Then you know what keeps me from it,' Lancaster said quietly. 'As you say, Hal, if I were to take the Crown from Richard, I would plunge England into civil war. Edmund is harmless enough but Thomas is ambitious. He could see himself as King easily enough. And then there is Mortimer. If Richard died without issue, his sons would be nearest the Crown. Who will keep them from it, Hal? Only I have the strength and power for it yet I still need the support of the barons.'

'I should have thought you have more than enough of those at your beck and call,' Hal said bitterly.

Lancaster laughed. 'Do you think I am fool enough not to have taken their measure? Neville, Latimer, even your own brother, they work for the master who pays the highest wage and no man in England can pay more than I. I do not speak of such men. I need men who will give their loyalty for love of Lancaster.' He rose softly and poured wine for them both. 'Your blood is Lancaster, Hal. You were raised and bred for Lancaster. Why deny it?' He came and stood above him and held out the wine. 'I will not insult you with a bribe but loyalty has its own reward. John Neville rose at my word, Hal, he could fall just as easily. You know the truth of it, Hal, you've known it ever since we were boys. You were content with nothing but the mastery then. Will you be content with less now?'

He held the cup nearer and the ruby on his hand danced redly in Hal's eyes. 'Come drink with me, Hal; to England—and Lancaster.'

Hal stared at the brimming cup and Lancaster's long fingers curled round the stem. If he took it he took more than wine. He'd heard the promise implicit in Lancaster's words. John Neville's fall would mean his rise. For that he would sell himself to Lancaster. Yet if he looked into his heart he wanted it, he had wanted it all these years and only Margaret had held him back from it. But Margaret was dead and there was nothing to keep him from it now. Slowly he took the cup and raised it high. 'To England,' he said, 'and Lancaster.'

Gilbert Umfraville's face was blood-red with choler and his breath rattled in his great barrel chest yet he could still drink enough for ten men. He peered at Hal with his bloodshot eyes.

'So you've joined Lancaster then?' He spat noisily onto the soiled rushes of his hall. 'Well, I dare say I would have done the same if I'd been younger.' He gave a shrill cackle of laughter. 'Too old now to care whose arse sits on the throne.' He buried his face in the great tarnished hanap, licking the droplets of wine from his beard. 'Not much to choose between them anyway, eh, Percy? Proud Lancaster and sly Mortimer and between them a lad that looks and smells like a maid.' He shook his head and his slack jowls quivered mournfully. 'Christ, Percy, where has all the glory gone?'

Hal turned away from the raddled drunken face in disgust. The hall where he sat was high and wide, the hangings mildewed and threadbare, for the Lord of Angus spent nothing except on his wine. He did not even know why he had come, save that Prudoe lay on his way north and, if he was truthful, it was a chance to cast his eye over the crumbling fortress that would one day be his. He glanced warily at the still figure of the Countess. Her face was small and pinched in the tight circle of her wimple and she had not spoken except to murmur a restrained greeting. Hal remembered their last meeting and it galled him a little that she should treat him with such scant courtesy.

Umfraville refilled his cup and set the ewer between them with a thud that slopped its contents onto the soiled cloth. 'And what's

181

this we hear that His Grace of Lancaster has allied himself to the heretic Wyclif?'

'Hardly that, my lord,' Hal said. 'John Wyclif is no heretic, a gentle priest who holds no greater ambition than that the common people should be able to read the gospels in their mother tongue.'

Umfraville pulled a derisive face. 'So worthy a cause.' His elbow nudged Hal's hand from his cup. 'But more than that I think—eh, Percy? Since when has Lancaster cared about common folk?'

'His Grace of Lancaster never does aught that is without profit to himself,' the Countess said. 'Lord Percy should know that well enough.'

Hal turned his head to meet her disdainful eyes.

'The reformer Wyclif also preaches against the wealth of the Church,' she went on. 'He calls for the dispersal and reversion of Church lands—but reversion to whom, my lords? As His Grace of Lancaster sees it, the sons of the fathers who purged their consciences with gifts of lands and money. A cheap reward to his henchmen without cost to himself.'

Hal's eyes hardened at the deliberate insult, though he could not deny the truth of her words. Lancaster did not cosset the outspoken Wyclif for the good of his soul. He would use him, as he used everyone, including Hal himself. But then he had known that from the moment he had joined him.

Umfraville leant forward, his red-rimmed eyes narrowed in resentment as he stared at his wife. 'Once again we lesser mortals must thank my lady wife for a lesson in statecraft. You should have been a man, Maud, and might as well have been for all the good you've been to me.' His wet sneering mouth set Hal's teeth on edge but he said nothing till Umfraville was diverted by the whisper of his slovenly steward. Then, covertly, he glanced at the Countess's pale face. She was smiling, the bright intelligence of her eyes hooded by her heavy lids. If for nothing else, he could admire her for her self-possession.

Umfraville tapped his sleeve with a grimy forefinger and nodded to where the cages of screeching fowl were being borne aloft. 'A wager, my lord? Ten marks on the blue ribbon?'

With a flurry of feathers the cocks were thrown together. They landed a foot apart and stood scratching the rushes, the silver fighting spurs gleaming dully in the feeble light. Then the boot of a knight drove them together and there was a roar from the men as the first stabbing beak drew blood. Umfraville yelled and thumped the table, thrusting his boot between the hounds who leapt snarling from beneath the cloths. The spurs gouged and spurted dark blood and suddenly Hal wished he had not come. Harry was waiting for him at Alnwick; his brother Tom was home from France and he was wasting precious time here. He only had leave of absence for a month. That brought an assuaged smile. How Margaret would have wept to see him now. Before her death he had been no man's but his own; now he was Lancaster's, at his beck and call, his tongue stifled by policy, Lancaster's policy. Even Northumberland took second place, for Tom had sent him word a dozen times that Douglas's men hunted his forests with impunity. That would only be the beginning. Douglas had given him warning enough.

Black Douglas had come to Westminster two summers ago with his brother the earl and the newly crowned Robert the Steward. David Bruce was dead and forgotten; none mourned him and the page was quickly turned. Robert was King of Scotland now and a hundred times the man the Bruce had been. And England had showed them all her weakness; its feeble king, its sickly heir, the frail princeling, all overshadowed by mighty Lancaster.

Douglas had sought him out, as Hal had known he would. He had seemed little changed; the raven hair shot with grey, the lines around the granite mouth grown deeper and more severe, but outwardly still the same Douglas who had confronted him at every turn of his life. Gladness had mingled with raw memory; Margaret had been alive the last time they had met.

'So, my lord, Scotland has itself a new king?'

Douglas had smiled dourly. 'An improvement on the last, would you not say?'

'That depends on which side of the fence you happen to be, my lord,' Hal answered him with amusement. 'As an Englishman, I preferred the Bruce.'

The Douglas nodded slowly, then he said abruptly, 'I have not come to gloat.'

'I did not think you had, my lord,' Hal said softly. 'But I doubt if His Grace of Scotland will treat us so tenderly.'

'Can you blame the beaten dog if he leaps at the first chance to bite his master?'

'What did you come for then, Douglas?' Hal demanded harshly. 'To give me fair warning?'

'Perhaps.' Douglas turned away from the eyes that in unguarded moments still disturbed him. His own eyes wandered round the lofty room and saw the wealth of England; the sumptous hangings and the gilded plate, the rare softness of the Turkey rug beneath his feet. He was not an envious man but even his heart was soured. So much, and all ill-gotten, while most men in Scotland counted themselves fortunate if they had enough food for the year, let alone a gilded platter to eat it off. At last he said slowly, almost reluctantly, 'It's come, my lord. It's come at last.' He turned to face him, his eyes kindled to blazing life. 'We've waited a long time, have we not? Twenty years since that day when David Bruce sold himself and Scotland to Edward Plantagenet. Do you remember that day? Do you remember the pledge we made then? Each to the mastery, no quarter given?'

'I remember it.' Hal knew what Douglas was trying to say. England was weak, preoccupied with her losses in France, turned inward on herself in petty squabbles. Douglas had come to warn him, to renew the challenge of their first meeting. Was it twenty years ago? So many to have slipped through his fingers unnoticed. He had been a boy then, full of a boy's bravado and rash chivalry and the years had shaped him far from the ideal he had seen of himself then. But all through those years Douglas had run, the recurring thread in the pattern of his life. Yet why him, why had Douglas singled him out, one enemy among so many? Then he saw, in the clear steady glance of his eyes. Douglas knew, he had seen and recognized all those years ago what he himself only saw now. The seeds of destruction were in him, growing, festering, out of his control—and that was the thread that bound them. Neither knew whether it was his own or the other's.

'So be it then,' he had said in a soft easy voice that concealed

184

the sudden hammering of his heart. 'But without malice, my lord. You once said it; to the mastery, but without malice.'

He started, as if from a dream. The Countess's narrow face swam into his vision.

'Shall we retire to more pleasant surroundings, my lord?'

He glanced down at Umfraville, slumped across the table, snoring loudly. The rest of the company roared drunken verse round the stiffening corpse of the vanquished cockerel while the victor crowed his victory from the shoulder of a knight.

'My lord will put himself to bed,' the Countess smiled maliciously. 'It is his usual custom.'

The upper room was full of light and warmth. This was her domain, the costly hangings brought from her manor at Cockermouth, the plate from her castle at Langley. In the soft shining light even the broad-faced Lancashire wench who attended them took on an air of grace. She poured wine into small gilded cups emblazoned with the silver fish of her house. 'You look surprised, my lord,' she said with her quick smile. 'Had you despaired of finding anything of beauty at Prudoe?'

Again she had him at a disadvantage, as if every word and gesture were shaped to that end. 'My lord Umfraville does not care too much for ceremony,' she went on. 'As long as he has sufficient wine in his cellar to drink himself nightly into a stupor, then he is a happy man.'

'And you, my lady? What makes you happy?'

'You need not be courteous with me, my lord,' she said lightly. 'You have seen me shamed enough times to know that I do not care what others think. You are not interested in my happiness and I do not expect you to be. No more am I interested in yours.' She watched his face harden into dislike and smiled. She would rather have that than the meaningless courtesy he gave to others, though perhaps not so often now. He had changed so much since she had last seen him, his face planed to sharp austerity by grief, the remembered mockery of his smile quenched by loss. There was no laughter in him now and his eyes were always cold, save when he spoke of his son Harry.

'There is a difference between courtesy and ill manners, my lady,' he retorted sharply. 'Perhaps as yet you have not divined it.'

185

'You think me ill-mannered because I speak plainly?' Her eyes kindled with dull fire. 'Well then, I'll speak plainer still. I know why you have come to Prudoe—to cast a proprietory eye over your new domain. Oh, do not look so shamefaced, my lord. I know of the entail that gives you Prudoe when Umfraville dies. Your father's sister was wed as a child to the Earl's son Robert, and Prudoe was settled on them and their heirs. Well, there are no heirs and therefore Prudoe reverts to the eldest male of the Percy house.' She laughed softly to herself. 'Poor Gilbert. Three sons, and not one of them lived to manhood and then he had the misfortune to marry me who could give him none. We have that in common at least, we are both doomed to extinction.'

Hal stared at her in sudden burning dislike, at the plain drabness of her gown and the pale unadorned face thinned by malice. 'Madam,' he said with soft cruelty, 'you flaunt your barrenness like a whore flaunts her body. You cannot always use it as a shield against life.' He regretted it the minute he had said it. For a moment the fine dark eyes were laid bare and he saw the sad unloved creature beneath. 'My lady, forgive me.' He rose and crossed the room, but by the time he had reached her she had recovered. He touched her hand tentatively. 'Forgive me, I did not mean . . .'

She moved away from his touch. 'It is late, my lord,' she said harshly, 'and no doubt you have seen all that you came to see.' She turned to face him and he almost recoiled at the look in her eyes. 'You will have noted which of Prudoe's walls need repair, which towers are crumbling and need rebuilding. The moat also has become silted by the postern gate—but I'm sure that you will remedy all these things when you become master of Prudoe.' She smiled happily as she saw the colour drain from his face. 'You are not a patient man, I think, my lord, but Umfraville will not keep you long. He is old and sick, not likely to last more than a year or two. Of course, I might delay you a little longer, as I retain all his property for my lifetime. But then I expect you know that.' She leant close so that he could see the amber glow of her eyes. 'It must be galling for you, my lord, to see me in such good health.'

Every word struck him like a blow in the face. He saw the pointed smile stretch to the corners of her mouth. The dark velvet

186

eyes stared him out and probed into the heart of him, stirring the rage that had slept so long into murderous life. 'You graceless, foul-tongued bitch,' he whispered and saw her smile widen.

'Unchivalrous, my lord,' she mocked him. 'And you always so mindful of your manners.'

She laughed and the soft malevolent sound wreathed around him like a mist. He saw her face, smiling with delight, the red lips drawn back over the small predatory teeth and he trembled to strike her into silence. But she had sensed her danger and moved within call of the wench who slept outside the door. Even then she could not resist a last thrust.

'But we must not keep you, my lord of Northumberland. No doubt your time is at a premium and His Grace of Lancaster will soon be chafing to have you at his side again.'

The reference to Lancaster sobered him. His vision cleared and he saw her sharp and clear again, the drab little sparrow whose only joy was pecking at the eyes of her fellow creatures.

'Of course.' The rage receded and slipped back into its dark corner and left his face smiling and untouched. 'And I must not keep you from your bed, madam. Sleep eases the frustration of mind and body and you are in greater need of it than I.'

'Do not pity me, Northumberland,' she snapped. 'You'll need all your pity for yourself before you've done with Lancaster.'

He smiled above the dull remembered ache of anger. 'Pity is the last thing I would offer you, my lady. I shall keep that for the poor wretch that is your husband.'

He left her, as always, with the sharp taste of enmity in his mouth, and in the draughty ill-lit chamber where he slept he relived the dreadful savagery of her scorn. A single cresset wreathed black smoke across his bed and the bare walls ran with trickling damp. Prudoe was old and crumbling, but yes, since she had said it, one day it would be his. When Umfraville was dead, when she was dead—his mouth hardened at the remembrance of her words. The dog grew like his master daily. Now he too waited for dead men's shoes.

The Londoners stood silent at his passing and that pained him more than any shouted insult could have done. He kept his eyes averted from the sea of threatening faces and fixed them on the broad swaying back of his serjeant-at-arms who rode ahead to clear the way. Then a clod of mud struck the hindquarters of his horse, another spattered the pale silk of his doublet. His serjeant rode roughshod into the crowd and he heard the scream of trampled flesh. The hostile roar of the crowd turned him cold, yet he kept his pace though his hands were sweating beneath the fine gloves. He set his teeth hard together. His conscience was as raw as the wind that blew in sharp clean gusts up from the river. He had earned every catcall, every shouted insult. He was Lancaster's man, all bought and paid for; he counted up the tally— Marshal of England in Mortimer's place, Captain of the Marches of Calais, custodian of Mitford, and the lucrative wardship of the Strathbogie heiresses, prospective brides for his sons Ralph and Thomas. His brother Tom was Constable of Roxburgh and—the greatest prize of all—he had stemmed the tide of Neville's rise. Lancaster had been as good as his word; out of favour and out of grace, John Neville kicked his heels in obscurity at Raby. But even the satisfaction of Neville's fall did not compensate for the utter betrayal of all he was, yet it was what he had wanted, what he had freely chosen. There was no going back now.

On Temple Bar a felon hung in chains, his rotted limbs swaying in a courtly dance. Eyeless, toothless, his flesh gnawed to the bone by the wild dogs who roamed the city ditches, a stark warning to any who thought to defy Lancaster. Hal knew this man's crime was solely that of defiance, but he had seen him hung, not once or twice, but six times till life was a mere whisper of breath in his tortured lungs. Each time he had been cut down and whipped to agonized life and each time his blackened pain-filled eyes had opened they had strung him up again till they had glazed over in agony and his tongue had thrust blackly through his bloody lips. It was a fine art, the executioner had told him proudly, to judge the exact moment when life would be finally extinguished.

He rode on, quickening his pace through Ludgate, the image of the corpse still before his eyes. Like a ravening beast Lancaster's revenge ran on unchecked. De la Mare still languished in his northern dungeon, Bishop Wykeham was out of office on trumped-up charges that harked back ten years to his days as Chancellor. And even then Lancaster had not been content; the Bishop had been hounded by letters and writs and forbidden like a leper to come within twenty miles of the Court. And all for what? The Duke's revenge, which was more for the old whispered slur of changeling than because Wykeham had stood out against him, had achieved nothing but to bring the fury of the Church down on their heads. Lancaster could not manipulate Holy Church as he had done Parliament, and for once the bishops had the support of the people. Yet even now, none had the courage to attack Lancaster direct; they nipped at his flanks and rear but never at the figurehead itself. The scapegoat now was John Wyclif, dragged from his seclusion on charges of heresy. He glanced over his shoulder to where the frail priest rode on his gently pacing gelding alongside his protector Lancaster. He seemed unmoved by the jeers of the mob and the grimy hands that snatched and tore at his robes despite the swinging staves of Lancaster's guard; another lamb being led to the slaughter on the altar of Lancaster's ambition.

The mob surged dangerously close as they turned into St Paul's. Filthy bare-footed 'prentices swarmed the wall of the churchyard and aimed missiles from the anonymity of the crowds, chanting derisive lampoons as Lancaster approached. A hand snatched at Hal's bridle and he looked down into a grimy urchin face contorted with hatred. He spurred his horse forward but the beast baulked at the intensity of the crowd. The urchin swung on his bridle till the horse shrieked in pain and lashed out with its hindquarters into the crowd. In desperation he brought his Marshal's staff down hard on the clenched determined fist and heard the crack of broken knuckles. Sweating, he rode through the gap his guards had made and saw Lancaster, pale and shaken, closing fast in his wake. A voice hurled his name out of the crowd and was caught and taken up by a thousand like it. *Lancaster, Lancaster! Death to the traitor Lancaster!* They roused a painful echo in his own mind. Once he had thought likewise and, more painful still, was the thought that perhaps he still did.

Beneath the dim vaulting of the church the mob crowded

together in hostile silence. Quietly threatening, they let him pass till he reached the broad transept. There they surrounded him on all sides, blocking his path, whispering insults that fell like soft rain in his ears. Lancaster was at his back, pale with impotent fury.

'Walk on, my lord,' he hissed. 'We do not pause for knaves and villeins.'

As if they had heard, the crowd closed about them. Hal saw the greasy sneering faces and breathed the stench of their unwashed bodies. His breath came sharp and painful in his throat as he shoved at the heaving wall of flesh and tattered clothing. A face thrust itself into the angry blur of his vision.

'Percy dog, Percy dog,' it mimicked softly. 'Percy dog that licks Lancaster's arse!'

With savage pleasure he brought his Marshal's staff down on the loathsome face. Blood sprang beneath the gilded tip and the angry murmur of the crowd swelled to a roar as the man fell senseless to the ground.

Lancaster gripped his arm in panic. 'For Christ's love, Hal! They'll tear us limb from limb.'

Strangely it was Bishop Courtney who saved them. 'My lords.' His loud voice carried before him as he swept down from the chancel arch. His light eyes rested first on Lancaster and then on Hal. 'My lord of Northumberland. Is it fitting that you should manhandle God's defenceless creatures within His house?'

'No less fitting than that you should allow them to bring their own grievances within His doors,' Hal answered him coldly.

Courtney's long mouth drew up in outrage then Lancaster spoke, anxious to get away from the bulk of the crowd. 'My lord bishop, we are not here to judge the King's Marshal. Shall we proceed with the business that brought us here.'

Wordlessly Courtney led them to the small chapel that lay behind the high altar. Here all the leading churchmen sat in sombre ranks and, at their backs, the aldermen of the city took their mood from their hostile bishop. Hal glanced along the rows of smug and complacent faces and saw how the matter was already settled in their own minds. There was no need for this parody of a trial; John Wyclif was judged and condemned before

190

he had uttered a word. Only one face held his eyes, the narrow cunning face of Alexander Neville, Archbishop of York.

Courtney took up his stance before the altar and waited while Hal and Lancaster seated themselves before the assembly. Then Hal rose and stared pointedly at John Wyclif, still on his feet. 'My lord bishop, it seems that we lack a place for Master Wyclif.'

Courtney's face did not move but his eyes hardened. 'Let him stand,' he said. 'He is charged with heresy.'

'Then as he has all the more to answer, he should have the softer seat,' Hal said softly.

Courtney's face flamed with anger. 'Let him stand. The prisoner must stand.'

Lancaster rose lazily to his feet. 'Then if Master Wyclif must stand, so shall I, and then perforce you must all stand.'

There was shouting from the churchmen and Bishop Courtney's voice was loudest of all. 'I did not think to see the day when you would lend your countenance to heresy, my lord duke.' He leapt down from his place in a flurry of glittering robes. 'You have come here today for no better purpose than to thwart justice, God's justice, upon a corrupt heretic whose infamous teachings attack the very heart of Holy Church.'

'God's justice or *your* justice, my lord bishop?' Hal intervened. 'Or perhaps no justice at all save the spiteful pronouncings of men who see their comfortable livings threatened by a harmless priest who has more of God in him than all of you put together.'

Courtney gibbered with rage and glanced wildly at the aged Archbishop of Canterbury to see how far he could go, but Sudbury only blinked mournfully and worked his hands within the sleeves of his cope. Then Courtney thrust a trembling forefinger at Hal. 'See the Devil's mouthpiece,' he cried. 'Lucifer's servant grown rich on the wages of sin.'

'Remember, Courtney, who you are and to whom you speak.' Lancaster was on his feet and white with anger. 'For all your noble blood you can still be brought low.'

'I trust in God, my lord duke, and not in my family,' the Bishop said loftily.

'Just as well then, my lord,' Lancaster shouted. 'For they'll have enough to do looking to their own needs to stir themselves for the son who brought ruin on them.'

It was out, the threat uttered and witnessed by every churchman in England. They rose as one man from the benches in protection of their fellow bishop and from behind their disordered ranks the aldermen spilled out, shouting wildly, running out into the main body of the church to spread the word. The Lady Chapel seethed like a cauldron and Hal grabbed the bewildered Wyclif as Lancaster's guard came thundering down the nave. The bishops milled about in panic as the outraged howl of the mob rose to the roof. He saw their faces pressed against the tracery of the chancel arch that barred their way.

Then a calm voice spoke at his elbow. 'The sanctuary door, my lord. Behind the screen. Take Master Wyclif out that way.' Alexander Neville smiled cautiously. 'Quickly, my lord, before it is too late.'

Dragging Wyclif with him and shouting to Lancaster to follow, Hal thrust his way through to the little sanctuary door. Outside, the pale frost lay unmelted on the shadowed ground. Hovels that were no more than coverings of filthy rags stood huddled round the smouldering warmth of the charnel house. Huts of rotting timber stuffed with mud and straw leant drunkenly against the churchyard wall and in the open spaces the pale ash of dead fires blew like chaff in the fetid air. The filth churned thick and stinking beneath their feet in the narrow alleyway that even in broad daylight was dark and full of shadows. Sometimes the shadows moved and turned filthy desperate faces toward them before retreating back into the stench and darkness of their crumbling dwellings. Hal supported the trembling priest as they stumbled toward St Martin's Lane and stared appalled at the filth and disease. And Holy Church lent its name to this? The reality was more than he had bargained for, this twilight world of thieves and murderers, safe from the gibbet only within the confines of sanctuary ground, existing on the slops dispensed nightly from the church and what they could steal or beg. He swallowed hard on the sickness that rose in his throat. Surely even death was better than this.

An urchin darted from a doorway and ran across their path.

His legs were thin as broomstraws and bowed like an old man's. 'A penny, lords,' he whined. 'A penny for bread?' Hal stared at the pinched face crusted with ugly sores turned up toward him. The child could not have been older than ten but his eyes were full of ancient cunning. He moved closer and stretched out a skinny hand to Hal then a blow sent him reeling on his back.

'Move on, my lord.' One of Lancaster's men gripped his arm. 'Move on. If you give him anything we'll have them all after us and then we'll never get out alive.'

The child rose up on his haunches, his large eyes blazing in his face. '*Bastards!*' he screeched. 'Bastards, whores' sons, bitches' spawn!' His virulent cries pounded in their ears as they ran into the clean air of St Martin's Lane.

Lancaster leant in the shadow of the wall. 'Thieves and cut-throats, all of them,' he snapped viciously and glared disgustedly at the stinking mud that spattered his hose.

Hal smiled thinly. 'Yet I wonder sometimes, my lord,' he said quietly, 'how are we better than they.'

In the richness and warmth of William Ypres' house it was easy to forget, they could even laugh about it—though Lancaster less easily, for his dignity was everything to him and not easily put aside. But at least some good had come of it; the bishops had dropped their charges against John Wyclif and allowed him to return to Oxford. Lancaster had let him go willingly; the priest had served his purpose and the Duke never kept stale meat in his larder for long. Hal's mouth twisted in a private smile, wondering when his own turn would come. He had no illusions about Lancaster now, or about himself. Each used the other to gain his own ends and both were aware of it. When Lancaster had no further use for him, he would cast him off with as little conscience as he had cast off John Neville before him. And the man to fill his place loomed ready on the horizon: the Duke's youngest brother, Thomas of Woodstock. Lancaster wooed him like a virgin maid and young Thomas, floundering and unskilled in policy, had lapped up his brother's promises like a greedy cat—another threat against him turned aside with soft words and empty pledges. Hal drew his breath soundlessly through his lips. He was safe for a space yet; while the old King lived Lancaster still needed him. Edward still lingered, though he had been sickly for months and rarely left his palace at Shene, but in all else Lancaster was king; despite the Church, despite the mob, only his voice could be heard above the seething discontent.

Lancaster laughed aloud, his indignities forgotten under the adoring smile of his mistress Lady Swynford, and even the careful cut of her gown could not disguise the fact that she was with child again, the third by Lancaster. The Duke flaunted her openly, but none could blame him for that. Constanza was but a means to an end and seemed content to remain at Kenilworth with her army of zealous priests and the swarthy little daughter she had grudgingly borne that summer. Hal's glance slid without interest to the coy maiden who sat beside Lady Katherine, another in the long line of heiresses Lancaster had attempted to foist on him. She was young and comely enough and sole heiress to a broad swathe of land in Lincolnshire—but not enough to tempt him; his heart was still sealed up in that cold little grave at Warkworth.

Then he turned his head sharply toward the window. He heard, they all heard, the sound of a single horse being ridden hard. The narrow street took up the echo and threw it from wall to wall; then suddenly only the echo remained, drowned by the thunder of a mailed hand upon the door.

Lancaster was on his feet, straining to catch the voice that rose above the creak and rattle of bolts. He glanced at Hal and then back at the door and his shoulders eased as they heard the dull murmur of Lancaster's serjeant. No enemy then, or he would have not got past the guard. The other voice, hoarse and winded, they still did not know.

Then Lancaster was at the door, flinging it wide as his serjeant came abreast.

'Your Grace,' began the serjeant. He brought forward the man who trailed wearily behind him. 'Ill news, Your Grace.'

Lancaster grasped the man's arm and pulled him inside the door.

'My lord duke—' His dust-rimmed eyes glanced quickly around the room and lighted on Hal. 'My lord of Northumberland. The mob have run riot. Lord Percy's house is already

194

sacked and now they are turning back toward the Savoy. You must leave quickly, my lords, they are out for blood and mean to have it before the night is out.'

Hal threw a glance at Lancaster's ashen face and went to the window. The casement bellied out over the dark street and at the corner by St Paul's a lantern swung and marked the watch. In the distance, muffled by the squat towers of St Martin's, he caught the dull angry roar that was the mob tearing his house to pieces.

'My lords—' the messenger's voice was loud and urgent in the silence of the room, 'you must make haste. They were turning back down Fleet Street when I left. If you do not leave now you will be cut off. There is an escort below and His Grace's barge waits at Queenhithe. Your only hope is to put the width of the river between you.'

They needed no second bidding. Cloaked and anonymous, for the second time that day they ran for their lives.

The Duke's barge rode in low water beneath the green–slimed landing stairs, its oars unshipped and ready. Wordlessly they climbed aboard and sat beneath the dark awning. The watermen bent and the long white oars stirred the blackness of the water and only when the waterfront had faded into pinpoints of light did Lancaster speak.

'Christ's blood! I'll have their heads for this. I'll hang every dirty little villein so high. . . .' His voice tailed off into impotent fury and Hal saw the white shadow of his hand clenched on the painted housing.

He said nothing and kept his eyes fixed on the receding bank. For some strange reason it gave him a small measure of satisfaction to see Lancaster afraid. The mob was beyond his influence or revenge; there were no high offices to be forfeited, no lands to be surrendered or privileges to be lost. They had nothing to lose but their poverty. He should have been afraid himself, afraid and angry at the humiliation and the loss, yet he felt nothing save a mild amusement. It was a small price to pay for loss of conscience.

He turned to Lancaster as the shadows on the far shore resolved themselves. 'Where to, my lord?' he murmured drily. 'Are we to take refuge in the stews of Southwark?'

'Kennington,' Lancaster snapped, 'we're bound for Kennington. There is nowhere else fitting or safe.'

Hal raised his brows. Even better. He would not have missed the sight of Lancaster begging shelter from the Princess Joanna for the world.

She received them coldly at first, then, all the more galling for Lancaster, with open amusement when she heard. She eyed Hal with mocking triumph. 'You see, my lord,' she whispered when the Duke was out of earshot, 'you see what befalls you when you consort with thieves.'

Hal swallowed his own grim laughter and followed her into the small privy chamber where servants ran to light fires and bring wine. At first he hardly saw the boy, almost swallowed by the dark oak of the chair in which he sat. Then he rose with his own peculiar grace and came toward him. Hal had a sudden vision of a child tottering toward him, his hands outstretched for his ball. A long time ago, when he had been free of Lancaster and Margaret had filled his life.

'Your Grace,' His voice was hoarse with memory as he knelt before him.

Richard smiled as if he too had relived the moment. 'My cousin of Northumberland,' he said in his soft childish voice.

Lancaster paused before his privy council, driven by rare passion. 'You talk of precedent, my lord bishop?' he shouted. 'England's history is riddled with precedent. Search your manuscripts and you will find it so.'

The Bishop of Hereford pursed his lips stubbornly. 'In the past, Your Grace, I grant you that in the past strict hereditary procedure has not been followed, but—'

'That is all I am concerned with.' Lancaster cut him off and stared round at the small assembly. 'All I say is that the Salic law be implemented if the Lord Richard should die without issue. Parliament will surely see the wisdom of this, that to leave England's governance in the hands of children for another generation would be total folly.'

Hal listened in silent admiration; so credible, so virtuous, so outwardly without fault—no mention of the obvious flaw that even the Bishop of Hereford had seen but dared not put into plain speech. He rose slowly to his feet, his admiration tinged by irritation. Such a submission would make them a laughing stock. He was a little tired of always looking the fool. 'Your Grace, with respect—' He went on, undaunted by Lancaster's frown, 'it occurs to me that the Earl of March will not sit idly by while you disinherit his sons.'

'I said nothing of disinherit,' Lancaster glared at him furiously. 'All I say is that it would be more in the interests of England if the French Salic law should be employed. Where the succession comes from the female line it should be set aside in favour of the male.'

'And has it occurred to Your Grace that to do so would render your father the King's claim to the throne of France meaningless and, if I may say so, also your own claim to the throne of Castile. Both are through the female descent.'

Lancaster stared at him coldly. 'We are grateful, my lord of Northumberland, for drawing these matters to our attention, but we are not speaking of France or Castile. England is all that concerns us at the moment and that, in the event of the demise of the Lord Richard without issue, the Crown should devolve on the male heirs of my father the King.'

'And for those among us who are as simple-minded as myself, do we take that to mean the House of Lancaster?' Hal snapped. 'Or, more to the point, *yourself*, Your Grace?'

Lancaster was on his feet. 'Yes, you can take it to mean that. It is no secret among the adherents of the House of Lancaster. If the choice is between myself and Mortimer's brats, then I shall be king. I did not think there was any doubt in the mind of any here as to that, my lord, least of all yours.'

Hal's mouth twisted in open disdain. 'Of course, Your Grace, least of all mine. A foolish dog indeed, that bites the hand that feeds it.'

In the ensuing silence he glanced round at the closed and shuttered faces: the Chancellor fiddling distractedly among his parchments; Hungerford picking absently at a torn fingernail; even the Bishop of Hereford who had sided with him sought sanctuary from his eyes in the back of Arundel's head. Dear God, he thought, how ever had he become one of their number—mindless, grasping time-servers who followed Lancaster no matter how their heart and inclination went against it? The stink of intrigue threatened to choke him and he glanced desperately behind Lancaster's head where the likeness of the old Duke stared stiffly from its gilded frame. It had been a joy and a privilege to serve Lancaster once; there had been no shame and dishonour in his heart then.

The Duke came to his chamber at sunset, when the last of the long rays lay level with the water's edge. Unannounced, without ceremony, he sat in the high-backed chair placed to catch the last of the sun. 'What ails you then, Hal?' He smiled his disarming smile. 'Have I not given you enough?'

Hal turned to face him and Lancaster saw his mistake. Quickly he said, 'Why then, Hal—? Why do you go against me when we have almost won?'

Hal laughed aloud at that. 'Your memory is short, my lord. It was less than three months ago that we were fleeing for our lives and, if it was not for the good offices of the Princess Joanna, we might still be.'

'That's past,' Lancaster said irritably. 'It's *now* that matters, and what's to come.'

'And what is to come?' Hal moved so that they were face to face and Lancaster flinched visibly under the long raking stare. 'Richard dead and Lancaster in his room? Is that what is to come? Remember, my lord, the first man in England, *after the King*.'

'And so it shall be, but not after Mortimer's whelp. I'll not suffer a Mortimer to mount the throne before me and mine.'

'And there is your flaw,' Hal flung at him. 'You take no account of any but yourself. I had once thought Mortimer the more dangerous but now I see that I was mistaken. You think all men are fools and can be bought and sold at your pleasure.'

'And can they not?' Lancaster said sharply. 'I thought I had proved otherwise.'

'Sometimes the price is too high, my lord,' Hal said quietly. 'Sometimes the cost becomes too great to be borne even by the greediest of us. I am Lancaster's man but not to the exclusion of all honour. I'll not condone treason, not at any price.'

Lancaster grinned. 'So it's conscience, Hal.' He came and laid a hand on his shoulder. 'You have no need of it. Neither of us has need of conscience, Hal. What we do is for England's weal.'

Hal flung off the soft restraining hand. 'Give me the courtesy of honest speech, at least, my lord,' he said savagely. 'Spare me the drivel you dole out to your minions. What we do is for Lancaster and no other. Let us at least acknowledge that between us.'

Lancaster averted his eyes to the balas ruby that glinted on his hand, the colour of Lancaster's rose, the colour of blood. 'And if it is? Are not the two the same? Will England flourish the better under the heirs of the second son of Edward than under those of the third? What difference will it make to England whether my son or Mortimer's is king?'

'None, my lord, none at all—unless you force the issue. You read too far ahead, my lord. It is all conjecture and surmise. *If* Richard should die young, *if* he should bear no sons—as if in your mind the thought will bring about the deed. For God's sake let it lie. If you try to disinherit the Earl of March's sons you'll set all England against you.'

'I thought they already were,' Lancaster said. 'And who is all England? That rabble out there who think they are above the law? Since when has Lancaster concerned himself with the opinions of villeins?'

'When they are hard on your heels with their hands an inch from your throat,' Hal told him sharply.

Lancaster laughed softly. 'You'll not let me forget that, will you?' Again his arm slid onto Hal's shoulder. 'Come, let us go down. We have talked enough to make my throat dry as tinder.'

Within the compass of Lancaster's arm Hal moved toward the door. He'd had no answer to the question that burned his conscience, no satisfaction of the niggling self-disgust; as always Lancaster had turned the blade aside when the thrust came too near. At the head of the stairs they paused and the hand on his shoulder tightened fractionally. Then Lancaster moved forward a pace and stared down into the well of the hall where the gentlemen of his retinue crowded together. From their midst a figure detached itself and the gilded leopards on his tunic leapt with awful clarity to his eye.

'Your Grace.' The man was down on one knee at the foot of the stairs and even before he spoke Hal read the words in his hollow eyes.

The King was dead. Edward was dead. Now it would begin.

Westminster

'Henry, by the Grace of God, Baron Percy, Earl of Northumberland, Lord of Petworth and Dagenham, Earl Marshal of England, enters here.'

Harry felt his stomach churn in excitement as his father rode into Westminster Hall. Tall and upright in the saddle, his face pale and taut against the crimson and miniver of his earl's mantle, he filled all of Harry's vision. His brow was banded with the gold circlet of his rank, and from beneath, the thick curling hair sprang brighter still—only the hard brilliance of his eyes betrayed the fact that he was ill at ease. Beside him, Lancaster rode flank to flank down the crowded hall, clearing the stragglers from the aisle. Three thousand candles lifted the great dark hall into the brilliance of day and around the walls the banners of the merchant guilds swayed against the rich hangings; the lion's head and chalice of the goldsmiths, the crossed swords of the cutlers, the wool sacks of the dyers, all ramped in scarlet and blue and fringed in gold.

Harry glanced at the boy beside him and smiled. His cousin and namesake, Harry Bolingbroke, as near to his age as made no difference. A handsome boy with pale slumbrous eyes that belied his sharp wits. They were friends, at first because their fathers had wished it, and then because they themselves wished it. The chosen companions of the Lord Richard, the three had formed a bond that had discounted rank and precedence. Together they had been knighted by the old King, together they had hunted and hawked and shared their boyish imaginings. Now Richard was set apart from them by his kingship. Now they were only two.

They both leant forward as the first of the heralds came through the high doors. Norroy and Clarenceaux in their scarlet and gold tabards, then Lancaster and Windsor and the pursuivants Blue Mantle and Rouge Croix. Harry's eyes strained past the brilliance of the King of Arms. He saw the tall slim figure shadowed by the arch of the doors; his pale comely face was drawn with fatigue but he held his head high beneath the irksome weight of the crown. The trumpets screamed and the slight glittering figure slipped from shadow into light. Harry held his breath. He had not expected him to be so changed. He glanced sideways at Bolingbroke and saw his full mouth turn sulky when Richard's eyes did not seek them out. Aloof and apart, pale as death in royal purple, Richard moved on to where all England's nobility waited in glittering silence. His eyes gleamed as brightly as his crown and his mouth was curved in arrogant pride. Harry looked away in disappointment. A King indeed and as far removed from them now as God in His Heaven.

From his vantage point beside the King, Hal saw his son's face as a pale anonymous blur. He had no stomach for the endless courses of rich pungent food that were borne aloft amid trumpets and rattling drums; he had no eyes for any save the pale little King—and, of course, Lancaster. Attentive, assiduous Lancaster, so jealous and insistent on all his rights and privileges; as Duke of Lancaster bearing the Sword Curtana, as Earl of Lincoln carving before the King, and Lord High Steward by right of his earldom of Leicester. All through the long coronation mass Hal had watched him and seen every shift and change of his face. Lancaster had been the first to pay homage to the newly crowned King, his face a mask of duty as he had kissed Richard's pallid cheek. Only the sudden tremor of his mouth as he had risen had betrayed him. How he must have wished that it was he who sat, regal and enthroned, receiving the homage of all England! His brother Thomas of Woodstock had followed him, swaggering with the importance of his new dignity as Earl of Buckingham; then John Mowbray, Earl of Nottingham; and Edmund Mortimer, Earl of March. When it had come to his own turn, Hal had trembled as he placed his hands between Richard's. The King's hands had not even covered the half of his, white and delicate as a maid's, his fingers drooping with the weight of rings.

'I, Henry, become your liege man of life and limb and of all earthly worship and faith, all truly bear unto you, to live and die with you against all manner of folk. God so help me.' Strange how the words had stuck in his throat, as if he had grudged them, as if he knew their falsehood. *'To live and die with you against all manner of folk.'* Against Lancaster? He had forgotten that he was Lancaster's man, all bought and paid for. But no more. It was finished. He could not side with Lancaster against a helpless boy. The pretence of loyalty had become reality the moment his mouth had touched those pale childlike hands.

The high silver note of a trumpet dragged him back. Down the centre of the hall the great stallion came, its shod hooves striking sparks from the polished stone. On its back, clad in silver armour, the King's Champion rode into the hushed brightness. The King of Arms stepped to the front of the dais. 'If any person of whatever degree, high or low shall deny or gainsay our Sovereign Lord Richard, King of England and France, Lord of Ireland and Duke of Aquitaine, rightful heir to the Lord King Edward of blessed memory, here is his champion who says that he lieth and is a false traitor.'

The gauntlet skimmed the polished tiles and came to rest at the herald's feet. Hal glanced wildly at Lancaster's face and saw his eyes resting quietly on the glove. His face might have been carved from stone, save for the tell-tale pulse that beat like a drum in the hollow of his throat.

Pick it up, Lancaster, Hal thought savagely. Pick it up and let's have done with it. And he was not alone; every eye rested on Lancaster, every mind held the same thought. Only this fair young boy stood between Lancaster and the reality of his dream.

The gilded staff lay on the table between them, rocking gently beneath the weight of Lancaster's hand. 'Why? In God's name, why?' he demanded angrily. 'As Earl Marshal you have more power than any man at Court.'

Hal drew in his breath slowly, taking his time over the answer he knew would set the two of them at odds again, perhaps for the last time. 'My lord, I fear the labourer is no longer worthy of his

202

hire.' Only that, softly said, but Lancaster read the insult in his eyes.

'You ungrateful cur!' he yelled and flung the Marshal's staff into a corner.

'My lord, my lord,' Hal chided him softly. 'Does the tutor berate his pupil for having learnt the lesson too well? It was you who lit the fire, Lancaster. Do not complain now when it burns you.'

Lancaster's eyes narrowed. 'And the reason? Yes, there must be a reason. Because Richard is King now? Is that why you have turned against me?'

'Why should you think I have turned against you, just because I have had my fill of your treachery and deceit?' Hal answered him coldly. 'I am neither for nor against you. It is of small matter to me whether you are King or not. All I want is to return to my lands and mind my own affairs.'

'And you think I will let you?'

He met threat with threat. 'Do you have a choice, Your Grace? Familiarity has dulled your memory. I am not one of your upstart minions to be brought down at your whim. You cannot command me as you do Hungerford and Latimer. And if Your Grace should think to hound me with trumped-up charges as you did Bishop Wykeham, then think again and look to your own safety. If I fall it will not be quietly, Your Grace.'

It was out, blunt and clear, the words he had longed to say since the day the old King had died. The threat hung starkly in the cold silence that crept between them.

Lancaster half rose, his hand trembling above the gilded dagger that hung at his belt. He saw it now, oh so clearly, the disdainful insolence of Northumberland cried it aloud. He was caught in his own trap; Northumberland had got what he came for and now he, Lancaster, was being cast off. And all the while he had thought himself the master, that he had led and Hal had followed. The mocking blue eyes spelt it out with painful clarity; Neville's fall, the advancement of his son and brother, the coveted earldom—all won with ease, without effort or scathe to himself. The shameful truth dawned. He had been used as he had meant to use Northumberland. 'You ungrateful cur,' he said again, 'you false, ungrateful bastard.'

Amusement warmed the coldness from Hal's eyes. 'False, my lord? What did I ever promise you that I have not kept? I have been your man as far as honour would let me and sometimes beyond. I have schemed with you and stayed silent when you have exceeded the limits of your rank and privilege; I have run and hidden and shared in your disgrace and sometimes tried to keep you from the consequences of your own folly. But now you ask more than I am prepared to give. Now I am done.'

'Go then,' Lancaster turned his back and only the heaving of his shoulders told of his rage. 'Get back to your savage north, my lord, and pray that you do not regret the day you turned your back on Lancaster.'

'Let us both pray for it, my lord,' Hal said softly. 'I doubt if the two of us are finished yet.'

The night wrapped Alnwick in shadow and silence. From the roof of the Constable's tower he looked down into the valley where mist and darkness merged the grey abbey into the hills and downstream, a shadow among shadows, the tower of Warkworth thrust from the lip of the ravine above the Coquet. He knew all the shadows, every dark cleft of moorland, every obscure stretch of river and marsh, every huddle of houses and glimmer of grey stone. This was his kingdom, as far as the eye could see and further, and there was not a man within seven days' ride to whom he owed homage or deference.

He leant against the merlons where the frost glittered deep in the weathered cracks. Beneath him his men scurried between hall and tower, pausing to exchange a word, and sometimes a whisper of laughter floated up to him. There was no need to mind their words here, no pricked ears to carry an unguarded remark to higher quarters. Westminster and the Court were far distant now and he had never had a moment's regret about leaving.

Harry had come less willingly; the glitter and excitement had mattered to him and he had wanted to stay close to Lancaster's son and the young King. But Richard had more than his share of place-seekers: Arundel, Warwick, the young de Vere, and a handful of deserters from Lancaster who thought there was more to be gained from the untried young King than from wily Lancaster.

His own departure had been marked by no more than a brief wagging of tongues that had been quickly stilled by greater events. In defiance of Lancaster and with the King's approval, Parliament had dismissed his petition for the Salic law without a hearing and named Mortimer's son Roger as England's heir. Richard himself had filched Lancaster's castle of Hereford for his own use and the council appointed to guide the young King's steps had significantly included neither Lancaster nor his younger brother, Thomas of Woodstock. For the moment Lancaster was in eclipse; all eyes were dazzled by the bright new star that was Richard.

And Hal was content to let it be so. He'd had his fill of kings and princes and in the end the north had been the physic to make him whole again; the clean healing winds, the soothing emptiness of moor and sky, the grey familiarity of Alnwick, all steeped in painful memory. But it was the pain of forgotten grief; love was a distant half-remembered thing, a memory roused when he looked at Harry. Only at night was he still vulnerable and then she came to warm away the loneliness of his bed, timeless, ageless, incorruptible in his mind; it was only he who grew old. And he had his sons, his beloved Harry, handsome as the Devil and twice as proud; Ralph and Thomas whom he knew and loved less well and the little maid Mary, his father's child, with whom he was hardly acquainted. But they kept him young and filled the emptiness of him. For that at least he was grateful.

He turned and drew his cloak a little closer. The wind was rising from the north, sharp and cold, laden with the scent of heath and moorland; and something else, sharp and distinct, the unmistakable smell of smoke. His eyes raked the distant skyline. There, beyond the threatening line of the Cheviots, in the dip in the hills where Yetholm lay, he saw the red virulent glow of flames. The moon slid out from behind Yeavering Bell and showed the dark shapes of scurrying sheep on Middleton Crag, and darker still, a solid wedge of horsemen, moving fast along the moorland track that led back toward Scotland.

The smithy hung by his neck from the roof. He swung gently on his chain above the embers of his forge, turning rhythmically like a carcass on a spit. He was naked, his body blotched and seared by the mark of his own branding irons.

Hal turned away and kicked through the charred timbers. It was almost dawn, the sky touched with pearly cloud and the smoke a grey drift on the horizon. He stepped over the sprawled bodies that lay face down in the narrow street; all men, no women save the few that had resisted too strongly and now lay among the slain; the rest had been herded out with the cattle to provide their captors with a night's amusement.

A child lay in a doorway, its throat cut as clean as a pig's. One of his men grabbed an ankle and dragged it toward the mounting pile of the dead. The head lurched back on its hinge of shattered bone and gushed fresh blood into the mud.

'In God's name, pick it up,' Hal shouted, and turned away as the man ran, shamefaced, to do his bidding. What did it matter, he thought wearily. They were beyond pain and humiliation now. He stared around him with eyes red and smarting from smoke and lack of sleep. Here in this small village his father had built the church that showed the gaping wound of its charred roof to the sky, and he himself had once cut thatch and wattle to rebuild their houses when the floods had come. All for nothing; there was nothing left except the blackened stones of the church, the rest blew like chaff in the cold smoke-laden wind.

He knelt and cleared a spar of timber from the frozen ground and saw the churned imprint of unshod hooves. Scots then, but not Douglas's men for only the wild border clans rode such horses. Yet Douglas would know of it and had not kept them back. Nothing moved on the Border that the Black Douglas did not sanction. He had timed it well; Edward dead, and England trembling in the unsure grasp of a boy.

He thrust his clenched fist against his mouth to stem the sob of rage. He felt it now, the first sharp outrage, the anger and grief of violation, but this was only the beginning. Soon he would be hardened to it again; in a year it would not even touch the edge of his consciousness. This was Douglas's herald, the messenger of his intent. The peace was over, the waiting done; now they could begin.

The smell of smoke hung over Norham and pervaded even the scented air of Bishop Hatfield's hall. From the long windows the burning shell of Roxburgh could still be seen and, where the flames still clung greedily to the dry peat moor, the smoke was dense and black as night.

Hal rose to his feet for the third time to address the council, his temper frayed by hours of fruitless wrangling. All morning they had struggled back and forth, this motley gathering of bishops and lords, and not one of them free from personal bias that could sway them this way and that according to the desires of their absent masters. His angry eyes swept round their faces: the Bishop of Durham and Mortimer for the King; the restored John Neville and the mealy-mouthed Bishop of Hereford for Lancaster; Mowbray of Nottingham; his own brother Thomas, and the lords Musgrave and Heron. These last were with him; their lands had suffered equally with his and Tom was Constable of what was left of Roxburgh.

'My lords. His Grace the King must make additional provision for the defence of the Border. The royal castles are undermanned and such troops as they house are fit for nothing. I have three hundred knights and five hundred archers and men at arms under my personal command—eight hundred in all and not enough should the Scots attack in any strength.'

'What makes you think they will attack, Northumberland?' Bishop Hereford interposed. 'We have a treaty with King Robert.'

'And do you have a treaty with the Earls of Douglas and Mar?' Hal snapped. 'Look around you as you ride home and see the proof of Scotland's "peace".'

'What of the levies?' Mortimer said. 'As Commissioner of Array for the North and Lord Warden of the March, you can summon every lord and knight within the hundred miles or more.'

'Levies take time, my lord,' Hal answered him wearily. 'A day for the summons; another, perhaps two, to reach the Border—and that always supposing the lords are not absent in Westminster.'

'Are you saying that you cannot defend the Border then, my lord?' John Neville thrust his dark aggressive face toward him.

'Perhaps the Border has been in the hands of the Percys too long.'

'And you could do better?' The cold disdainful eyes shifted from Neville and swept over the assembly. 'Could any of you do better? I cannot count more than a dozen here who deem attendance at Court less important than the protection of their lands.'

'You are the Warden of the March,' Neville shouted. 'The Border is in your hands. Do not seek to lay the blame for your failure upon others.'

'My lord Neville.' Bishop Hatfield's cold thin voice made itself heard above the sudden uproar. 'It might be more to the purposes of this council if you confined your remarks to the business in hand.' Then maliciously he added, 'Is it a Neville trait, my lord, to venture opinions where they are least wanted?'

Neville subsided in sullen anger at this pointed thrust against his brother the Archbishop, who had alienated Durham by his high-handed interference in the Bishop's affairs.

Then Hal's brother Tom spoke. 'My lord bishop. I am with the Earl of Northumberland in this. Roxburgh lies in ashes and French gold is pouring into Scotland. I need not remind you that the French do not part with their money without cause. They are mustering an army while we do nothing. They burn and slaughter at will, for every town they burn of ours we burn one of theirs. But nothing is accomplished save the destruction of life and property. If we are ever to regain our former ascendancy over Scotland then we must strike at the very heart. We need an army, my lords, to settle the question for good.'

'Armies cost money,' Hereford said. 'Where is this money to be found?'

'Where it has always been found,' Hal replied furiously. 'From the people who pay half their miserable wages in taxes to keep the King in his silks and velvets. In return they are at least entitled to his protection.' His bitter gaze made the Bishop lower his glance to the floor. 'I hear that Westminster never sleeps now,' he went on, 'that feasting and pageants take up all the King's time. Well, take my duty to His Grace, and tell him that when he next sits down to his dinner another score of his subjects will be dead, robbed and murdered by Scottish scum. I trust that it will not turn him from his food.'

Amid a shocked and uneasy silence he left them and smiled as he heard the whispers break out at his back. He had given them fuel enough to fire Richard against him, and did not doubt that by morning the tale would have been further enhanced to suit Lancaster's willing ear. It would be worth it if it stirred the King from his contemplation of himself and his royal dignity.

Outside the smoke still blew in choking drifts across the Tweed. The land was barren again, a graveyard of smothered life and stunted trees where the faceless enemy hid behind the grey Lammermuir hills. He'd had some small respite this last month; the enemy had turned west, raiding as far down as Carlisle. Time to count the dead and maimed; eight hundred since Christmas and more to come from the hundreds that had fled to the hills and would starve there.

He'd had some small revenge: tit for tat, Dunbar for Roxburgh, Lauder for Yetholm, and a dozen or more nameless villages. But he was chasing shadows that came and went by night, retreating into their protective hills at the first glimpse of him. He'd not had sight of Douglas yet but he knew he was there, waiting and watching, playing out the game they had begun more than twenty years ago. 'Without malice,' Douglas had said. It was hard to remember that now.

'A fine speech, my lord.' Edmund Mortimer came out from the shadow of the postern tower and stood at his shoulder. 'I see the years have not laid a curb on your tongue.'

'Ah, my lord of March,' Hal smiled down into the dark waters of the Tweed. 'It is you, come to tell me the error of my ways, no doubt.' He turned and gave his chilling smile. 'You never could leave well alone, could you, Mortimer?'

The earl smiled thinly. 'It is a shared fault. Neither of us is content to let injustice gain the ascendant.'

Hal laughed. 'Shame on you, my lord. I had not thought to see you add hypocrisy to your crimes.'

'Gently, my lord. I am not the callow youth you once could insult with impunity. We have both changed, I think, my lord.'

Hal leant his back on the river-damp stone. 'How have we changed, Mortimer, save that you have lost your pimples and I have gained a few grey hairs?'

'I cannot believe that you have not changed, Northumberland. You turned your back on Lancaster, did you not, when once nothing I could have offered you would have induced you to do so.'

'For my own reasons, Mortimer. Because I was tired of playing the courtier and it pleased me to play Lancaster at his own game.' His sharp green gaze held Mortimer silent. 'I have no plans to become such again, not to any man.'

'I had not thought it, my lord, but . . .'

'What do you want, Mortimer?' Hal said impatiently. 'You are beginning to weary me.'

Mortimer's mouth trembled with the beginnings of anger but he held his voice steady. 'To give you the truth, Northumberland, as it concerns you.'

'*Your* truth, Mortimer?' Hal leant close and his eyes were momentarily peaceable and bright with the distant echo of laughter. 'Tell me, my lord. I am eager to hear how it differs from Lancaster's truth.'

'No, not just *my* truth,' Mortimer said urgently. 'The truth as any will give it to you who are not in Lancaster's thrall. Ask Bishop Hatfield, ask Warwick or Arundel why the King leaves the north starved of aid. By Lancaster's word, my Lord.'

Hal moved away to stand at the top of the narrow stairs that wound down to the inner ward. 'Go on, my lord,' he said softly. 'Let us hear all.'

'His Grace of Lancaster has not abandoned his lust for kingship, he merely casts his eyes elsewhere; Castile, to be precise. He has petitioned the King to allow him to raise an army for Spain. It follows then, does it not, that outright war with Scotland would put paid to any hope of that.'

The words fell like stones into the whirlpool of his mind; the ripples spread, carrying him along on the swift current of thought. He could believe it well enough. Had he not felt the heat of Lancaster's ambition and almost been burnt by it himself? It blazed too strong for either Richard or Mortimer to douse. Castile was second best, but enough to keep the fire bright, enough to sacrifice both him and the north to get it.

Then Mortimer was at his elbow, soft and mocking in his ear. 'Did you think to be free of him so easily, my lord? Did you think he had forgotten that you cast him off? You heard his henchman Neville questioning your competence on the Border—Lancaster's words, a taste of the calumnies he whispers in the King's ear. He says that it is you yourself who provoke war with Scotland and urges that he be given control of the March.' He laid his hand softly on Hal's arm. 'It is well, my lord, that there are those to speak for you at Westminster.'

'Not *for* me, Mortimer. Only against Lancaster.'

Mortimer shrugged. 'What difference? If our enemy is the same can we not be allies? Protect yourself, Northumberland. Protect yourself or he'll surely bring you down.'

'And the King?' Hal asked slowly. 'What says the King to all this?'

'Richard is not his own man yet. He plays for time and lets his erstwhile councillors squabble amongst themselves. But he's not the puppet that Lancaster thought him. He has a mind of his own and his fair share of cunning as well. We too must play for time, my lord. No man can defeat Lancaster outright. He must be worn down gradually till he is blunted by age and failure and Richard is strong enough to look to himself.'

'You have it planned to a fault, my lord.' Hal raised his eyes, smiling over the fierceness of his thoughts. 'And where is your place in this, my lord? It does not sit well upon you to play the innocent.'

'We come full circle, Northumberland,' Mortimer answered evasively. 'Back to that night off La Rochelle when you told me that if ever it came to it, I should not be your choice. Have you changed your mind yet, my lord?'

'No, I have not, nor will I,' Hal said bluntly. 'I have done with factions, yours or Lancaster's or Richard's.'

'A truce then, my lord. A pledge between us that you will not act against me or mine for Lancaster and in return I'll protect your interests at Court when I can.'

'You can have that, for what it's worth,' Hal agreed mockingly. 'If our paths run together against Lancaster then so be it, but there is an end to it.'

'Agreed, my lord, but there is a better way. One that would set my mind more at ease.'

'Ah, now we come to it.' Hal drew his breath in an elaborate sigh.

'It's no bribe, Northumberland, before you say it. Bribes are easily swallowed and forgotten. I had in mind something more binding, something more lasting.' He paused and looked unflinchingly into the ruthless eyes, like a man aiming a shaft that dare not miss. 'Marriage, my lord. My eldest daughter to your eldest son.'

Hal drew his breath between his teeth in a painful little gasp. Then, softly, the sound bubbling like wine in his throat, he began to laugh. 'Oh my lord, no bribe you say! What greater bribe could you offer a man than the thought that one day he may be the grandsire of kings?'

Yet still he held back his answer, though all the while the ambitious little flame at the heart of him burned higher. It would have afforded him more than a little pleasure to see Lancaster's face when it was announced that Percy and Mortimer were to be one, to walk again that knife-edge between success and failure. But the choice was not his to make. He'd not make Harry walk the precipice with him against his will. The decision would have to be Harry's.

The hounds poured out from the dark undergrowth, muzzles dropped to the damp earth. The horsemen followed close behind, crashing through the barren branches, swerving wildly over the stagnant burns that ran unseen under their covering of winter leaves. The horn screeched and sent a herd of young deer scurrying from their path; the huntsmen chivvied up the baying dogs who milled about in the empty clearing, snapping at the dense bracken. Hal reined in his horse and wiped the sweat from his face while the huntsmen whipped the dogs back. Then suddenly, with a heave and crack of branches, the boar broke cover. Hal yelled to the men and the horn set up its raucous wail. The hounds leapt forward in a tangled flood, the tall boar-hounds in the lead, the heavier-jawed mastiffs pounding behind.

Dragging desperately at his horse's mouth, Hal plunged back into the thicket, heedless of the thorns that clawed at his face. Close behind, his brother Tom cursed his bulking mount over a tangled hedge. Then they were in the open. The boar was a black streak jerking through the bracken and the dogs were closing; but not fast enough, outrun by the short powerful stride of their quarry. Tom yelled in anguish as the beast swerved towards cover, as lustful for blood now as the panting hounds. Harry rode hard at his flank and Hal heard his joyful shout of laughter above the shrill of the horn. Musgrave was down, limping clear of the oncoming horses, his own running on free.

The boar was tiring, its thrusting stride slackening as it turned for the scattering of trees. The hounds lost precious time in the turn and the beast pulled ahead, finding a last desperate strength in the sight of the forest. Then it stumbled, screaming, as the snapping jaws tore at its haunches. It pulled free and ran in a frenzied circle, searching for escape, then turned at bay, its head lowered to charge. The small red eyes glowed like hot coals above the lethal tusks; the long black snout twitched with fear and dripped mud and spume from the cavernous nostrils. Its breath came in great vaporous clouds as it turned its head from side to side, the small close-set eyes taking in the snarling dogs, the waiting silent men and the trembling horses. Then its head came down and its haunches quivered in one final effort. It was down and finished within a hundred paces, its body writhing and jerking between the slavering bloody jaws. Hal took the long bladed knife from the huntsman; the beast twitched beneath his hand, its eyes glazed with the knowledge of certain death. He set the sharp blade to the short muscular throat, then glanced up to see Harry's eyes fixed pleadingly on his face.

He smiled and tossed the knife toward him. 'Take him then, Harry. Clean and quick. He has given us a good run.'

He flung himself down on the winter leaves. Above his head the sun pricked through the bare branches and dabbled the tall oaks with pallid light. Harry dropped lightly beside him, his black curls tangled with thorns. Dried fronds of bracken clung to his clothes and his hands were still wet and red with the boar's blood.

Quietly Hal said, 'The Earl of March has offered his eldest daughter in marriage.' Then as Harry said nothing he added brusquely, 'Do you want her?'

He watched as Harry's eyes narrowed and then widened again.

'Mortimer's daughter?' he whispered. 'Since when has the Earl of March had any love for us?'

Hal scooped up the yellow leaves and crushed them to dust. 'Since he has known that the Duke of Lancaster and I must be enemies.'

'And are you?'

Hal smiled grimly. 'Not yet, not openly, but it will come.'

'Then, if it is what you want. . . .'

'No, Harry. Not what *I* want, not this time. The choice must be yours, whether you'll take a maid of nine years old, who you've never seen and who could not be more than a sister to you for years to come.'

'But she's the King's niece. That must count for something.'

'It may count for much one day, Harry. Can you wait that long? And more than that, will you set yourself against Lancaster? If you wed Elizabeth Mortimer then my quarrel will become yours, and if I suffer then you will suffer also. I do it for love of it, Harry, to tempt Fate, to see if I can turn her from the course she has laid for me. I would not ask so much of you.'

Harry kicked thoughtfully at the tumbled leaves. He had not thought of a wife; he knew no love but the blind adoration he had always felt for his father. When had he ever countenanced anything that was not his father's will; when had their paths not run as one? He knew what was being offered him; Elizabeth Mortimer was a prize that no man in England would think twice about. He was man enough to feel pride and ambition, but not man enough yet to shake off the necessary dominance of his father. There was no choice for him but his father's will.

'My answer is still the same,' he said. 'Whatever you want me to do, then I will do it.'

Hal sighed and watched the huntsmen carrying handfuls of steaming offal to the ravenous dogs. 'Then let it lie, Harry,' he said. 'Let it lie for a while.' The fire was laid, it but needed the spark. But why, in God's name, after all this time, was he so reluctant to be the one to provide it?

The bell was a distant echo in his mind, part of his dream yet outside it, stirring him from warmth, drawing him from the well

214

of memory. Then the cold horny hand of his steward shook him wide awake. He sat bolt upright; the tocsin bell still rang frantically with hardly a breath between peals.

'Berwick, my lord.' The steward's voice trembled with panic. 'There's a messenger come. He says the Scots have taken Berwick, my lord.'

Colder than the flags beneath his feet, the words brought him leaping from his bed. 'Berwick taken?' He sounded like a halfwit himself as he stumbled into his clothes.

The steward held out his shirt and hose. 'The Governor, Sir Robert, is slain and all the garrison with him.'

'How many are the enemy?' Hal snatched his surcoat from a sleepy page and thrust it over his head as he made for the door.

'No more than fifty, the messenger says—' the steward panted in his rear, 'led by Sir Alexander Ramsay.'

Hal closed his eyes in cold anger. Berwick taken by less than fifty men and led by that stripling Ramsay! He did not need to ask the reason why. Boynton and his slovenly garrison had as like been drunk and sleeping at their watch. He pressed his lips hard together. It was just as well that none of them had lived to tell the tale.

William Besset, Deputy Governor of Berwick, waited wet and wretched on the castle ramp. Hal glanced across the dark gulf of the moat and saw the drawbridge hanging drunkenly by a single chain.

'We cut down the piers on the town side, my lord,' Besset explained. 'When they lowered the bridge to storm the town, it collapsed. They are trapped, my lord. There is no other way out.'

Hal nodded and glanced up through the forking rain. On every tower an archer stood; on every walk between, the shapes of men could be clearly seen. He counted forty men and perhaps that was all there were, but it was enough to hold Berwick against any assault that he could bring, at least until reinforcements came. And that was what the Scots were waiting for: help to come from across the Border. Alexander Ramsay was the Douglas's close kinsman; he did not doubt that aid was already on its way. He smiled grimly in the shadow of his hood. They'd not find easy pickings this time; this time he'd be ready and waiting and

Berwick would be strangled by the cord of his troops. None could get in but then none could break out either. He had them caught like rats in a trap and if he had his way, by the time they did come, he'd have that Scottish rag down from the keep and the lions of England in its place.

All through the next day the levies came pouring in: Clifford with his squad of Cumberland archers; the lords Grey and Scrope; and John Neville, come to gloat on what he saw as Northumberland's failure to keep the Border intact. By nightfall the wide meadows of Tweedside were black with men and still no sign of the Scots.

At the bottom of the dry moat, a dozen men worked with picks and mallets, hacking doggedly at the sandstone rock beneath the curtain wall. Their blows echoed through the great shell keep, slow and measured strokes that resounded like a drum in the void of the walls. John Neville had kept himself in the background, grudging Hal any mark of respect or precedence, but even he could not keep silence on this.

'In Christ's name, what good is your pecking and burrowing?' he sneered. 'You'll never breach the walls. You might as well set a pack of rats to chew their way through.'

Hal shifted his gaze from the master mason's solemn countenance. It was a long time since he and Neville had met face to face without the restraint of court or council between them, and still he could not meet those cold grey eyes without thinking of Margaret and how he'd held his hand against Neville in those early years for her sake. There was none to plead for peace between them now, or soothe the grudges and bitter jealousies that had burned between them for as long as either could remember.

'You have a better course then, my lord of Raby?' he asked coldly. 'Let us hear. Let us hear how you propose to take Berwick, my lord.'

Hal's voice was loud enough to turn heads toward them and Neville flushed. 'I did not say that I had a better way,' he snapped, 'But at least if we mounted an attack they would see that we meant business.'

'Proceed then. You have my leave to lead your own men in an

attack.' Hal smiled his soft provoking smile. 'It should provide good sport for the rest of us to see your men picked off by the Scottish archers before you get to within fifty yards of the walls.'

One of Mowbray's esquires was unwise enough to laugh out loud and Neville's face grew purple with rage. He took an unsure step forward, his head lowered. Hal laughed softly and his eyes fell to the Lancastrian collar that heaved on Neville's chest. 'The Neville bull,' he mocked, 'and ringed and collared by his master for all to see.'

There was a silence, broken only by the trembling of the canvas walls. Neville's hand twitched upon his sword hilt and the angry colour faded to sickly grey as the memory of their last combat filled his eyes. He was growing old, plagued by a sluggish heart, worn out by too many half-won victories and near-defeats. His dream of Neville supremacy had faded, rendered impotent by this man's contempt for life and power, as if it was all some foolish game he played; the outcome might amuse Hal Percy but it would never touch him or disturb his outer calm. He stared at him through tear-filled eyes; still erect as a young larch, resplendent in Flemish velvet, that hated arrogant face unmarked by age or sickness, the malevolent bones still strong and sharp beneath the bronzed fleshless cheeks. His hair was greying, but even that so subtly that you could not tell where the gold ended and the silver began. And all so effortlessly, everything fallen to him like windfall apples: the earldom that he himself would have sold his soul for, the undisputed sovereignty of the north—as if the more he defied Fate the more she heaped honours upon him. And that was what galled John Neville most of all, not what Northumberland held but what he could have held and had turned his back on with such contempt, while he who had given all his life to Lancaster had not received a quarter of it.

He lowered his eyes to the golden collar that hung on Northumberland's broad breast: marguerites, with hearts of shining topaz. That was where it all began and ended; he'd not forgive him for that any more than he had ever forgiven her. Northumberland had taken the flower of his life and crushed it to death and in exchange he'd had Maud; fat, stupid Maud Percy, who'd given him nothing but his two sons, and then only grudgingly.

Unwillingly he looked again at his enemy's face. He knew what he would see, not triumph or jubilation—he could have under- stood that—but Northumberland's eyes were serene and cloud- less as a summer's day, and filled with a secret amusement that showed him his defeat as clearly as if he had looked into a glass. That was what was so unforgivable; Northumberland did not kill quickly, he tormented his victim to death.

Then a figure thrust itself between them, tall and thin as a starved hound. Hal saw eyes as cold and grey as new cut stone, and a mean spiteful mouth overhung by a long curved nose; a sharp clever face that had no semblance of youth, despite the dark uncertain growth of a boy's beard upon his narrow chin. Ralph Neville smiled, the gracious effacing smile of a born courtier.

'Remember also that a bull has horns, my lord,' he said quietly. 'Take care that you do not impale yourself upon them.'

A shadow drove the laughter from Hal's eyes and left them empty. He felt the hair rise on his neck, the same intuitive feel of the huntsman knowing that his quarry was near, waiting to spring the moment his guard was lowered. 'I'll take care, nephew,' he answered slowly, 'And give you my thanks.'

'For what?' Ralph Neville glanced at his father's pale face and then back to Hal.

The old mocking smile touched Hal's lips briefly. 'For warning me,' he said softly, and turned his back, eager to shut out young Neville's face. He beckoned his brother from his corner. 'No sign of the Douglas and his men yet?'

Tom shook his head. 'I've had scouts as far in as Melrose and there's not a rabbit stirring. Perhaps the Douglas will leave his rash young kinsman to stew after all.'

'He'll come.' Hal stared across the dark lapping water of the Tweed. 'There's time yet.'

He rode between the sprawling tents. The darkness crept slowly from the hills and blurred his vision. Beyond the river, beyond the treacherous marshland, the grey hills merged with the twilight and here and there the tall solid shape of a peel tower showed black against the sky. Douglas was there, waiting, watching, knowing his every move. If he did not come, then it was because he knew defeat to be certain.

He turned and rode back toward the town, dismounting at the foot of the slope that flanked the castle's east wall. A mason crawled out of the ditch, his face red with blown sandstone. 'Ready, my lord.'

On his belly Hal followed him down into the well of the gully, hugging the overhang that was their only protection against the hail of enemy arrows loosed evey time they showed their faces within ten yards of the walls. Master William, the chief mason, was down on his knees, crouched in the hollow of rock that ran back beneath the foundation of the curtain wall. Every crack and fissure was stuffed with faggots and pitch and his hands were cupped round the reluctant flame that hissed and spat and finally all but died against the damp stone. The mason breathed it back to feeble life with a prayer, coaxing it with dry twigs till it roared into glaring life.

Hal smiled and glanced into the mason's dour face. 'How long?'

Master William spat the dust from his mouth. 'Four days, my lord,' he said. 'Four days and Berwick will be tumbling round their ears.'

But before the four days were out Hal had word that the Scots under Douglas were advancing with five hundred Frenchmen in their van. And Berwick still stood out against him; four days and nights the fire had burned beneath its wall, kept at furnace heat till the rock glowed white and the mortar dried and crumbled into dust. On the fifth day he assembled his men on the ramp, a bare yard out of bowshot. For two hours he watched the black-ened walls tremble and groan as the mortar flaked from between its joints. Harry was beside him, pale with excitement and tense as a coiled spring as the wall bulged and sagged and then with a roar spewed stone and rubble into the ditch.

Even before his father's voice had cried the attack, Harry broke like an arrow and plunged down into the ditch, clambering over the smoking stone into the jagged breach. The rock was still hot beneath his hands and shifted and settled with clouds of blinding dust at every touch. On either side the standing shells of masonry leant precariously together, their core of rubble spilled out into the ditch. He threw himself flat against the sliding rock as a hail of arrows skinned his back. Then with a last thrust and a painful scraping of flesh he had gained the ridge. He was aware of his father's voice somewhere at his back as the main body of the assault swarmed over the rim and into the outer ward. Yet he had been first and was first to run the gauntlet of arrows to the archway of the inner ward where the Scots defenders took a first and last stand. He drew his sword, his eyes smarting with dust and smoke and only for an instant, in that first unlooked for moment of mouth-drying fear, did he waver. Again he heard his father's voice; *'Esperance, Esperance Percy.'*

The shock of the first blow almost knocked the breath from him, then after fear came exhilaration and the feel of blood pumping hard through his veins. The world narrowed to the tall shadow of his adversary. The Scotsman outreached him and his hard swinging strokes were powerful enough to lift Harry clean off his feet, but he lacked the speed and lightness of youth, and for every long thrust, Harry could swerve and lunge beneath the dogged blade till he caught him off balance. He brought his blade hard up against the mail gorget and had braced himself to spring back before he realized that his blow had struck home. The warm stickiness of blood seeped between his fingers and he stared appalled and quivering as the Scot fell and retched blood at his feet. His sword dangled from his nerveless hand as a figure came at him out of nowhere. Then a hand snatched at him and flung him against the wall; from the corner of his streaming eyes he saw his father fling off the blade that would have cleaved his head in two had he hesitated a moment longer. With trembling limbs he fell in at his father's back and fought with stiff and clumsy strokes till Musgrave's archers had gained the higher ground. He felt his father's eyes upon him as the prisoners were herded up. The Scotsman's blood dried and stiffened upon his hand, his first kill, the first time he had taken a man's life in anything but thought. But the horror was fading under his father's bright glance. Then Hal's eyes turned from him and swept along the handful of Scottish knights who had survived, and this time the golden eyes held death. 'Hang them,' Hal said harshly. 'All of them.'

The corpses hung from the walls of Berwick and the sharp withering wind that had sprung up from the river flung them gently against the crumbling stone. Harry kept his eyes from their distorted faces; he had seen them hung, he had seen their eyes widen and bulge from their heads, seen the feeble threshing of their legs as the breath was choked out of them. And all the while his father's eyes were upon him. He had read the warning from their cold clear depths. This was war—not the chivalrous game he had imagined it, but blood and death and hunger. He had held his own life cheap for a taste of glory and now he was being punished for it.

His father's eyes looked away to the distant figures of approaching horsemen. John Mowbray galloped up, shouting his message before he reached them. 'They're retreating, my lord. The Scots are retreating, falling back toward Melrose.'

Harry saw the assuaged smile touch his father's lips. Was it disappointment he saw in his eyes, or relief? Who could tell what went on behind that cold empty glitter, least of all him.

Revenge was not long in coming. A week later Coldstream was burnt and twenty villagers gutted like rotten fish. In his fury Northumberland had sacked Melrose and loosed his men on the scattered hill towns that harboured Douglas's moss troopers, burning and scouring every bolt-hole till there was nowhere for them to hide but the wild barren hills of Galloway. Then, when he was almost within sight of the enemy, their salvation came in the guise of a royal writ. Hal read and reread the offending document till the first disbelief had hardened into cold fury. He, Northumberland, was forbidden by royal command to proceed against the Scots. He did not need to look for the reason—the writ was signed by the King and then by Lancaster as Lord Lieutenant of the Marches.

So Lancaster had won. Now Northumberland's word ran second on the Border. He thrust the Parchment into the depths of the fire and watched it curl and blacken. Then he called for his own clerk and waited with unaccustomed patience while he made his parchment ready. Then slowly he said, 'A letter to the Lord Mortimer, Earl of March and Ulster. Tell him that his offer is accepted. Tell him the marriage can take place as soon as ever he desires.'

221

1381–1396

'The nightingale, that clepeth forth the fresshe leves new'

—Chaucer

It was two years since he had seen her, yet if anything she seemed younger, her eyes brighter, her tongue sharper. 'Umfraville is dead, my lord,' she said in her soft resonant voice. 'I thought to be the first to tell you.'

Hal leant back in his chair and regarded her through half-closed eyes. She looked so small and thin against the vibrant warmth of the hangings, so drab and insignificant in her widow's garb. 'Yes, I know,' he said softly. 'Should I congratulate you or grieve with you, my lady?'

That brought a faint smile to her mouth. Umfraville was dead and she did not mourn him. He was a loss only in as much as one missed the warmth and comfort of a familiar garment. She lifted the hanap of malmsey to her lips, then laid it down sharply when she saw how her hands were trembling. She was aware of his eyes upon her, questioning and faintly amused. How much more amused would he be if he knew the reason she was here? She had come to sell herself and had not known till now how great the pain would be if he refused her. It had taken weeks for her to find the courage for this and now it was gone in one brief moment beneath the cold scrutiny of his eyes. What if she had misjudged his ambition? How far would he go to gain a weapon against Lancaster—to the extent of marrying her? Better to say nothing and go away empty handed than always bear the shame and pain of his scorn. Yet what was pride to her now, what comfort was there in loneliness and the empty days ahead without meaning or purpose?

'Well then, my lord, you are one step nearer Prudoe,' she said harshly. He said nothing and she rose abruptly to her feet, finding courage in the quick catlike movement of her limbs. Slowly she turned to face him. 'Why stop at Prudoe?' she said and her voice almost broke with emotion. 'Why not Cockermouth and Langley and the twelve manors in Cumberland and Lincoln?'

He sat very still, the oblique smile clinging resolutely to his mouth. He knew what she was asking, yet he had to hear, he had to see the wound exposed and bleeding again. He wanted to feel all the pain of her broken pride. 'And the price?' he asked softly.

Her chin came up sharply and he saw her mouth trembling and vulnerable. 'I am the price, my lord.' She swallowed on the painful tears. 'Marriage to me and the pledge of you and your heirs to bear the Lucy arms with your own. And in exchange, all my lands and honours to you unconditionally and the revenues of the Umfraville lands for my lifetime.' It was out; for good or ill, she had said it. There was no going back now.

He did not move but the smile had gone. 'A poor exchange from your point of view, Countess.' His eyes were suddenly cold and wary. 'I can give you nothing that you do not possess already. It could be purely a marriage in name only.'

She smiled, even though every word cut into her like the lash of a whip. He could not have said more plainly that he could never love or desire her. A marriage in name only—but better, so low had she come, than no marriage at all. 'Better the devil you know than the devil you don't,' she said lightly. 'I am content to have it so, my lord.'

He smiled then and for once she saw it touch his eyes to a fleeting warmth. 'Shall we drink to it then, my lady?' He rose and came round the table to fill her cup. 'Shall we drink to the Countess of Northumberland?'

Across the touching rims she saw his eyes, bright and acquisitive with the echo of laughter in their depths, and knew that they saw only the promise of her lands and wealth. For that he would suffer her, and in that moment, with his hand covering hers, it was enough.

The heat rose in a mist from the lake and warped Maud's vision of the tall elms that clustered at its edge. She trailed her hand in the cool water and caught a stray flower that had escaped from the child Mary's industriously worked chaplet; a marguerite, soft and white, the yellow heart trembling with tears. She crushed it in her hand and flung it back into the water. She needed no added reminder of Margaret Percy; her image was everywhere, at Alnwick, at Warkworth—even here at York her device was worked into every hanging, it was even carved upon the great ornate bed where Maud still slept alone. She smiled above the little tremor of despair. Half a year gone since she had signed over all she possessed to Northumberland and she was still his wife only in name. Yet what more had she expected? The bargain had been fairly struck and fairly kept. She was Countess of Northumberland and he had warned her that he had nothing else to give. She had been woman enough, though, to hope that once the deed was done he might turn to her. But if he had need of a woman he never let it be seen; if he had need of love he found it in his memories and the son who was the living reminder of his mother. She was left to find comfort in the children who were almost as much outside his love as she was.

She smiled indulgently as she watched their light-hearted squabbling through the screen of tall reeds. Thomas was almost fifteen now, a grave, quiet boy who held himself aloof from all except his precious hawks. Ralph was a year younger, a happy, laughing child whose sole purpose in life was teasing his father's Strathbogie wards, Bessy and Philippa. Out of all of them Ralph was the only one who had shown her any love or kindness, except perhaps Mary. Old Lord Percy's daughter had become her special charge, the orphaned little misfit who belonged nowhere. Maud had found a kindred spirit there. So much love to give and none to receive it till she had come.

And then there was Harry's child-wife, Elizabeth; pale, lovely Elizabeth with hair the colour of the Welsh gold they dug from the mountains where she had been born. A strange, quiet child, full of secrets and premonitions. Maud glanced to where she sat curled with a manuscript beneath the concealing fronds of willow, remembering the strange illumination of her face when she had told her that her father the Earl had been slain in Ireland. No tears, no sign of grief save the almost imperceptible trembling of her mouth.

'It is the curse of the Mortimers,' she had said. 'Our punishment for the death of the second King Edward. Did you know that my great-grandfather murdered him, that he had his bowels burnt out with a hot iron for love of Queen Isabella?' She had smiled, her strange unearthly smile. 'We carry the seed of our own destruction. When my brother Edmund was born the horses in my father's stables were found standing in blood. So it will be with him. He'll die amid blood and violence like all our house.' So calm and unemotional, as if she had told no more than the time of the day. It had made the other children afraid of her.

Maud called sharply as Ralph shoved his betrothed dangerously close to the water's edge. The sun had cooled and lodged in a fiery ball between the spires of the Minster; she rose and beckoned Elizabeth from her dreamy contemplation of the water. Mary came running toward her, holding out the snowy garland of marguerites. Maud smiled and grasped the flowers reluctantly, feeling the coolness of the spiked petals on her hand. Then she felt Elizabeth's glance upon her face. She was smiling, a bright all-knowing smile that told her she knew and delighted in her discomfort. With unreasoning anger Maud flung the chaplet into the lake; it bobbed and spun upon the still, green surface, nudged by the fish that rose inquisitively in search of food. Elizabeth's smile widened.

'Let the fish have it,' she said softly. Then with her eyes intent upon Maud's face she added, 'The silver fish will devour the flower in the end.'

In her chamber, Mary dressed her hair, her cool blunt fingers combing and braiding the heavy coils. Maud's face was flushed with summer heat and the remembrance of Elizabeth's last remark. She glanced at the hanging above her head where the blazon of Northumberland gleamed from dark velvet: the Percy lion quartered with the silver fish of the Lucys.

The silver fish will devour the flower. Was she foolish enough to take the trite sayings of a child for truth? She was desperate enough to grasp at anything that would ease the constant ache of neglect. Margaret Percy was dead, only a shadow that hung in the dark corners of Northumberland's mind. Maud was the substance, she was real and, if she had the courage, perhaps she could make it truth. But there was the flaw. She had no courage left.

Mary lifted the silk gown from its pole, grey and soft as a dove's breast, drab as a shadow, as she was. All her gowns were alike, dark and anonymous, lest she should shine too brightly and have Hal think she courted him. She could bear a lack of interest in his eyes but not contempt. She did not have the courage for that. She stared at herself in the long mirror. Nearly forty, yet her body was firm and lithe as a girl's and the lines that etched her mouth and eyes were of discontent rather than age. She strained to see herself. Would it be so hard to love that face, to touch her flesh with any semblance of desire? She swallowed hard against the knot of tears that lodged in her throat. Hard enough it seemed, too much to hope for, remembering the cool impersonal way her husband acknowledged her presence. Carelessly she fastened the collar of garnets at her throat and rose impatiently, almost before Mary had settled the wide headdress into place. She did not look again before she went down to greet her husband.

She knew every moment that his eyes rested upon her face. He had paused only long enough for his knights to acknowledge her entrance; no word or look for her above common courtesy. He paid more heed to the falcon that clung to his sleeve and fed greedily on the morsel of flesh between his fingers. She smiled in greeting at the faces that she knew; the lords Clifford and Mowbray, Tom Musgrave and, beside his father as always, the tall handsome figure of Harry Percy. Her eyes lingered longest upon his face for he did not raise his eyes nor stir from his place at her approach. His dislike was almost a tangible thing; like heat or extreme cold, she felt it the minute she entered his presence. And over the months it had become mutual—of all Margaret Percy's sons, Harry was the one who kept his mother so fiercely alive. If Hal had noticed the subtle discourtesy, he let it go unchallenged and turned back to his companions.

She knew of what they spoke, though they pitched their voices low. Lancaster was in the north, entrenched at Bamburgh while he pursued the humbling truce with Scotland, a truce that had been gained at the cost of ceding disputed land to King Robert. No price, it seemed, was too great to loose English troops from the threat of a Scottish war and leave them free to follow Lancaster to Castile. The protests of Henry and the Border lords had gone unheard. Mortimer was dead and Richard overborn by the counsel of his royal uncles.

It was as it had always been; there was no louder voice in England than Lancaster's.

She heard Musgrave say, 'Could we not appeal to the King?'

Mowbray pulled a grim face and stretched a languid arm along the back of his chair. 'All appeals to King Richard must go through Lancaster and his brother Woodstock. And besides, I fancy that the King has more than enough to contend with keeping the Kentish rebels at bay.'

'I heard that they hung a tax collector in Dartford for questioning their tally,' Musgrave remarked gloomily.

Maud took up a length of thread and stuck her needle into the corner of the linen square. She had heard that and worse this past month. As near as Lincoln there had been riots, led by renegade priests and mercenaries come home from the French wars. They had found a ready source of discontent in the oppressed villeinry already crushed by crippling levies. Now the King's newly devised poll tax—a shilling for every citizen over fifteen, rich and poor alike—had swept away the last of their restraint. Only last week in the Minster churchyard, a barefoot priest had incensed the rowdy 'prentices to near-riot. They had a saying now, passed between them like a war cry: 'When Adam delved, and Eve she span, who was then a gentleman?'

She glanced up at her husband's face and wondered if he even knew or cared, if he ever heard or saw anything but Lancaster. The Duke's presence in the north seemed to have drained all the life out of him. His mouth was turned in constant bitterness, his eyes cold empty pools of ice water, and he'd not even let her share in his hatred. She stabbed her needle hard into the stiff linen. She had new enemies now. The pain of longing, the ache of hopeless love.

———

York

Maud paced out the confines of her solar, pausing in panic at every footfall and sound that came through the heavily barred door. The casement was closed despite the heat, and a bee rapped irritatingly against the horned panes, seeking escape from the smoke that drifted on the heavy air. They were burning Archbishop Neville's palace and even from here she could hear the roar and crackle of flames.

She collapsed into a chair, her limbs suddenly weak with fear. All morning they had been penned in this hot little room while the noise of the mob erupted all around them, their only news the little that her servant had brought from the rooftops. Clifford's house was already in ruins, his furniture and hangings flung into the street and burnt. Now they had turned back toward Walmgate and the still air was full of their clamorous cries and the battering of their axes upon the doors. She rose, striving to keep her thoughts calm. She had done all that could be done. Word had been sent to Hal at Beverley but she held out no hope of seeing him before the evening. In the meantime her only defence was a handful of servants who had remained loyal, and one or two aged knights. Little enough to pit against the rabble army that roamed the streets, burning and destroying everything in their path. She turned, calling sharply to where Thomas and Ralph sat in high complaint against their confinement. Elizabeth was curled on the windowseat, reading a manuscript of verse with irritating calm, while Bessie and Philippa snivelled quietly in Mary's arms. She gnawed at her lip as the sound of voices grew louder and beat fearfully on her ears. Then from their midst came one she knew, close by, calling from behind six inches of oak. With trembling fingers she unlatched the door and through the

228

furtive opening caught a glimpse of her servants, armed with staves and borrowed swords. The steward shoved his short squat body into the room. His face was streaked with sweat and smoke and he had cast off his livery for a threadbare jerkin of home-spun.

'It's madness, my lady. All the world's gone mad.' He shook his head and grasped eagerly at the wine that Mary had poured. 'The Archbishop's house is burnt to ashes, and they have hanged two of his clerks. Praise God that he is absent in Westminster or else he would have joined them.' He shook his head and lowered his voice. 'It was one of the Archbishop's men who attempted to collect the tax. He is still alive, my lady, but only just. They are drawing him through the streets on a hurdle, poor wretch.'

Philippa's wail drew them all to the window. Through the misty panes Maud saw the wavering shapes of men running through the pleasaunce. Slapping Philippa to silence she opened the shutter cautiously. The smell of smoke and burning thatch caught at her throat. She saw a ragged figure swing his axe at the bole of a tree; another ran to the rose arbour, smashing the fragrant blooms with his stave. Then the whole garden was covered with them as they swarmed the walls, swinging on the covering vines. She shut the window with a crash, her face pale and angry. Heron drew his sword and went toward the door, but she called him back.

'No,' she said sharply. 'If they see a drawn sword they'll have no mercy on us.' She glanced back to the window and heard the crack of a stone against the shutter. 'I'll speak to them,' she said faintly. 'They'll not harm a woman.'

'My lady!' The steward had caught at her wrist. 'For Christ's sake, my lady, you do not know what you are about!'

She shook off his hand. 'Perhaps not, but I'll not stay here while they burn the house around us.' She was at the door before he could stop her. 'Bolt it behind me,' she said calmly.

Once outside her legs gave way and she was forced to lean against the wall. The bolt had ground home behind her; she could almost feel the weight of her men pressed against the oak, listening and ready should the mob turn against her. Yet for the moment she went unnoticed as they trampled the gardens. They

229

had fired the stable block and the scream of horses jerked her out onto the wide steps. They they saw her, the dreadful silence falling and crying her presence louder than any shouted warning. A dozen men advanced toward her, ragged and filthy. The tallest came and laid his foot on the lowest step, his chin thrust up toward her, flecked with red hair like a sow's hide.

'What do you want?' she said and was surprised that her voice was so strong.

'Justice,' the man answered, 'justice and freedom.'

'And you think you will get it this way?' The uncertainty of his eyes gave her courage. 'By killing and burning, how are you better than those you decry?'

She had gone too far and the man lifted his stave to her threateningly. 'There are only women and children here,' she called desperately. 'Do you make war on such, the helpless and the weak, those for whose cause you say you fight? Would you be so bold if the Earl himself stood here in my stead?'

'We are not afraid of Northumberland or any like him,' a voice shouted from the rear.

'Then prove it.' She advanced closer and stood near enough to smell the sour wine on his breath. 'Leave us in peace and bring your grievance before the Earl when he returns. If there is justice to be had then he will obtain it for you.' She raised her voice so that they could all hear. 'Which of you can say you've ever had aught else at his hands? Which of you can say that you have suffered because of him? The man you want takes his ease at the Scottish court, bartering England's rights for his own gain. Lancaster is the man you want, my friends. Lancaster—King Richard's counsellor and mentor who keeps the Treasury empty to keep alive his pretension to a foreign crown. And now he brings his corruptness to the north, Lancaster and his pack of lordlings and tax gatherers. It is they who keep you poor and hungry in Northumberland.'

She smiled in quiet triumph as first one voice then another took up the cry. 'Lancaster, Lancaster, death to the traitor Lancaster!' If she could have conjured him up they would have torn him limb from limb and she would have looked on smiling to see it done.

She beckoned to their leader. 'Go now, and when my lord

returns I will send him to you. If there is aught to be done he will do it.'

Almost meekly the man nodded and called the others to him. Maud leant back against the door, sick with relief as she watched them go. She smiled triumphantly. They still understood the magic of the name Northumberland.

He walked alone among the dead fires, and the night wind fanned latent sparks from the shimmering skeleton of the Archbishop's palace. On the trampled meadow the rebel banners stirred and quietly flaunted their crudely daubed messages of freedom: 'For King Richard and the Commons . . . Death to the traitor Lancaster.' That brought a tired smile to his chilled lips. Lancaster was on the run and no man who could shed his livery was wearing it today. His Duchess Constanza had fled for her life to Pontefract and had been refused entrance, and Lancaster himself had been proclaimed outlaw by the King; a small comfort for the humiliating months watching Lancaster usurp his power in the north, feasting himself at the Scottish court while he signed away the rights that had been so bitterly bought with English blood. The Border needed peace, but not this shameful one-sided peace that Lancaster had wrought for his own ends. The warmth of his hatred brought a film of sweat to the palms of Hal's hands. He had underestimated the force of Lancaster's power and had thought himself inviolate. But Lancaster had struck where it could wound him most, at the Border and Northumberland. He would not hesistate again and hold his hand against the Duke of Lancaster.

He kicked at the long-dead fire and sent a flurry of fine ash into the warm air, staring round at the deserted field that two days ago had housed a ragged villein army. It was over now, the rebels sent home with empty promises, for that was all he had to give them. He had no power at Westminster and what he'd had in the north had been gradually eroded by Lancaster. He had never felt so helpless, so aware of his isolation from the heart of power. He had promised them justice, sustaining their pathetic belief that the young King would right their wrongs. Yet Richard was still an unknown quantity, the head that wore the crown while his

231

body and limbs were Lancaster and Woodstock, ruling through him, for him, but only so far as it suited their own aggrandizement. He had had nothing from Westminster except the panic-stricken missive appointing him Captain against the rebels and ordering him to seal the Border fortresses. No word of how Richard fared, save that the Kentish rebels held the city and that the King and his counsellors were captive in their own Tower. His brother Tom was one of them. He smiled wryly. Perhaps that in itself was a good omen. Somehow Tom always managed to be on the winning side.

He walked broodingly to where his horse cropped the trampled grass. For all he knew, Lancaster's dream might be accomplished. For all he knew, Richard was already dead.

The messenger awaited him in the dark courtyard of his house in Walmgate. Flushed with hard riding he came out to meet him, speaking low and swift against the horse's neck.

'My lord, I come from Sir Matthew Redmayne, Governor of Berwick. The Duke of Lancaster has crossed the Border and demands admission to Berwick. Sir Matthew will not admit either the Duke or his men till he has your consent.'

Hal slid slowly down from his horse. 'Sir Matthew did rightly,' he said quietly. 'Permission to enter Berwick is only granted to those who hold the King's signed writ. Does His Grace hold such?'

'Hardly, my lord. His Grace has only recently come from Scotland.'

Hal smoothed the long curve of the stallion's neck. 'Then permission is denied.'

'But my lord! To the Duke of Lancaster?'

Hal smiled. 'Especially to the Duke of Lancaster,' he answered softly.

A week later Hal listened in quiet and appalled silence as his brother unfolded the tale, so gross a tale of death and destruction that it made the recent happenings at York seem as nothing.

'They came from Blackheath and overran Southwark in a day. The Marshalsea and King's Bench prisons were wrecked and the felons loosed.' Tom's voice shook with remembrance. 'Yet the city was safe, till that treacherous bastard Sybyle lowered the bridge.' He shook his dark head in disbelief. 'So many of them, Hal. Thousands, tens of thousands.' He shook his head again. 'None of us could count.'

Hal stared at his brother's grim face in disbelief. 'In Christ's name, Tom, could you not fight?'

'Fight?' Tom looked at him bleakly. Yes, he had wanted to fight, in the beginning, before old Salisbury had worn them down with his cautions. They had been so few; the King and his uncle Woodstock, the Holland brothers and the earls of Warwick and Salisbury. Harry Bolingbroke had been there and the stripling de Vere – boys, callow youths and old men. And he and Salisbury the only experienced soldiers among them. Even now those two long days came to him with an air of unreality. The blazing June day fanned to furnace heat by the burning city, and they, complacent and smug behind the Tower walls, had refused to believe that it could happen.

That first night he had stood with the King on the Tower roof, ringed by fire and choking smoke that crept up through the narrow arched windows and hung like cloud drift beneath the jutting merlons. Beneath them the river was streaked scarlet and darkness touched the sky like a timid shadow. To the north Treasurer Hales's Highbury manor still burned, and westward all that was left of the Marshalsea belched black clouds into the reddened sky. The Savoy was no more, fired and blasted to a pile of blackened stone; the Inns of Court were smoking ruins, Lambeth too, the face of London changed in a day. He had looked down into the shrouded city and seen the rebel fires on St Catherine's Hill, so close and only the wall of the Tower between them. The rebels had set up their own makeshift block by Cheapside Standard and the Londoners had taken savage revenge on the rival Fleming merchants. A hundred had died that day alone. He had heard that the gutters into Thames Street ran red with blood. Now the sound of their drunken revelling floated up on the burning air. *Jack the Miller grinds small, small, small. The King's son of Heaven shall pay for all.'* He had glanced at the King and seen tears trembling on the fair lashes. He was no more than a child yet there was a kind of courage in the soft mouth, and he would be in sore need of it before the next day dawned, trapped between the rebels and his bungling counsellors who weaved this way and that and wearied even Tom with their long and fruitless deliberations.

There had been one vain bid at peace. That evening the King had gone by barge to Greenwich and made a futile attempt to parley with the rebel leaders. But in the face of the clamouring, yelling hordes that had lined the river bank, Salisbury had lost his nerve and ordered the barge back to the Tower with nothing accomplished save his own loss of face. Now there was nothing to do but wait.

In the King's presence chamber they sat in unnerving silence. Woodstock paced the floor, chewing at his thrusting underlip till his teeth pricked blood. In a corner to themselves Hales and Archbishop Sudbury sat in quiet resignation. It was their heads the mob clamoured for, theirs and Lancaster's. Tom glanced to where young Bolingbroke stood by the narrow window slit. His pale eyes were drained and white as glass; the same thought was in both their minds. If not Lancaster, then his son would serve as well.

Richard came last into the chamber, with de Vere and Mayor Walworth at his back. Tom watched him as he took his place: pale smooth cheeks downed with gold, the round proud eyes and vain womanly mouth; a boy still, but already with something of a man's cunning in the light blue eyes.

'Well then, my lords,' he said suddenly, 'have you lost your tongues? What say my erstwhile counsellors now?' His voice, hoarse and newly broken, held a note of malice that brought a dull flush to the older men's necks.

'We must treat for peace,' Salisbury said heavily. 'There is no other way.'

'Treat?' The King's eyes blazed with outrage. 'Treat with villeins and serfs?'

'What else then, Your Grace?' Salisbury said wearily. 'They have us trapped. The Tower is surrounded.'

'I still say we fight.' Walworth might have been their equal instead of an upstart grocer the way he strutted in their midst but

234

he had the young King's favour and that was enough to make himself heard. 'We have two hundred men at arms within the Tower and more could be raised once we gained the city.'

'Two hundred?' Warwick snapped. 'Against how many? They would tear us to pieces before we'd time to draw our swords. As my Lord of Salisbury has already pointed out, there's no room for fancy charges in the London streets.

'And also,' Tom put in quietly, 'once we leave the protection of the Tower, the lives of Treasurer Hales and His Grace the Archbishop would be forfeit.'

'Then we must needs devise a plan whereby his Grace and the Treasurer can make their escape,' the King said with childish simplicity.

The Archbishop rose, his tired face grey and sickly. 'I could countenance naught that put my safety before yours, my liege,' he said. 'Our first concern must be for the King. If my death can accomplish that then I am content.'

Tears sprang into Richard's eyes as he clasped the primate's withered hand. 'Oh my lord Archbishop , if I had half such loyalty from the rest of you, I should be happy indeed.'

Woodstock turned away, scowling. 'Easy enough for an old man to barter away his life,' he muttered. 'But I'll not give up mine so easily.' He turned back to the King. 'Well then, my liege, it seems that our problem is solved. If His Grace the Archbishop is happy to martyr himself for your cause, then let him offer himself to the rebels. His life for yours, my lord King, a noble and worthy exchange.'

Richard stared at his uncle with burning dislike. 'I do not see you offering yourself up, my lord,' he shouted.

'Nor will you, my liege,' Woodstock snapped back. 'It is not *my* head that the rebels call for.' He stabbed his long finger in the direction of the Archbishop. 'It was not *I* who hatched up the ingenious tax that has brought half of England to revolt.'

'No, but you did not speak against it either, my lord,' Richard yelled. 'For one whose voice is always so loud in council I cannot believe that you would have sanctioned aught that did not meet with your approval.'

'It was necessity, my lord,' Gloucester threw back at him.

235

'When the King disperses his revenues to merchants and favourites, something must needs meet his demands for a new coat.'

Richard's eyes flew wide as if he had been slapped and the burning colour flooded his cheeks, then drained away to leave him white and staring.

'My lords!' Salisbury intervened hastily and stepped between the trembling boy and his view of the insolent Woodstock. 'We will achieve nothing bickering among ourselves.' He laid his hand on Richard's velvet sleeve. 'You must calm yourself, sire, if you are to win the victory.'

Obedient to the sop of Salisbury's words the royal rage departed as swiftly as it had come and left no mark but the spiteful curve of Richard's mouth.

Salisbury turned his quiet gaze from the King and looked at the Archbishop. 'The King is right, Your Grace, in as much as both you and the Treasurer are at risk; also my lord Bolingbroke. If we could draw the rebels away from the Tower it would give you all the chance to escape.' He turned back to the King. 'It could be done, my liege, if you have the courage. If we arranged a parley, outside the city. Face to face, yourself and the rebel leaders.'

'Christ's blood, Salisbury! Are you mad? To suggest that His Grace expose himself to that rabble?' Warwick interrupted.

'I doubt if the King himself has anything to fear from the rebels. You heard their cries: "*For King Richard and the Commons*". They have faith in the King to right their wrongs and besides, my lord, it is our only chance. They must be dispersed from London. We are helpless while they hold the city.'

'And what good will a parley do us, my lord?' The King asked sharply. 'They'll not disperse till they have what they came for. You know their terms; abolition of villeinage and boon work. They all want to be free and work for a shilling a day. You suggest that I agree to all this? I'll not demean myself bargaining with villeins.'

'Promise them anything,' Woodstock said. 'None will hold you to terms given under duress. If it sends the fools home then what does it matter?'

Salisbury nodded. 'Aye, my lord. For the moment we must seem to yield, to give us breathing space, till we have possession

236

of the city. By that time word will have reached the other lords. We shall be strong again.'

Richard folded his white hands in his lap, a gentle childlike gesture, yet his eyes were not the eyes of a child. He stared round at the set faces and saw the uncertainty that bordered on fear. They were helpless, stripped of their power by an army of ragged scum, who would tear them limb from limb if they showed their faces beyond the Tower walls. Laughter bubbled deep in his throat. For the first time they had need of him for more than the signing of their charters. His limbs twitched in sudden pleasure as if he had been released from chains. He was free, free from the stranglehold of their carping counsel. For the first time he was in truth the King.

He rose with slow deliberation, walking among them, and their silence was music to his ears. They waited on his word and seeing their fear he made them wait the longer. Then, slowly, tasting the sweetness of every word before it left his lips, he spoke. Woodstock he sent scurrying like an errand boy, and Warwick to attend Mayor Walworth while he sent word to the rebels. Salisbury he left alone and took his pleasure from the tight disapproval of his mouth. His cheeks were flushed and he smiled like a happy child. Pride and the glorious feel of his power drove out fear. He was King and in the morning he would lead his council out and let the world see them hiding behind his skirts.

The day dawned bright and clear, the morning sun burning the pale river mist to a rainbow haze. From the roof of the Queen's Tower Tom watched the black tide of men that surged through Aldgate towards Smithfield, a grey colourless wave of drab humanity, and here and there the violent splash of a banner against the mocking cloudless sky.

But the streets below were still lined with vociferous crowds and even Salisbury's soothing voice could not quell the panic in the Archbishop's eyes. 'They are waiting for the King,' Salisbury said. 'They will follow on when the King has ridden out. They are only waiting for a sight of the King.'

And indeed he was a sight worth waiting for. Bathed and perfumed, his hair was dressed in sleek golden waves round the pale, deceptively innocent face, his surcoat stiff and glittering with silver thread and the sheen of pearls. He thrust his impeccably shod foot into Warwick's cupped hand while his Holland brother held the wide jewelled reins. Then Richard turned, smiling that bright malicious smile that sat so oddly on his child's face. 'Come then, my lords,' he said. 'Let us go to make our peace.'

The thin impertinent chime of St Nicholas Cole ringing the hour for lauds disturbed the soft clinging silence of the room and stirred the King from his fitful sleep. He lifted his head from his mother Joanna's shoulder, his face blank with sleep and streaked with tears and dirt. 'What hour is it?' he whispered.

'Almost midnight, Your Grace,' Salisbury answered him distractedly. He had aged ten years in as many hours, they all had. Warwick paced out the tiny room with an old man's gait and even Woodstock's tongue was stilled. They still reeled from the shock of it. The Tower had fallen, invincible, impregnable, yet not against the treachery of the guards who had let the rebels in. Hales and his snivelling clerk Legge were dead, their heads paraded through the streets of London still. And gentle Sudbury, dragged to the block with the Sacrament still moist upon his lips. They said it had taken eight strokes of the rusty axe to separate the Archbishop from his head. Only Bolingbroke had survived; like his father, Lancaster, he had the knack of survival. And while it was done they had humbled themselves before knaves and thieves at Mile End. The King had conceded all, glibly, smilingly, holding nothing back, even to yielding them his royal banner to give the semblance of right to what they did. Even now the Chancery worked into the night, issuing pardons and manumissions as proof of his good will.

And all for what? For every rebel who had been sent home content with the King's pledge there were two who had stayed. The rebel leaders were still camped outside the fallen Tower, Wat Tyler and the renegade priest John Ball, clamouring for more than even the seemingly pliant King could yield, even if he'd had a mind to.

Tom glanced to where the King slept, his finery soiled by smoke and the touch of a thousand grubby impertinent hands.

Tomorrow they would begin again, swallowing their anger and outraged pride in one last attempt to persuade the rebels to disperse. And to buy themselves another day's bargaining time. All their hopes were pinned on the King. Tomorrow they would stand or fall on the courage of a boy of fourteen.

They rode out at first light, crowding close in the narrow streets, averting their eyes from where the headless corpses of the Flemings lay stinking in the Cheap. Through Ludgate and Temple Bar, where the scar of the Savoy still blew pungent smoke in their faces. The wide Strand was littered with debris from the Bishop's houses and at Charing a corpse in Lancastrian blue dangled from a makeshift gibbet. They turned north towards the dark threatening towers of St Bartholomew outside the city gates. Behind the church lay Smithfield and a smell of dung so strong that it turned their stomachs before they had come within sight of the market square and the huddle of poor dwellings that hedged it in. Today the square was black with men, dirty ragged men with wild vociferous voices that spoke all at once. The King had halted, nodding to Salisbury and Mayor Walworth to draw in close. Tom glanced along the rebel ranks and saw the longbows strung and turned toward them. It would have been foolish to say that he was not afraid when all the while his heart hammered painfully against his ribs. One false move and they were all dead men.

Then a man broke from the crowd and cantered across the square toward them, raising his hand to the cheers of the mob. Wat Tyler's face was large and fleshy and dark with a week's rough growth of beard.

He reined in his shaggy colt close to the King but did not dismount, careful that they should mark each small disrespect. His narrow eyes ranged over them all and came at last to rest on the King. 'What now, brothers?' His voice was loud and arrogant. 'Come to send us home like the foolish lackwits you would take us for?'

The King's voice began faintly then gathered strength. 'I have come here to ask that you disperse as was agreed. Why are you still here when we have granted all that you ask?'

'Come to *ask*, have you, my lord?' Tyler grinned as he saw the angry flush creep into the King's cheeks. 'Ask away all you like but you'll not be rid of us that easily. We want more than scribbled parchments and fancy banners.'

'What more?' Richard asked faintly.

Tyler pursed his mouth in sly deliberation. 'Lancaster's head for one and no lordship but yours. No serfs, no lords, no man to bend the knee to, save to yourself.'

'And if it is refused?'

Tyler grinned and jerked his head to the waiting crowds behind him. 'Then we'll take it, Lord King and more besides.' He spat loudly into the tall grass at Richard's feet. 'Perhaps then we might not even need a King.'

Richard swayed slightly in his saddle and his smooth cheeks pulsed with angry blood. 'Take him,' he screamed, 'take him and shut his foul insulting mouth!' Walworth's sword was only half out of its scabbard before Tyler struck with the long dagger thrust in his belt. But the blow miscarried and Walworth's sword caught him hard in the chest.

Tom edged his mount close to the King, his eyes on the crowds that pressed dangerously close. He heard the roar of clamorous voices and then the sudden deathly hush. Tyler's horse turned and bolted across the square, dragging its bleeding rider in the dust. Then the bows were raised, the shafts fitted and aimed while they stood frozen with fear.

Tom laughed harshly. His hands were damp with sweat, remembering. 'You should have seen him, Hal! He rode straight at them and told them bold as brass that he would be their leader. He put us all to shame that day. A beardless boy with ten thousand ruffians at his back, leading them off to Clerkenwell Fields as meek as lambs.'

'The King is safe, then?' Hal said.

'Oh, more than safe, Hal. He's top of the dungheap and crowing fit to burst. Woodstock has let him off the leash enough to let him do the council's dirty work for them. They needed a scapegoat and Richard of his own inclination has offered himself. As soon as the rebels had dispersed the King ordered the immediate revocation of all pardons and charters. Given under

240

duress, he said, and therefore invalid. He told them to their faces: "Villeins you are and villeins you always will be." Then with that bloody cut-throat Tresilian at his back he ordered a commission of assize. I rode with Woodstock against the men of Essex. He herded them up like cattle and slaughtered them with less thought. The King himself ordered fifty men to be hung in Canterbury and Tresilian had fifteen men in St Albans hung, drawn and quartered, the priest John Ball among them.'

'Without trial or hearing?'

'Without even a prayer.'

Hal thought of the wild and joyful faces he had seen in York: grown men weeping and dancing in the streets, waving their paper liberty. They were free. There would be no more bondage, no more scything their lords' corn while their own rotted in the field, no more boon work or crippling fines. It was a dream that he had never believed. But they had believed it. The King had told them so.

He raised his eyes slowly to his brother's face and saw the quick sideways shift of his eyes and the way his blunt fingers worked at his sleeve. He gave a deep and audible sigh. Now they were nearing the thing Tom had come to say.

'And Lancaster?' he asked softly.

Still Tom kept his eyes turned to the floor. 'The King's punishment of the rebels must needs be his defence of Lancaster. His Grace has sent to Westminster for a safe conduct and I am charged to tell you to give His Grace honourable escort to Reading where the King awaits him.' He drew the parchment from his tunic and laid it on the table between them. It tipped and rolled under the weight of the royal seal, so small, so inoffensive, the instrument of Lancaster's freedom, and of his own defeat.

Hal smiled, a broad generous smile. 'If the King commands it, then so be it. His Grace of Lancaster shall have his safe conduct and escort. He'll have nothing to fear with five hundred Percy knights at his back.'

'Richard, by the grace of God. . . .' The oft-repeated words lifted a little of the petulance from the King's mouth as he entered the crowded hall. He was never tired of hearing them. Richard,

King of England and France, Lord of Ireland, Duke of Aquitaine. It was the solemn avowal of his kingship, a constant reminder of who he was, though he himself had less need of it than the lords who bent the knee to him today. His pale eyes swept over the gaudy ranks and marked those who were slack in respect, those who kept their eyes upon him instead of cast down to the floor and whose obeisance was no more than a grudging bend of the knee.

He mounted the dais to the trumpets' blare, careful of the train that dragged its jewelled weight on the steps behind him. His esquires ran forward to lift clear the long sleeves that had consumed a full twelve ells of tarse silk; his doublet was of white velvet and the high collar rimmed with rubies leant a nebulous colour to his face. He inclined his head and gave his hand to Archbishop Courtney who had so swiftly replaced the martyr Sudbury. Not his choice, but then nothing of importance was ever his choice. He was a nonentity, whose thoughts and desires were of less account than the humblest knight at his Court. His brief freedom of the Hurling Time had been swiftly curtailed, forgotten amid the general relief that they were masters again. But he had not forgotten; every moment was stamped in glory on his mind. It was he who had saved their miserable skins, who had brought them out of it without scathe and restored the balance with savage reprisal. He had been King indeed then. Now he was King of naught but what his counsellors allowed him, and that was little enough. He marked them with his wide child-like gaze. Arundel, with his thick stumbling tongue and insulting mien; Woodstock, whose grudging fealty mocked his royal dignity with every breath. And Lancaster. The last was a mere rush of air between his teeth. Lancaster, who fettered him about with his restraints and devious counsel and filled his Court with men of his own choosing, old men, cautious men, who diverted his revenues into their own hands, men who looked first to Lancaster, then to the King. Richard Scrope had the Exchequer, John Neville held the privy purse, and even Archbishop Courtney had joined his former enemy in an uneasy alliance against him. He could not draw breath but Lancaster knew of it first.

How he had yearned to give that villainous scum what they

had clamoured for: Lancaster's head. Did he himself want anything less? Caution smothered the hot spark of hatred that brought the tell-tale colour flooding into his cheeks unaware. Not yet, not alone, with Woodstock and Arundel so set against him. Once there had been Mortimer to ease the weight against him but Mortimer was dead now and none had risen in his stead. He had his own men, the new men, hungry for land and power. His old tutor Burley, and Robert de Vere, Oxford's son, who was more than friend to him; Mayor Walworth, possessor of that special loyalty incumbent on the self-made man; Tresilian, with his clever legal mind and enough ambition to bend it to the King's will; de la Pole, the merchant's son, for all his worth, spurned by the greater lords because of his humble ancestors—he was not one of them nor ever would be. It made the King hold him that much dearer. There were others, trembling on the brink of desertion from Lancaster—Archbishop Neville and Chancellor Scrope. There would be more, all of the same breed, all owing loyalty to none but him. He smiled like a happy child. He could wait. The youth that had weighed so heavily against him now would be his salvation. He was young and Lancaster was old, worn out from chasing his tarnished dream of a crown. At least he could keep him from that. He had time, Lancaster did not.

He glanced up as a shadow fell across him and dimmed the glory of his thoughts. He saw a face, shaped and hollowed by the raw north wind like weathered stone. The granite mouth was unsmiling and the burning eyes sunk deep into caverns of polished bone watched him like wolves in ambush.

He stared at Northumberland in preconceived dislike, remembering the insulting message that had come down from the Border last year. Here was another who thought that rank and ancient privilege absolved him from respect, but this one was not so far out of his reach as Lancaster. His eyes were cold as he held out his hand. He did not have to show a meek and yielding face to Northumberland as he did to his uncle of Lancaster.

Hal brushed the extended hand with dry lips and breathed the cloying scent of rosewater. The cold kingly gaze filled him with indifference and perhaps a faint amusement. He saw the boy struggling too soon to be the man, smothered by the outward

243

trappings of kingship and so tender of his dignity. And beneath the lofty pride and inward gaze that saw nothing but himself, a glimpse of the mean, vindictive streak that had sent five thousand common men to their deaths.

'So my lord of Northumberland graces us with his presence.'

Hal did not need to turn his head to know that Lancaster stood behind him. 'We had thought that the affairs of your own kingdom might keep you from us, my lord. 'Tis true enough, is it not my lord? None save a king could forbid Berwick to the Duke of Lancaster.'

Hal turned slowly, his face impassive save for the dangerous gleam of his eyes. He felt a mild surprise that Lancaster should spoil for a fight so openly, and here, before the King, who held his royal uncle in no great esteem. But perhaps they had both gone beyond caution now, and Lancaster still smarted from his last thrust. He had given him his escort, not grudgingly but with full honours, flaunting him through the streets of York where rebel heads grinned down from Micklegate, through the silent villages where the victims of the King's revenge still hung in the market square. The streets had been lined with men, the same dirty ragged men who had seen their pathetic trust in the King's justice trampled into the dust; broken bitter men and twice as dangerous in defeat. And Lancaster had been forced to suffer it, the jeers and catcalls, the clods of mud and filth that were flung at him, aware that one word from Northumberland and they would have torn him limb from limb.

'I obeyed such orders as I had,' Hal answered calmly. 'They made no mention that the Duke of Lancaster was exempt.'

'You took the law into your own hands and read what you wished into your orders,' Lancaster shouted. 'Such actions are treason, my lord Northumberland.'

Hal looked back at the King. 'Forgive me, sire, perhaps I mistook your intent. The word that I received was that none should be admitted to Berwick or any Border fortress save that he carried the King's commission. His Grace the Duke was then outlaw—on your word, sire—and therefore did not hold such.'

Richard writhed beneath the icy gaze, the colour coming and

going like an angry tide in his face. He opened his mouth to speak then looked wildly at de la Pole.

'My lord Northumberland—' De la Pole rose smoothly to his cue. 'At that time the realm was disturbed. The King was under considerable pressure. We cannot put too much store by writs issued under duress.'

'Am I to take it then that the King's word is worthless? That I also number among the poor fools who found that his writs were not worth the parchment they were written on?'

In the appalled silence the King's breathing was loud. 'They were scum!' he shouted before he realized that a king would not need to justify himself. 'Villeins and treasonous scum who presumed to challenge their King.'

'And also your subjects, sire. Or perhaps Your Grace does not acknowledge those without the right to coat armour?'

'You presume too much, Northumberland, to dare to tutor the King in manners,' Lancaster said loudly, one eye on the rising colour of the King.

Hal turned to face him. His breath was caught painfully in his throat and for a moment his vision blurred on the familiar features. He felt the crushing weight of rage on his chest and struggled against it, trying to turn his eyes from the smile that goaded him like a hot iron and showed him the vision of his own hatred, all the more potent because it had taken so long to wring it from him.

'Let's make an end to it then, my lord.' His voice was so quiet that only Lancaster heard. 'Once and for all, to the death.' The crack of his gauntlet on Lancaster's cheek drove all sound from the room. 'Take it up!' Hal shouted. 'Take it up and make an end to it!'

The King was on his feet, trembling with the beginnings of his royal rage. He thrust a trembling finger at Hal. 'How dare you!' he screamed. 'How dare you profane the presence of your King!'

None moved, none even looked his way, then into the trembling silence the King's thin scream burst. He lurched down from his seat, his long unwieldly train wound about his legs, reeling from step to step like a drunkard. His eyes were pale and staring and spittle clogged the narrow corners of his mouth. 'Take him!' he screamed. 'Arrest him! Get him out of my sight!'

Hal neither heard nor saw, his gaze was locked fast on Lancaster, shut in the small private world that contained only the two of them and where the ranting of the King only reached him above the whispering of old memories. How had it come to this? How had that first small spark grown to such a blaze? And yet he himself had fanned it to full heat with grievance and bitter words. He could not complain now if it threatened to consume him. It was Lancaster himself who broke the spell. He stretched out a hand; to touch him or ward him off, neither of them knew. Then he turned away, the mark of Hal's challenge still livid upon his cheek.

'Take him away,' he said harshly. 'Have him conveyed to Windsor till the King's pleasure be known.'

For an hour Maud waited in the crowded ante-room filled with clerks and giggling pages. She wore her quietest gown of nunly black, for the King did not care to be outshone, even by a woman. Richard kept her waiting, as she had known he would; the petulant act of a petulant boy, but she did not grudge a minute of it. She would wait all day if it meant Hal's freedom.

Since Tom Beauchamp had come with the news of his arrest she had been like a thing possessed. 'He had provoked the King,' Warwick had told her, 'by questioning his treatment of the rebels.' She had managed a faint smile at that. How like Hal to risk himself for a handful of peasants who meant nothing to him. But did they? Perhaps she also had misjudged him there. A man of the people, she had heard it said, and it was true enough that there had been little discontent in his earldom during the Hurling Time. But the people could not release him from Windsor's dungeons.

She rose impatiently at the sound of the King's boyish laughter coming through the doors. What was de la Pole about to let him keep her waiting so long? Then she bit her lip, remembering that it was she who had cause to be grateful. All day she had roamed the Court, humbling herself to rake up old forgotten favours in a vain attempt to find someone to speak for Northumberland.

There she had seen at first hand the measure of their fear of Lancaster; Warwick she could count on, yet the King was more than wary of any above the rank of knight. De la Pole had been more difficult and hard of access, and she'd had to bribe her way to him through a chancery clerk. Yet he was a northerner and honest, one of the few men around the King who would speak without fear or favour. She turned distractedly as a clerk touched her arm. De la Pole was beckoning her from the chamber door.

She kept her eyes turned to the floor until she reached the King then sank in low and humble obeisance. She laid her hand upon his jewelled shoe. 'My gracious liege,' she said and saw him smile.

The gesture pleased him and he raised her up. He knew why she had come and his former irritation was soothed somewhat by her manner. Already he regretted the outburst that had seemed to range him too openly on Lancaster's side. Northumberland's only crime had been one of disrespect to the King, in his eyes far more heinous than refusing Lancaster admission to Berwick. His show of temperament had allowed Lancaster to take the bit firmly between his teeth. He had called for Northumberland's arraignment before Parliament and Richard was not so sure, King or no, that he could stop it now.

'My liege.' The Countess's warm and somehow sensuous voice released him from these unpleasant thoughts. She raised her eyes, glazed with meekness. 'We are so isolated in the north. All through the rebellion we were plagued with rumours of Your Grace's safety and welfare. His Grace of Lancaster had been a month in Scotland concluding the truce and when he came to Berwick there were certain Scots knights in his train.' She paused, unable to resist a final thrust at Lancaster. 'In view of the uncertainty and talk of plots against Your Grace, my lord thought it better to err on the side of caution till we had more certain news.'

She saw the angry flush creep into Richard's cheeks and lowered her eyes as if she had looked too brightly on the sun. 'Our brother Sir Thomas Percy told us of your courage and daring against the rebels, Sire. The people love you, Your Grace, and if Northumberland dared to speak against their punishment it was because he would not see that love destroyed by over-zealous counsellors who act in your name.'

Richard swallowed the lie like a greedy fish, his vacillating mind rejecting all that did not please him. Yes, he could see that. It was not his fault that his officers had read more into his orders than he had intended. Woodstock had been too savage with the Essex men, and perhaps even Tresilian himself had gone too far with his merciless execution of the rebels at St Albans. Northumberland had always kept himself to himself, not always meddling and calling him to account as Lancaster did. De la Pole spoke readily enough of him and Walworth declared him a stout man. His smile widened, the gracious condescending smile of one about to bestow a great favour. Northumberland would have to face Parliament, he could do nothing about that, but he could release him. Earl Warwick and de la Pole were willing to stand surety for him and that was good enough for him. Yes, he would let him go and add the joy of Lancaster's fury to the gratitude of Northumberland and his Countess. Still smiling, he beckoned to his clerk to bring his seal.

Once outside the royal presence she breathed freely. So much meekness did not become her and for a few moments she allowed her contempt for that arrogant young popinjay to overcome here. But she had what she had come for, Northumberland's release, signed, sealed and witnessed and clutched firmly in her hand. Tomorrow he would be free again.

She went quickly down the ill-lit passage and paused in the deep embrasure that showed the grey strip of the Thames backed by brittle winter trees. The darkness came swiftly at this time of year, the grey sunless days merging into night almost unnoticed. She loved the night and the deep engulfing silence, the shadows and the candlelight that stripped ten years from her age. She thought of Hal and wondered if he thought of her.

She turned her head at a familiar voice, too distant to catch the words but clear enough for her to know it was Harry. She heard his soft intimate laughter and then another voice that drove her back into the shadows. What did Harry want with Bolingbroke?

She watched him come toward her. How strange to see that arrogant walk slowed by stealth—or was it shame? He was smiling and humming softly to himself. Her face grew white with anger. How dare he smile and sing while his father languished in Windsor!

She stepped out and barred his way. She saw the smile fade and the dark colour creep into his face. 'Something amuses you, Harry?' she said sharply. 'Something my lord of Bolingbroke has said?'

Harry felt the guilty colour creep into his cheeks. Yet what had he to be ashamed of? He had not even sought Bolingbroke out. He had come to him while he had sat alone and inconsolable over his father's arrest. The door had closed quietly behind him, so quietly that Harry had not even realized that he was in the room till he had spoken his name.

It had been a long time since they had exchanged more than a few words, a long time since those inseparable days that had ended so abruptly.

'It's not our quarrel,' Bolingbroke had said in answer to his silence. 'We need not be enemies because our fathers are.'

Easily said, but where did the dividing line between new loyalty and old friendship begin and end? He smiled faintly. 'I think that they will make it our quarrel, Henry, whether we like it or not.'

Bolingbroke came and sat beside him. 'We swore eternal friendship once. Remember, Harry—you, Richard and I, the inviolate triumvirate, the earthly trinity, bound until death?'

Harry smiled, remembering the childish vow. 'Richard forgot,' he said. 'When he became King he had no need of us.'

'He has de Vere now,' Bolingbroke said with a flash of open jealousy. 'He has given us up for de Vere.'

Harry threw a curious glance at him. He had changed, grown older than his years, the solemn cautious streak in his nature overshadowing the humour and daring that had kept them close in those early years.

'Shall we swear again, Harry, the two of us?' Bolingbroke's pale eyes held him like a vice. 'Whatever our sires do to each other, it will not affect us. We shall always be friends. Bound until death.'

So harmless—a childhood pledge made new by the bond of chivalry: where was the shame or guilt in that?

249

Maud's voice probed coldly from the shadows. 'What can you have to say to Henry Bolingbroke that needs must be said behind closed doors?'

He glared at her in open dislike. He hated her for the plainness that shadowed his father's magnificence and, more, because she had the place that had once been his mother's.

'Nothing that concerns you, madam,' he said hotly.

'It concerns me that you consort with our enemies.'

'Henry Bolingbroke is not our enemy!' he shouted.

'His father is, and therefore so must he be till he has proved otherwise.'

'Well, he has proved it to me. Bolingbroke is not like his father.'

'And no more are you like yours, that you can laugh and exchange fair words with Bolingbroke while your own sire is confined on his father's word.' She came out of the shadows, her face white and pinched against the black gown. 'Your father would have thought more of honour.'

'You speak of honour? You, who sold yourself to my father like a sack of wheat?' He snatched at the cloak which bore her crest. 'There is your bill of sale, madam! All that you were worth to him or ever will be!'

He left her trembling against the wall. '*All that you were worth to him or ever will be.*' Not true, not true, there was more; there had to be more. The tears welled up in her tired eyes; the King's warrant crackled beneath her clenched hand. She turned away and stared out into the comforting darkness. There was no more and she knew it.

She stood in the dark doorway, out of the chill wind that ruffled the sheen of her furs and laid ice upon her cheek. She watched him come through the archway, tall and erect, that proud unassailable head turned up toward the wintry sun. De la Pole and Warwick walked by his side and he dropped his head to catch Warwick's dry murmur and laughed. They came on across the entrance yard white with glistening frost. She saw him look about him, his eyes roving from face to face like a questing hawk till they came to rest on Harry. The first face he looked for, the first hand he clasped. Nothing for her, except an indifferent smile. Behind the broad span of his shoulders she saw Harry's proud and jubilant smile.

Elizabeth's clear and virginal voice filled the solar where she sat at her lectern. She grew fairer each day; the childish roundness had fined down to show the delicate shape of perfect bones and the hair that cloaked her to her knees was like fire in the sun. Yet there was still that air of aloofness about her, that air of untouchability that the others felt and because of it left her alone when they could.

Maud sighed and turned her attention back to the steward's accounts: all ink blots and scratched wording and some dubious figures that did not fit her tally. Five hundred pounds of wax with vermilion and turpentine for red wax—£40. One thousand pounds of tallow wax and the same of Paris for candles—£12 14s. For linen cloth for the Earl's chaplain—£43 17s. For fifty-two tuns of claret wine for the Earl's house at York—£52 15s. For six barrels of sturgeon—£19. ... She pressed her lips together and laid a mark against it: too much when sturgeon could be had in York for a mere £2 a barrel. She supposed it to be another of the steward's frequent perquisites. Fifty ells of blue silk for livery. ... One hundred pieces of samite, mixed, for gowns. ...

She paused and glanced again at the slim figure curled like a cat in the sun. Elizabeth was fast outgrowing all her gowns, even her best of fine Italian brocade was strained at the seams. Not that she complained, unlike Philippa and Bessy; she would have worn her gowns till they turned to rags. Maud laid down her quill pensively. The sun was tempting, slanting in wide beams through the open casement and falling just short of her feet. All was warmth and slumberous air; Warkworth had that special quality, as if the sun itself was impregnated in the golden stone. She rose and looked again at Elizabeth. Her head was bent over the inevitable manuscript. Elizabeth would not miss her. Elizabeth had need of none but herself.

Outside, the air was sweet with the smell of fresh scythed corn and near the church, where the masons worked, full of whirling golden dust that lay in her mouth like sand. It was a year since the revolt, less than that since she had wheedled Hal's release from the King. She'd had some thanks for that, a softening of his manner that was almost affection, and for a little while she'd had some hope. But all too easily they had slipped back into the old ways. He had little time to spare and there was always Harry between them.

He'd gone to Parliament in the spring, arrayed and accoutred like a prince, with five hundred armed men at his back. The Londoners had cheered him through the streets and to add insult to injury had refused Lancaster and his army admittance when he came a day later, forcing him to camp on open ground outside the walls. Richard had welcomed him warmly, though less so when he saw the size and magnificence of the force he had brought with him. Parliament, packed with Lancaster's men, had judged him guilty of insult to the Duke. The King had seen to it that the punishment was harmless: a public apology to Lancaster that Northumberland had delivered with such largesse and warmth of amusement that its receiver was left more insulted than before.

She herself had been left to her own devices. She'd found a passive contentment in the care of the children. The sisters Philippa and Bessy were wed to Ralph and Thomas now and already pestering for their own households; Mary was betrothed to John, Lord Ros. That was joy and sadness come together, for Maud had grown more than fond of Mary. It would be a hard day for her when she lost Mary.

She looked round at the tall ring of towers. It was the first time she had been to Warkworth, while Alnwick was being cleansed and sweetened for the winter. A year's neglect had done nothing to dim its beauty. The tall new-made towers sharp and clean against the sky, the great hall that could house a thousand men and behind it the blue smoking warmth of the kitchens. And the new church, rising again out of the green heart of the bailey, had filled the shuttered rooms with insidious dust that had taken her a month to dispel. But no amount of beating and scouring could rid Warkworth of Margaret Neville. She had died here and was buried here; she lived in the golden stone and was the heart of the great church. Maud moved nearer the tall lancet windows that watched her like empty eyes. The roof was open to the sky and funnelled the sunlight into the half-finished nave where the whirling stone dust lay thick and glittering as frost. She watched a mason set his punch to a column; the chips of yellow stone flew like chaff and out of nowhere a flower bloomed, the long flat petals of a marguerite.

She turned back, her feet heavy on the wide steps. She paused at the foot of the stairs and then abruptly went along the dark passage that led to the old chapel. It was dark and the air was heavy with the smell of long-snuffed candles, peopled with the shadowy figures of saints. She went to the altar and stared down at the dusty slab that lay behind it: so plain, so unadorned, with nothing to say who lay there. Then she whirled at a sound from the door. Elizabeth stood there smiling, her hair like an intrusive flame in the gloom.

'She is not there,' Elizabeth said simply and smiled again, that strange unearthly smile that raised the hair on Maud's neck.

'She is where my lord has laid her, in the hermitage down by the river.'

The sun was warm upon her back and brought a beading of sweat to the downy lip of the page who rowed her downstream. She stood for a long time staring at the narrow doorway cut into the face of the cliff before she plucked up the courage to go in. It was cold and damp inside and after the sunlight it seemed dark, despite the tall candles that burned at each corner of the effigy. She stared round at the smooth white walls of the chamber that ran back under the rock. There was a small doorway that led to another room; she heard the faint drone of plainchant from its darkness.

She went and looked down at the recumbent figure that almost filled the chapel: Margaret, as she had been all those years ago at Harbottle; pale, perfect, incorruptible. The long sensuous body was draped in cloth of gold, her small feet rested on the horned head of the Neville bull.

Maud felt the angry tears well up in her eyes. Had he mourned her so much that he'd had to build a shrine to her where he could come in secret? Was this where he came when he could no longer stand the sight of her? How drab and ugly a comparison she must have made to Margaret's remembered loveliness. Did he still come here? Did he still weep?

She gave a little startled cry as she heard a movement behind her. A priest stood quietly watching her. 'Can I help you, my daughter?' he asked.

'No.' She looked back at the effigy. 'No', she said again. 'No one can help me now.'

Elizabeth ran wildly through the long grass, heedless of the dew that drenched her slippers or the coiling brambles that tore at her skirts. The wind blew her hair in a fiery cloud; she loved the wind, the harsh unrelenting north wind that only drew breath to blow again stronger. It sent the scudding clouds racing ahead to plunge the valley into sudden shadow. Like her, the wind was answerable to none.

She sank down in the hollow of trees where the sun never came. It was dark and cool and the trailing branches blotted out the bland, smooth moorland and the grey hills that rose one behind the other, like a mirror image. It was her secret place, where she, Elizabeth, was queen. The sun pricked vainly at the clustering screen of leaves. She thought of her brothers Roger and Edmund, squirming under Arundel's wardship, and of her sister Philippa, betrothed out of hand to his son. She thought of the silver valley of the Usk that rose on Black Mountain and ran down to Caerlon where the prince magician Merlin had been born. In her mind's eye she saw the mountains; the Beacons, Pen Y Fan and Long Mountain, their flanks clothed in tumbling green. And Ludlow with its soaring towers, the angry peaks of Wales at its back, the gentle roll of the Shropshire March at its feet.

She lay back against the mouldering leaves and closed her eyes against the prick of tears. There would be no more Roger, no more Edmund or Philippa with her foolish merry face; no more of Wales and its wild dangerous beauty. She opened her eyes abruptly, wide empty eyes that had no true colour of their own and stole it from the thing they looked upon. They were green now and flecked with yellow points of distant sunlight.

Above her the green canopy of leaves tossed in the wind. The lower branches were grey and leafless through lack of sun, twisted and locked into strange ugly shapes. She breathed the deep and reverent quiet. As if in homage to her presence the birds had stilled their bickering and sat with feathers ruffled against the chill of silence. She smiled. They knew what others only felt. She was Elizabeth, of the devil's breed Plantagenet, descended from the Welsh princes of Powys.

She hummed an ancient song, taught to her by the Welsh woman Morganna who had raised her. She had taught her many things; of herbs and potions that could reduce a strong man to a whimpering child and of the fairy folk who lived beneath the rock of Snowdon and danced on midsummer's eve in the Giant's Ring. It was she who had seen and fostered Elizabeth's gift, cherishing the childish foresight until it had become the power to see beyond mortal shapes; the ancient power of the enchanter Merlin. Morganna had told her that she was Merlin's child. Again that cold little smile touched her mouth and she closed her eyes anew, revelling in the solitude that had once been forced upon her and was now hers by choice. She needed none. Philippa and Bessy she despised, and Mary she pitied. The Countess Maud was possessed of too sharp an intellect to be pitied and perhaps if there was any she had respect for it was her. Northumberland she feared, and did not know why. Perhaps because she knew him to be the only one outside her influence. And Harry, who treated her with the same vague amiability that he bestowed on Philippa and Bessy, as if she were a sister to him instead of his wife. They were alike in pride and vanity, save that hers was tempered with a soft cunning and a knowledge of things that would have made his blood run cold if he had known.

Near to her hand a spider crawled across a dry leaf and dropped on a silver thread into his web. She watched the fly, no larger than a mote of dust, hovering on trembling wings above the dew-hung silk. Then blindly, as if it knew no other course, it plunged into the heart of the web where the spider sat curled and waiting. She smiled and dashed the web with a swift movement of her hand. So it would be with Harry when the time came.

———

It had not rained for a month and even the bay tree was withering in the heat, the leaves brittle slivers of dusty green that scattered at the touch of Maud's hand. The earth was dry and iron hard, the budding jasmine shrivelled before the first flower had shown, the clumps of sweet cicely burnt to bare brown twigs. By the wall, where the sun did not reach, white marguerites drooped on parched stems.

Maud's gown raised wisps of smoking dust from the ground as she walked the narrow winding path of the pleasaunce. She looked down at the imagined coolness of the river; it was at low ebb and showed a green-slimed line along its banks, and the Bow Burn on the east side that fed the castle well had dried to a brown trickle of steaming pebbles. If it did not rain soon they would be short of water. The sky held no promise, clear and blinding bright, the early morning drift of vaporous cloud burnt up by the sun. All was dry and parched and slowed to crawling pace by the burning heat.

She turned her back on the glaring fields and felt the prickle of sweat beneath her gown. It would be cooler within, where the solid walls gave perpetual shade, but she dreaded the thought of that great empty hall where every footfall sounded loud as a thunderclap and a hundred men barely filled a corner. There were none who needed her now. Mary was gone, blissfully happy with her new husband John Ros. Thomas and Ralph were with their father at Carlisle, and Bessy and Philippa merely added to her irritation. Of Hal she saw little. She did not wait on his coming now. There was no joy in the sight and sound of him as there once had been—only pain and the renewal of loneliness. Elizabeth knew, and she was beginning to hate the feel of those cool river-deep eyes upon her. Did it show so much? The agony of her longing, the desperate need? Perhaps only to Elizabeth.

All her former defences had gone. The wit and intellect that had been her salvation all those years with Umfraville were blunted in Hal's presence. She had acquired the fatal habit of obedience and adhered blindly to his wishes. She trailed from manor to manor as the season demanded, her quick agile mind starved of news other than that the steward's wife at York had been brought to bed of another daughter or that the wine at Rothbury had turned sour.

She walked back along the eastern wall. The grudging breeze fanned her cheek and brought the smell of new bread and cinnamon from the open door of the bakehouse. From the constable's tower she heard the sound of laughter and the click of dice, and louder the whine and yelp of the dogs fretting in the heat. Old Siward growled softly at her arm as she passed. He was old now and slowly dying. He had never ceased to pine for Bebba. The bitch had been so badly mauled by wolves that it had seemed kinder to put her out of her pain. They had only been able to save one of the pups she had carried. Hal had named him Ceolwulf after the ancient King of Northumbria.

She paused a moment in the tunnel vault of the gatehouse. After the sunlight it was black and cold, the whisper of her breath loud in the narrow airless void. A blast of damp stinking air and the scuttle of rats came from the grille of the dungeon pits. She smiled wryly and passed out into the sunlight of the courtyard. It did not need iron bars to make her feel a prisoner at Alnwick.

In the solar Elizabeth sat curled like a serpent on the window ledge, reading aloud.

> 'Once again the White Dragon shall rise up and will invite over a daughter of Germany. And little gardens will be stocked again with foreign seed and the Red Dragon will pine away at the far end of the pool.'

Philippa lifted her head from the small shivering dog that snuffled on her lap. 'There are no such things as dragons. Even I know that.'

Elizabeth stared in cool resentment at her sister-in-law's vacuous face. 'The dragons are symbolic,' she said stiffly. 'An allegory. See—as here.' She turned back a page of the stiff little book.

> 'In the day of the lion, gold shall be squeezed from the lily flower and the nettle. And silver shall flow from the hooves of lowing cattle.'

She smiled. 'Merlin prophesied this. 'The lion was my great-grandfather King Edward, and the lilies are the French, the nettles the Scots.'

'What are the dragons then?' Bessy picked mournfully at a loose thread that hung from her over-tight bodice.

Elizabeth smiled with heavy patience. 'That is in the future,' she said. 'We shall not know till the time comes.'

'What good is a prophecy if you do not know what it means till it has happened?' Philippa objected, and went back to caressing the dog who yelped at the pressure of her heavy hands.

Elizabeth shut the book with a contemptuous snap as Maud came into the room. She watched her for a little while as she took up her embroidery, then bent her head again to the book.

Maud's needle darted without pause through the detested altar cloth. She heard the distant toll of the Vespers bell from the abbey and still the sun clung defiantly to the lip of the sky. A page came to light needless candles and smiled boldly at Elizabeth, stooping to retrieve the little book that had slid unnoticed from her lap. Maud watched him as he moved across the room, and saw how his covert glance never left her face. Elizabeth would have no lack of admirers even if Harry was too blind to see what he had. She thrust her needle deep into the strip of white linen, thinking of the last time she had seen him. So handsome, so perfect, lording it over his brothers and they hanging on his every word and look. They were not together often and for that she was grateful. She found it hard to bear his enmity, and worse, she feared he might transmit it to his father.

She glanced up and found Elizabeth's eyes upon her. 'Why do you stare Elizabeth?' she said sharply. 'Have none told you that it is ill-mannered to stare?'

Elizabeth did not remove her gaze. 'I would not stare if there were naught to see,' she said softly.

'And what do you see? A plain ugly woman who was wed for her lands. Are you pitying me Elizabeth? Is that why you stare?' Her voice was trembling with anger and pain. How tired she was of the knowing looks, of the covert jests on the fact that she slept alone, of always giving and receiving nothing.

Elizabeth said, 'No, my lady, that is not what I see, but it is what you see. I pity you not for what you are but for what you think you are.'

Maud stared bitterly at the lovely face. What would she ever know of loneliness and rejection? Even now, Elizabeth could have had a hundred men at her feet if she chose. She rose and flung the altar cloth to the floor. 'I have had other opinions than my own,' she said grimly as she went towards the door. 'Two husbands and my own mirror have told me all I need to know.'

In her chamber she sat alone, closing her ears to the timorous knocks of her women against the closed door and the whispered conjecture of the silence. Her cheeks were mottled red by the sun, her eyes swollen with the tears that ran down her face and into the lines around her mouth. Old, ugly and useless—that's what she saw, that's what they all saw. With a little scream she tore off the restraining headdress and dragged the pins savagely from her hair. The gown of amber silk ripped loudly under her clawing hands and she tore it strip by strip from her body and ground its shining softness beneath her feet. She was trembling as if from the cold, she wanted to scream but the sound stuck fast in her throat, smothered by tears. She stared wildly around the chamber, at the dark ceiling of banded oak, the costly hangings and the tapestry that swung on tenterhooks, creaking beneath its own jewelled weight. Against the wall stood the sandalwood press that held her finest linen, another held her timid mouse-like gowns. The great bed took up almost half the room; silver fish leapt against a sea of blue velvet and swam incongruously beside the Percy lion. Her 'bill of sale', Harry had said. Her receipt for Prudoe and Langley and the vast estates of Cockermouth.

The candles grew suddenly bright against the swift descending dark. The thought calmed her, she loved the night, the anonymity of darkness, the oblivion of sleep. Slowly she rose and went to the window. The sun had finally set, leaving the sky drenched with purple shadow. The air was so still and heavy, held between the last of the long day and the coolness of night. She closed her eyes and thought of Hal, wild shameful thoughts that sent the blood pounding in her face. Yet she could indulge herself in that, it was all she was likely to have of him. Once it had been enough to be in sight of him, to hear his voice, to meet his every need as best she could, until she had realized that he had no need of her; no need of any except of his beloved Harry. And she had waited on him like a begging dog. Oh, where was pride? He must have known. He must have seen it in her eyes each time he looked at her, and cringed at the thought. She closed her eyes against fresh tears and lifted her face to the whisper of the night breeze. She did not hear the gentle knocking on her door or the creak of its opening.

'My lady?'

She spun round, anger dilating her eyes. Elizabeth stood within the door, her hair blowing in the sucking draft. Maud snatched a robe from the carved stool by the bed, furiously aware of her wild dishevelled hair festooned with silver pins and the trampled gown that lay between them. 'What do you want?' she snapped.

Elizabeth closed the door. 'I wondered if I might sleep here tonight?'

'What for?' Maud thrust her bare arms into the velvet coat. 'What is wrong with your own chamber.'

'I am afraid.'

'Afraid?' Maud came close and tilted Elizabeth's face toward her. 'Of what?'

Elizabeth shook her head. Her eyes were dark and shadowed with unknown fear. Her face was pale and for once she looked the child that she was.

Maud touched a strand of the fiery hair. A child, who had need of her, perhaps only this once. Tomorrow Elizabeth would have recovered from whatever nightmare had driven her from her bed; she'd be wrapped again in the cocoon of secrecy and aloofness that protected her from a hostile world. But tonight she had need of her; perhaps tonight they had need of each other. She wrapped her arms round the narrow shoulders and drew her close. She realized suddenly that Elizabeth's flesh was as cold as death.

They were burning her alive. She could feel the searing heat upon her limbs, her lungs were choked with smoke, her eyes blinded by the bright glare of fire. Then Elizabeth was pounding her awake, shaking her so fiercely that she screamed in panic. The chamber glowed with a fiery light that turned the hangings black and stained Elizabeth's face like blood.

She flung herself from the bed and stumbled to the window. A sheet of flame leapt into a vermilion sky and rolled like a tidal-wave across the bone-dry fields. She strained her eyes through the rain of burning chaff and saw a black undulating shape moving apace of the flames toward Alnwick. It took her a few moments to realize they were horsemen.

She ran, dragging Elizabeth behind her, kicking her sleeping attendants awake and screaming like an eelwife at the pages who slept outside the door. 'The chapel bell!' She hauled the boy to his feet and thrust him toward the stair. 'Sound the chapel bell!'

They assembled in the great vaulted hall. Philippa was screeching like a butchered pig and the four chaplains sent up a chorus of discordant prayer. Yet it was Elizabeth's face that struck fear. Stripped of that unnerving calm it filled Maud with more panic than all of Philippa's wailing.

The steward's voice was soothing and meant to reassure. 'You're safe enough here my lady. 'Tis no more than a raid. They'll burn their way around us and be content with that.'

So lightly said—as if the ruined harvest and the burning town were of no account. 'Can we get word to the Earl?' she asked faintly.

The steward shook his head. 'No man could get through, my lady. We are only a hundred men. All we can do is wait till they pass on.'

She sank down in the chair he had placed at the edge of the dias. Elizabeth sat mute and still upon the step, her eyes colourless as glass. Philippa and Bessy were huddled among the women. She gnawed at her lip, listening to the thundering feet, the raised and strident voices of the guards, the grumbling chains of the inner portcullis being lowered. The heat was a physical presence now, consuming the air so that her throat burned and she found it hard to breath. She rose abruptly, holding out her hand to Elizabeth. 'Come,' she said. 'We do not have to suffocate to death.'

If anything the air outside was less breathable and whirling thick with smoke and sparks. The half-moon towers of the keep glowed red with reflected flame and spurts of fire licked greedily at the wooden roof of the bakehouse. Holding Elizabeth close

Maud crossed the bailey, darting between running men laden with arrows and grooms struggling with terrified horses. New sounds arose to strike fresh horror: she heard the high whine of a scream quickly bitten off, the clamour of voices and pummelling fists outside the postern gate. She caught at a guard's sleeve. 'Open the gate, the town's people are trying to get in.'

The guard shook her off with a look. 'Aye, my lady, and half the Scots force with them.'

He left her staring at the trembling gate. She saw it heave and strain against the heavy bars. A hand thrust itself beneath the iron spikes, a woman's hand, short and rough, scrabbling vainly against the stone. Then it lay still, the outspread fingers dabbling in the blood that flowed like a slick of oil beneath the gate. She turned her head away, fighting down the nausea that rose in her throat. She sharpened her voice to call for the captain of the guard but none heard her. She had no authority here. In this place pity and compassion were as useless as blunted arrows.

She stood transfixed by the screams and sobbing. She heard a dull rushing of air in her ears and a man's headless body lay at her feet, his broken bones inert upon the flags. The ragged stump of his neck still pumped gouts of black blood and collared the coarse homespun of his shirt with red. She felt the hard hand of the steward beneath her elbow. She heard his voice, distant, exasperated. 'Come away my lady. There's naught you can do here.'

From the roof of the Ravine Tower she relived it all. The black deserted fields that still glowed red beneath their blanket of ash, the smouldering shell of the town, the narrow streets choked with burning thatch. In her mind's eye she could see the bodies heaped outside the postern door. The Scots still rode around the walls, yelling their strange unintelligible clan cries. On the ramp a chieftain stood, the eagle's feather in his bonnet straight as an arrow. She saw his thick bare legs clamped hard to the shaggy sides of his horse, his broad shoulders swathed in plaid. He was laughing, his mouth wide and black against his beard. It was almost as if she had loosed the arrow herself, so great was the force of her hatred then. She saw it plough a furrow into his broad chest. He jerked back in the saddle, then fell heavily against his horse's neck. Smiling, she watched him slip to the ground. She wondered if he was laughing still.

She sank down in the shadow of the wall. Elizabeth was still awake, her arms clasped round her knees. Maud slid an arm round her cold shoulders. 'Was this what you were afraid of?' she asked softly.

Elizabeth nodded and closed her eyes. Sometimes she cursed her powers. It only meant that she suffered twice as long as others.

The fields still smouldered and drifted grey smoke a week later when Hal rode down from Carlisle. The town was a ruin of blackened stone, the stumps of walls leaning together like broken teeth. And not only Alnwick, every village in a line from the Border had been stripped and fired with such meticulous care; nothing had been left standing, no blade of corn, even the meanest of hovels had been razed to the ground. All was scoured and picked clean with such thoroughness that he could not help but lay it at the Douglas's door.

The castle wards were still crammed with survivors who looked at him with dirty expectant faces. There would be more to come; not a day passed without it brought a huddle of starved and terrified folk out of hiding in the forest. There was little food, and water was rarer than wine.

He had sent Maud and the children to safety at Prudoe and still his conscience pricked him that he had not even asked how they had fared. He had heavier things on his mind now. He had heard that very day that Berwick had fallen and now his brother Tom was come with worse news. He had been judged guilty of treason for the loss of Berwick.

He smiled into his brother's solemn face. Dear Tom, always the bearer of ill news, his messenger of disaster. The thought passed swiftly through his mind—Lancaster's man once and could be again? But no, Tom was the King's man now, chamberlain of the royal household and high in Richard's favour.

Tom said, 'Lancaster convened a parliament as soon as he heard. All Lancastrians, primed and ready to scream for your head. His brother Woodstock is backing him to the hilt, and

Arundel too. You were arraigned, tried and judged before you ever left Carlisle.'

'And the King?' One never knew which side of the fence Richard would come down on, save that it would be the one closest to his own interests.

'The King refused to sign your death warrant for my sake. He could do no more than that, while Berwick is in enemy hands.'

Hal resisted the desire to laugh. Could it be true? Tried and convicted on such a flimsy charge? He was not the first man to lose a royal fortress to the enemy, but twice in two years, that's what counted against him. Neglect of his duties against the weal of the kingdom. He had seen men fall for less when the prize was great enough and his earldom was bait enough for men like Woodstock and Arundel.

Then Tom said, 'They have taken the Countess and the lady Elizabeth.'

'Taken?' His skin pricked with sudden cold. 'Taken where?'

'To Leicester—as surety for your surrender.'

Rage and anger seethed within him but his lips were still turned in the semblance of a smile. 'How long do I have?'

'Not long enough, Hal. Parliament meets again in two weeks. I doubt if I could hold Lancaster off any longer. You'll need more than that to retake Berwick without help. You are an outlaw now, Hal. None will ride with you save your own men.'

'Not even you, Tom?' Hal's eyes shone with sudden malice.

His brother flushed. 'No, not even I,' he flung back angrily. 'I'll be more use to you at Court keeping Lancaster and his pack at bay.'

Hal looked away. It was strange how he could never bring himself to trust Tom; after all these years the distrust was still there, not far beneath the surface of their outward amity. But this time it was without cause. Tom had done his best and the bond between them had been strong enough for him to come and give him warning. He touched his arm in mute apology. 'So you will Tom,' he said. 'So you will.' He smiled. 'Get to it then. Perhaps we'll beat him yet.'

He called him back before he reached the door. 'If it should go against me, Tom—' He paused, unwilling to say the words less he should tempt Fate too strongly. 'If it should go against me, you'll look to Maud and the boys for me?'

By midnight he had reached Berwick and camped his men a mile from the town. For the second time in as many years he viewed the impregnable walls but this time he was alone. There would be no levies to come rallying to his banner this time.

The King rose, slowed to an old man's gait by the weight of the jewelled robe that stood out from his long limbs as stiff as coat armour. His hair gleamed and his beard was carefully oiled and dressed in clustering curls around his mouth. He held his neck stiffly, above the chafing rubies that edged his high collar; it gave him the look of an inquisitive bird.

He stretched out a languid white hand and took the parchment from his chancellor, de la Pole. He read the brief clipped sentences and his petulant mouth eased into a smile. So Northumberland had retaken Berwick—and in such a manner, bribing his way in to the hefty tune of two thousand pounds. And what pleased him most: out of his own pocket too. Richard laughed outright. He liked that. All the more because it was the second time he had cheated Lancaster.

He paused, waiting while the pages who trailed in his wake lifted his finery clear of the low couch; one bore his wine, another a bowl of rosewater, the last held the velvet cushion on which rested his crown. He took the heavy goblet between his long fastidious fingers, sipping it delicately while he mused on the merits of a man like Northumberland. Not so pliant as his brother Sir Thomas, who watched him now with eyes that spoke of more than a willingness to serve. Richard was naturally wary of the power of independence that lords like Northumberland wielded, yet Lancaster's persecution might drive Percy into a corner. If he could be brought round, he would be the obvius weapon to use against Lancaster.

He smiled contentedly at the small and intimate gathering. His bride Anne, young and plump and biddable. She inspired no passion in him, but then few women did. She was plainer than he would have liked, and dark, but there was compensation in that she made all the better foil for his fairness. Beside him sat his well-beloved Robert, his prop and confidant. More than a friend, more than a brother. Only Robert understood him and shared his bitter resentment at the repression of his royal dignity. It was Robert who soothed and comforted him after the violent rages that left him so weak and vulnerable. Yet he was learning. If his council thought him content with with the sop of Kingship, then let them. Oh, if he shouted loud enough he could make himself heard, but he had found a better way. His power was growing, slowly, subtly, almost without any being aware of it. Archbishop Neville was his now and Scrope almost so. Michael de la Pole was chancellor and served as a buffer between him and the stingy grumbling Commons. His Queen had brought him a ready source of untapped power in the multitude of needy Bohemian noblemen who had accompanied her to England; penniless and dependent entirely on his favour.

Lancaster's song was almost ended. The first note of discord had already been heard. He and his brother Woodstock were at odds over the marriage of Lancaster's son Bolingbroke to the younger de Bohun girl. Woodstock had been so sure of all the de Bohun estates falling to him. It was the sole reason he had married Eleanor de Bohun. Her younger sister had been content in her convent, leaving Eleanor sole heiress, until Lancaster had dragged her from her cloister and wed her overnight to his son. Richard smiled happily. Woodstock was not a man easily crossed and there was no telling what might happen when thieves fell out.

Lancaster still hankered after the Spanish conquest. Parliament never met but he pestered them for leave to raise an army. Grudgingly Richard had given consent for a volunteer force but Lancaster needed more than volunteers. He needed an army and only a king could sanction that. He gnawed at his red underlip. The temptation to be rid of his uncle was almost too great. He longed to be free, he longed for the day when his every word and deed did not have to be seconded by Lancaster. But he saw the danger in letting him rise so high. He might style himself King of Castile, but it was a far cry from the reality. Once it was true, once he *was* king of Castile, he would be his equal. Might he not then cast about for further conquests? It would not be such a long step then to England's throne.

Richard set his teeth together against the old shiver of fear, yet it was not so strong now. Northumberland's self-reprieve had lessened his dread of Lancaster and shown him as less than invincible. Could he not do more? He, the King, from whom by right all power should come? And he needed a diversion, something to placate the Commons who were forever whining about the cost of his household and the Queen's lack of dowry. His thoughts turned back to Northumberland. The Earl had pressed for an army against the Scots, as Lancaster had for Castile. A show of favour to Northumberland would be as good as a slap in the face to Lancaster. Yes, his irresolute mind grasped eagerly at the new idea—a war against Scotland and he, its leader. He closed his eyes on the image of himself in damascened and gilded armour.

Ceolwulf growled softly at his approach, then subsided into a joyful whining at the sound of his voice. Hal paused, halted by the sleeping silence of the house, and the dog padded eagerly toward him, dropping his grey muzzle to his hand. It was all the welcome he had. All else was darkness.

A single cresset burned in the stripped and naked hall and showed the walls dark and patched where the hangings had been. He stared around him. So Lancaster had anticipated his fall to this extent. For the first time in weeks a smile touched Hal's lips. It would make the reparation all the sweeter.

He sat on the hard wooden bench by the door. The escort of knights he'd sent to bring Maud from Leicester slept by the empty hearth. He did not disturb them. He had need of nothing except rest. He sat very still, wrapped in the void of silence. His limbs were cramped and cold yet still he did not move. He watched the shadows trembling in the corners; his own, black and crooked on the far wall, and others, dark threatening shapes that moved with the leap of the cresset's flame—the demons of his mind come out to taunt him. He had come so close to disaster, and the memory of those agonizing days and nights outside the walls of Berwick, when he had begged and cajoled and finally bribed his way to possession, still raised a sweat on his hands. He closed his eyes in weariness. He felt sick and tired—and old. The afterthought made him raise his lids in mild surprise. It was the first time he had ever noticed the drag of the years. He was forty-two.

He braced his hands against the wooden bench and pushed himself slowly to his feet. The silver spurs at his heels rang softly and brought the hounds to their feet again, the fog of their breath clouding the cold air. They watched him with soft melancholy eyes as he went out into the dark passage.

At the head of the stairs a strip of warming light showed beneath her chamber door. She was still awake—waiting for him? He laid his foot on the creaking stair. Strangely, it had been her face before him all those days at Berwick, her voice whispering in his mind, driving him on till he would have beggared himself to buy her free. The vision of her, despoiled and dispossessed because of him, had added to the crushing guilt of his neglect. He had taken all she had and given her nothing. Yet what had he ever had to give? He was nothing but an empty shell himself.

Maud opened the door to his hesitant knock. Her hair was loose and warm as amber wine in the firelight. He stared at her for a long time before he closed the door behind him. He watched her as she set a jug of wine to warm by the fire. The silk robe clung softly to her limbs and showed the gentle curve of her breasts.

'You and the little maids were treated well?' he asked roughly.

'Well enough, my lord,' she answered lightly. It sounded trite and unfeeling but she had longed so much for the sight of him that now it was come his presence stripped her of all reasoning thought. And what was there to say about the three long weeks she had spent at Leicester, waiting for word of him and hearing nothing but whispered chilling rumour? Fool that she was—she had thought only of him, suffering agonies of imagination as to his fate. Elizabeth had been her only comfort, quelling the worst of her fears with those calm green eyes, feeding her the reassurances that she had wanted to hear. As always, she had been right. They were free and he was with her again—and so close that she trembled at the very nearness of him.

He sat on the edge of the stripped and naked bed. A scrap of torn silk fluttered close to his cheek where the hangings had been carelessly ripped away. His eyes were half closed, trembling on the edge of sleep, and the stark deathly shape of bones gleamed beneath the bronzed and polished flesh. She had held him every night in her sleep, touched the imagined warmth of his flesh. She had kissed the anguish from his mouth and felt his breath quickening with need against her own. Foolish, empty dreams that she had only allowed herself against the fear that she might never see him again. But now reality was back, hard and sharp against her heart. All would be as it had been, save that she would be emptier than before.

He took the wine from her and shivered as a soft coil of hair brushed his hand. He looked up into the warmth and vibrance of her face. Her eyes were soft and dark and the firelight touched her face with a soft inner beauty; not the pale heart-rending beauty of Margaret, but warmth and kindness, a refuge for his starved and empty heart. She was warm and he was cold, so bitterly cold. Gently he drew her close to him and laid his trembling mouth on hers.

Spring came early that year and April was a month of blustering wind and brief violent showers that drenched the fields and dried as quickly as a child's tears in the smiling sun. It was early morning when Hal rode down from the crest of Cushat Law and followed the line of the river to Warkworth. The long curving line of the hills folded the valley in shadow and it was still cool enough for mist to cloud the dark ugly pits of last summer's raids. On the higher ground the signs were not so easily hidden. At Holystone the spars of the burnt-out and abandoned mill stood like jagged teeth against the sky, the useless wheel creaking softly against the placid flood of the Coquet; at Thropton the gutted cots still stood empty, the sagging walls grown over with weeds. At Rothbury they had begun again; the barns were patched and mended and the church scraped clean of soot and washed with lime. A group of ragged urchins came out to watch him pass; they stood wide-eyed and hungry, hopping from one bare foot to the other and giggling behind their hands when his glance fell upon them.

He rode on past the newly fenced byres where the heavy ewes waited to drop their lambs. In the fields they had begun the harrowing, and flights of screeching crows wheeled and pecked in the ploughs' wake. The men nearest the road paused and touched their caps to him: all alike, bent and stooped like old men before they were thirty, their faces battered by the north wind into the same harsh lines. He beckoned to one, a man who would have been tall save that his legs were bowed from years behind the plough. His face was leathered and brown as a walnut but his eyes were bright and held a look that might have been judged by some as too proud for a villein. Hal recognized him as the reeve's son Will.

Hal nodded to where the oxen lumbered between the sodden furrows. 'How goes it, Will?'

Only the barest flicker of the man's eyes betrayed his pleasure that his name was remembered. 'Fair enough, my lord. The earth is wet and heavy and slowing us a mite but we'll get it done right enough.'

Hal smiled. 'I'll not keep you then, Will,' he said. He saw the man's dour face ease into a smile then suddenly he was down on his knee, his mouth pressed against Hal's hand.

'God keep you and the young lord,' he said. 'We're all of us glad to see you safe and well again, my lord.'

Why should that give him such a surge of pleasure? Perhaps only because it recalled another time. He had been the young lord once and it was still there, the bond that held the common people to him, even above the King. His smile had a touch of malicious amusement, remembering their faces the first time they had laid eyes on Richard; polite, incredulous amusement as if he were one of the painted and jewelled effigies that the abbey paraded on saints' days. Still they looked to him; to them he was the reality and King Richard no more than a distant echo of the awe in which they held Northumberland.

The farce of the Scottish war was over and Richard had returned to Westminster in January to sulk and lay the blame for its failure on any whose shoulders were broad enough. It had been doomed to failure from its hasty and extravagant conception. To the King it had been little more than an opportunity to parade himself in silver gilt armour before the gawping populace: to the barons who came with him it had been a chance to air and settle old grievances. Even before the royal army was fully assembled a quarrel had broken out at Beverley. The King's half-brother John Holland had slain the Earl of Stafford's eldest son: a small pebble in a large pond, but the ripples had reached out and touched them all. Ralph Stafford was a favourite of the Queen and allied by marriage to half the nobility and Holland stood even higher. By the time they reached York the army was split and divided and seething with discontent which the King had inflamed even further with his favourites. He had taken refuge in his royal rage, as he always did when faced with a decision which was not to his liking. It was Richard who had set the pace. With smiling innocence he had played them off one against the other, raising his royal uncles Edmund and Thomas to the dignity of dukes as a buckler against Lancaster, and flaunting his disregard for the lesser lords by bestowing the earldom of Suffolk on the commoner de la Pole. De Vere was fastened to the King's side like a bloated leech, replete with the King's subtle contrivance of a marquisate that placed him only fractionally below the royal dukes but above every other lord in the kingdom.

Lancaster had joined them grudgingly at Durham but with such a show of force that the King had visibly blanched and taken it as a personal affront to his royal dignity that Lancaster's men almost outnumbered his own. For the rest of the campaign he was at great pains to let every man know that he bore his uncle's company only under sufferance. Hal himself was in high favour, the King's trusted confidant and adviser—though in truth Richard listened to none but himself. The northern lords' pleas to divide the army and protect the road to Carlisle had been dismissed on the advice of de Vere; it was also de Vere who had favoured the disastrous eastern route by Berwick that left all the north open to attack. Hal had accepted his sudden elevation to favourite with mild amusement and knew that each smile, each show of favour, was less for him and more a slap in the face for Lancaster. He himself was past any feeling of triumph. It was the first time they had met since his acquittal and they met as strangers, common courtesy strained to the least that could be said between them. The King was not so cautious. He had gained a precarious confidence from his burgeoning household of place-seekers and beholden kinsmen; foreign upstarts for the most part but here and there a known face, the old adherents of Lancaster who had shrugged off their worn-out loyalties with the ease of serpents shedding their skins. Archbishop Neville was there and, less happily, Richard Scrope. There were new faces too, and one in particular that still roused a feeling of disquiet in Hal: the sharp angular face of Ralph Neville.

Thus they lumbered on in precarious unity to the Border, hampered by the King's unwieldly baggage train that contained all but his plate and hangings. They found no enemy. The Scots had had warning enough and a day wasted at Berwick, while the King veered this way and that on strategy, had given them ample time to retreat into the hills. They advanced at a crawling pace up the Tweed valley toward Melrose. The Scots had abandoned none of their old strategy under French influence and if anything had gained a little from it—only the French had more experience at running from a fight. All they found was a deserted empty land; nothing stirred, every pig and chicken driven into the hills to await their passing. They fired the abbey at Melrose and turned north to Edinburgh, circling the fortress on its sheer impregnable rock and turning the town at its feet to ashes. Farther west at Stirling the news came that the Scots had crossed Solway into Cumberland.

At the end of the month the royal army camped alongside the broad estuary of the Forth, trapped between the glare of water and the high September sun. Behind them lay black smoking devastation; beyond the river the lush grassland dwindled into bog and moorland and rose again into the grim foothills of the Highlands.

The King's face was flushed and his petulant mouth turned down in displeasure. His yellow beard was lank with sweat and his fair skin burned beneath the blistering weight of damascened armour. He glared round at his counsellors and singled out Lancaster to bear the brunt of his floundering rage.

'Well then?' he shouted. 'What now?'

Lancaster rose unperturbed. 'As I have already said, sire. We should turn back and follow the Scots' line of march. We can then cut off their retreat into Scotland.' Neither he nor any of the other lords reminded the King that they had already foreseen the Scots attack and begged for troops to protect their rear. Now Clifford's lands were devastated and Carlisle surrounded and they were entrenched halfway into Scotland with the enemy at their back.

De Vere, the puppet master, spoke. 'So His Grace of Lancaster would have us floundering through the Westmorland passes with winter approaching? What of our supply of ships? How are we to transport those through mountains?' He rose and laid his hand possessively on the King's sleeve. 'A risky venture at the best of times, my lord, but doubly so when we have the precious person of His Grace the King to protect.' His jewelled fingers clenched on Richard's arm and his high girlish voice was soft with insinuation. 'But perhaps His Grace of Lancaster has already thought of that.'

Hal looked on despairingly as they argued the issue and though he had no love for de Vere he was with him in this. They'd had disasters enough without plunging this great discontented, leaderless army into the treacherous mountains of Westmorland. He glanced at the King, who grew flushed and pale in turn. Primed to the pitch of his royal rage by de Vere, Richard heard nothing of the reasoned argument of the other lords. His pale eyes were fastened on his uncle and narrowed with suspicion as Lancaster persisted.

'The Scots have managed it,' Lancaster said. 'How are we less than they?'

'They are only a quarter of our number and less heavily laden,' Richard shouted. His face grew purple under the beading of sweat and he shaped the noiseless working of his throat into a scream. 'If you are so keen, my lord, then take your *own* men and attempt it,' he yelled. 'It will not be the first time you have led men to their deaths.'

Hal saw Lancaster grow as pale as death but still he smiled, the small conciliatory smile that to any who knew him well was a greater sign of rage than all of Richard's tantrums. He bowed low over the King's trembling hand. 'I look for no other leader than you, sire,' he said pleasantly. 'Wherever you lead then I shall follow.'

Hal watched as the smile became strained and finally faded under the King's cold eyes. Lancaster was not ready to abandon his dream of Castile yet. He needed Richard for that and even if it took the price of his pride then it seemed that he was willing to pay it.

So they had turned tail and lumbered back toward Berwick, with nothing achieved save the King's loss of face and the squandering of five thousand pounds.

Hal slowed his horse to the steep and twisting path that led down to the valley. The river ran wide and clear till it plunged into the narrow gorge below Warkworth. He could just see the golden turrets tipped by the mid-morning sun and, beyond, the sloping hills of springing green where the first flowering of the gorse shone like yellow beacons. He smiled, a rare deep smile of contentment. Once, all this had been enough, the land, his sons, the knowledge that there would always be a Percy in Northumberland. He had not seen himself growing empty, he had not noticed the insidious passing of the years that had sprung age and loneliness upon him in one fell swoop. Twelve years, a long time. Twelve years since he had bedded any woman save a whore. Then suddenly there had been Maud, with so much love to give him that he could have drowned in it. He had been cold for so long that he had forgotten the warmth of love. Not the wild uncontrollable passion he had felt for Margaret; this was softer and less painful, and stronger perhaps, for his need for love was greater now.

He had come to the place where the river looped and turned back on itself below Warkworth. Out of habit he glanced down the cliff to the dark concealed door of the hermitage. It was a long time since he had been there.

Maud walked with a quick light step along the airy passage. Windows were thrown wide and the morning breeze drove the fresh rushes against the long tables where a dozen clerks were sifting parchment in preparation for the daily business of the Earl's court. Through them the steward's voice came as a thunderous roar chivvying the pages to their duty.

She stepped over the dogs who basked on the sun-patched

landing. Ceolwulf rolled on his back and swiped at her skirts with a giant paw. She scanned the faces of the petitioners whose rank saved them from a long chill wait in the bailey. The abbot of Herne, his pallid face set in the wheedling lines of a favour-seeker. There were two shabby knights come for the second time to beg relief from their yearly rent. She smiled ruefully. And they would get it. Hal was renowned for his generosity. Outside there were more: weavers, tanners, fullers, a few merchants come from Rothbury, the rest simple peasants come to argue over pigs and corn tithes. He would hear them all, sitting long into the day so that no man returned home without justice. It was no wonder that they loved him so well.

She smiled softly. But not so well as her. Even now she found it hard to believe. He loved her. Perhaps not in the fierce passionate way she had always dreamt of, but gently, generously, with all of the heart that was left in him. It was enough, more than enough. That first night he had done no more than lie in her arms. He had not touched her, though her body had ached for him. She had kissed him to quietness and wrapped him in her warmth; she had wept out of pure happiness while he slept. There had been a passion between them since. All those empty years filled in that first night he had lain with her. He had taught her how to love, to touch, to kiss, and every moment of the learning had been joy for both of them.

She looked down to the sheltered little garden below the terrace and saw the sheathed white buds of marguerites nodding on their long stems. For the first time she really believed that Margaret Neville was dead.

The King was in high spirits, the jewelled core of a glittering assembly that revolved around him in breathless anticipation. His own breath came in pleasurable little spurts, his narrow breast heaving beneath the coruscation of cloth of gold and diamonds. His hands trembled in eagerness as he watched his enemy approach. He closed his eyes against the bright sun that probed beneath the silken canopy and fingered the jewels at his throat; he opened them again on the smiling face of the Duke of Lancaster.

Joyfully Richard laid his rouged mouth to the gaunt and weathered cheek; beyond the broad velvet shoulders he saw the faces of the Court. His uncle Woodstock, Arundel, and his brother Bishop Thomas, smiling with quiet triumph—even the parchment–stiff faces of the clergy were eased into grudging smiles of relief; there was not a man among them who was not glad to see Lancaster and his pack leaving.

It had cost him dear, a grant of twenty thousand marks from his own privy purse to subsidize that of the Commons, half a year's pay in advance for the army that had gathered so swiftly at the promise of easy pickings in Spain. But money well spent; he would have paid twice as much for his freedom if need be. He averted his eyes from the Duchess Constanza's dark and swarthy face, his fastidious nostrils dilating at the sickening stench that rose from beneath her gown. Here was another he would be glad to see gone from his Court, with her pious mutterings and unclean habits, but he steeled himself to kiss her oily cheek, hurrying through the formal speeches of farewell. He was eager now to see it done.

His parting gift was the final irony: gold crowns for each, blazoned with the arms of Castile and Leon. He smiled softly as he set it on Lancaster's head. He did not grudge him a crown now, so long as it was not his.

He rose and linked his arm through Lancaster's with studied malice. The Court pressed close, the ladies in their high gauzy hennins like a fleet of full-masted ships; his own Queen, her plump cheeks rouged to a fevered brilliance; and so weighted with jewels that she had to be helped from her chair. De Vere was never far behind him, his comfort and his mentor. It was their shared triumph. He felt almost drunk as he kissed Lancaster for the last time. He was free; no more of Lancaster's meddling and tedious caution, no more of his heavy hand in his dealings. He laughed softly in his throat, then turned and looked into the cold ruthless eyes of Henry Bolingbroke.

Elizabeth had gowned herself with special care and the soft Italian silk clung seductively to her limbs. Her hair was coiled on either side of her face and anchored with emerald-tipped pins, the stiffened velvet headdress making her look older than her fifteen years. She sipped delicately at the rich malvoisie wine, watching the faces that crowded the hall, seeing the expressions that came and went in their eyes, the unconscious tell-tale gestures with which they elaborated their flat courtly speech.

Beside her, Harry sparred playfully with his brother Ralph, but now and then his eyes would stray possessively to her face. She smiled her secret woman's smile, remembering how he had stormed her virginity with the violence of an enemy assault. If there had been no answering spark she had not let him know it. She was not ready to cross him yet. His rash ungovernable temper had earned him the name of Hotspur, and he was, even in the dark confines of her bed. With cool detachment she watched him flirt openly with Musgrave's wife. He was handsome enough: the black tumbling hair; the large grey eyes that were always bright with laughter or darkened by rage, with no happy mien; the warm lazy smile that had half the women at Court at his feet; even the quick stumbling speech that afflicted him sometimes only added to his charm. That he had mistresses and two bastard daughters in Lincoln she knew. The discovery had not concerned her greatly. He would have no need of mistresses now. He would have no need of any save her.

He would have to be schooled in diplomacy, the rash outspoken speech tempered with caution, the violence and latent ambition channelled to her own ends. He was still too much under his father's dominance, content to be Northumberland's heir with nothing of his own save what Hal chose to give him.

Briefly her eyes lost their detachment. She thought longingly of her brothers. Roger would be almost a man now, and Edmund not far behind. It was six years since she had seen them, six years since she had received any news, save that Arundel grew fat on the revenues of their lands and, even though the King had named Roger his heir, the resurgence of their power was smothered by Lancaster's influence. But Lancaster was gone now, chasing his illusory dream of a Spanish crown. Only his son remained to guard his interest. The thought brought her eyes back to her husband's face. He would have to be weaned from Bolingbroke, and swiftly too, before he committed himself irrevocably. It had already begun, the struggle for power that Lancaster's presence had held in check. They had heard that morning. Suffolk was down, and half the Court party with him. The hounds were loosed and their teeth bared at Richard's throat.

The same thoughts passed through Hal's mind. That which all but the King had foreseen had become accomplished fact. Woodstock had stepped swiftly into his brother Lancaster's shoes, and feelings ran high enough against Richard and his favourites for him to be able to push through Parliament that which might otherwise have been obstructed by both Lords and Commons. Woodstock and his henchmen were out for blood, more particularly De Vere's blood, yet for the moment his birth placed him out of their reach. Suffolk was to be the whipping boy, impeached on such a long and transparent farrago of charges that even Parliament had winced for shame. The King had reacted with his customary spleen and removed himself and his uneasy household to Eltham. There he had sent word to Woodstock that he would not remove even the meanest scullion from his kitchen at Woodstock's command.

Hal mused upon the five lords who had laid their name to Suffolk's impeachment. Woodstock and Arundel were no surprise; but Warwick? He would not have thought that Tom Beauchamp had the stomach for rebellion. Thomas Mowbray, Earl of Nottingham, was the waverer, torn between old friendship and the influence of his father-in-law Arundel. And the last name—Harry Bolingbroke, Lancaster's son. He would have expected to find Lancaster's hand in it somewhere. Like father like son? He felt the stirring of old doubts. Was there more to Bolingbroke's attack on the King than met the eye? He glanced at his own son. Harry and his cousin Bolingbroke were still close, the boyhood friendship still held. Did Harry know more than he was telling? He tore his eyes sharply away. No, Harry would not deceive him. He was imagining slights where there were none. But then Lancaster's name always had that effect on him. Even after all this time he was not free. Abruptly he turned his head and saw that Harry's wife was staring at him. He smiled absently and raised his cup. He wondered afterwards why that pale pointed face should fill him with such unease.

Elizabeth was late in rising. They had not reached London till long past midnight and it seemed that she had no sooner fallen into bed before the dawn was up and she was being shaken awake. She lay in the darkness of the bed hangings, reluctant to leave the warmth and her pleasurable thoughts. The windows had been thrown wide and she could hear the slow rumble of carts coming through Aldersgate and the shrill birdlike cries of hucksters bound for the morning market at Cheapside. She stretched lazily, shivering as her naked limbs touched the icy outer limits of the bed. It was probably the last time for a while that she would enjoy such freedom. Harry would arrive today and when they were together he came to her almost nightly. She closed her eyes against the memory of the angry passion that left her so empty and bewildered. There was no love between them, only desire on his part and, for her, the need of an instrument for her own ambition. Abruptly she flung back the covers and leapt from the bed. It was enough. She had no more need of him than that.

She rinsed her mouth in honeyed wine and called for one of her women to dress her. She craned eagerly from the window for her first sight of the city. The domes and clustering spires of a hundred churches rose into a clear sky. The streets were narrow and dark, barely a cart's width and choked with people even at this hour. The noise seemed thunderous after the quiet of the north, yet beneath it all there was unease. She saw the glint of armour at every street corner: Woodstock's men and, here and there, the dull burgundy of Arundel's livery. Her heart leapt. Her brothers were here in Arundel's train, brought from their Sussex obscurity to give a semblance of respectability to Woodstock's cause, and perhaps as a hostage for King Richard's good behaviour. She smiled softly. She would see them no matter how closely they were kept. Harry would see to that.

In the solar Philippa Percy's strident voice filled the chamber, complaining that the water was cold, the wine sour and there was no clean linen for the babe that snivelled persistently in its cradle by the window. She was with child again, her great belly thrust before her like a ship in full sail. Her round face was unhealthy with blood. Elizabeth smiled maliciously. She did not blame Thomas for abandoning her for Castile.

Philippa dipped her finger in honey and stuck it into the babe's mouth. She glared at Elizabeth. 'So, my lady Elizabeth has graciously consented to rise from her bed,' she snapped, and gave the little maid who had brought the linen a vicious slap.

Elizabeth only smiled. Her sister-in-law's dislike of her and her aggressive pride in her frequent child-bearing left her unmoved. She did not care for Philippa, and cared even less for the thought of motherhood. There were ways to avoid it, potions in which Morganna was skilled. She laughed softly and gave Philippa a pitying look over her shoulder. It would be a long time before she looked like that.

She ran down the narrow turret staircase. One of Northumberland's squires grinned cheekily and pressed himself against the wall to let her pass. She did not even glance his way but she knew the look in his eyes. It did not disturb her. Most men looked at her like that.

The doors of the Earl's apartments stood open. Six men staggered under the weight of the great Crécy tapestry; she watched it as it was heaved into place, the jewels seen unfolding inch by inch. She smiled acquisitively. She had marked it for her own the first time she had seen it.

She wandered listlessly along the narrow passage. A page sat counting tallow dips as a penance and raised his head to stare at her. The minstrels' gallery that flanked the hall was deserted, silent save for the rumble of men's voices that came from below. She craned inquisitively from the shadows. Northumberland was there, and that great bear of a man Lord Clifford. The others were strangers, yet she knew before he spoke that the tall aggressive-looking man was Thomas of Woodstock.

Hal had risen to his feet. He wore the bland smile that all who knew him knew concealed distaste. 'My lord of Gloucester, and Arundel too.' His smile broadened into open mockery. 'I am honoured, my lords, and had I known where to find you I would have saved you this visit.' His eyes gleamed with mischief. 'I had heard that you were already lodged in Westminster Palace itself.' He came down slowly from the dais and faced Woodstock. 'And how is the King, my lord? I take it that he still is the King?'

Woodstock flushed. 'We have no wish to harm the King.' He controlled his voice with an effort. 'In fact, quite the contrary, my lord. Our quarrel is with the evil men who surround him and bring him to bad governance.'

Hal smiled. Richard's refusal to yield up de Vere had put the needed weapon into Thomas of Woodstock's hand. He had pressed his advantage to the limit and now the list of the accused ran far beyond de la Pole and de Vere. Archbishop Neville and the lawyer Tresilian were fair game, but old Simon Burley and Nicholas Brembre . . .? Brembre might have feathered his own nest at the King's expense, but Burley's only crime was loyalty.

'Evil men?' he said scathingly. 'Suffolk? Whom the council themselves set up as the King's guardian. Simon Burley? The King's tutor since boyhood and his father's faithful servant before that. You did not think them evil men before, my lords. What has so suddenly lifted the scales from your eyes?' He paused, and brought his eyes to rest coldly on Woodstock's face. 'Perhaps only the absence of your brother Lancaster.'

A voice came from the back of the hall. 'I speak for Lancaster, my lord of Northumberland. Whether my father is here or not, Lancaster has lent his approval to the actions of the committee for reform.'

Hal looked past the heaving shoulders of a silent and furious Arundel. 'Ah, it is you, fair cousin. And Nottingham too, skulking in the shadows. Come and be counted, my lords. Let us see how many of you there really are.'

He stared at Henry Bolingbroke's flushed and angry face, so like his father—yet his mouth had a look of iron determination that his father's had always lacked. 'I had not thought to see you in such company Henry,' he said softly. 'I thought that, of all men, Richard had a friend in you.'

'Not now, my lord,' Bolingbroke answered stiffly. 'The King has his own friends whom he chooses to favour to the detriment of England.'

Hal smiled. That was what irked them all the most. They could bear to see one of their own raised up and favoured, but not upstarts like Suffolk and Brembre.

Then Woodstock spoke. 'We have the backing of Parliament, Northumberland. We do not stand alone in this.'

Hal gave him a scathing look. 'Parliament answers to the loudest voice, as well you know, my lord. And that honour undoubtedly falls to you, Your Grace.'

'Are you telling us that you stand with de Vere then?' Arundel broke silence in a spluttering roar.

'I am telling you nothing, my lord, save that I will not see the King brought down,' Hal said grimly.

'But they are one and the same. De Vere rules, not Richard,' Nottingham said unguardedly. 'England is ruled by the Duke of Ireland.'

'And you would put the Duke of Gloucester in his place?'

'My lord!' Gloucester said loudly and quelled the rash reply that rose to Nottingham's lips. 'We are wasting our time. The Earl of Northumberland has made himself clear.'

Hal bowed mockingly. 'As you yourself have also, I think, Your Grace.' He passed between them, moving slowly and leisurely towards the door, but the gesture of dismissal was clear. He paused on the threshold and turned back to Woodstock's outraged countenance. 'By the way, Your Grace—the King has commanded me to Eltham tonight.' He smiled malevolently as he saw the flush of consternation creep into Woodstock's face. 'I'll tell him how assiduously you all labour for his welfare.'

In the gallery Elizabeth stood pressed into the shadows. Her hands pricked with sweat and her breath came loudly through her parted lips. The sight of him had been like a physical blow, a scream of warning from the depths of her mind. She knew now, more surely than she had ever known anything. The enemy was not Northumberland. It was Henry Bolingbroke.

Hal rode to Eltham that same day. He knew why the King had summoned him and knew even better what his answer would be. All the Court knew, except perhaps Woodstock and his party, that since the beginning of the summer de Vere had been drumming up troops from the west. Tresilian and his band of legal cut-throats had armed the King with enough evidence to proclaim Woodstock a traitor, but Richard needed an army to enforce it and that was why Richard had sent for him. Unbelievably, the King would plunge England into civil war rather than give up de Vere.

He spurred his horse grimly. He was in no hurry for his meeting with the King, yet better to get it done with. He did not have the answers that Richard looked for; he was the King's man in all but this. He'd not risk open warfare to save a man like de Vere.

And his own son Harry was Bolingbroke's man. He'd had proof of that after Woodstock had departed that morning. He'd told him what had passed between them and Harry had said nothing for a while. Then he'd glanced up, with that uncertain look in his eyes that made him look more of a boy than a man.

'And will you take the King's side?'

'Would it trouble you so much if I did?'

'Yes, it would.' He hesitated and then blurted out, 'I'll not side with that perverted whelp de Vere.'

Hal smiled. 'Then I take it that you stand with your cousin Bolingbroke?' Deliberately he chose his name rather than Woodstock's.

'Yes, I'll stand with him, because he is right. Woodstock is right. Richard is weak and thinks of nothing but his own pleasure and that of de Vere.'

'And has it not occurred to you that perhaps both Henry Bolingbroke and Woodstock might have some other motive?' Hal asked him.

Harry looked away from his father's eyes. 'He'd make no worse a king than Richard, if that's what you mean,' he snapped. 'Nor Woodstock either, for that matter.'

Hal stared at the pale angry face he loved so well. 'Has he told you this?' he asked quietly.

'No, but there's plenty who think it. Richard is weak, I tell you! He'd break England in two and give half of it away if it pleased de Vere.'

Hal rose abruptly. 'It's as well we are alone Harry,' he said coldly. 'What you have just said could land you in the Tower if the King came to hear of it.'

283

Harry faced him defiantly. 'I had not noticed you so cautious before my lord. I've heard you say worse to his face.'

'Then hear me say this. If Bolingbroke reaches out one hand to bring Richard down he'll let all hell loose. There's none who'll fight to save de Vere but there are many who'll fight to save a crowned and anointed King—and I am one of them. I warn you, Harry, leave Richard be. De Vere, Suffolk, Tresilian, you can have them with pleasure, and fetter the King with counsels till he has learnt to mend his manners. But Richard must be left King. And remember, Richard's heir is neither Bolingbroke nor Woodstock, but your own brother-in-law Roger Mortimer.'

Harry stared at him. 'Christ, my lord! You talk as if I'm Bolingbroke's man.'

Hal smiled grimly. 'Are you not, Harry?' he said. 'In your heart, are you not?'

Still he did not know if that grieved him. In his heart he could not blame Harry for it. He had been under Lancaster's thrall long enough himself.

The King received him in the ornate and suffocating grandeur of his bedchamber. Robed in a plain black velvet gown, his fairness was quite startling. He wore no jewels, and Hal smothered an ironic smile as he kissed the ringless hand. This was a new portrayal; this was Richard the martyr.

'You see how I am used, Northumberland,' Richard whispered pathetically.

Hal inclined his head in sympathy and looked past him to the men who stood at his back. Suffolk, released by the King in defiance of Parliament's decree; Archbishop Neville, driven irrevocably into the King's camp by the persecution of Arundel. De Vere was not there, nor Brembre. No doubt both were well occupied sounding out the King's strength. All through that summer Richard had had his scouts out to test the temper of the north and west. But, like Hal himself, none would be drawn, not while the King had de Vere at his elbow.

'Well my lord,' the King said when both were seated. 'What word do you bring from Westminster? Do my enemies flourish?'

'His Grace of Gloucester is well, sire, if that is what you mean.'

Richard nodded rapidly. 'You know he means to depose me?' he cried shrilly. 'He threatened me with it here at Eltham. Unless I returned to Parliament and agreed for my lord Suffolk's removal as Chancellor. He forced that unholy toad Arundel on me and shackled me with another council.' He jerked to his feet; he was trembling, the long slender hands plucking at Hal's sleeve. Then Archbishop Neville came out from behind his chair.

'Calm yourself, Your Grace,' he said soothingly and pressed Richard back into his chair. He glanced archly towards Hal. 'I'm sure my lord of Northumberland has good advice to offer.'

Hal inclined his head. 'My lord Archbishop credits me with too much widsom,' he began, but Richard had already snatched at the bait.

'Yes, yes.' He gave a little cackle of laughter. 'You are past-master at eluding the chase. Remember how you bought yourself free at Berwick?' His smile faded a little, recalling how Lancaster had been the enemy then. How could he have known that, by ridding himself of the one, he had opened the gates for another, twice as strong?

He leant forward and laid his hand on Hal's shoulder. 'You know that Woodstock plots against me. His men are everywhere in the city and there are more assembling in Essex. How many could he bring against me if it came to it my lord? Could you match his strength?' The flower–like mouth thinned to a crafty line. 'You would not stand alone, my lord. Brembre has the city in hand and my lord of Oxford has the promise of four thousand Chester men. If you declare yourself, others would follow. Be-tween us we could send Woodstock and his rabble packing.'

Hal eased himself from the King's clinging hand and turned to look into his face. Richard's cheeks were flushed like an eager child, yet his mouth had the look of an old man's cunning. Was it really possible that Richard would plunge them all into civil war just to keep de Vere by him? The fanatical gleam of his eyes said he would, and not because he loved de Vere so much but because he could not bear to be denied; because of the royal prerogative he clung to with such pathetic stubbornness. Parliament panted for de Vere's blood but perhaps they pursued the wrong quarry. De Vere or no de Vere, Richard was all the man he ever would be—and that was none at all. The King himself was the danger. If de Vere was put down there would soon be another to take his place. Richard would always be in need of a whipping boy.

'And you think that one man is worth this sacrifice?' Hal said critically.

Richard's smile faded. 'It is not just one man,' he snapped.

'It might have been if you had consented to the original reforms,' Hal answered mildly. 'They would have been content with de Vere.' Then, bluntly, he continued. 'You asked for my advice, sire, and I'll give it for what it's worth. Get rid of de Vere, Your Grace.'

Richard's smile froze on his face. 'Those are Woodstock's words, my lord. I had not thought you one of his minions.'

'No more am I,' Hal said wearily. 'I speak for your own good, for England's good.'

Richard leapt from his chair. 'I am England!' he shouted. 'King of England! Sworn and anointed!'

'That does not give you the right to abuse your kingship, sire,' stated Hal calmly. 'I have no love for my lord of Gloucester but you yourself have put right on his side. You rule a court of parasites, foreigners and upstarts who bleed you dry and then send you cap in hand to the Commons to beg a loan. Your patronage of de Vere has alienated men who have been loyal to you all their lives with no reward and none looked for. De Vere is doomed, my lord, with or without you. It is up to you whether you fall with him or not.'

Before Hal was half done the King was out of his chair and trembling. His teeth chattered and spittle flecked the perfection of his beard. 'Lies, lies!' he screamed. 'Filthy perjured lies that the traitor Woodstock has put into your mouth!' He fell back into his chair, his hands clenched and straining upon the velvet arms. 'Woodstock wants me dead. You all want me dead. You'll persecute me till I'm friendless and alone.' Tears of self-pity pricked his eyes. 'I had thought you loyal, Northumberland. Of all men, I had thought you loyal.'

Hal stared in disdain at the blotched, tearful face. At the King's elbow Neville stood poised to halt and soothe the mounting rage before it rendered Richard incoherent. De la Pole stared at his feet, his old tired face blank and withdrawn. Hal brought his eyes wearily back to the King's face.

'You *have* my loyalty, sire, and that of almost every man in England. But neither my loyalty nor theirs runs to the protection of a man like Robert de Vere. De Vere must go,' he added loudly over the scream that rose in the King's throat. 'If you want to be King then act like one, my lord. Kings stand alone. They have no need of favourites.'

He turned, then, and walked away in disgust, the shrill sound of the King's rage ringing in his ears. Richard or Gloucester—was there such a difference between them? The only choice lay in which rotten apple had the fewest maggots.

The first snow fell quietly, melting as soon as it touched the black leaded roofs of the Tower. There was black ice underfoot, slowing the horses to a careful mincing walk over the cobbles, and though the narrow street throbbed with the sound of mounted men, beneath the noise there ran the alien quiet of fear.

Hal rode between Archbishop Courtney and the Bishop of London. The Bishop lagged behind on his pot-bellied palfrey and was forever glancing nervously about him at the soldiery that filled the streets. The Archbishop stared straight ahead of him and his face spoke of a deeper resentment than even he would have dared put into words. Like all the lords who attended the King today, he was here under sufferance, his loyalty given only because Richard was King, and against his better judgement.

By Galley Quay a group of soldiers in Arundel's livery drew back to let them pass. There were more, crowded beneath the Tower walls, encamped in makeshift tents down by the river. Five hundred of Woodstock's Essex men crammed the lower guard and blew on numbed fingers against the cold. In the narrow constricting passages of the White Tower there was hardly room to pass between them.

On the threshold of the King's apartments Hal paused. They were all there: Thomas of Woodstock, Duke of Gloucester, close to the King and smiling in quiet triumph; Arundel, red-faced and truculent as ever, and his brother the Bishop quivering with spite; the Earl of Warwick, nervous as a rat, sat beside young

Mowbray; and a little way apart, staring from the narrow window slit, stood the dark solitary figure of Henry Bolingbroke.

Dear God, Hal thought, no wonder Suffolk and Archbishop Neville had fled for their lives. There would have been little mercy for them here. He advanced slowly into the room, keeping pace with the Archbishop's shorter step. They were the peacemakers, the appointed mediators between the King and his uncle Woodstock. Yet what was there to say or do now, except see that Woodstock's demands were kept within bounds? The King was beaten. All knew it save Richard himself. He sat pale and solemn, drained by the spasm of rage that had taken all morning for the gentleman ushers to quell. Still he persisted, buying time with storms of angry tears. His last hope had gone with de Vere's crushing defeat at Radcot Bridge and eventual escape to France. His beloved de Vere was gone—not so beloved, Hal had noticed, that Richard had stirred himself from his refuge in the Tower to lead the half-hearted army that de Vere had scraped up from the Western shires. Even that last piece of bravado had been doomed to failure. No man wanted to fight for de Vere alone, and without Richard at their head the rebel force led by Bolingbroke had scattered them before they came within fifty miles of London.

Woodstock's purge of the King's household had thinned them to a handful of old and blameless retainers. The gaps had been filled by Woodstock's men, honest men some of them, but nevertheless Woodstock's men. The list of the treasonable had come down to a mere dozen. Brembre they had, penned up in the Tower; Tresilian would soon be flushed out from his hiding place in the city. The rest were unimportant household knights, a vindictive replacement for the loss of Suffolk and de Vere that even ran to include the King's confessor. It was old Simon Burley that was the stumbling block. Even at this last pass the King refused to sanction his death, protecting him with the same passion that he had once protected de Vere, to the extent of the Queen spending three hours on her knees before Arundel to plead for his life. The King was on sure ground here. There were more than enough ready to plead for Burley, Hal for one. But Woodstock was not going to be cheated this time; every man in

288

the room was aware that it was Burley's head or civil war.

He listened with half closed eyes as Bishop Arundel stated, for the hundredth time that week, the terms under which Woodstock was prepared to disband his army. The tight clipped voice filled the room, hurrying over the oft repeated phrases. The Bishop wore his irritation like a hair shirt.

The King heard the speech through and rose with strenuous calm. 'I agree to all this—' he paused and slid a spiteful look at his uncle, 'saving my royal prerogative.' Again that magical phrase that Richard used like a protective armour and that gave him licence to undo all that his counsellors might formulate.

The Bishop snapped his mouth shut and opened it again and looked to Woodstock for prompting. Then Bolingbroke spoke softly from his corner.

'There are no choices, Your Grace,' he said. 'Only a simple alternative.' He took the King gently by the arm and led him to the window. Through the narrow slit the rebel armies were black as ants round the Tower walls. 'See there, Your Grace—there is your choice. You either yield Burley or we will take him.'

The King stared up into his cousin's face and read the threat implicit in the cold eyes. Burley's life or his—that was the choice that none dared put into words. He turned back into the room, his bloodshot eyes darting from face to face, and saw for the first time the extent of the contempt and disgust for himself that he had failed to estimate. He knew the truth. Even men he counted as his own would not move to save him now. Piteously he stretched out his hand to ward off the hated faces that closed in on him.

'So be it, then,' he whispered. 'Take Burley, take who you like but leave me alone.'

The wind blew cold from the east and blew fiercely in the faces of the long cortège that came down the city road toward Tyburn. The crowds had been gathered at the crossroads since early dawn, some huddled together on stalls and benches dragged from the nearby houses, some perched like crows in the creaking elms. There were beggars stationed by the roadside rattling their bowls. A pieman hawked his wares loudly through the waiting

289

crowds. It might have been a holiday, if it had not been for the stark reminder of the gibbet that stood by the road.

The King rode straight-backed, pale but resplendent as ever in crimson velvet and sable. At least Woodstock had allowed him the trappings of a king. Hal watched Richard's face as Tresilian was dragged to the scaffold. If he grieved he did not show it. His eyes were blank and meek as a child's. He did not look up even when the crowd roared his name.

Hal watched as the halter was placed round Tresilian's neck. Who would have recognized him now: the great hooked nose splintered and spread across his face, the mean spiteful mouth fallen in across his broken and bloody teeth. But the crowd recognized him; there were many who had come a long way to see the man who had condemned John Ball to the same shameful death. Hal was close enough to see his eyes, narrowed to slits between swollen flesh, dull and glazed as a blind dog's. He tried to gauge their expression and failed. Not fear: Tresilian was not afraid of death, for him the wait for death would be the agony. Only once, when they rested briefly on the King, did they show any sign of life. Hal wondered how Tresilian felt now, seeing the master for whom he had laboured so long and arduously come to watch him die without lifting a hand to his defence.

He looked away as the halter was placed round his neck. He heard the creak of the gibbet as they jerked him up, the loud wheezing of air being squeezed from the constricted throat, the crack of bones as they let him drop. The crowd howled with joy as they hawled him up again, roaring with laughter as his spindly legs threshed the empty air, yelling with derision as the executioner gave the signal for him to be let down again. Tresilian was an old man. He'd not give them the sport they had hoped for.

The executioner felt for Tresilian's flagging pulse and lifted the swollen lids from the bulging eyes. The crowd had fallen silent, trampling each other for a better view. The women shrieked with raucous laughter as they stripped him naked, sniggering at the fat mound of his belly and the shrivelled manhood.

Hal glanced at the King and saw that he was sweating; he flinched and swayed slightly in the saddle at the plunge of the knife. The cut was clean and expertly done, the first springing of blood spreading like delicate flowers across the white skin. He shuddered as Tresilian screamed. Was it possible that a man had strength and will enough to fill his lungs with air and scream that dreadful scream while his gut was slit and steaming? The executioner plunged his hand into the gaping wound and the rip of muscle and sinew was loud in the breathless hush. He withdrew his gory prize and held it aloft to the crowd, blood trickling down his bare arm and smearing his cheek. He was smiling with pride as the mob cheered him. He still smiled as he dashed the severed entrails to the ground and trampled them beneath his feet.

Tresilian had stopped screaming. They could not see his face and the only sign that he still lived was the feeble rise and fall of his chest. It would not be long, thank God; the executioner was already wielding the great two-handed sword for quartering the body.

The King made a little noise in his throat, and for a moment Hal thought he was weeping. But his eyes were dry as he raised his head. He looked neither at Hal nor at the mangled body of Tresilian. His eyes saw nothing but the smug arrogant face of Thomas of Woodstock.

Alnwick

The light was almost gone, faded to pale glowing streaks on the horizon. In the Earl's apartments above the hall the candles burnt brightly and drew the moths in from the courtyard. The air was warm and still and smelt of sweet summer hay.

Carefully Maud stitched at the length of green silk that was to be the skirt of Philippa's new gown; a waste of good cloth, she thought, and remembered Philippa as she had seen her last, stuffing herself with sugared violets. The tight velvet bodice had merged her huge breasts into the rolls of fat that girdled her waist and her bare swollen feet were thrust into wooden clogs. Philippa was like yeasted dough: she rose in the heat. She tried to smother the feeling of dislike that the plump greasy face always gave her.

291

Philippa was a victim of neglect. She'd not seen her husband Thomas in two years and only had word of him through his father the Earl. None spared her a moment's interest, even though, as she constantly harped, she was the mother of the heirs presumptive to Northumberland. That was her only saving grace; two sons to her credit and not yet twenty.

This thought reminded Maud of Elizabeth. She had watched her tonight, curled in her favourite window seat, one hand stroking the head of Siward's pup, the other idly turning the pages of a book. Harry had sat playing chess with Ralph but Maud had seen that his eyes were more often than not on Elizabeth, dark with longing and—the ridiculous thought had struck her—enchantment. The boy was sick with love, but then she reminded herself that he was no longer a boy. He was a man now, twenty-two years old, as tall as his father and twice as hot-headed. An unlikely match for Elizabeth and her cool frigid smile. Fire and ice—Maud wondered which would devour the other first. Yet it was Elizabeth who had eased the friction between herself and Harry. He acepted her now and sometimes there was even a tepid warmth between them. Only where his father was concerned did that old coldness spring up between them. And she in her turn had accepted that. Harry would always have the lion's share of Hal.

She turned her head and smiled at the sound of Hal's laughter from outside the door. It was a rare sound since he had returned from Court, and even now she did not know the full truth of his feelings toward the King. She had seen Richard only once before they had left for the north; a meek and placid figure beside his plump little queen. It was that very meekness that she had found so disconcerting.

She laid aside the half-finished gown as Hal came into the room. She watched him strip off the fine linen shirt. The bronzed and ageless flesh was firm and supple as a boy's and she touched the downward curve of her own cheek, remembering the fine wrinkling beneath her eyes that even the Welshwoman's unguents could not stave off. He came and stood behind her, sliding his hands over her breasts.

'I am growing old,' she said sharply.

He laughed and kissed the top of her head. 'And I with you, my love.' He lifted her up and carried her across to the bed. 'We shall grow old together and make joy of every moment.'

He lay down beside her on the soft velvet and kissed her with such agonizing tenderness that she could have wept. His mouth was soft and teasing yet his eyes were still strained and uneasy.

'What is it?' she asked abruptly. 'What troubles you?'

He rolled away from her and stared up at the gilded darkness of the canopy. 'Nothing,' he said, and smiled. 'Something I had thought dead. I am afraid that it is coming to life again.'

'Is it Harry?' she said.

'Yes, I suppose it is.' He closed his eyes. 'I'm afraid for him, Maud. He's too close to Bolingbroke.'

'You think that Bolingbroke can harm him?'

'He could. He could harm all of us if he had a mind to. It's not finished yet. They all think they've got Richard well to heel. But he'll not forget.' He was thinking of Richard's eyes the day of Tresilian's death. 'He'll not forgive or forget. In his mind he has all five of them marked down for revenge. Woodstock, Arundel, Warwick, Mowbray and Bolingbroke. I don't want Harry to stand with Bolingbroke.'

Harry, Harry, Harry. That was all he ever thought or felt. She leant over him and kissed his throat, tracing the long line of the scar that ran to below his heart. She forgot that she was over forty and should know better. She was young enough in her heart and she could still rouse him as well as a young girl.

In her chamber Elizabeth disrobed hurriedly, dragging the pins and twisted threads of gold roughly from her hair. She waited impatiently while her tiring woman unlaced her gown and her hand slid to the still flat plain of her belly. It was two months since there had been any sign of bleeding, a month since she had begun to feed herself with the evil potions that did nothing but make her purge and vomit. She closed her eyes in sudden despair. The thought of a child turned her sick with rage. She would become another Philippa, with pendulous ugly breasts and a sagging belly, always smelling of sour milk and whining

293

about chills and draughts. Savagely she snatched up the cup and gulped it down; the bitter taste of hoarhound turned her sick but she'd suffer anything rather than be with child.

She climbed into the high bed and closed her eyes. Harry would come tonight. She'd seen it in his eyes and heard it in his voice, and the thought of the hot animal passion that neither she nor his two Lincolnshire mistresses could seem to satisfy brought tears of resentment to her eyes. She bit her lip hard. She would not weep; tears were weakness and she could afford none where Harry was concerned. When he came she would be ready. She was skilled enough to bring him quickly to an end.

She knew the very moment he entered the room, though he trod softly as a cat. She lay quite still and did not open her eyes until he spoke her name. Then she turned her head, and stared at him through half-closed eyes as if she had been asleep. He was naked beneath the long velvet robe and the dark soft hair on his chest ran unbroken down to his belly. She looked away as he slid into the bed beside her. His body was fever-hot against the marble coldness of her own.

He turned her face gently toward him and touched her cheek. Her eyes were closed but he knew that was only so he did not see their coldness. The lovely flaming hair was deceptive. Elizabeth was devoid of passion and he'd had enough women to know that her sighs and moans of pleasure were feigned. The knowledge made him all the angrier at his own need for her.

Even now he did not know if he loved her. She had been part of his life for so long that he had hardly noticed her become a woman. And then suddenly she was there, so young and lovely—and his for the taking. It was his natural instinct to want to possess a beautiful woman, but Elizabeth was more to him than a need of his body. He wanted her more than he had ever wanted any woman, perhaps because he possessed only what she allowed him. He bent to kiss her. Her mouth lay inert and passive beneath his own and he raised his head to look at her.

'Do you dislike it so much?' he asked roughly.

She did not answer and turned her head away, knowing that she provoked him. He was angered easily enough when he was sober, but drunk he was as dangerous as a mad bull.

'Do you ever feel anything, Elizabeth?' he said angrily. 'Pain, pleasure, grief, joy—do you ever feel any of these?'

She turned to face him. 'What would you have me feel, Harry? Wild and abandoned like your Lincoln whore?'

'Yes,' he said softly. 'I would have you like a whore.' Suddenly he had covered her with his weight and pinned her arms above her head so that she could not move. 'I would have you scream with pleasure and cry for more.' His eyes were cold and hard as sharpened steel. 'I would have you weak with lust and begging for my body as I do for yours.'

She knew that he had meant to shock her and she stared him out, though her heart pounded painfully against her ribs.

'Then you'll wait a long time,' she said coolly. 'I have no more need of you than the page who fetches my supper—'

The last words were broken off by her own scream. He had struck her hard across the mouth and he laughed as she cried out in pain. 'So you can feel that at least, my lady, if nothing else.' His face was close, white and angry, his eyes almost black with the agony of his lust. She felt his panting breath upon her burning cheek and whimpered as he bit the soft flesh of her breast. His hands bruised her shoulders as he held her down. He raised himself on his elbows and gazed into her face.

'Now, my lady,' he said savagely, 'let us see what else you can feel.'

He entered her with such violence that she screamed aloud and writhed against him in pain and shock. Each savage thrust took the breath from her and plunged her deeper into an agony of torn and bruised flesh. She sobbed against the hard imprisoning pressure of his mouth. His flesh was damp and burning hot. His hands were entwined in her hair.

'Elizabeth,' he whispered. 'Love me, Elizabeth.'

She heard his voice from a long way off and closed her eyes against the sudden warmth. His kiss was gentler and she tasted the salt of his tears in her mouth. She raised her arms and slid them round his neck. She never knew when the pain ended and the ecstasy began.

She woke before dawn and left him sleeping. With only a robe over her nakedness she ran swiftly down to the river. The sun peered from behind hazy cloud and the grass was wet and cool against her bare feet. She crept beneath the long overhanging branches that trailed in the still water and slipped the robe from her shoulders. Her body was stiff and heavy as lead and still bore the marks of that long joyful night. She smiled softly to herself and slipped silently into the river, shivering as the cool green water lapped her skin. She thought unashamedly of the hard magnificent body she had kissed and caressed to such a pitch of ecstasy that he had wept. He had had his wish. She had been his whore, his lover, his mistress, anything he had asked, as long as he had kept her in that world between agony and delight that she had not even known existed.

She turned and floated lazily on her back, her hair fanning out around her face like a sunburst. At first she thought that it was the drumming of the water in her ears, then as the sound grew louder she turned her head toward the bridge, and saw four horsemen riding single-file across the rattling planks. She swam stealthily for the cover of the trees, waiting till they had disappeared behind the high flanking tower of the postern gate before she emerged from the water. She wrapped the robe tightly around her and climbed back up the grassy bank. The horses were tethered in the outer ward, lathered and dusty. She stared at the blazon on their trappings; the crimson saltire-in-chief of Neville. Her eyes narrowed in premonition. What did Neville want here—that had him ride so hard and long to get it?

She ran, oblivious of her wet, streaming hair and the wide amazed stares of the grooms. Her feet left a damp imprint on the sunbaked steps as she ran up to her chamber. Men stumbled past her half-awake, thrusting their arms into padded shirts as they ran. She heard the Earl's voice echoing through the great cavernous hall below her.

Her chamber was empty save for Morganna moving noisily round, twitching back curtains and dragging the tumbled sheets from the bed.

'What is it?' Elizabeth asked.

Morganna turned a sour face toward her. 'The Scots are over the border,' she said in her clipped, sparing voice. 'Slipped through in the night and as far as Durham already.' She stared at

296

Elizabeth's sodden robe and the pool of water that had formed at her feet. 'You'd better get some clothes on before you catch your death.'

Obediently Elizabeth sat while Morganna rubbed her limbs dry. Though she could not help but see the weals and bruises on her body, she said nothing, but her mouth turned down in disapproval and perhaps her hands were not so gentle as she squeezed the water from her hair and bound it into a loose knot.

When she was dressed Elizabeth ran down to the hall. The Earl paced the length of the dais with his long cat–like tread. Harry stood by the hearth, his eyes intent upon his father's face till he saw her. He sent her a quick, loving smile, heavy with memory, but he did not move from his place. Elizabeth moved to where Maud stood pale and anxious, still in her morning robe with her hair loose and dishevelled. The Earl beckoned his sons to his side. Elizabeth watched Harry's face and saw how he looked at his father when he spoke to him. She saw the blind eager adoration in his eyes. The pride and love between them was almost a visible thing. She smiled faintly. She had no rivals now, except for Northumberland.

All through that long dreary day Elizabeth waited. The sun was hot in the tiny solar and Philippa's brats wailed and giggled in turn, careering across the rush floor to plant sticky hands upon her skirts. She did not even know what she was waiting for; there would be no news of Harry before nightfall, and when there was she did not doubt that she would be the last to hear it. She smiled ruefully at her thoughts. Who would have believed that she could care so much? She glanced down as Philippa's elder son, another Henry, staggered against her. He was like his father, blond and blue-eyed, yet his features were plain and flat like Philippa's. She looked across to where his mother steamed and sweated in the summer heat. She had almost forgotten that she was to have a child herself.

Sunset came, red and thunderous, and still there was no word. Troops were still coming in from the outlying manors, filling the wards with the drum of hooves and shouted voices. From the high turret room of the Auditors' Tower that looked clear south over the flat open plain toward Warkworth. Hal watched and saw nothing.

'It's early yet.' Old Clifford's eldest son Tom stretched his length on the hard wooden bench that normally seated all six of the Earl's chancery clerks. 'Old Heselake will take his time. I doubt if he will cross the Tyne before dawn.'

Hal did not take his eyes from the velvet shadows of the valley. It was not the Bishop of Durham's progress that worried him. He ground his teeth together in frustration. He'd been outplayed this time—outplayed and outmanoeuvred, and all so easily. He should have known that the Douglas would not risk his men so far into England without a reason. The Scots force raiding Durham was only the half of it, a diversion planned to hold his attention while the Douglas himself plundered down to Carlisle at his leisure. Ten thousand men, the greatest army Scotland had ever raised, and he was powerless to stop them. He'd committed every man he had to the defence of Durham. Then he jerked his head and swore softly. His thoughts had carried him so far adrift that he'd been watching an advancing horseman for at least a minute without realizing it.

It was Grey of Heton. In the dusk of the courtyard his eyes showed like tallow-dips in a mask of dust and sweat. He swilled his mouth with ale and spewed it out again before he spoke. 'The Scots have taken the coast road. They've passed Newcastle and are advancing toward Morpeth.'

Hal nodded and turned with Grey towards the keep. In this at least he had been right. 'And my son?' he asked.

Grey slid a knowing sideways glance at him. 'Staying put, but under pressure,' he admitted. 'There was a skirmish of sorts outside the gates of Newcastle between Harry and Jamie Douglas. A lot of shouting and knightly threats, but Hotspur lost his pennon to Douglas. It was as much as we could do to stop him riding after him there and then.'

Hal frowned. How like Harry to risk everything for a square of embroidered silk. It was his one worry: that Harry would override him and take affairs into his own hands. 'Has Durham come up yet?'

'No sign of him,' Grey said. 'And there'll not be till morning.

The roads are awash with carts and cattle. There's not a village standing between Durham and Newcastle.'

They had come full circle and Hal halted, staring absently at the groom who walked Grey's steaming horse. Would Harry wait that long? He must, if they were to have any chance of success. Pennon or no, this once he'd do as he was told. He turned to Grey.

'Tell Harry to wait—all tomorrow if he has to. If Durham has not joined him by then, send word to me.'

He watched Grey mount and ride out. He turned back toward the keep and paused for a moment to stare up into the sky. It was a clear bright night; the moon was new, a sharp silver crescent riding high in an indigo sky. The badge of the Percys. Was it an omen that, as he looked, it slid behind a grey drift of cloud that seemed to have appeared from nowhere?

For the second time in as many days they were dragged from their beds before dawn. Elizabeth stood at the top of the narrow stairs that spiralled away into shadow and half light, isolated from the din of voices by fear, her own private fear that she had nurtured against her will these past two days. Harry was dead? At the hard chilling thought she broke into a run, stumbling over the hem of her robe, bruising her hands on the walls. No, not dead. She'd have known, she'd have felt something more than this numbness. She'd not have needed the battered blood-stained little troop who had ridden in to tell her that.

On the threshold she paused. The hall was full of faceless men, dirty, exhausted men with despair in their eyes. Tom Grey was there, his face drawn and sagging like an old man's. On her knees beside him Maud staunched the gaping wound in his thigh. The blood shrieked warning; though she could barely hear Grey's weary voice she did not come any further into the room.

Grey spoke between his teeth, his voice hoarse with pain and hard riding. 'He could not wait, my lord. He had marched out of Newcastle before I could reach him.'

Hal said nothing, listening to Grey's voice confirming all that his mind had already conjured up—one rash hot-headed mistake after another. Harry had not waited for Durham and had embarked his army on a long exhausting night march with an unknown destination. That was his first error; the second was not to reconnoitre more carefully the heaven-sent gift of the Scots asleep and unaware, camped at Otterburn.

'It was dark, my lord,' said Grey, as if that excused it. 'We attacked instantly and almost had the victory when a second body of the enemy fell on our flank.' His voice stumbled and broke. 'We fought for almost four hours and at the end of it there was nothing to show but half our army dead. Jamie Douglas is dead. Harry killed him and a dozen others.'

Hal lifted his eyes then. They had come to it, the thing he was almost afraid to ask, the answer that Grey had withheld since he came. 'And my sons?'

'Taken my lord. Both grievously wounded. Ralph was so badly hurt that the Scots allowed him a priest.'

Hal heard Elizabeth's pitiful little cry from the door; he saw Maud's face jerk into his vision as she stumbled to her feet. Slowly he turned and walked away from them.

He went straight to the turret room at the top of the Auditors' Tower, where he had watched Grey of Heton ride in less than five hours ago. Harry had been safe then. He had still been free and whole. His body jerked and writhed in rage and grief. Harry, Harry, Harry—damned bloody fool that he was, yet all that he cared for, all that he lived for. He slammed his fists against the wall. He was beaten now and oh so thoroughly. The Douglas held the masterhand while he held Harry, knowing him impotent. He was one of the few men who knew how much Hal would give to save his son.

He began pacing; there was comfort in movement, release in the short jerking strides that held off the tears of anger and despair. He must be calm, he must think. How badly was Harry hurt—badly enough to die? The painful lurch of his heart stopped him dead in his tracks. There'd be revenge for Jamie Douglas's death and what better than to take it on the man who had killed him? He stared his own fear out and saw it fade. No, Douglas was too shrewd for that. Harry was more valuable to him alive than dead, a weapon to use against him and finally beggar him for ransom.

He sank wearily to his knees. It was daylight outside and the candles had burnt down to spluttering stumps. 'Let him live,' he whispered. 'That's all I ask, let him live.' He stayed there a long time, so lost in his thoughts that he did not hear the door open.

Maud touched him gently on the shoulder. 'My lord?'

He did not move for a moment, then he turned his head and rose slowly to his feet. She had brought him wine and oatcakes.

'What will you do?' she asked quietly.

'There's nothing I can do till Douglas states his terms,' he said. 'He'll ransom Harry in the end, but it's what he'll demand in the meantime. . . .' He pushed the wine violently away from him. 'Christ,' he groaned, 'I wish I knew how badly he was hurt.'

Maud laid the pitcher of wine down sharply. 'Harry,' she said coldly. 'Always Harry. What about Ralph? Didn't you hear what Grey said, that he's so grievously hurt that they called a priest to him. He might be dead now for all you know. It's time you remembered that you have other sons beside Harry.'

The reproach caught him on the raw and stung all the more because it was true. He jerked his head up, his eyes blazing with anger. 'Yes, I *have* other sons!' he shouted. 'And none of them yours—remember that, madam, before you interfere.'

If he had struck her he could not have hurt her more. He saw the colour drain from her face, her hand upraised as if to ward him off. He stumbled from his chair and caught her wrist as she turned from him.

'Dear God!' He pulled her close, holding her so tightly that she winced in pain. He dropped his head onto her narrow shoulder. 'Forgive me,' he whispered. 'Forgive me.'

She raised his head and touched his cheek, feeling the wetness of the unwilling tears squeezed from his closed eyes. 'It's all right,' she said softly. 'It's all right. All will be well. They'll be safe.'

It was Douglas's victory; there was no doubt of that. Added to the bloody defeat of Otterburn was the Bishop of Durham's cowardly rout. When eventually he had brought his forces north, too late to find anything but the wounded and fleeing blocking the road to Newcastle, he had joined them. The Scots had gone home unhindered, their carts and wagons laden with booty and half the north's chivalry in chains. And after them had come the stream of Northumberland's messengers and envoys asking for news of his sons. If he'd had to, he would have begged on his knees to fetch Harry home.

They met on the wind-scarred heights of Hungry Law, within clear view of the men of both sides who waited uneasily in the valley below. For a long time they stood unmoving, the stretch of winter grass between them. The Douglas spurred his horse toward him, his cloak flung out like the black wings of a crow. Neither dismounted, but edged their horses close so that they stood neck to neck. The watchers squinted and strained on the edge of the ridge but heard nothing except the howl of the wind.

Hal stared into the Douglas's face; an old man's face, pitted and scarred, the hollow cheeks seamed and furrowed with hardship. Old and stubborn and intractable—but then was *he* so very different? Neither of them had ever known when he was beaten. He looked down into a well of memories. Was there anything left of that old reluctant friendship? Christ knew that both had tried to stamp it out. It should have been long buried by now.

Then, abruptly, the sun came out from behind its screen of clouds and shot full into his eyes. He turned his head away, momentarily blinded. 'My sons?' he asked, long before he meant to. 'Where are my sons?' With any other man he might have kept up a pretence.

'Safe and well,' Douglas smiled gently, 'their bones mended and waiting to come home. Did you expect aught else of me?'

Hal nodded, blinking fiercely on his tears. Perhaps he had. The thought had been there, discounted swiftly but not for the right reason.

Then Douglas said, 'I wonder which of us had the victory out of this.'

Hal glanced up into his eyes and saw the truth written on the parchment-white of his face. Only when he was with Douglas did he feel the futility of it all. There was no victor now, nor ever would be. No victory, no peace, only war and death. 'And the price, my lord?' he asked cynically. 'What price am I to pay for your solicitous care?'

Douglas smiled with rare humour. 'Do you remember you once said that those who could not match you in the field must be prepared to pay the price for failure?'

Hal gave a dry smile. 'To the victor go the spoils. . . .'

'Three thousand pounds then,' Douglas said sharply. 'For each of your sons, together with the release of the Scots prisoners that were taken at Otterburn.'

Hal met his challenging gaze calmly. Six thousand pounds: more than all his revenues for a year, yet he should be grateful that it had not been more. Both of them knew that whatever Douglas had asked, he would have paid it. 'Six thousand pounds then. Before Christmas.'

Douglas nodded, silent with the awkwardness of parting. Then he touched Hal's arm briefly in salute and turned his horse. 'Till the next time then, my lord,' he said and turned his horse back to his men.

It was three days before Christmas and the snow had just begun. In the gay bough-hung solar at Alnwick the two women waited; Maud pacing before the frosted casement, Elizabeth by the fire, one hand on the cradle where the newborn babe slept. The child was a girl and a disappointment, red and scrawny, and in her eyes unbelievably ugly. When Maud had first put it in her arms she stared at it with disbelief; so much pain for such a plain little thing, and a girl at that. Yet what did it matter; she was free again. They were both free. In a few hours Harry would be home and they could begin again.

The wind howled down the chimney and flattened the leaping flames with gusting smoke. The babe whimpered and before Elizabeth could rise, Maud was there, lifting it into her arms, crooning soft endearments into the tiny wrinkled face. Elizabeth smiled. Maud treated the child as if it were her own, a fact that Philippa had noticed spitefully and commented loudly upon at every opportunity. Elizabeth was content to have it so. The child's demands wearied her, and her insistence on a wet nurse had shocked and surprised both Maud and Philippa.

She rose gracefully, smoothing the flat line of her waist. In a way, she was glad that Harry had not seen her swollen and ugly

303

with child. The thread would run on unbroken from that last night they had spent together. She leant close to the window and watched the stars of fresh-fallen snow melt upon the glass. It would not be long now, it was no more than two hours' ride from Roxburgh where the exchange was to be made. She smiled at her own impatience, she had waited long enough, almost a year; it was strange how this last hour seemed to be the longest of all.

Maud cradled the drowsy child upon her lap, smoothing the down of red–gold hair with a possessive hand. She had been careful at first, smothering the craving for possession as she had with Philippa's sons. It was not her child, she had no rights save those of the doting grandmother. Yet Elizabeth had seemed more than happy to abandon the babe to her care; it was hers by default now and she loved it with all the pride and fierceness that should have been Elizabeth's. She placed the child back in its cradle and glanced resentfully to where Elizabeth stood, wondering if there was anything she cared about save herself. She'd watched her these last months, fretting and spiteful while she carried the child; her joy at its birth had been more the relief of ridding her body of a cumbersome burden than any mother-love. She loved Harry, certainly, but with a strange possessive love that was almost frightening. She had waited out the long months of his captivity in that secret shadowy world she had lived in when she had first come to Alnwick. None could reach her save the Welshwoman Morganna. It was only these last few weeks that she had begun to come alive again.

Then Elizabeth turned, her eyes wide and luminous. 'They're here,' she whispered. 'Harry's here.'

They both ran, Maud lagging behind Elizabeth's flying skirts. The drift of pages and squires coming out of the hall drew back to let them through. Maud heard the shout growing louder as it passed from mouth to mouth.

'*Hotspur, Hotspur! Hotspur is home!*'

She set her mouth grimly as the great outer doors were pulled back. There was no point in fighting against it. That was the only name they ever heard now. She went forward beside Elizabeth. She saw Hal's face, white and grim, his hands supporting Ralph. She could have wept when she saw him. He was so thin and pale and the badly healed broken leg was twisted under him from below the knee. The elfin laughing face she loved so much was seamed with red ugly scars. Then she looked at Harry, so whole, so handsome, his face unmarked except for the pallor of confinement. Her mouth tightened in renewed dislike. It would never be Harry who suffered, even though all this could be laid at his door. His arrogance had led countless men to their deaths, beggared his father and maimed his brother for life, yet she knew that there would be no rebuke for Harry. Harry Hotspur was perfection in all eyes but hers.

Elizabeth stood at the head of the stairs. The cressets at her back edged her with flame, her hair floated out from her unseen face, radiating light. Harry looked up through the whirling snow and saw her. Like a man blinded, he went toward her with outstretched hands.

Hal raised his cup again as yet another toast acclaimed the King, but he did not drink. The wine was dark and strong and so heavily laced with cloves that the very scent of it took his breath away. The food was worse, exotic delicacies swimming in pungent sauces that numbed the palate and burned the stomach. There were quail and heron, pheasant and peacock, even skinny fleshless larks stuffed and tortured into feathered splendour: thirty courses in all and each one a greater extravagance than the last. Beside him, the shrill voice of Woodstock's duchess clacked over his head. It was the first time for five years that he had been to Court and he liked it even less; the noise, the smells, the artifice all jarred. He longed for the cleanness and freedom of the north. He was too old now to dance attendance on kings, especially a king like Richard. For the first time in his life he felt old and tired. Yet how much of that was grief? His son Thomas's death had hit him hard. It was his own private sorrow, shared by none, and perhaps harder to bear because he had never loved Thomas as well as he should. The guilt was a greater burden than the loss.

It had been May when the news had come and the evening air had been soft and enticing and full of the promise of summer. Down by the river the deserted maypoles had trailed long bright ribbons in the muddy ring left by the children's feet. In the town square, bonfires had roared beneath twenty spitted and dripping oxen, and the sound of laughter had floated up to him on the scented air. He watched from the parapet of barbican tower, smiling as they had shouted his name and flung garlands of May blossom into the air. He had watched the man ride toward him curiously, straining his eyes to see his face. He was thin to the point of starvation, his shoulders stooped as if with an old sickness. He looked at the horse; the blazon on its saddle was his own.

'Tom.' The name escaped from his lips in a whisper of disbelief. Tom—his brother Tom, so old and stooped. He had called his name and seen the man turn his head. He was sure then. It was Tom.

He'd run down the stairs and out across the courtyard, his arms outstretched. He was all bone and shrivelled flesh, so light that Hal could lift him clean off his feet. 'Tom, Tom! You old devil, when did you get back? You should have sent us word.' His laughter faded as he saw his brother's face clearly for the first time. There was more than the hardship of war in the sunken cheeks and the yellow jaundiced eyes. There was sickness and hunger and near-death. 'Christ, Tom—was it so bad?' he asked.

His brother grinned and showed loose yellow teeth.

'Bad enough for me to long for the north.'

'Let's go inside,' said Hal. 'You look half starved. We must feed you up.'

Tom smiled. 'Not yet,' he said. 'Let's sit awhile. I am not used to civilized company yet.'

'How long have you been back?' Hal asked and sat beside him.

'A month. I stayed a week with the Duke in Westminster before coming north.'

'So Lancaster's back then?'

'And in favour too,' Tom said, and smiled as he saw the quick startled movement of his brother's head. 'Of course—' he added, 'you don't know do you? I'd forgotten how isolated you are here in the north.' He leant forward, his elbows on his straddled knees. 'There has been a revolution, my dear brother. Bloodless and so swift that half the Court is hardly aware of it even now. Woodstock's out and Lancaster's in—and by the King's wish at

306

that. It was Richard who commanded the Duke's return and then, all innocence, he summoned his council and asked Woodstock point blank how old he was. "Twenty-three, Your Grace," says Woodstock, all unsuspecting. "Then I'm old enough to manage my own affairs," says the King and promptly demands the seals of office from Arundel.' He laughed shortly. 'It was done, a fait accompli before Woodstock could draw his breath. The King is his own master again, Hal, with Lancaster at his side instead of at his throat.'

Hal shook his head in disbelief. 'In God's name why, when he moved heaven and earth to be rid of him?'

'Better the devil you know than the devil you don't,' Tom said. 'And Lancaster's harmless now compared to Woodstock and Arundel.' He stared out into the darkening evening. 'He's finished, Hal, a broken man come home to die in peace.' His voice took on a queer weightless quality. 'We were lucky that any of us got out alive. There were so many dead—fever, starvation, pestilence, we suffered them all. Out of all the men who sailed with Lancaster I doubt if even half have come home.'

So Lancaster had not lost the knack of leading men to their deaths. Hal turned to speak and saw his brother's eyes. 'Thomas?' he said sharply. It had never occurred to him that his son was anything but alive and well.

'Thomas is dead, Hal,' his brother had said quietly. 'It's what I came to tell you.'

His head jerked up sharply. The King's shrill laughter cut through the painful thoughts like a knife. Hal looked to where he sat, jewelled and resplendent as a peacock beside the soft roundness of his Queen. Six years wed and still no sign of an heir. Some said the King was incapable; others, more malicious, said he took his pleasure among the mincing effeminate courtiers that he still loved to surround himself with. It was hard to believe it, looking at that round cherubic face. But then they had all underestimated Richard. Thomas of Woodstock's swift and resounding fall was proof of that. There was little that those pale indolent eyes missed and more than a hint of ruthlessness about the small red mouth. Whatever he had learnt from that year beneath Woodstock's heel had changed him. His very mildness was unnerving. That he had

307

held his hand against the rebel lords was out of character in itself. Thomas of Woodstock had had the good sense to absent himself for a year on crusade but the Arundels were still at Court, though notably powerless. Warwick likewise had returned tactfully to his estate, while Tom Mowbray had thrown himself on the King's mercy and had been taken back into favour with such ease that he had been in a nervous sweat ever since. Bolingbroke had been safe by virtue of his father Lancaster but even now, four years on, they still waited for the reckoning which had never come.

Hal frowned. The pieces did not fit; there was something else, something they had all missed. This newly acquired docility was at odds with what he saw in the King's eyes. He seemed as bent now on raising up the old nobility as once he had been on keeping them down. Lancaster had been the prime recipient. Richard had created him Duke of Aquitaine for life and made the Duchy of Lancaster a palatine, thus bestowing on him all the powers of a pocket king. The Percys had not been forgotten. Hal was Privy Counsellor now, and his brother Tom, Chamberlain of the King's Household. Harry had his Garter and was Governor of Carlisle and Warden of the West March. So much for so little—? He wondered how long it would be before the King demanded payment for his favours.

His eyes dwelt musingly on the pink smiling face. Richard was inclining to plumpness, the flushed soft roundness of good living and malmsey wine. Only twenty-seven, but already he had the high unhealthy colour of his father. Another, more sobering thought came from nowhere: his father had been dead before he was forty.

His eyes went sharply to the man who sat beside the King. Lancaster, Lancaster, always Lancaster. The old hatred grown cold these past years sprang into virulent life. He felt suddenly numb. Harry and Ralph so nearly lost to him and now Thomas gone, rotting in some Spanish grave. Strange that he could not even recall his face now, though he had looked on it a thousand times, as if death had killed the memory. Perhaps it was less painful that way. There were enough remembered griefs in his heart already.

A last defiant flame fled sulkily among the smouldering ash of the near-dead fire. Hal watched it with tired eyes, as it crept feebly along the burnt-out length of crumbling wood and died, only to reappear with a vicious little spurt. He closed his eyes and the image remained, a bright persistent shape against the darkness of his lids. He sighed and shifted his weight from the hard uncushioned ribs of the chair; like Lancaster, the flame was always there, waking or sleeping, inescapable, always at the back of his mind. Tom had been right. The Duke was a broken man. There were no dreams left now, only the sour unpalatable fact that he would always be second. For Hal it should have been triumph, the enemy vanquished, yet where was the enemy in the weary disillusioned man who had faced him that day six months ago at Reading? It was the first time they had met for almost four years. Richard, malicious to the last, had demanded their public reconciliation and if he had thought to see a confrontation he was disappointed. It was so easily done, the joining of hands, the exchange of a kiss. Both were masters of the arts of deceit and subterfuge. Out of all those watching, perhaps only the two of them had known it for the meaningless empty gesture that it was.

With the fire gone it was growing chill. Little Bess stirred in Maud's arms and slid her hands beneath the fur edging of her gown for warmth. Hal looked to where Elizabeth knelt at her husband's feet.

' 'Tis time the child was in bed,' he said loudly.

The slight movement of Elizabeth's gleaming head was the only sign that she had heard. It was Maud who swept the sleeping child up and silenced her little cries with kisses and soothing words. Elizabeth only looked up when Maud carried Bess to her.

'Kiss your mother goodnight, sweeting.' The child stared stonily at her mother and inclined her plump cheek for the usual frigid kiss. Then she was away, climbing onto her father's knee to fasten her plump arms round his neck.

Harry laughed and loosed the vice-like grip. He ruffled her hair and cupped the rosy face in his strong hands as he kissed her. 'Go to bed, lovedy. Tomorrow I'll take you riding if you're good.'

Hal watched Elizabeth's mouth tighten with disapproval. She

disliked anything that would take Harry's attention from her—
and that included both Bess and himself. She was beautiful, he
granted her that, exceeding by far the promise of the quiet gawky
nine-year-old who had married his son. But it was a shallow,
introspective loveliness that was saved only from utter coldness
by the intelligence of her clear colourless eyes. She was clever in a
sly cunning way. She had weaned Harry from him as adroitly as
she had foisted her child onto Maud. Her father's daughter in
every way, she had the Mortimer's inbred hatred of Lancaster.

She glanced up and saw his eyes upon her. She rarely met his
eyes squarely, as if she were afraid she might see too much.
Her own eyes slid away from him now, save that this time she
covered the movement by rising and pouring wine into fat-bellied
goblets.

'I heard a rumour that Queen Anne was with child,' she said
lightly, and smiled softly to herself. 'Another false alarm. I saw
no sign of it today.'

She came and held out the wine to him. Hal took it with
measured slowness so that she could not move away as quickly as
she would have liked.

'I also heard a rumour—that you once had a daughter,' he said
coldly. 'I see no sign of that either.'

She flushed and almost spilled the wine in her haste to snatch
her hand away. 'I have better things to do than play nursemaid,'
she snapped.

Hal smiled cynically. 'Such as, madam? Scheming to place that
milksop brother of yours on the throne?'

Her colour faded as quickly as it had come. 'My brother Roger
is the King's designated heir,' she retorted. 'It is only natural that
I should look to his interests.' It was a lame answer and she knew
it, but the chill amber eyes forbade the soft dissembling that
worked so well on Harry.

Hal threw back his head and laughed—a great roaring belly
laugh so full of scorn that it set her teeth on edge. 'You deceive
yourself, Elizabeth. Roger Mortimer will never make a king.'

It was the laugh more than the remark that angered her. 'And
who *would* then, my lord?' she screamed. 'Harry Bolingbroke?'

Harry sprang to his feet; from the corner of her eyes she could see his white and angry face. 'For God's sake, Elizabeth! You're obsessed with Bolingbroke!' he shouted.

'And you are not, I suppose?' She sprang to face him. 'A boyhood friendship, you say. Well you're a man now, Harry Percy, and should long have outgrown such things.' She laughed shrilly, gone too far now to be checked by the growing coldness on both men's faces. 'You can't see, can you?' She encompassed Hal with her long green glance. 'Neither of you can see. You're both blind—besotted by Lancaster, pretending that Richard will never die, that you'll never have to choose. You think that he'll save you all at the eleventh hour by siring an heir. Well, he will die and there will be no heir. You'll have to choose, like it or not. My brother or Harry Bolingbroke. Can't you see that he is waiting—waiting for Richard to die?'

'As *you* are.' Hal rose slowly to his feet. 'You Mortimers can never resist meddling, can you? Your father was the same, always seeing himself as greater than he was, quick to pounce on anything that he could turn to his advantage, whatever it cost him in loyalty.'

'Loyalty?' Elizabeth tore herself from Harry's grasp and advanced across the room toward him. 'You talk of loyalty when you have changed your coat more times than any man I know? Lancaster's man, Richard's man, Mortimer's man. Whose man are you now, Northumberland?'

He stared coldly into her furious eyes. 'The same as I have always been—my own. It does not matter to me whether your brother is ever King or not. You may have bewitched my son but your scheming is wasted on me. My advice to you, madam, is to attend more to your duties as a wife and mother and less to adorning Roger Mortimer's foolish head with the crown.'

He turned abruptly, and all the time it took him to walk the length of the room her eyes never left his back. Silently she cursed him, and so great was her rage that as he slammed the doors she spoke the words aloud.

'Elizabeth!' Her name, sharply spoken, broke the spell. Harry's eyes were dark with warning. 'Take care, Bess,' he said softly. 'He is my father and well loved.'

'Yes.' She spoke the one word for no reason, to gain time and cover the dreadful blunder she had made. Deliberately she moved away from him so that the small oak table was between them, the candles set upon its surface lighting her face and hair to warmth and fire.

'I'm sorry,' she said and raised her green tear-filled eyes to his face. 'It's just that sometimes I'm so afraid.' That was true at least. She was afraid of Northumberland and even more so of Harry Bolingbroke.

Harry came round the table and tilted her face toward him. 'Afraid of what?' he asked gently.

She shook her head. 'So many things. . . .' She leant against him, feeling the strength of his arm encircle her. 'The King did Roger no great service when he named him his heir. You think I am obsessed with Bolingbroke. Yet you know him, Harry, better perhaps than any of us. If Richard dies without sons, do you think he'll stand aside and let Roger be King?' She lifted her face and saw the shadow of doubt in his eyes. 'He's Lancaster's son. He's been bred thinking that he had even a better right than Richard to the crown. Will he accept a Mortimer? Will he suffer any who has a better blood-right than he? If we had a son he would be close to the throne, closer than Henry Bolingbroke. Would you love him so well if he threatened your own son?'

She moved toward him and felt his body harden against her. 'You want a son, Harry.' She kissed his trembling mouth. 'If you had a son you'd not see him trampled by Bolingbroke. . . .' The words were smothered beneath his hungry mouth. She closed her eyes and shivered with pleasure at the hard cool pressure of his hands upon her breast. Tonight she'd see the fulfilment of her own prediction. Before the morning came she'd be with child again.

Slowly Maud laid the letter down on the smooth polished surface of her lectern. Bessy Percy's illiterate scrawl sloped untidily across the single page, blurred by tears and spattered ink. Poor stupid Bessy, she'd not even the wits to spell her own name aright. She turned her head away violently. Ralph was dead, her dearest child, the nearest she had ever come to a son of her own. Vision upon vision crowded her mind. Ralph at thirteen, regarding her with hostile curiosity when she had first come to Alnwick.

He had been the only one to really accept her; she remembered the first shy kiss he had dropped on her cheek, the way he had championed her against Harry's sullen criticism. The last vision was more painful: Ralph maimed and crippled, all the joy and laughter driven out by his constant pain. She'd almost been glad when he'd gone back to Bessy. She could not bear the travesty of him limping after his glorious brother any more than he could.

She rose and folded the letter carefully. There was still Hal to tell. Could he bear any more grief? Two of his sons dead in five years: it would make Harry all the more precious to him, if that were possible. Her mouth set in a grim line. It was all Harry's now, nothing to share or divide, yet she did him an injustice to think he'd be glad of that. Elizabeth might be, but to give Harry his due he had always loved Ralph well enough.

She walked stiffly out onto the sun terrace. Philippa's son Henry sat crosslegged, attempting to teach Bess the intricacies of dice. She paused to watch them. The child was so lovely. All her mother's beauty, without the streak of inhibiting coldness. She had all her father's open charm and his wildness too, apparent as she struck the dice cup from Henry's hand with a shriek of childish rage. Maud passed on and let the unseemly show of temper go without rebuke. She was a fool to love another woman's child, especially a woman like Elizabeth. Was it wishful thinking on her part to suppose that Elizabeth didn't care? She showed little interest in this child except when it claimed Harry's attention. The pose of motherhood was kept solely for his eyes and if this next child was a son, Maud doubted if there would be anything to spare for Bess. Sons were useful weapons in the hands of women like Elizabeth.

Quickly she went through the walk shaded by cypress trees. The grass was thin and patchy here from lack of sun but the brambles flourished in the damp and shade, spreading long tentacles across her path. She reminded herself to see that they were cut back in the morning. Round the angle of the gatehouse she saw Hal, his back against a tree, his face turned up to the sun he loved so well. Thomas, Lord Bardolf, sat beside him, laughing at something he had said. In the crook of the tree above them Harry sat whittling an arrow head with solemn precision.

She did not move, and saw his shoulders stiffen into awareness that he was being watched. Hal raised his head sharply and she smiled tremulously. It was a moment she always waited for, that first softening of his eyes as he saw her.

He beckoned her forward and Bardolf scrambled to his feet, spreading his cloak with the clumsy gallantry that was part of his outsize charm.

Hal smiled affectionately at him. 'I have been telling our rustic Bardolf here that he must alter his dress if he is to be a success at Court. Skin-tight hose that show all of your manhood and doublets to accentuate a delicate waist.'

Maud forced a smile at Bardolf's outraged bellow. Hal grinned and turned his head toward her.

'It seems our volatile sovereign is about to grace the north with his presence,' he said with dry amusement. 'The Londoners have provoked the royal rage with a refusal to lend the King a thousand pounds—and what's more, they have beaten to death the obliging Lombard who did.' Then, more soberly, he continued, 'Richard's had the mayor thrown into prison and has removed the Court to York—Chancery, Exchequer, Wardrobe and all.'

'The York merchants will be pleased,' Bardolf said. 'The King spends more in a day than all the northern lords in a week.'

Maud glanced up into Hal's face. 'Will there be trouble?'

'Only for us, in as much as we will have to attend the King at his new Court.' He smiled wryly. 'I'd forgotten what a blessing it was to have King and Court three hundred miles away.'

Maud looked away from his vivid eyes. Bardolf was talking, but she did not hear him. Her fingers plucked listlessly at the tiny pink-tipped daisies that thrust through the clipped grass. She knew that he was still watching her. Then Bardolf's deep voice tailed off into silence. She lifted her head and became aware for the first time that her face was wet with tears. She looked at Hal.

'Ralph is dead,' she said abruptly, and saw the life drain slowly from his eyes.

The abbey bell tolled out its monotonous repetitive note. Three for a death, and one for every year of Ralph Percy's life.

314

Thirty in all, then the briefest pause before it began again. Elizabeth paced out her chamber, pale in mourning black and sable. She disliked black, especially the hastily made gown that had none of the elegance and careful seaming of her others. In this her belly seemed swollen to twice its size.

She met Morganna's blank stare. 'You'll do the babe no good pacing like that. He'll not thrive on your ill humours,' Morganna said.

Elizabeth gave her a baleful look. The babe—that's all they ever harped on now, as if she were nothing, the means to an end, that end being an heir to Northumberland. It would not be so bad if Harry were here instead of dancing attendance on the King at York. He'd come back fast enough if he thought she'd borne a son. She glanced sharply at the Welshwoman's dark face. 'You're sure it will be a son?'

Morganna smiled slyly. 'Do you not know it, my lady? It is you who has the gift.'

Elizabeth laid her hand on the mound of her belly and closed her eyes. Yes, she had the gift, but only for others. She could see death and grief in another's face but in her own there were only shadows.

Then Morganna laid her gnarled hands upon her shoulders. 'Rest easy,' she whispered. 'It will be a son. The signs are all for a boy.'

Elizabeth nodded uneasily and shook off the iron grip of Morganna's hands. She walked quickly toward the door. In Maud's chamber there would be laughter and easy chatter, however tedious. For once, she felt the need of company other than her own.

Maud was seated by the hearth, stitching placidly at a froth of silk and Alençon lace. At her feet, flushed and rosy in a patch of sunlight, Bess played with an ivory doll. She looked up and unaccountably began to cry at the sight of her mother.

Elizabeth advanced through the unwelcome silence she had made. She did not spare a look for the knot of women who unconsciously backed away at her approach. Her eyes were fixed irritably on the child who wailed and blubbered and held out her plump arms to Maud. 'In God's name, Maud, is there no nursemaid to see to the child?' she snapped.

Bess screeched aloud at the sound of the sharp hostile voice. 'There is no need,' Maud said calmly, scooping the child onto her lap. 'I am content to see to her myself.'

Elizabeth smiled maliciously. 'And content also to wean her away from her mother?'

Maud looked up with hard angry eyes. 'That was your own choice, Elizabeth. I did not steal her. I merely picked up your leavings.'

'And if I should change my mind?' Elizabeth's eyes glittered with spite. 'If I should decide that she would be better cared for by Morganna?' She saw the leaping fear in Maud's eyes and suddenly felt ashamed of herself. 'Rest easy, Maud,' she said in a gentler voice. 'I'll not claim her now. She's more yours than ever she was mine.'

Maud said nothing and smoothed the child's shining curls, watching Elizabeth as she paced restlessly round the room. Seven months gone with child, and she had lost none of her beauty, except that the discontented line of her mouth gave her a hard and brittle look. Sometimes she almost hated her. It was so easy for Elizabeth, she had so much—too much, if she could discard her own daughter as if she were a gown that did not please. It rankled that Elizabeth could cast away something that she would have given half her life to possess. And then there was that all-consuming fear that Elizabeth had just put into words. Maud held the child tighter; Elizabeth had misjudged her there, if she thought she'd hand Bess back without a fight.

She beckoned to one of her women to take Bess and kissed the protest forming on the red petulant mouth to silence. The tiny half-finished gown lay where she had discarded it at Bess's first outcry. With her eyes still on Elizabeth she picked it up and retrieved her needle.

'When do you expect to see Harry back?' she asked casually.

Elizabeth's mouth drooped. 'I don't know,' she said. She'd see him when he chose to come. When he was welcome in her bed again and had had enough of drinking himself into a stupor every night at the expense of the King. Bolingbroke would be with him, stamping out the seeds of distrust that she had planted so carefully. She had failed there. Harry was not so easily turned from

316

his friendship. Just when she thought she had him where she wanted him he slid away from her, turning her from her purpose with smiling evasiveness. That was his father's doing; a woman's place was by the hearth, mending sheets not meddling in the affairs of men.

Then abruptly Maud said, as though she had been reading her mind, 'Why do you hate Henry Bolingbroke so much?'

Elizabeth hesitated for a moment, then said, 'Because he is all that you once thought his father to be. He thinks to be King of England in my brother's place.'

Maud raised her brows. She'd heard all this from Hal, it seemed that she'd been hearing something very like it since Richard was in his cradle. They'd lived so long with the threat of Lancaster's kingly pretensions that she was immune to it now. 'The House of Lancaster has been waiting for Richard to die since the day he was born. Naught has come of it yet, nor ever will in my opinion. The King is contrary enough to outlive them all.'

Elizabeth turned her head and smiled. 'Oh, he will die soon enough. I know it, I have seen it.'

Maud laughed. 'Another of your predictions Elizabeth?'

The tight, pointed smile faded. 'I would have thought you the last to mock,' Elizabeth said softly. 'It served you well enough once when all you had was hope.' She leaned closer. 'You cannot see the wind, you do not know where it comes from or where it goes, but you can feel it on your face. You know it is there. Well, I also know that no son of Richard's will ever sit on the throne. It will be Mortimer or Lancaster, and I mean to see that it is Mortimer.' She laid her hand on the hard rise of her belly and the child kicked against it as if in answer. 'My son will be a Mortimer.' She turned her lovely face toward Maud. 'Have you thought that if Richard and my brothers died tomorrow my son would be heir to the throne?'

Maud rose slowly to her feet. 'You're crazed, Elizabeth,' she breathed. 'Dear God, what are you leading us into, wishing away men's lives as if they were nothing.' She caught Elizabeth's arm and turned her toward her. 'Your son, if it is a son, will be a Percy. He'll be heir to Northumberland and nothing more. Be content with that.'

317

'Content?' Elizabeth sneered at her openly. 'What is this contentment you offer me? Sewing and spinning and getting myself with child every year till I'm old and fat? Have your never felt ambition Maud?'

Maud smiled. Once she had felt nothing else. She remembered how she had sneered at Margaret Neville once for being content. But that was a long time ago, before she discovered what an empty thing ambition was unless it was tempered with love and compassion. She doubted if Elizabeth had ever felt either. Suddenly, for all her beauty, Maud pitied her.

1396–1403

'The jalous swan, ayens his deth that singeth'

—Chaucer

For the fifteenth time Elizabeth rose to acclaim her husband's victory. His victim this time was a Frenchman and unpopular with the crowd. Even before the first course had been fully run, Harry had lifted him from the saddle with expert precision and put him on his back amid a clatter of armour and the delirious roar of the crowd. She watched their avid faces as they shouted his name: *'Hotspur, Hotspur!'* He held them cupped in the palm of his hand. The Londoners loved him, the dazzling extrovert figure who never rode through a town but that there was free ale for all. Even the lords of the Court were in awe of him and paid grudging tribute to the skill and reckless courage which to their old and cautious eyes sometimes verged on madness. To the young impressionable knights he was a god, the mirror of chivalry, the knight par excellence. To her, he was all these things and more, he was the man who would help to place her brother on the throne of England.

Strangely enough it was the King himself who was her greatest ally. In the five years since her son had been born the game had gone her way as if worked by her own will. Queen Anne had died the year before and the King had crushed all hopes of an immediate heir by marrying himself to the seven–year-old daughter of the mad King of France, an unpopular choice, especially as it had cost England the surrender of Brest. Lancaster's Duchess

319

Constanza was dead and the Duke had married his mistress, Katherine Swynford, to the outrage of the Court. Such a heaven-sent opportunity for mischief-making had been eagerly pounced on by the King. Lancaster's bastards had been swiftly legitimized—the eldest son John Beaufort made Earl of Somerset, to her delight and the chagrin of Henry Bolingbroke. She smiled with malicious satisfaction. Bolingbroke was not as self-assured as he had been. Richard had them all on the defensive—Bolingbroke, Arundel, Warwick and Mowbray, pinned in the corner into which he had been slowly driving them for the past ten years. She admired his patience; only once had the mask slipped. At Queen Anne's funeral mass, Arundel had not even had the grace to be punctual and had added insult to injury by asking to be excused. Richard had snatched a warder's staff and struck him to the ground. She had seen his eyes then and marvelled that he could have held his hand so long. If it had been her, their heads would have rolled on Tower Hill years ago.

She gave the King a careful sideways glance. His face was blotched and raddled by wine and there was something unnatural in the way he fawned on his child Queen. He was safe there, none could expect him to do his duty in that quarter for at least another seven years. She looked away and stared out over the trampled grass of the tourney field. She knew with cold triumphant certainty that Richard would not see forty; there would be no child, no heir to oust her brother Roger's claim. But there the vision clouded and she was plunged into uncertainty. Roger himself was the stumbling block; he lacked the burning ambition of herself and their brother Edmund. He had to be pushed into every strategy, goaded into asserting himself above men like Bolingbroke. If it were not for her and Edmund, he would have quit the Court long ago and been content to keep to his land like a cowherd. Suddenly apprehensive, she scanned the gaudy banners that edged the field. The white lion of March roared tamely beside the scarlet splendour of the Lancastrian rose. Roger was there, bending to the girth of the heavy-boned Spanish horse that the King had given him at Christmas. She could not see his face but the red–gold Mortimer hair marked him like a beacon.

She rose suddenly, murmuring an excuse to the other ladies in the lodge. At the back of the tents the armourers sat knee to knee, hammering out dents and mending torn mail. She picked her way carefully through the piles of broken and discarded lances, turning her nose from the steaming piles of horse dung that seemed to litter every available space.

Her brother Edmund was sprawled on the grass in front of his tent, his face buried in a jug of wine. She called to him softly and smiled as he turned his handsome face toward her. It was her one regret that he, not Roger, was the younger.

'Well?' She drew him back into the shadows. 'What did he say?'

Edmund shook his head. 'I can't dissuade him. He insists on going to Ireland. He says that he'd rather secure the lands he's got than hang around at Court waiting for new ones.'

Elizabeth's mouth tightened in anger. 'Dear God—what ails him that he'd rather risk his life among a lot of savages than mind his place here by the King?'

Edmund shook his head again. 'You know Roger. He couldn't care less about being Richard's heir.' He raised his dark intense eyes to her face. 'Christ, Bess—I wish it were me! I'd give anything for the chance that he's got.'

'And he treats it as if he were being offered some worthless bauble,' Elizabeth snapped. Then she laid her hand on his arm. 'Well, we'll have to make do without him. If Richard. . . .' She paused, suddenly aware of a shadow falling between them. She looked up and saw Harry leaning against a tree, watching them.

'Plotting again, sweetheart?' he said drily. 'And you Edmund, you should know better than to encourage her.'

Elizabeth smiled. 'Ah, it is you, fair Hotspur,' she said mockingly. 'The new Alexander come to boast of his conquests.'

Harry grinned and came toward her. He had stripped off his armour and the linen shirt, open to the waist, clung damply to his skin. He slipped his arm round her waist and she saw how the muscles of his chest gleamed with sweat and steamed like a hard-run horse.

'I never boast,' he said and kissed her lightly on the cheek.

Elizabeth said with malicious sweetness, 'Why should you,

321

when all the world does it for you? Do you not find that such adulation palls? I must admit I am increasingly seized with a desire to see you laid flat on your back for a change.'

Harry laughed and glanced up at Edmund. 'Will you excuse us? I am famished and dirty and have a sudden need to beat my wife.' He swept her abruptly off her feet and carried her amid shouts of laughter to the little grove of trees at the edge of the field.

Elizabeth brushed furiously at her skirts. 'For God's sake, Harry, must you treat me like a trollop—in front of my own brother at that.'

'You *are* a trollop.' He grabbed her wrists and pulled her to him. 'Deny it and I'll take you here and now and prove it.'

She leaned against him, her anger fading, aware of the hardness of his body and the mingling scents of sweat and leather and horseflesh that came from him. She laughed softly and looked up into his face. 'Then I'll not deny it,' she said. 'Though I might if we were not within staring distance of a thousand pairs of eyes.'

He smiled and kissed her willing mouth. 'Then your lack of virtue has saved you,' he whispered. 'For the moment.' He flung himself on his back and closed his eyes. 'Christ, I'm tired and sick,' he said.

'Sick?' She sat up sharply, her eyes anxiously scanning his face.

He smiled. 'Sick of the city and of playing the courtier to that juvenile little French brat.' His smiled faded. 'Let's go home, Bess. I'm sick for the north.'

Sick for your father, she thought with sudden anger. It was only these last few months since he had been away from Northumberland that he had become hers so completely. All hers— save for that small part he kept for his father. She hated the Earl for that. He could block the course she had steered so carefully with one word; one look could bring Harry back under his influence, and temper that hot reckless streak in him that was her greatest asset. If she faced the truth, Harry was only really hers when he was plunged deep into her body. The rest of the time he went his own way. She could lead him only so far, then unpredictably he would break away, back to the north, back to his father, as he was doing now.

Abruptly she said, 'Roger is set on going to his estates in Ireland.'

Harry opened his eyes. 'Then let him go. He's got more sense than the rest of us.'

'And let someone else fill his place by Richard's side?'

Harry propped himself up on his elbow and looked at her with a mixture of admiration and amusement. 'You credit others with your own morals, Bess,' he said. 'Not everyone is hankering after Richard's crown—and least of all, I think, Roger himself.'

'I know one that is.'

'Ah yes, of course,' Harry sneered. 'We must not forget our villainous cousin Bolingbroke, poised with itching fingers to snatch Richard's crown.'

She turned furiously to face him. 'You can mock, Harry Percy, but you'll see one day. The King believes it. He's set on bringing Bolingbroke down, and soon.' She smiled in triumph. 'Henry Bolingbroke is a doomed man. If you need proof, look into the King's eyes next time they rest on Bolingbroke.'

'And who says all this? The little demon you keep inside your head or that Welsh hag who stirs you up in case you ever forget you are Mortimer bred?'

'I need no telling, and neither would you if you had the wit to read the signs. Even if you've forgotten, the King hasn't: De Vere, Suffolk, Burley, Tresilian—did it ever strike you as strange that the King took it all so meekly? You know him, Harry, you grew up with him. When was the King ever meek or forgiving? When did he ever forget the smallest slight? Yet he saw all his closest and dearest friends slaughtered and banished without a murmur.'

Harry sat up and stared at her. 'Allowing that you're right, why now and not then? What is so different now?'

'Three thousand Cheshire archers at his back night and day. He was weak then and now he is strong. There is no de Vere now to keep the nobility sitting on the fence. How many would go against Richard now to save Woodstock and Arundel?'

'Lancaster, perhaps, if he thought his son was threatened.'

Elizabeth laughed. 'Lancaster's old and finished, and so firmly in Richard's pocket that even Bolingbroke could not prise him out of it. He has other sons now, remember—three Beaufort sons, hungry for power and entirely dependent on Richard for it.'

Harry said nothing but his eyes never left her face. She was so lovely, and with the mingling of hatred and triumph lighting her face unusually so; lovely enough for him to turn a blind eye to the evil malignant streak that sickened him every time he was faced with it. In a strange, incomprehensible way he was almost afraid of her and that dreadful singleness of purpose that nothing could turn her from. Any means justified the end; himself, her brothers, even her son—none was exempt, none too great a sacrifice to make if it brought her what she wanted.

'Leave it, Elizabeth,' he said harshly. 'For God's sake—let it alone before you bring grief and misfortune down on all our heads.'

Elizabeth dressed with exquisite care, sitting with unaccustomed patience while Morganna combed and plaited and braided and finally hid the burnished copper coils beneath a high-pointed hennin. She stared at her own reflection and smiled. Her eyes were long and green as a cat's beneath finely plucked brows, her skin pale and glowing as Italian marble, the high cheekbones subtly rouged with henna. Her mouth was red and voluptuous from crushed juniper berries, her neck and wrists touched with the aphrodisiac vervain. Morganna came, arms outstretched, and laid the gossamer veil over the needle point of her headdress. She waited as it settled into place, and pulled the long trailing end over her shoulder. Then she rose; she was ready. Like a man fully armoured she went down into the hall.

Harry was waiting, sprawled on the long settle by the window taking wine with the knights of his retinue. She paused at the top of the stairs to observe him. He wore the Percy colours, azure velvet edged with gold, and in deference to her he also wore the silver rose of Mortimer. She smiled; so he had forgotten. How like Harry, his anger went as quickly as it came. By the time she reached the foot of the stairs he wouldn't even remember that they had quarrelled.

Beneath the austere magnificence of the King's new hammer-beam roof, the nobility of England bruised their lips on his long beringed fingers. He was dressed in cloth of gold and so crusted with diamonds that the brilliance of him almost hurt the eyes. Beside him his little French queen Isabella lisped broken English. She looked pale and sickly in burgundy velvet, almost as magnificent as her lord but not quite. Richard was always careful that none outshone him.

Elizabeth watched from her place at the end of the high table. Woodstock glowered at all and sundry, tapping his bony fingers on the cloth as Richard blatantly passed him over and made much of Lancaster's new duchess. His own wife sat beside him, stiff with outrage. She had almost baulked at ceding Katherine Swynford precedence but a look from the King had silenced the spiteful outburst that still lay smouldering beneath her flat bosom.

Elizabeth glanced with interest at the woman who had not only held the Duke of Lancaster's interest for nearly twenty years but married him. Not the harpy and strumpet that Eleanor of Gloucester would have the Court believe, by the look of her. She must be forty now but the fine bones of her face still maintained the illusion of beauty and she had a quiet dignity of her own. Her Beaufort sons were there; John, now Earl of Somerset, and Henry the clerk, plucked from his learned studies at Oxford and abruptly manoeuvred into the wealthy bishopric of Lincoln before he was sixteen. Elizabeth's glance slid maliciously on to Henry Bolingbroke. She wondered how he felt, seeing his father's new and unexpected family raised so high. Her eyes moved on down the hall. The inevitable Cheshire bodyguard lined the walls and at the lower tables the redundant garrison of Brest got loudly drunk, making the most of the King's largesse before they were finally pensioned off. Harry was dancing with Joan Beaufort, already rumoured to be betrothed to the recently widowed Ralph Neville. Northumberland would not like that, she thought, the plum of the newly sprung Beaufort tree going to the Nevilles.

With detached amusement she watched Harry tease the girl with his eyes as their bodies briefly touched in the rhythm of the dance. His hands lingered round her waist, bringing a rush of colour to her cheeks. Elizabeth smiled. Harry was so susceptible to women, especially young pretty ones. It did not bother her unduly; she had no rivals now. Harry was wholly hers in that respect. He'd not get what his body needed from a young untried girl like Joan Beaufort.

She turned, smiling, as a hand touched her shoulder. Her smile faded as she looked into the cold blue eyes of Henry Bolingbroke.

'My lady.' He bowed courteously over her grudgingly given hand. 'Will you do me the honour of partnering me in the dance?'

She had no words except a muttered 'My lord'. His hand was cold and steady as he led her onto the floor, and she was aware of Harry's amused stare. She recovered quickly, turning toward him as the first throbbing notes of the tabor announced a rondo. She was almost as tall as he was and glad that she did not have to look up into his face. It was the first time she had been so close to him. They had met and exchanged greetings and she sat in mute and aloof silence on the few occasions she had dined at Leicester; but never face to face, eye to eye. She had not realized that his eyes were quite so pale or that his mouth was quite so ruthless.

She turned beneath his arm and spread her skirts in a low curtsey. They joined hands again and swayed toward each other.

'Does it hurt so much, my lady?'

She stared at him blankly.

'Dancing with me,' he explained with a smile. 'It shows. You have such an expressive face. The waiting tells on you.'

'The waiting for what?' A stupid clumsy remark when she had meant to be so witty and clever.

He smiled again. 'We all wait for different things—though perhaps not we two.' He glanced swiftly at the King then back to her face again. 'Perhaps we wait for the same thing but to different ends, Elizabeth.' It was the first time he had ever spoken her name. She was surprised at the sound of it in his mouth, almost caressing. She could have laughed out loud. Dear God, surely the man was not trying to court her? She held his eyes though her heart began to pound with excitement. He could not have said more clearly that they both wished Richard dead.

'Perhaps we do,' she answered softly, 'but I *can* wait, my lord. It strikes me that perhaps your own patience is wearing a little thin.'

He laughed, a harsh mirthless sound which grated on her ears. 'I think that you would tempt me to treason, Elizabeth.'

'You are already there, my lord, in thought if not in deed,' she retorted, and watched the sudden hardening of his eyes.

'We both are,' he murmured quietly. 'But then our thoughts can do us no harm. It is our deeds that count against us.'

Elizabeth smiled. 'As perhaps you are beginning to learn to your cost. The King has a long memory.'

He came close to her again. 'Not long enough, I hope, to remember that it was a Mortimer who murdered his great—grandfather.'

If he had thought to rouse her with that he was disappointed. Still smiling she said, 'Did you ask me here just to insult my blood?' She glided three paces away from him and turned beneath his outstretched arm. 'Why did you ask?' she added as she swept back to face him.

'Every good captain always consorts with the enemy.'

She raised the invisible arch of her brows. 'A prior skirmish, my lord? What makes you think that I am your enemy?'.

'I know that you try and turn Harry against me and that you'll employ every wile in your devious little mind to put that brother of yours on the throne.' He smiled and showed his teeth. 'I promise you this, sweet Elizabeth. Your brother will never be King of England.'

She stood quite still, her hand limp in his grasp. He brushed it formally with his lips and she waited till his eyes were on a level with hers again before she spoke. 'And you *will* be?' she asked him softly.

He laughed, avoiding the trap he saw in her eyes. 'If I ever am,' he said, 'it will be my first royal duty to wipe that arrogant smile from your face.'

She did not know whether she was pleased or angry. It was a confession of sorts. He had committed himself, not openly but in a devious and roundabout way that she could understand. She had been right. Her intuition had not failed her. Henry Bolingbroke saw himself as the next King of England.

Harry was waiting for her, mildly drunk and sitting by his uncle Tom Percy. Elizabeth smiled a lukewarm greeting; she had

327

never been able to make up her mind about the Earl's brother. Dislike was too strong a word, indifference fell a long way short; one could never be indifferent to a man like Thomas Percy. Then Harry said, gently sneering, 'So the white rose and the red rose come together! A charming bouquet, if it were not for the stink of intrigue.'

She showed her small teeth in a savage smile. 'Jealous, my lord?' She looked pointedly at the rounded prettiness of Joan Beaufort, 'I thought you had a taste for roses yourself, albeit of the hybrid variety.'

Harry grinned. 'Peace,' he said and pulled her down beside him. He glanced up at his uncle and then at Elizabeth. 'Tom has sent for my father the Earl. He thinks there will be trouble.'

Elizabeth stiffened. 'Trouble—what kind of trouble?'

Tom looked doubtfully at Elizabeth. He did not care for women overmuch, especially clever ones, and Harry's wife was a born meddler. But then that was Harry's concern; if he could not keep her down it was no business of his. He glanced uneasily behind him toward the royal dais, then said, 'The King is like a cauldron at full boil. I could be charitable and say Queen Anne's death has turned his mind but I think it's more than that. He seems hell-bent on committing financial suicide. The Treasury is empty, the jewels of Aquitaine already in pawn, and now there's a truce with France the London merchants are demanding that the war tax be abolished. Thirteen florins in every hundred, enough to make them squall loud enough in wartime let alone when Richard squanders it on a Frenchie queen.' He paused and gulped a mouthful of wine. 'It's Woodstock that's stirring up the trouble and the King knows it. Woodstock's been holding secret meetings with merchants, inciting them to rebel. There's going to be sides taken before long and such an almighty furore that we'll be lucky if any of us come out of it unscathed.'

Elizabeth stared past his dark thin face. It was come: the first ripples of the tidal wave that would sweep the privileged ground from under Bolingbroke's feet. And there, enthroned and resplendent as a popinjay, was the architect of the deed.

The King was drunk, pleasantly so, not enough to addle his wits but enough to allow a little of his true feelings to show in his eyes. He smiled as Thomas Mowbray leaned close and filled his cup. Dear Thomas, stupid Thomas, ungrateful and faithless Thomas. It would be one of the headier pleasures of his vengeance to see Thomas Mowbray grovel for his life.

Richard glanced around at the smug satisfied faces that he always kept before him. Lancaster sat beside him, the weary smile that he always wore a little strained as the King's eyes rested upon him. Did he still doubt, after all this time? But then that was an essential part of the game he played. Doubt, uncertainty, seeing them all waiting for the reckoning that never came. Perhaps Bolingbroke knew. He would have liked that, to think that his quiet scheming had not gone unnoticed. He liked an audience, especially one that could appreciate the finer points of his performance.

Then, slowly, like a child leaving the choicest morsel to the last, he looked at his uncle Woodstock. Oh, that had been joy, to see that sour-faced wife of his have to suffer the Duchess Katherine! He stared hard at his face, committing each detail to memory: the dark heavy brows that almost met above the long Plantagenet nose, the dark brown eyes like a dog's, beneath the white fleshy lids. In his mind's eye he saw them bulging with pain, the clacking insulting tongue thrusting through blue swollen lips and slowly turning black. Richard started as the eyes were suddenly raised to his.

'And now I suppose we'll have a plague of unemployed soldiery running riot,' Woodstock was saying loudly. 'Perhaps Your Grace has given a thought as to how they are going to live, now that you have deprived them of their livelihood.'

Richard smiled thinly. 'They will be provided for,' he said calmly. 'They have been billeted near London till work can be found.'

'What work?' Woodstock's loud voice filled the hall. 'My father bred a nation of soldiers and you have turned them into a nation of useless clods. My God—' he thumped his fist on the table, 'I remember a time when Frenchmen walked in fear of the English! Now they just snigger at us behind their hands and ask what colour hose the King of England is wearing today.'

Richard's face grew pale and sickly but he said nothing. Give Woodstock enough rope and he would hang himself.

'Perhaps Your Grace should try risking your life to capture a city before you go handing back those that your father and grandfather shed good English blood for.' Woodstock shoved his chin forward, his lip curled in a sneer. 'You'll be giving them back Calais next, I suppose.'

'How dare you!' The words escaped the King's lips in a whisper of outraged air. 'How dare you insult me!'

'I dare because I am an Englishman and proud of it. I'll not stand by and watch you give England away and tax her into penury to satisfy your perverted tastes.'

The King was on his feet, swaying like a drunkard. 'Get out!' he screamed. 'Get out before you stir my memory too well and I remember old treasons! Get out while you still have legs to walk upon!'

'With pleasure, Your Grace.' Woodstock rose from the table and bowed mockingly low. 'With the greatest of pleasure.'

With supreme self-control Richard lowered himself into his chair again, aware of all the anxious uneasy eyes that clung to his face. He'd had him there and let him go. He smiled as he felt the blood rushing back in his face. He could wait a little longer. Not one, but all. It must be all of them. He'd not be cheated again.

Amid the strained and uneasy silence Elizabeth watched as Woodstock quit the hall, the knights of his retinue firmly at his back, his Duchess trailing in their wake. She swallowed down the bubbling little laugh of triumph. Her eyes sought out Bolingbroke and she smiled as she saw that his face was as pale and still as death.

London

It was August, hot and sultry, without a breath of air to lift the heaviness of the long day. The timid little breeze that had sprung up from the river had died away at noon, after wafting the stench of rancid meat over the low walls of the house at Aldersgate. From her perch in the low-branched elm Elizabeth could see the

330

haze of flies that marked the Shambles and Newgate, the soaring spire of St Paul's blunted by a mist of heat. A frown creased the white perfection of her brow. Edmund should have been here at noon and it was now long past two o'clock. She tilted her head back and stared up into the brilliant greenness of the hushed branches: so quiet, so still, the broad flat leaves curled and limp in the heat, trapped and motionless as she was. With sudden violence she jumped down. Her feet were bare and the long uncut grass was cool against her skin. She heard the discordant muddled chiming of a dozen bells. It was three o'clock. Edmund would not come now.

She ground her teeth together in irritation. Jesu, how she wished she were a man instead of always waiting, having to be content with the scraps of information that Harry fed her, and then only as much as he thought she should hear. All she'd had these past few weeks since Woodstock's quarrel with the King were rumours: that Woodstock and Arundel plotted the King's death, that the King had ordered his uncle's arrest, that Woodstock was dead, that Bolingbroke was dead. That last was wishful thinking on her part. The only thing she knew for certain was that the five lords marked for Richard's vengeance had beaten a hasty retreat from London.

She wandered out from the shade of the tree and the heat struck her like a physical blow. In the grove of aspen trees behind the herb garden her children played. Between them Maud sat with the inevitable embroidery on her lap, her face still pale from the sickness that had swept through the city. Maud had recovered but in the poorer quarters there had been as many as a thousand dead. She smiled as Bess painstakingly built a tower of coloured bricks and little Hal knocked it down again with a gleeful shriek.

Elizabeth eyed her daughter coldly as she noticed the way she shrank a little closer to Maud at the sight of her. She noticed also that her gown was crumpled and stained and that a strand of red hair had escaped from the neat little cap. She looked like a young savage. Yet nothing could detract from the loveliness of her features. She was as fair as her mother, perhaps fairer, with the bloom of youth and innocence on her cheeks. Elizabeth remembered that she was ten years old now, about the same age that she had been when she had married Harry.

She smiled as little Hal staggered toward her. His mouth was full of comfits and a sticky dribble adorned his chin. She picked him up and scrubbed his mouth before she kissed him. There was no doubt who held her heart. The kiss was so full of love and tenderness that Maud looked away in anger. Poor Bess; she had never had anything but sharp words and criticism.

'I want to go out,' the boy said plaintively. 'I want to fly the merlin that grandfather gave me.'

'Soon, my sweet,' Elizabeth said. 'Tomorrow perhaps. Morganna said there have been no deaths in the city for a week.'

'Then if Morganna says it, it must be true,' Maud said sharply. 'When has Morganna ever been wrong?'

Bess stared stonily at her mother's narrow back. 'Grandfather says Morganna is a witch,' she said loudly.

Maud opened her mouth to reprove the child but Elizabeth forestalled her.

'If she were, then my lord would have been burning in hell fire long before now,' she snapped.

Elizabeth looked away from Maud's shocked and angry face. It was true. If the wish could have become the deed she'd have seen him in purgatory. When the Earl was present no other voice was heard. Since his arrival two weeks ago she'd seen her influence with Harry wane sharply. Maud had been right about that. It had been a mistake to make an enemy of him so soon. Yet what other course had there been? All the usual wiles had failed. Even the sharp antagonistic wit which could draw most men out fell on stony ground. She'd become used now to the quiet rebuff of his eyes. It could only hurt her when she saw the echo of the look in Harry.

She turned her head fractionally. Maud continued to stitch in stony silence and Bess had begun to toy with the bricks again. She scooped her son up from the seat and disentangled his fingers from the chain around her neck.

'And see that child is decently gowned before she comes down to supper,' she said over her shoulder as she left them.

She waited late for Harry and it was past midnight when he eventually came. He lounged in the doorway, stripped to the waist, his shirt and doublet trailing from his hand. He watched her for a little while and then said, 'Waiting on the corpse, my little vulture? Could you not sleep till you had tasted blood?'

'And have you brought me a corpse, Harry?' She smiled and uncurled herself on the bed, aware of his eyes on her loosened hair and the shadows of her body through the thin silk.

'Three, to be precise.' He threw his tunic down on the bed and poured himself wine. 'Woodstock was taken at Pleshy last night and Arundel and Warwick are being brought to London for trial on charges of high treason. That snivelling little rat Mowbray betrayed them. He is prepared to swear that he was present when they plotted the King's death at Arundel last month.'

The pent up breath left her body in a long pleasurable sigh. She watched Harry come toward her. He was naked now and sweat filmed his throat and chest. Her eyes moved down to the narrow ridged muscles of his belly, the long hard line of his thighs veined with the white threads of old tourney scars. She smiled as she saw her glance arouse him.

'And Bolingbroke?' she said longingly. 'What of Bolingbroke?'

He came and knelt beside her, grasping a handful of her hair and twining it round his wrist like a rope. He pulled her slowly toward him. 'Not yet, my little vixen,' he said softly. 'You'll have to wait a while for Bolingbroke, my love.'

She did not have to wait long. By September Arundel was dead, having run the gauntlet of a sham trial and a rigged Parliament not a little swayed by the menace of two thousand Cheshire archers at their back, to end on the block at Tower Hill. His brother Bishop Thomas was down, exiled and out of office, and they said the King had wept for joy to see the look of bleak and foolish amazement on the prelate's face when he had been told. Warwick had saved himself, but only just, wailing and weeping through his trial like an old woman, and secretly laying such a wealth of evidence in the King's lap that Richard had openly declared that Warwick's confession pleased him more than all of Arundel's and Woodstock's lands put together. Did it implicate

Bolingbroke, Elizabeth had wondered? It would be like Richard, to set one thief to catch another. Of Thomas of Woodstock nothing more was heard or seen save the brief and tongue-in-cheek announcement of his death in prison at Calais. Murdered ... All knew that. Elizabeth knew it, and the knowledge sweetened the final waiting. It meant that Richard would not be cheated at any price.

Yet Mowbray and Bolingbroke remained unscathed, Mowbray because he was still useful to the King and Bolingbroke because he was Lancaster's son. The King heaped them with even higher honours; the dukedom of Norfolk to Mowbray, Hereford to Bolingbroke. Elizabeth had smiled when she had heard. The higher Richard raised them the further they would have to fall.

Then in December it had come. Mowbray had been the first to break. All the honours and favours had not been enough to mask the threat of the King's vengeance and he'd been fool enough to run to Bolingbroke with his fears of persecution and plots. They were the only two of the five left. He knew for a fact that Richard and his Holland brothers schemed for Bolingbroke's death.

Bolingbroke had still felt himself secure enough to lay Mowbray's treasonous rantings at Richard's feet. Mowbray when summoned had denied that he had ever said it, and had in turn accused Bolingbroke of treason. So the quarrel had grown, burgeoning into a feud of accusation and counter-accusation, while the King had watched happily as both had fought and squabbled their way to destruction. Then it had seemed for a moment that both she and the King might be cheated of victory. Bolingbroke had appealed to the court of chivalry and elected trial by combat; a fight to the death. Had the same thoughts run through Richard's mind as hers? That there could only be one victor and the odds were heavily in favour of it being Bolingbroke? It seemed that they had. The trial had been set for September, a cold day; the King had worn miniver and sable against the chill. All was ready. The marshals had examined and approved the weapons; the armourers, squires, surgeons and confessors had retreated behind the barriers. The two combatants waited for the King's signal. It never came. At the eleventh hour Richard had stopped the trial.

'The crowd went mad,' said the knight beside her, who had been there. 'Some had trudged miles to see the combat. For half a groat some would have lynched the King himself when it was announced that the trial was to be abandoned and that sentences of exile were to be imposed instead.'

Elizabeth smiled. Ten years for Bolingbroke, life for Mowbray. How clever of Richard to kill two birds with one stone. She herself would have preferred Bolingbroke dead. Yet exile was enough to silence the voice that had stirred Richard up against her brother Roger; badly enough for the King to summon him back from Ireland to attend the Lent Parliament at Shrewsbury. Crowds had turned out in their thousands to greet him. The streets had been red and white with the Mortimer colours, the air a trembling roar of his name. She could imagine Bolingbroke whispering in the King's jealous ear: 'Jesu, sire—it seems my lord of March thinks himself King already.'

If only they knew that beneath his golden handsome exterior there was a man who'd rather be a cowherd than a king.

She glanced toward the Earl. He had been at Coventry. Had he pleaded for Bolingbroke? Had his been one of the voices that had forced the King to reduce the sentence of exile from ten years to six? It would not have surprised her. The Earl always favoured the underdog, even when it was the son of his bitterest enemy. Tomorrow he'll be gone, she thought exultantly. Back to the north, taking sickly Maud with him. Harry would be hers again in mind as well as body. Then she could begin.

She turned her head sharply as if a voice had spoken in her ear. Edmund was here. Edmund, weeping and calling her name, She stared frantically round the hall. Candles burnt with frightening brilliance, plunging all the faces into shadow. Then Edmund was standing in the doorway, his chest heaving, his eyes red–rimmed and staring. The shadows converged on his face and swallowed him up. She saw a field—green verdant grass slicked with mud. A horse was coming toward her, dragging its rider from the stirrup. There were men—strange, wild-looking men in pelts and furs. The horse had shaken its rider loose and ran on free. The men closed, howling, stabbing, hacking. In their midst she could see the dreadful mangled thing that had been her brother Roger.

335

Edmund touched her arm. 'Elizabeth,' he whispered. 'Elizabeth.'

She raised her eyes and saw how his tears trickled into the creases around his mouth. 'Roger is dead. At Kells. Oh God.'

He was blubbering like a child and she slapped him hard across the cheek. 'Tell me,' she said quietly.

Edmund dragged his sleeve across his mouth. 'It was a mistake,' he said. His voice had dropped to barely a whisper yet it echoed like a drum in the silent staring hall. 'He was wearing an Irish cloak that he had captured from one of the chieftains. He rushed on too far ahead of his own men and in the fighting he was mistaken for the enemy.' He began to weep again. 'Dear God, Bess. They tore him to pieces. There was nothing left of him.'

Elizabeth closed her eyes. No, nothing left except an empty useless dream. She began to scream. She had not beaten the curse after all. Roger was dead. He was only twenty-four years old.

Maud opened her eyes to the half darkness. The acrid smell of vinegar and rue made the air heavy and hard to breathe. There was no pain. Morganna had seen to that. She smiled a little to herself. Whoever would have thought she would have waited on the coming of that old Welsh crow with such eagerness?

She turned her head toward the light. He was still there, staring out from the high window, turning his head fractionally to follow the flight of a bird that skimmed the leaden panes of the Tower room. He had not heard her move and she watched him a little longer. His hair was almost grey now and his face was thin almost to the point of emaciation. Yet nothing could destroy the stark splendour of bone and eyes. They were almost black as he turned to look at her, the gold a long way down like points of sunlight at the end of a shaft. He smiled and came to sit by her.

'Are you well?' he asked softly. 'You slept for a long time.'

She nodded. 'Yes, I was tired. I feel better now.' She smiled and picked up the small jewelled book beside her bed. 'Will you read to me?'

'Not scurrilous Langland, I hope?'

She smiled. 'No. Chaucer. He's in more need of support.

Elizabeth told me that he was forced to ask the King's protection against his creditors last year.'

Hal sighed. 'And so of course you sent him a crown or two?'

'Or three,' she admitted. 'It seemed such a small price to pay for so much beauty.' She closed her eyes as he began to read.

> 'The lyf so short, the craft so long to lerne,
> Th'assay so hard, so sharp the conquering,
> The dredful joye, that alwey slit so yerne,
> Al this mene I by love . . .'

She smiled. Once that was all she had known of love. The assay so hard, the dreadful joy. . . . She clenched her teeth hard on her lip as a spasm of pain stabbed through her chest and stirred the racking cough of life.

He lifted her upright from the bolster and held the cup for her to drink.

'Go on,' she said, smiling over the raw agony of her lungs. 'Go on. It's nothing. It will pass.'

She kept her eyes on his face. The sight of him warded off the pain better than any potion; his eyes, his mouth, his hands, long and brown against the pale silk of the book. She'd always loved his hands, gentle and strong, steel and silk, the instruments of so much pleasure and pain.

> 'Ther mighte men the royal egle finde,
> That with his sharpe look perceth the sonne. . . .'

How apt, she thought. He had reminded her of an eagle the first time she had seen him all those years ago at Harbottle. The tawny hair, those wonderful golden eyes that had stared at Margaret with such dreadful lust.

> 'Ther was the douve, with hir eyen meke;
> The jalous swan, ayens his deth that singeth. . . .'

They were all there. Margaret the dove, Elizabeth the fey swan. The false lapwing full of treachery was Lancaster. Harry could have been the strutting cockerel and she the nightingale, the drab little bird with the silver voice.

She closed her eyes on sudden tears. Oh, my love, my dearest, dearest love. What will you do when we are all flown?

He had stopped reading, thinking her asleep. She opened her eyes. 'I love you Hal,' she said quietly.

He smoothed back her hair from her damp brow and kissed her. She suddenly realized that she had never actually heard him say it; even among the passionate whispered endearments of their lovemaking, it had never been there.

'You've never told me,' she whispered. 'You've never said that you love me.'

He raised his eyes to her. 'Did I have to?' He took her hand and held it to his mouth, so small and thin, like the starved little claw of a bird. 'I love you,' he said simply. 'More than you ever knew. I married you for what you brought me—and never dreamt it would be so many years of happiness.'

'More than you loved Margaret?' How childish, how stupid after all these years—yet he answered her honestly.

'I've loved you both,' he said, 'equally and without favour. Each of you fulfilled a need in me. My need of you is greater because I have had it the longer.'

'And when I am gone, what will you do for love then?'

He did not answer her with lies or deny the truth of what she said. She was dying and they both knew it. He smiled. 'The memory of you will last me until we are together again.'

'Margaret will be there too.'

'Yes. All three of us together, as it was in the beginning. Are you still afraid of her, my dearest love?' He took her hand and slid it beneath his doublet till it lay against the warmth of his breast. 'My heart is yours,' he said softly. 'Take it. She would not grudge it to you now.'

He stayed beside her till she slept. The sound of her tortured breathing filled the room and turned his heart within him. How long—a day, perhaps two, and then he would be alone again. He stared out across the hills. The thin horned moon drained the world of colour, the grey of stone, the stark whiteness of the fields and the blackness of the forest that heaved and struggled from its blanket of snow. He had lived in a world like that before, without warmth or colour, without love. Suddenly he felt old and tired and full of fear. Yet afraid of what? Himself, his certain loneliness, that old fear of self-destruction that had drained the joy out of half of his life. He could perhaps have welcomed that now. Peace, oblivion, the obliteration of memory and thought. The coward's way.

He turned quickly back to the bed and watched the fragile movement of her breast, the shallow thread of her breathing broken by pain. Not long, not long. Oh, dear God, a little longer! Let me have the fire a little longer. He stared blindly round the high chamber. So many memories here. The spartan stone of his father's day was smothered in silks and velvet now, the great bed where he had lain with Margaret—Hal had been born in that bed, Harry and Ralph and Thomas. His own mother had died in it. Now Maud would die in it. All his life crowded into this one room, and one by one the candles that had given it light and life were being extinguished. Margaret, Ralph, Thomas, now Maud—leaving him in darkness and isolation. Only Harry left and Harry was tainted with that Mortimer bitch.

Outside the room the shadows were worse, all the old faces gone. Arundel, Woodstock, John Neville had died; old Warwick was immured on some God-forsaken island; Mowbray and Bolingbroke in exile. Lancaster was still there, an old man—all old men now, being ploughed down to make way for the new. And there were enough of those, springing up like weeds from the devastation of the fallen earldoms. Ralph Neville was earl of Westmorland now, wed to Lancaster's bastard Joan Beaufort. His brother Thomas had the earldom of Worcester, though Hal did not grudge Tom his reward. He had earned it well enough. And at the head of it all, Richard mad with his own power, drunk on the blood of Arundel and Woodstock. In three days the cowed parliament of Shrewsbury had placed more power in Richard's hands than even he could ever have dreamed of. The tenth of all revenues, the subsidy on wool and leather for life. Richard was King indeed now, answerable to none but God.

He shivered, blown by the cold wind of premonition. The room was almost dark, the fire burnt down to white glowing ash. From the hall below he heard the sound of singing. Of course, he had forgotten. It was Christmas Eve.

Maud began to cough, the first fretful sound rising to long rasping gasps as she struggled for breath. Softly, so as not to wake her, he lay down beside her and gathered her in his arms. He could feel the heat of her wasted limbs through the furs—so warm, and he was so cold. Dear God, he was so very cold. Quietly he began to weep.

Death, like the raven, never came alone. By February all but the last candle was snuffed. Lancaster was dead, slipped quietly away with a meekness that he had never possessed in life. There had been a final reckoning, a last feeble clash of swords before they were sheathed. A week before the end, Lancaster had sent for Hal. He had gone, eagerly, not out of triumph but because, without this last sight of each other, it would be unfinished.

Lancaster received him propped in a chair. He was bareheaded and swathed from head to foot in a heavy velvet robe that hid the thinness of his limbs.

'So you came then,' he said. 'I did not know whether you would.'

'I came because the Duke of Lancaster commanded it,' Hal said stiffly.

Liar. You would have come anyway. You could not have let him go without a last word.

Lancaster's pain-filled smile echoed the thought. 'And since when have you ever cared for the word of the Duke of Lancaster, Hal? Did you come to see the enemy vanquished? To taste the final victory?'

Hal stared at him. Jesu, where was all his hatred now? He did not even know why he had come. He had nothing to say. 'I see no victory, my lord,' he said, and cursed the tremor of pity in his voice.

'You are alive, Hal, and I am dying.' Lancaster clenched his teeth on the pain of his labouring heart. 'What better victory than that?'

For once in his life he was drained of words. There had been so many between them already, sharp, wounding unretractable weapons; like shafts once sped from the bow, no force on earth could call them back again. And then there was the dread that the man he had hated so hard and so long would catch the weakness

340

of his voice, that he might sense the hatred was not as strong as it used to be.

Then Lancaster said, 'Is it done, Hal? Is it really done? Was it all for nothing? All those years, all those dreams. Is this all that's left, a sick old man with his heir in disgrace and exile, and nothing to set against his name but a failed ambition and lost causes?'

'It's done my lord.' What could he say to ease the truth? Why should he even want to? He only knew that he did. 'It's done— finished. We're both finished, John.' Jesu, how long since he had called him that? Not since they were boys. They said that old age was a second childhood. Perhaps they had come full circle and were children again, with nothing but affection and shared blood between them. 'There's only Richard now,' he added.

Lancaster smiled faintly. 'Would I have made a worse king, Hal? Thinking on it now, would I have been so much worse?'

'Thinking on it now, no. Thinking on it now, I wish to God you had been king.'

Lancaster closed his eyes. After a pause, he said, 'Oh that was joy, Hal! To hear you admit that you might have been wrong.' He opened his eyes. 'A consolation to my dying hours,' he added with a flash of the old humour. 'And there's the irony of it Hal. A circumstance of birth, the difference of a year between two brothers. Edward's sons instead of my sons. It shouldn't be so, Hal. Such a chance advantage should not give a man the right to grind a whole people beneath his heel.' He shivered and drew the velvet robe a little closer. 'But then, what's done is done. It will not be my concern much longer. And by the way, I haven't thanked you, I know that you spoke for my son at the trial.'

'I did what I could. There was not much anyone could do. The King was not going to be thwarted.'

'So you know then?' Lancaster eased himself in his chair. 'He's mad, Hal. He thinks himself God, with the power of life and death over all of us. You have heard of his latest notion to extract more money from the people? He's had lists prepared of all those men who were involved in Woodstock's rebellion. He's forced them to buy pardons and sign blank letters of confession. *Pleasaunces*, he calls them. There's not a man in England now who does not walk in terror of him and these Cheshire thugs that are always at his back.' He glanced up and the faded blue eyes held a glow of amusement. 'Are you afraid of him, Hal?'

Hal smiled slowly. 'You would know me for a liar if I said that I was not. But it's an old man's fear, not too deeply rooted. I've not so many years left that I count them all that precious.'

Lancaster laughed softly. 'Oh the world's not finished with you yet, Hal. You've cheated the years better than most. Come closer Hal, where I can see you. My eyes are not so good as they were.' He watched him as he came toward him. Tall and lean in his mourning black, an old man's face, gaunt and fleshless, the lambent eyes set deep in the hollows of bronzed and polished skin, yet there was an ageless quality about the cast of his bones. That arrogant walk could have belonged just as easily to a young boy. He felt the stirring of envy. Perhaps that was all it had ever been; envy that life, outwardly at least, had not seemed to touch him. Envy that he'd always gone his own way, even at the price of his own ruin, that he could not be bought or bribed or threatened. He'd almost had him once; almost, like England and Castile, almost but not quite, the reality always eluding him at the last. Was Hal Percy still beyond price? He must have thought so or he'd not be steeling himself to ask a last favour of the man who in all the world had least reason to grant it.

'Sit by me, Hal,' he said faintly. The long hand with its winking sapphires came out from beneath the robe, hovered uncertainly over Hal's, then clenched itself hard on the arm of his chair. 'My son Harry—I'm afraid for Harry.' He breathed deeply to control the distorted spasms of his breathing. 'Richard will never let him come back. When I'm dead Harry will have everything. More than I ever had. All of the duchy and his de Bohun lands as well. Too much for one man unless it is Richard himself.' He raised his pale eyes to Hal's face. 'Will you stand by him, Hal? See that he is not cheated? See that he comes to his inheritance without scathe?'

The years rushed back and left a roaring in his ears. Another Lancaster, another lifetime, but the same words. Was this what the old duke had seen in the shadows? It was hard to speak, harder to tear his eyes away from Lancaster's.

'I'll do what I can,' he said. 'If it comes to it, I'll speak for him.'

'Swear it.'

The hand was on his sleeve now. He could feel the hard pressure of the bony fingers against his wrist. Irrelevantly, Elizabeth's pale pointed face rose before him. 'I swear,' he said softly.

Lancaster's grip relaxed and he leaned back in his chair and closed his eyes. 'I am content,' he said. For a while he lay quietly, then with his eyes still closed he said, 'Will you take one last cup of wine with me, Hal? For old times's sake; for the times before the old times when I won your precious gyrfalcon from you and you bloodied my nose in the tourney in revenge.'

Hal smothered his laugh. 'You cheated,' he said. 'You always did cheat at dice.' He rose and poured the amber liquid from the pitcher beside the bed.

'The old toast,' Lancaster murmured softly. 'To England and Lancaster.'

'The last time you said that I ended up running through St Paul's sanctuary with a pack of screaming Londoners at my heels.'

'Jesu, yes.' Lancaster smiled. 'It seems like only yesterday.' Then he said, 'You remember when I came back from Castile and Richard insisted that we exchange the kiss of peace at Reading?'

'I remember.'

'Is it too late now, Hal? Without pretence, without enmity?'

Hal stared down at him. Without pretence, without enmity. Was there enough truth in him to admit that it was so? Was he so mean in spirit that he could not yield just this once; a last affirmation of what they had both known since he had walked into the room. He stooped and laid his mouth against the pale hollow cheek.

'Without enmity, John. For the times before the old times.'

Lancaster nodded, his eyes closed on tears. 'Go now,' he said hoarsely. 'I'll not have you in at the kill.' He dragged his trembling hands across his face. 'When you see Harry again—tell him my thoughts and love were with him. Ask him to treat Katherine and my Beaufort sons kindly. They've loved me well. I would not see any hurt come to them.'

343

'I'll tell him, my lord.' He was almost at the door when Lancaster called to him.

'Such a waste, Hal. Together we could have held the world by the throat.'

Hal turned and smiled. 'Aye—and choked the life out of it as we almost did each other.' He held the pale eyes a moment longer. 'God be with you, my lord,' he said quietly, and closed the door.

It was the last time they had ever met. But the chain still held, tighter in death than it had ever been in life. It had dragged him here to Westminster today and accomplished in a week all that twenty years of bribes and threats could not do. As Hal walked into the King's presence a grim smile touched his lips. All this for Lancaster. Who would have believed the day when he risked his neck for Henry Bolingbroke?

From the raised height of his throne, Richard watched him approach the oasis of jewelled and perfumed light that was himself and that only the chosen and privileged few could enter. The rest remained outside—shadows, nonentities, who fell to their knees in respectful awe should his gaze happen to fall upon them. Yet suddenly the jewels did not seem so bright, the light no longer so pure and perfect. The shadows came impertinently close; one in particular, tall and full of smiling malice. He closed his eyes on the sudden irrelevant fear. He was prey to visions lately. His poor Anne, pussed and swollen with pestilence, wringing her hands and weeping. His beloved de Vere with his thick strong legs and tender mouth; a corpse now, all his beauty gone. He'd righted that. *An eye for an eye, a tooth for a tooth.* Arundel draining out his blood on Tower Hill and Woodstock choking beneath the weight of a feather mattress. Silly Thomas pining away among strangers. And Bolingbroke, that was the lasting joy, Bolingbroke dispossessed and forgotten. *If thine eye offend thee then pluck it out.* Laughter bubbled softly in his throat. He was safe, more than safe, anchored to his throne by the weight of diamonds and damascus cloth, inviolable, untouchable, God's anointed. What need had he to fear a man like Northumberland? He opened his eyes.

344

'Well then, my lord of Northumberland?'

Hal straightened from the deep obeisance and looked full into the King's face. It seemed a long time since he had seen him, though in reality it was less than six months. But then Richard never showed the same face twice. The pale unstable eyes were narrowed in suspicion now, the womanly mouth pursed and haughty as an outraged virgin. A mean spiteful parody of a king, but a king nevertheless. Richard never let any forget that.

'I am disturbed, my liege,' he said with careful irony, 'and incensed at these rumours which call my King's name into disrepute.'

'Rumours?' Richard blinked rapidly. 'What rumours?'

Hal smiled pleasantly. 'That the King of England's word is worthless,' he said amiably. 'That since the death of the Duke of Lancaster you have banished his son, Lord Bolingbroke, from the realm for life and denied him his inheritance. That his estates are already being given out piecemeal to worthless favourites. Of course—' he paused as the tide of colour that flowed into the King's face reached its peak, 'of course, I know this cannot be true, Your Grace. I myself was present when you said that on his father's death Henry of Bolingbroke would come into full possession of his estates.'

The King gulped the air noisily and looked wildly to his Holland brothers for support. The Earl of Kent rose obediently to his cue.

'It has been agreed that Henry Bolingbroke is a threat to the peace of England,' he said loudly. 'Therefore it has been agreed—'

'Agreed?' Hal's voice was soft and liquid as honey, but every man in the chamber heard it. 'I did not agree to it, my lord,' he said. 'And I can bring you a hundred others who could say the same.'

'I do not need your agreement!' Richard's voice shrilled round the chamber like an injured bird. 'Not yours, not theirs!' He flung his hand out to encompass the men who crowded uncomfortably close to Northumberland's back. 'I need the consent of none. You hear me? None. You are all nothing, you hold nothing save by my grace. You are all my chattels to use as it pleases me.'

345

Hal stood impassive, watching as a froth of rage gathered in the corners of the petulant mouth. The King's eyes were glazed with madness and the long fingers convulsed barely a hand's width from Hal's throat. Salisbury caught him by the arm and whispered in his ear, but Richard was too far gone for that.

'And since you love my lord of Bolingbroke so well and are so concerned at his exile, perhaps you would do better to share it.'

Hal lifted his amused gaze to the contorted face. 'I can think of worse company, Your Grace,' he said softly. He bowed and turned without waiting for the King's leave. Richard's voice shrilled round the chamber, calling him back, but he did not turn or break his stride till he was at the door.

He read the letter again. *'Richard by the grace of God'*—his eyes skimmed the lengthy list of high-flown titles—*'to our kinsman Henry Percy, Earl of Northumberland, greetings.'* Then the letter took on a complaining note and shaped itself suddenly into a threat: *'. . . that you present yourself to the King at Bristol without further delay under pain of exile and banishment.'*

Under pain of exile and banishment. Perhaps he had heard the threat too often for it to strike fear into him now, though he did not doubt for one minute that Richard was capable of it. Yet the alternative was little better, if his brother Tom was to be believed. Tom's message had come a bare hour after the King's summons: *'For God's sake, stay in the north. If you come within five miles of Bristol, the King will have you in chains.'*

Hal lifted his head and stared round at the strained and awed faces that crowded the hall. They did not believe it yet: that Lancaster had fallen, that Northumberland tottered on the brink. Did *he* believe it? Remembering the King's eyes the last time he had seen him, he did. He had been a condemned man from that day. He'd not come out of it unscathed this time.

Harry was watching him carefully. 'What will you do?' he asked quietly.

'Do?' Hal pushed the royal summons away from him and stared down at his hands. 'Nothing,' he said. 'I shall do nothing yet.'

What was there to do? Run? There were plenty of hiding places. Scotland and the mocking charity of Douglas. France and Henry Bolingbroke—he had said himself that there was worse company. But it had not come to that yet. He was safe while Richard played at war in Ireland. But for how long? It was only a breathing space, a postponement of the final reckoning. Was he going to sit and wait and let the King come and take him as he had done Arundel and Gloucester? There was another choice. It stared at him hard and bright from Harry's eyes. Rebellion, treason . . . Lancaster. Dear God! Why did he still cringe from it? It was fact now, he had made it so from the moment he had sworn that fatal oath to Lancaster. Perhaps even before that, when he had pledged his word to an old man at Leicester. And even if he had not committed all of his heart to it, then Harry had. It had been he who had urged the confrontation with Richard at Westminster and though he had tried to keep it from him, he'd had word from Bolingbroke through the emissaries of the ex-Archbishop Arundel.

He knew that Bolingbroke only waited his chance. And now Richard had given it to him by taking himself off to Ireland, as if he believed himself so inviolate that he could invite disaster unchallenged. But would Bolingbroke move? Richard still held his eldest son Henry of Monmouth as hostage. Would Bolingbroke risk his heir on the gamble that he could find enough support in England to force the King to reinstate him? If he dared it then the time was now, with Richard and half the English lords floundering in Irish bogs. He glanced sharply at Harry.

'Is he coming?' he asked, and smiled as he saw the gleam of colour touch his cheeks.

'Yes. He's coming,' Harry answered him defiantly and steeled himself for the look of cold disdain that he still dreaded. But it never came and he was asked nothing more and dared ask nothing himself. His father still had not spoken when the courier came with the news that Henry Bolingbroke had sailed that morning from France.

Elizabeth listened quietly to the carefully chosen phrases that Harry served up to her like comfits on a feasting dish. He might as well have saved his breath for her mind had locked fast onto the first dreadful words. She had lost; she was beaten, defeated. Bolingbroke would be king after all. She stared down at her hands and was surprised that the terrible rage only showed itself as an imperceptible trembling of her long ringed fingers. The topaz that covered her knuckle winked in jaundiced malice. It had all been for nothing.

She looked up and met Harry's uneasy stare. 'So Bolingbroke will be king, then,' she said tightly.

'Christ, Bess—' Harry said angrily, 'there's no thought of that in anyone's mind but yours. Harry Bolingbroke has come to claim that which he is entitled to, and nothing more. He's sworn on oath that he's come only for Lancaster.'

Elizabeth smiled. 'And you believe him?'

'Yes. I believe him and so do all the others who are flocking to join him at Pontefract.' He gripped her arm so tightly that she winced. 'There's nothing else to be done, Bess. Richard's mad. He'll make beggars of us all unless he's stopped. For God's sake, what else would you have us do? Sit back while he strips us of our lands? We're under sentence of exile. There's no other choice but to support Bolingbroke.'

'Only because your father spoke out for him,' Elizabeth snapped. 'If he'd kept silent and minded his own affairs we'd all have been safe.' She turned away from his hostile eyes. 'You're a fool Harry,' she said coldly. 'Both you and your father. You think that Bolingbroke is like his father, that he'll never have the courage to take what he wants outright. But this man has it, Harry. Oath or no oath, he means to be King in Richard's place—in my brother Roger's place,' she added. 'I have seen it, Harry; I *know*.'

'My God—I'm sick of your foresight and hindsight, your visions and premonitions!' he yelled. 'You know nothing, Elizabeth, only the blasphemy that that old Welsh hag has filled your mind with.'

He lifted his hands in a helpless gesture. 'Oh Bess,' he said softly. 'Must we always quarrel?' He touched the bare flesh of her arm. 'You've got to face it. Richard must be brought to heel before he destroys England, before he destroys us. He's not fit to be King any more.'

348

'And neither is Bolingbroke,' she said faintly. 'After Richard, the crown goes to a Mortimer.'

His hand dropped away. 'Is that all you ever see, Bess?' His voice was suddenly angry again. 'Forget Mortimer. You're not a Mortimer now, you're a Percy.'

'Then if I'm a Percy I shall remember that my own son has a better blood-right to the Crown than Bolingbroke!' she screamed back at him.

He moved away from her. 'Oh, no,' he said quietly. 'You'll not taint young Hal with your disease. I'll send him to Bolingbroke before I let you do that.' He smiled as he saw her eyes widen. 'Yes—that would hurt, wouldn't it my lady? Your precious Mortimer-bred son raised by Henry Bolingbroke. Well, take care then madam. Leave the boy be or I'll do it. Believe me, Elizabeth, I'll do it.'

He left her staring down at the topaz ring on her hand. Yellow fire, fire she could gladly have roasted him alive in at this moment. He meant it. If her disease was Mortimer then his was Lancaster and she had no cure for either. Perhaps Harry was right. Perhaps there was nothing in her save that which Morganna placed there, figments of her imagination conjured up by her own need.

'No.' She said the word aloud and jerked abruptly to her feet. With doubt came madness and destruction. 'Morganna!' she called sharply and the little Welshwoman came obediently from the outer room where she had been waiting. Elizabeth breathed the scent of hyssop and myrrh that rose from her gown and felt comforted. She clasped the small brown hands. So cold; there was no blood in Morganna's veins, only ice water from the mountain streams of Snowdon.

'Bolingbroke will be king,' she said faintly.

Morganna smiled. 'Did you ever doubt it, my lady?' she said, and lifted the high pointed headdress from Elizabeth's hair.

Elizabeth closed her eyes. No, perhaps she never had, any more than she had ever doubted Roger's death, but she had fought against both—and lost.

Morganna's hand loosed the ivory pins from her hair. 'You must not give up, my lady,' she said in her soft lilting voice. 'It is

349

written; Merlin himself has prophesied it—"*A giant, snow white in colour and gleaming bright, shall beget a people that is radiant.*" '

Elizabeth nodded. She would not give up, she would not believe that it was finished. She knew it to be truth, that one day a king with her blood would sit on the throne of England.

That night she dreamt with frightening clarity: a field of lush and verdant greenness and in its midst a single rose. The rose had grown and multiplied, covering the field with its blood-red flowers, its thorns striking blood from the earth, strangling all that tried to rise beneath it with its virulent growth. She had seen beyond the dream. The field was England, the rose Lancaster and the man who had planted it was Northumberland.

The fine summer rain shrouded Chester with a silver pall, a warm insidious mist that drifted in shining clouds over the high walls and around the man watching from the roof of Chester Castle, wrapping the city in the semblance of a dream.

Henry Bolingbroke pulled his sodden cloak a little closer. Was it a dream? The thousands of men who crowded within the walls and overflowed onto the flat meadows along the Dee were real enough: thirty thousand at the last count—and he had landed at Ravenspur a month ago with only thirteen. An unlucky number, the French captain had said, yet Fortune had done nothing but smile on him. Pickering, Knaresborough, Pontefract—all fallen to him within a week, with never a hand or voice raised against him. Even the elements had been on his side and had kept Richard and his army chained to Dublin awaiting a fair wind.

At Doncaster the northern lords had come, Willoughby and Ros, Neville and his sons—and the ultimate prize that he had longed for and dreaded at the same time: Northumberland and his son. It had been the affirmation of a long-held bond, that old childhood pledge come to its final fruition. He was sure enough of Harry; of the old man he was more wary. It was Northumberland who had all but forced him to take that oath at Doncaster that he had come only to claim his inheritance. It had been the truth then. He would have been content with that, before he had seen the extent of the power that had fallen so effortlessly into his hands, before he had seen how much the people hated Richard and loved him. At Bristol they had blocked the streets for a sight of him, screaming his name till his horse had panicked and reared at the tumult. He was their saviour, come to deliver them from the tyrant Richard. It had roused the old dormant dream, his father's dream. Was it such a long step to take? He had the means. All he needed was the courage.

At Bristol the dream had begun to crystallize into reality. The city had fallen without a blow being struck and had delivered Richard's henchmen—Burley, Green and Scrope, Earl of Wiltshire—into his hands. He had had them executed the same day. The Regent, his uncle of York, had abandoned the fruitless task of trying to control his reluctant army gathered in Richard's name and had surrendered. Only old Salisbury and his renegade army of Welshmen had still held out against him, and they had fled to Conway to await the King and his returning army.

Richard had landed at Milford Haven at the end of July. It had been his one moment of doubt. While Richard was in Ireland he had been supreme. Both York and Salisbury had failed because they lacked a rallying point. But with the King in England and at the head of an army. . . . He had almost panicked then, and the dream had taken on the dark colours of nightmare. He remembered how his father had been cursed: almost—but not quite; the cup of victory always dashed away at the last minute. His mouth turned in a wry smile. How could he ever have doubted?

With Richard's coming the dream had grown brighter, clearer—so clear that he could almost touch it. Once on English soil the King's army had melted away like summer snow. They had flocked to him in their hundreds: Lord Bardolf and Scales; Northumberland's brother Worcester; York's son Aumale. And Richard himself had fled disguised as a priest to join Salisbury and his meagre following at Conway.

He stared downriver to the wide estuary of the Dee. All he could see of Wales was the faint thread of its shoreline and the darker shapes of the mountains behind. On a clear day he could have seen the drum towers of Rhuddlan and Flint. But Conway was sixty miles away, below the northern spur of Snowdon. He knew Conway, walls fifteen-feet thick and surrounded by water

351

on three sides. Impregnable, as both Salisbury and King Richard knew. The King could lie low there for as long as he chose; till Salisbury had rallied an army, till the Welsh came out of their mountains? The Welsh Prince Glen Dwr was notoriously loyal to Richard. He chewed nervously at his lips. He dared not wait for that. He must get Richard out of Conway and into his possession. He would never be safe while Richard was loose. The thought came before he could stop it. *He would never be safe while Richard was alive.* He turned his back on the sight of Wales. Before him lay England—*his* England? Open and vulnerable, there for the taking, if he had the courage. Yet he must be careful. He knew that. He had all England at his back but until he had Richard he had nothing. And even then he must tread softly. There were some who'd baulk at outright usurpation. He must be patient, keep his own council for a while. That had been his father's mistake, letting all know his intentions too soon. It gave men time to think, to weigh the disadvantages, to examine their consciences if they had any.

And then there was his own son Harry. Still in Ireland, praise God, at Trim. Another of Richard's mistakes. If he'd kept Harry with him he'd have been a powerful weapon to fight him with. He'd sent Dorset to fetch him home. He would be here within the week. He smiled thinly. He would be able to move more freely once he knew Harry was safe.

That still left the King. He must have possession of Richard at all costs, and soon. If he could lure him as far as Flint for a parley! Yet who could he send that Richard would trust enough to abandon the security of Conway? Edmund of York? Richard would trust him well enough, but York was bound to bungle it. Northumberland? Richard believed that Northumberland meant him no harm, but did the Earl trust *him* enough to do his bidding?

He smiled with rare humour. Yes, he would send Northumberland to bring the King out of Conway.

The King viewed the small embassy with open hostility and at Archbishop Arundel he would not look at all. It was the second day of long and bitter negotiation; he was yielding slowly, but not without a fight.

'So, Henry Bolingbroke has come to demand his rights,' he said coldly. Yesterday he had screamed and ranted like the madman they thought he was: 'Bolingbroke has no rights save those which I choose to grant him!' Today he was calmer, soothed by Salisbury's counsel and the promise that Northumberland held out to him. He was to remain King providing he restored Bolingbroke's estates to him and declared for a free parliament. There would be more. There was bound to be more. A council to keep him to heel, and he would as like as not have to name Bolingbroke his heir—but what did that matter? Promises made under duress were not binding. Once he was enthroned at Westminster again he would see to it personally that Henry Bolingbroke had all that was due to him and more. He felt the warmth of returning confidence. He had faced confrontations like this enough times to be undaunted by them. He had been as low and had risen again like the phoenix: like the phoenix he knew himself to be indestructible. Bolingbroke was just another Woodstock, another John of Gaunt of the old days. He had beaten them both. He would defeat Henry Bolingbroke also.

Still, he was torn; Salisbury advised him to remain at Conway with an eye to a retreat to France. But he did not want to retreat to France or anywhere. He wanted to be at Westminster again, to be with his little Isabella, alone and defenceless without him. He wanted to see Bolingbroke's head on a spike, his eyes pecked clean and red by London crows. He would have his bowels drawn and burnt before his eyes, before his son's eyes, before the eyes of all the world. He'd have that snivelling traitor Aumale flayed alive. He'd heard that there was a man in France who could keep his victim alive for three days while he stripped the skin from him inch by inch. The wild thoughts ran on behind his fixed child-like smile while Archbishop Arundel laboured some point that Northumberland had made.

Richard spoke suddenly. 'And I am to remain King, with full prerogative?'

Hal gave Arundel a weary look. Was that all Richard cared about, the bauble of a crown? For two days the King had vacillated between rage and grief. This was the first coherent exchange they had had. He would have to make the most of it.

'That is so, my liege,' he answered formally. 'The Duke of Lancaster swore a solemn oath at Doncaster that he came with no other intent than to claim his inheritance.'

'And you believe him?'

Hal looked away from the bright fanatical stare. *Did* he believe him? He believed that Bolingbroke was a man of honour and would not break his oath. Beyond that he did not know: perhaps he did not even care. Harry believed him, and it seemed that these days it was Harry who led and he who followed.

'Yes, I believe him, sire,' he said.

'Then swear also.' Richard rose and came to stand before him. 'You are Bolingbroke's proxy. Swear on the Host that he means me no harm.'

Hal was silent, aware of Arundel's furtive nodding and that those of his own party had withdrawn a little from him. At the back of his mind he heard Harry's insistent voice: *'He must be brought out of Conway, one way or the other.'* Did Harry care which way it was? He was waiting for him ten miles away, with the fifteen hundred men that he would have brought right to the walls of Conway if Hal had let him. He knew that Harry would not have talked and wrangled for two days to get Richard to Flint.

His hesitation brought the ready flush of anger to the King's cheeks.

'You see?' he yelled. 'You cannot swear! You know the lie of it!' His voice was rising to the pitch that always preceded one of his rages. Archbishop Arundel moved a little closer to Hal but the sight of him only served to inflame Richard more.

'Your Grace,' Hal said with heavy patience, 'if you will only accompany us to Flint then the Duke will swear the oath himself.'

The King's eyes bulged from his head. 'I do not want *his* oath!' he shouted. 'I want *yours*, Northumberland!'

Hal inclined his head in resignation. 'Very well then, my liege,' he said quietly. 'If it makes you feel the happier, you may have it.'

He averted his eyes from the King's triumphant smile and heard Archbishop Arundel's sigh of relief loud as a north wind in his ears.

It was dusk before they reached the deep valley that swept down to Rhuddlan. The King rode slumped in his saddle. He was tired and—without the security of the stout walls of Conway—a little afraid. Perhaps he should have listened to Salisbury. He should have made Bolingbroke come to him if he wanted to parley. Even now it was not too late. They would rest the night at Rhuddlan. He would have time to think again. He still had the upper hand; fifty men to Northumberland's half dozen and two of those were priests.

He jerked himself upright as the Earl called a halt. The sun was low and heavy in the sky, struggling from behind great drifts of red, sullen cloud. The river Clwyd ran silently in the shadow of its steep banks yet now and then the King caught the glitter of water: there was no wind but the clumps of trees on the wooded slopes were moving. The King's eyes widened. Moving, streaming down the hillside and converging across his path on the valley floor—not trees but men, not water but steel armour.

He looked wildly at Northumberland. 'Treachery,' he whispered faintly.

Northumberland smiled. 'No, my liege. My son Harry. Do you expect us to ride in hostile territory without an escort?'

The King shivered, glancing behind him at the dark suspicious faces of his men and back again to Northumberland. 'If I thought you would betray me, Northumberland, I would have your head,' he said viciously.

Hal smiled wryly and watched his son come spurring toward them. 'If I betray you, my liege, then you may have my head and willingly,' he said softly. Was it just his imagination or did he hear laughter from behind the clouds?

The King could hear the bells of London from more than a mile away, a hundred clamorous silver tongues merging into a continuous peal of joyful welcome. But not for him; the bells would never ring for him again unless it was for his death. He blinked away the tears of self-pity. During the three weeks it had taken them to reach London he had veered between wild hope and utter despair, long days of deepest melancholy that turned suddenly and without cause into a wild euphoria that verged on hysteria.

355

There was only a painful emptiness in him now. All hope was gone. He had been a fool to think that there ever was any. He should have known his fate that day at Flint the moment he had looked into Henry Bolingbroke's eyes. Even the faithful wolf-hound he kept at Chester had betrayed him. They said that a dog was the first to smell a new master. The sight of Math fawning on Bolingbroke's hand had broken him more surely than anything he could have said. They could swear themselves sick with oaths and denials: he knew that Bolingbroke meant to have his crown.

Oh, but to give him his due, he kept it concealed well enough, the iron fist within the velvet glove. All would be done with at least the semblance of right. Even now he was shown no dis-respect. All was still done in King Richard's name. The writs for the coming parliament had borne his seal though he knew the value of parliaments like that: hand-picked men, primed by Bolingbroke. He should know. He had done the same thing himself enough times. Bolingbroke himself still addressed him as King and was almost lavish with respect. Richard smiled grimly to himself. No man spat upon the coat he was about to put on. He had them all deceived, all except him and he did not care any more. He would be glad enough to keep his life.

The clamour from the bells was so loud now that none could hear themselves speak. At Charing they halted and Hal watched as the King and a small escort were led apart, no more than a dozen and all Lancaster's men; Bolingbroke had seen to it that there were none among them to revive the King's spirits. Richard was to remain at Westminster whilst Lancaster made his triumphal entry into the city: Westminster, then the Tower, then what? He looked so frail and insignificant in his plain black robe. It was the jewels and the glitter that had made him a king. Without them he was only a man. Hal remembered the slim exhausted boy who could hardly keep his eyes open while he had stumbled and faltered through the coronation oath as if he had known then that he could not keep it. He remembered his mother Joanna that day at Bordeaux, and the bright golden child laugh-ing and clutching the gilded ball. Perhaps Richard remembered too. He turned a pale meek face toward Hal as he passed.

'My cousin of Northumberland,' he said softly.

Hal turned his horse sharply and rode to where Bolingbroke sat his horse impassively. He was bareheaded and in full armour, the reins of the black destrier looped easily over his wrist. A groom fussed around him, straightening the azure housings of his mount. He himself stared directly ahead, his eyes fixed on the road that had been empty a moment before and was now filled with the noise and panoply of welcome. He made only the slightest movement of his head as Hal reined in alongside him.

'Almost a royal welcome, cousin, would you not say?'

His quiet voice was almost lost beneath the blare of approaching trumpets.

Hal stared at the swollen profile. 'My lord—' he said harshly, 'if you remember, I gave my word that no harm would come to the King.'

Bolingbroke smiled faintly but he did not turn his head. 'Nor will it. His Grace will only be lodged in the Tower till Parliament has convened. Then it will be up to the people to decide.'

'I also swore a solemn oath upon the Host that you would not take the crown while Richard lived.'

Now Bolingbroke turned to look at him. 'I took no such oath,' he said quietly.

'You did to me!' Hal cried angrily. 'You swore at Doncaster that you only came for Lancaster.'

Bolingbroke regarded him coldly. 'Then we are *both* forsworn, my lord earl,' he said. 'We must both bear the guilt as best we can.'

In the dim uncertain light of St Paul's the likeness was not so very great. The effigy on the tomb showed only half the man. The shape of the bones were there beneath the pale alabaster flesh: the long Plantagenet nose, the close-cut beard. But the mason had missed the humour and weakness of the mouth, and the blank finely chiselled eyes gave no hint of the treacherous brilliance they had once held. He looked younger too. Cold, colourless, all he had never been in life—but that was the Lancaster of twenty years ago.

Hal touched the smooth ageless cheek; the place where his kiss had rested that last day at Ely House. He was glad now that they

357

had not parted enemies. He raised his eyes and stared out across the candlelit nave. Quiet and empty: full of shadows and the soft diffusion of golden light; full of memories. He recalled the day when the church had been filled with the howls of the mob: the obscene taunts, the rough, snatching hands and gentle bewildered Wyclyf. He remembered Lancaster at his back: *'Walk on, my lord. We do not stop for knaves and villeins.'*

He had been Lancaster's man then. He was Lancaster's man now. And if he had felt shame and guilt at it then he bore twice the burden now. He looked down into the blind sightless eyes. What was it Lancaster had said? *'Was it all for nothing, Hal? Only failed ambition and lost causes to be set against my name?'*

Hal smiled faintly. He wished he could have told him that a week ago his son had been crowned King of England. He closed his eyes wearily. Dear God! How had it happened? He had thought he could control it, keep Bolingbroke to his own pace as he had once kept his father. He had been too preoccupied with the lion roaring at the door to see the serpent sliding over the sill. Now it was done, accomplished almost before he had realized it. Richard, King of England, was deposed and Henry of Lancaster was King in his place.

Abdication. The word itself was a mockery. Yet that was what it had been. Hal had been present when Richard had yielded up his crown. A meek, resigned, unrecognizable Richard, who had signed his throne away to Henry of Lancaster with hardly a protest. There had been no force, not force that men would acknowledge as such. All the fears had been in Richard himself, intensified by isolation and the refusal of Parliament to allow him friend or counsellor or even the comfort of his little French queen. The grim damp walls of the Tower bred fear and perhaps Richard had remembered too vividly another king who had died in agony because he would not yield.

Even then he had had no real conscience over Richard, nor over the set-aside claim of Roger Mortimer's son. It was hardly a choice; a madman for king or a child of seven. Bolingbroke had been the only choice: all that a king should be, all that England needed him to be. So why did he still doubt? Why was he afraid?

It had been done in less than a day. Accused, judged, condemned

358

and deposed—without trial, without hearing, and not one voice raised in his defence except old Bishop Merke's, and he had since paid dearly for it. And he, Northumberland, what had he said? What had stilled that perverse, malefic tongue that had brought him close to ruin enough times for him to have lost all fear of it? Only the thought of Harry. Harry was all that mattered now, the last candle, the last warmth. Harry had smothered the doubt and the guilt of that broken oath. Harry had wanted Bolingbroke to be king, so he had wanted it too.

Hal had been well rewarded. Lord High Constable of England and the Isle of Man and all its dependencies annexed to his earldom. His Judas money. His brother Tom was Lord High Steward, Governor to the Prince of Wales, Treasurer, Admiral, Keeper of the Privy Seal and Governor of Aquitaine. Harry was Justiciar of North Wales and Governor of a string of castles that ran from Bamburgh to Caernarvon. Was loss of conscience such a high price to pay? It was for him. It dogged his every step. Richard's face was always before him, like the stinking fish hung round the neck of a cheating fishmonger. Where was Richard now? Kept in safe custody by order of Parliament, dragged from grim prison to grim prison. The last Hal knew he was at Pontefract.

Time seemed to have lost all meaning. Was it only eight months since Lancaster's death, less than two since that fateful day he had brought Richard out of Conway: a week since he had walked in that brilliant procession to Henry of Lancaster's coronation and sworn the same oath that he had sworn twenty years ago to Richard? Would he keep it as well?

He thought suddenly of Elizabeth. It must have been galling for her to have to kneel before Henry and acknowledge him as king. He had kept her there a long time and had smiled as he bade her rise. The smile had almost deepened into laughter as he looked into her face, as if they had some secret pact between them. Hal had wondered at it. It was rare for Bolingbroke to be amused.

He himself avoided Elizabeth when he could. It was still there, the deep ingrained dislike, for reasons that neither could quite grasp. Perhaps for him it was because she had seen the thing he had always tried to deny. His heart belonged to Lancaster. He stared down at the pale still effigy. But to *this* man, not the hard ruthless usurper he had helped onto England's throne. That was one oath he had kept. He had kept faith with Lancaster. He had seen his son come to his inheritance without scathe, and more.

Slowly he stooped and kissed the cold cheek. It was done. He was committed, it was too late to go back. He would not fight it any more.

She was home again, the first time in twenty years yet nothing had changed except perhaps that she was less in awe of it. The mountains where the giants lived did not fill her with terror now.

The light was almost gone, the crest of Moel Gamelyn already lost in shadow and mist. Only westward where the sun lingered did the mountains hold their colour and shape, soft ragged peaks like a strip of torn silk running down to Cader Idris and the sea. She followed the distant unseen line of the river in her mind's eye; from where it spewed out of Bala Lake and roared down to Llantysilio, then Corwen, Edeyrnion, Glyndyfrdwy—the names of her childhood—on to Llangollen in its cradle of hills. Against the evening sky she could still see the stark towers of Dinas Bran from where Madoc Ap Griffith had once ruled all of Powys. His bones lay at Valle Crucis, a mile downstream, buried and forgotten like the old Welsh dreams. Her kinsman Owain Glen Dwr held it now. He was the new Welsh dream, Lord of Glyndyfrdwy and Cynllaith, risen against the usurper Bolingbroke, the hope of Wales and of Elizabeth.

She closed her eyes and listened to the night sounds, the last obstinate shriek of birdsong from the sycamore grove, the steady distant roar of rushing water. Within the castle itself there was laughter. She heard the high sharp note of a harp, the softly rising cadence of a Welsh voice. It was here, to Chirk, that Ralph Mortimer had brought his dark little Welsh princess Gwladys Ddw nearly two hundred years ago. They said that she still looked out from the roof of the King's Tower, staring towards Aberfraw and the peaks of Snowdon. Elizabeth had never seen her but she had often heard her singing her lament for Wales. Sometimes she heard her own father's voice. He had loved to sing. A sweet young voice—they were always young voices; the Mortimers never grew old. She remembered there had always been music: the songs of ancient Wales, of Arthur and Merlin, the tales of the bard Prydydd Y Moch in praise of their ancestors Llywelyn Ap Iorwerth, Llywelyn the Great, Prince of all Wales, the son of Owain Gwynedd. She and her brother Edmund were the last of the ancient royal line of Gwynedd.

And now Wales was the enemy, its oppressor her own husband Harry. She too suffered the pangs of divided loyalty. She was Wales, she was England; she was neither, she was both, like the twin rivers of Ceiriog and the Dee that joined themselves below Chirk and flowed as one toward Chester. Yet tonight she was Wales; she was part of its magic and mystery, she shared its wild heart. She cried out with the same voice for revenge.

Richard was dead, murdered six months ago at Pontefract. Parliament had given out that he had starved himself to death but all knew the lie of that. You did not parade a corpse lapped to his chin in lead if he had taken his own life; you showed the world his fleshless bones and sunken belly. She had looked on his face when they had brought him to Westminster. It had not been the face of a man who had died for lack of food. Ironically it had been love of Richard that had signed his death warrant. That loyal Salisbury's brief and abortive rebellion had failed had been due more to treachery than to any love of Bolingbroke. Salisbury had lost his head for it, the Holland earls of Kent and Huntingdon too. It had been enough to seal Richard's fate. Bolingbroke had known that he would never be safe while Richard lived. Now the dead king was a martyr, his faults glossed over by the bards and rhymers. In Glen Dwr's hall they sang nightly the ballad of 'Sweet Richard'.

Even then the Usurper had been far from secure. The murder of Richard lost him the support of all but the very loyal. France was breathing down his neck, demanding the return of Queen Isabella and her dowry after spurning Bolingbroke's advances to wed her to his eldest son, Harry Monmouth. It was rumoured that the Comte de St Pol gathered a fleet at Harfleur and planned to join the Welsh against him.

The Scots spilled out across the Border, burning and harrying.

She had not been north for almost half a year but she had heard that there was food for neither man nor beast. And now Wales was in rebellion: in Richard's name, in the young Earl of March's name for he was still the dead King's acknowledged heir. And there was the danger, for the Usurper held both her nephews in close captivity at Windsor. If Bolingbroke had no scruples over the murder of a king, he would have even less over that of a boy of ten.

She turned toward her brother Edmund. Since the death of Roger he was doubly precious. Between them they held the only weapon that could topple Bolingbroke from his stolen throne—if they could bring the boy safely out of Windsor. They'd had the promise of Glen Dwr's support too—at a price.

'Tell me again,' she said. 'Glen Dwr's terms.'

'All of Wales,' Edmund said briefly, 'to be held absolutely by him and his heirs. Myself to wed his daughter Cathryn.'

Elizabeth turned away impatiently. A dream. A mad Welshman's dream, though he could have had all and willingly if it would drive Bolingbroke out. But out of her mouth or Edmund's it would just be an empty promise. Glen Dwr would not treat with any less than Harry or his father—and what hope was there of that, with Northumberland still doggedly loyal, though his lands were devastated and his troops starving for lack of money to pay them. But Harry was weakening. The death of Richard had hit him hard, and this last six months he had all but beggared himself to pay his army despite numerous appeals to the Usurper for their wages. In April, Conway had been betrayed to Rhys and Gwylm Tudor and though Harry had regained it after a month's strenuous siege, he'd been forced to pawn some of her jewels till the grudging tally had come from Westminster. And even then it was only for half what was due.

Edmund touched her arm. 'It's useless, Bess,' he said gently. 'There's nothing to be done. Richard is dead and Bolingbroke is King. We'll not alter that now.'

'No,' she said sharply and moved away from him. She would not believe that. Her pride was still scarred from that last meeting with the Usurper. He'd laughed at her, knowing that she remembered: *'If I ever am King it will be my first royal duty to wipe that*

362

arrogant smile from your face. But he had not. She had smiled at
him, radiant with her inner knowledge, the certainty of his fall.
He did not know her at all if he thought she'd give up as easily as
that.

Edmund said irritably, 'You're dreaming Bess. Even if we
could win Glen Dwr to our side, what good would it do? We need
more than the Welsh to bring Bolingbroke down. It might have
worked while Salisbury and Kent were alive, if Richard were
alive, but not now.'

'Oh Edmund, Edmund!' She turned her face toward him and
he saw it light up with that strange look which always made him
feel slightly afraid of her. 'Can't you see, Edmund, it has to be
now? The Usurper is hated. He's proved no better a king than
Richard; worse, for now he has the stain of royal murder on his
hands. Richard is beloved again. They have forgotten what he
was. Some are even saying that he is still alive, hiding in Scotland.
They want him to be still alive, Edmund.'

'We would need the north,' he argued stubbornly. 'Northumberland put Henry there. It would need Northumberland to
bring him down. You would never get the old man to treat with
Glen Dwr.'

'He might,' Elizabeth said softly. 'If Harry did.'

Edmund made a sound that brought a flush of anger to her pale
skin. 'Christ, Bess—' he said. 'You could not win Harry over
before Bolingbroke was king, what do you think you can do
now?'

'That was *then*,' she snapped back at him. 'A man always lusts
after a thing till he's had possession of it. With possession the
illusion is destroyed. Harry knows Bolingbroke for what he is
now. Usurper, murderer, liar and cheat.' She stared coldly into
her brother's eyes. 'Afraid, Edmund?' she taunted him. 'Afraid
you'll lose your head like Salisbury? What happened to all that
ambition, Edmund? I remember you once said that you'd give
anything to be in our brother Roger's place; to be King.'

'Perhaps I did.' He avoided her bright, pitiless stare. 'When
Richard was alive. It was different then. We would not have been
tainted with treason. And besides, it is not me who will be King, it
is Edmund.'

'What better?' she said. 'A boy of ten and biddable. You would be Regent till he came of age. You would be King in all but name.'

He stared at her and saw the brittle hardness of her, diamond-bright through his tears. She was looking at him as she had once looked at their brother Roger. How she despised weakness. Yet he was ready to admit that he *was* weak, he *was* afraid: he was human.

'Oh, Bess—' He groaned as if he were in pain. 'You know that if Bolingbroke got wind of this we would never see young Edmund or Roger alive again.'

'It will not come to that,' she said confidently. 'The Usurper dare not risk more blood on his hands. She could have said that there was another, ready, waiting, more surely under her control than either of her nephews. By right of blood her own son Hal could succeed.

She came close to him and laid her long tapering fingers against his sleeve. 'We'll do nothing yet,' she told him placatingly. Even Edmund she could only push so far. 'We will wait till Harry returns from Aberfraw. He attends the Prince of Wales there.' She smiled up into his face. 'Will it suffice if I promise to do nothing till Harry is of our mind?'

She felt the relief flood through him and the smile hardened fractionally. Even Edmund, on whom she had depended so much. But then perhaps she had always known that in the end the burden would be hers alone.

She stared out into the night. She felt stronger here; her power was almost a tangible thing fostered by the land and the wildness. It was Mortimer land, and perhaps for Edmund the tie was even greater than the lust for a crown. They had been Marcher lords long before they had been heirs to kingdoms. She fed the names greedily into her mind: the Irish lands, the fortresses of Chirk, Wigmore and Ludlow; the Welsh lordships: Maelienydd and Blaenllyfni; Gurthrenion, Cwmteuddur, Arwystli, Cyveilog and Caereineon; the magical sounds of her childhood. Enough, it should have been enough. It was enough for Edmund. But for her there were others who demanded more. She had seen them—in the swirling smoke of fire and torch, in the shadows of roof and corbel—clear, defined shapes come from the dark fields beyond her vision. The first Earl, Roger, the murderer—still warm from a Queen's bed when they hacked his bowels out of him, still alive. Her brother Roger—the heap of bleeding stumps and severed bone they had buried at Wigmore. Her father, her grandfather, his father before him—all dead in their prime, all grinding out their bloody penance generation after generation. She smiled her strange unearthly smile. Now they were absolved. The blood of another murdered king had set them free. The curse was Lancaster's now, on him and all his house, till the blood debt was paid.

She turned away from the window, her mouth hard and unsmiling. She would send word to Glen Dwr in the morning, despite her promise to Edmund. When Harry came back it would be accomplished.

They were whipping the boy: hard vicious strokes that bit deep into his soft young flesh and drew blood instantly. Beside the tunic they had ripped from his back Elizabeth could see the small pouch of silver that she had used to bribe him. The letter that he had been carrying to Glen Dwr was not with it. She saw it, a sliver of white in Harry's clenched hand. She turned sharply away from the window. She knew then; he had returned from Aberfraw a day earlier and must have seen the boy leaving her chamber. She swallowed on the little rush of panic. She must stay calm. He could do nothing. He could not whip her as he had done the page.

The boy's yelping cries had stopped. She was tempted to look again from the window. Was Harry still there? Had he stayed? Had he gone? Then she heard his footsteps on the tower stair. He was running but it seemed a long time before he flung open the door.

'You bitch!' he said. 'You evil, traitorous bitch!' He was parchment white, she had never seen him so white. His eyes were dark and narrowed with rage and hatred.

She turned her back on him, feeling sick with dread. 'It was for your own good,' she said wildly. 'I was tired of seeing you let yourself be trampled underfoot by Bolingbroke.'

He was behind her. She could feel the menace of his eyes on her back. 'Not Bolingbroke—he's *King* now, King Henry the Fourth of England.' He grabbed her hair and swung her round to face him. 'Say it!' he yelled. 'Say it! King Henry the Fourth of England.' He rammed her back hard against the wall. 'Say it, you bitch.'

She smiled her provoking smile. 'Very well then, my lord, I'll say it. King Henry the Fourth—Usurper, murderer, traitor. . . .'

He struck her hard across the face and she felt the blood spring into her mouth. Hot blood, red as wine and as intoxicating. She swore at him in Welsh and gloried in the madness that came into his eyes. Then she struck him with all the force of a year's hatred and bitterness. Blood flowed into the impress of her hand across his cheek. Then his hands were round her throat. She screamed as the collar of opals gouged her neck when he tore it off.

He was cursing her in French; garrison filth, every obscenity that he had ever heard. His fingers constricted her throat, she could barely breathe, barely hear her own agonized sobs. Somehow she reached his mouth. He bit her lip and tried to turn his head away but she wound her arms around him, pressing her mouth against his till the murderous grip was loosed.

'Harry, Harry!' Choking for breath she leant against him. 'Jesu, don't you know that I'd do nothing to hurt you? I love you, Harry. Your pain is mine, your pleasure mine.' Her hand slid down to his loins and she felt him spring blood-hard against her. 'I see things, Harry,' she whispered urgently. 'I told you once that Bolingbroke would never rest till he was King and I was right. He murdered Richard because he was too great a threat to keep alive. Now *you* are a threat, Harry. You and your father. You put him on the throne and you could just as easily drag him off it again. He knows it, Harry, and it makes him afraid. Fear can drive a man to madness. Soon he'll hate you as much as he once loved you because you only serve to remind him of how weak he really is. Oh, Harry, believe me! I've seen it, I've seen the blood—*your* blood, your father's blood. You can turn it, Harry; you can turn it away from you even now. Listen to me, for pity's sake, listen. Give him up. Give Wales up. Go back to the north. You've had no money from him for months. How many times have you written to him begging for money to pay his troops? How much of your own money have you spent because you couldn't bear to see them go without? Is this how a king

366

treats the man who helped him become king? Go back to the north, Harry. See then if I am right. See how much he loves you then, when you cease to be at his beck and call.' Her mouth moved against his throat, kissing the hard little pulse at the base of his neck.

He leant away from her, drained by his rage, suddenly passive against the torment of her mouth and hands. 'Dear God, you frighten me sometimes, Elizabeth,' he said hoarsely. 'What else do you see? What other world is behind those empty eyes of yours?'

She leant close to him. 'Shall I show you, my love? A world where pleasure and pain are one. Where there is no night or day, no beginning, no end. A world where there are only the two of us, your mouth on mine, your body in mine. Come, Harry. Let me show you my world.'

He closed his eyes against the caress of her voice, struggling against the ache of pleasure it gave him: he had been on the edge of that world so many times.

Like a child he let her lead him to the bed and like a child he let her strip him naked. He lay on his back, the sensuous warmth of fur against his spine and Elizabeth above him, glowing white in the dusk. Her smile was unearthly, wanton, turning his soul within him. He felt a strange humility, like a man would feel before death. Elizabeth, his life, his death, his love.

She kissed him, long devouring kisses that drew all the breath from him. Her mouth was on his throat, moving down to where his heart pounded visibly beneath his tawny flesh. Her teeth pricked softly on the hard muscles of his belly, her tongue lightly traced the scar that ran down into his groin. His hand reached out and twined itself in her hair.

'Oh, Bess, Bess! Don't torment me, Bess!'

Then the agony ceased and became a red, searing mist of pleasure that clouded his mind and drew him down into that other world. There were hands touching him. Every woman he'd ever had: the first time when he had been fifteen, the first virgin—the exquisite pain, the blood, the ecstasy; the first whore who had initiated him into undreamt of pleasures, his first mistress who had turned him from a raw boy into a skilled and insatiable lover. They were all there, a hundred tongues of flame caressing him to an unbearable furnace heat. And all with the same face—Elizabeth.

'Don't stop,' he moaned. 'Let it go on forever. Don't let it ever end.'

Then he was weeping, sobbing like a child against her. 'Elizabeth! Kiss me, Elizabeth! Let me feel you in my mouth. Let me taste you.'

He turned her violently on her back and the salt of his own passion burnt his mouth. She stared up at him, the knowledge of a thousand years looking out of her eyes.

'Oh, Hotspur, Hotspur,' she mocked him gently. 'Ride me hard, Hotspur.' Her body arched toward him at the first savage thrust. 'Harder,' she whispered, 'you are riding the Devil, my darling.'

They were both possessed: he by some alien spirit from that other world, insatiable, untiring, playing out each fantasy that had ever touched the secret corners of his mind. And she was the mirror of his lust, matching him in depravity, hour for hour, the eternal, unquenchable flame that would always consume him.

There was a darkness and a quiet in him like the end of the world. He lay very still, he could not move or speak. He knew that if he opened his eyes all he would see would be Elizabeth.

Northumberland stared up at his son, torn between irritation and admiration. For a moment he had seen himself again. Had he ever been that sure of himself, so indifferent? Only a Percy would have turned his back on the power that Harry had had out of pure spleen.

'So you found that your idol had feet of clay then?' he asked mildly.

Harry threw him an angry look. 'And I suppose you are going to say that you knew he was worthless from the start?'

His father's mouth turned in its oblique smile. 'I wish I had, Harry. I wish I had,' he said sadly. 'I might have saved us all this grief if I had.' He rose stiffly from his chair. He had lost flesh since Harry had last seen him. A tall lean cadaver of a man with eyes that burnt with a strange fevered brilliance.

Harry thought: He's eaten up with guilt; he blames himself for Richard's death.

His father said, 'What will you do now?'

Harry shrugged. 'Stay in the north. There's enough to do here. I am still Governor of Berwick and Warden of the East March.'

Hal frowned. 'And the King accepted your resignation of the Justiciarship without question?' It was not like Henry. He was too fond of giving the orders himself.

'No doubt he was glad to be relieved of the need to pay me. Despenser has taken my place. I shall be glad to see if he can keep Glen Dwr in check without money to pay his men.'

Hal nodded. He had fared little better himself. The cost of the Scottish war this last year had almost crippled him and he'd paid the wages and sustenance of the men himself rather than see them go hungry. Not that there was much to be had. The north was barren, and the cost of a bushel of wheat almost beyond price. The grudging and tardy payments that had come from Westminster had soon been swallowed up. Henry pleaded poverty and an empty treasury. Yet Hal knew there was money: the royal revenues and those of Lancaster. Richard's treasure, the crippling war tax. Enough to keep a dozen armies in the field for a year. But then it always cost dearly to keep men loyal. Neville and his sons had had their fair share of bribes. He was the King's brother-in-law now and at pains that all should know it. Hal doubted if Ralph Neville had ever had to go cap in hand to the King for money.

'He's used us!' Harry burst out suddenly, startling him. 'He's used us to fight his battles and keep him secure on his throne. And what reward have we had? If it were not for us he would not even be King.'

'I am not proud of that, Harry,' Hal said quietly. 'And besides—' His brows lifted in faintest mockery. 'I thought you did all for love of him. You should need no reward.'

'I ask for nothing more than I am entitled to,' Harry cried hotly. 'I could not fight battles with men who have both empty bellies and pockets.'

'I know, I know.' He had forgotten how quick Harry was to anger.

Then Harry said, 'There's a man in Radnor who says that Richard is still alive and that the dead man the people saw was only that of his clerk Maudelyn. He said that he had seen the King in Scotland.'

Hal lifted his eyes slowly, searching his son's face for the meaning he sensed behind the words. 'Richard is dead,' he said slowly. 'You saw him. I saw him. Do you think I could mistake a man I had known since childhood for a clerk?'

'There are some who wish it were so. That Richard was still alive.'

Hal kept his eyes on Harry's face. 'And you are one?'

'Are not you?'

They stood for a long time without speaking. Then Hal turned away, his voice uneasy. 'What's done is done, Harry. Richard is dead. Henry of Lancaster is King. We made it so. If we made the wrong choice then we must live with it.'

He had learnt to live with it: the shame, the dishonour, so familiar now that they troubled him less each day. He had left all his honour and pride at Conway two years ago. Now there was the guilt to add to it. He did not live so easily with that. He should have known: that cryptic little message from Henry's council—*If Richard the late king should be alive, as it is supposed he is, it is ordered that he be well and surely guarded. But if he be dead, then that he be openly shown to the people.'*

If he be dead! He *was* dead—starved, beaten, stabbed? None knew, for by the time any laid eyes on him there was only that pale, still, child-like face to look upon.

But what had they all been about that they did not even know till it was too late? He should have spoken up, demanded to know where and how Richard was kept. It had eased his conscience more not to know. He had not wanted to know. Perhaps in his heart he had never believed Bolingbroke capable of it. His father had not been. Constant fear did strange things to men. It turned them inward on themselves, made cowards of them. Bolingbroke was still afraid, even of him. He had sensed it when Henry had come north to lead that timorous and abortive Scottish foray. He had resented the obligation, the debt, the need to repay. Yet if he had known it there was no need. It had not been done for him.

He turned, suddenly aware that Harry was watching him. He

smiled and held out his hand to him. He would forget: all guilts passed in time. It would be easier now he had Harry by him again.

———

Warkworth
He coaxed the old lame dog from its place by the dead hearth, holding the great brindled head against him while it stretched and found its balance. He needed neither collar nor leash. Ceolwulf would follow him without question as he had always done.

Softly, like an errant child he crept down the silent passages, past the sprawled, inert figures of sleepers. None stirred yet. It was barely dawn though he had been awake for hours. He'd had a sudden desire to see the sun come up over Warkworth.

The morning air struck cold against his cheek and the long dew-drenched grass soaked his soft doeskin boots instantly.

He paced himself to Ceolwulf's unsteady, ambling rheumatic gait. The mist still lay heavily on the water and coiled in white vaporous clouds beneath the overhanging trees. He heard the furtive splash of water rats disturbed by his presence. Ceolwulf heard it too and raised his muzzle, scenting old trails, old long-forgotten delights.

Hal smiled and dropped his hand to the soft velvet ears. 'You'll not catch them now, boy,' he said quietly.

The dog looked up at him with steady amber eyes limned in black. Saliva dripped from the panting dish of his tongue and his sides heaved in short violent jerks. He must be all of fifteen now. An old man, content with a full belly and a place in the sun. The fate of all old men. An echo of laughter awoke in his eyes. He was past sixty himself. Would he ever be content with just a place in the sun? He remembered the dog's sire, the giant Siward, his dam, the gentle Bebba who had watched him so lovingly as he had set the knife to her throat. He remembered when old Will had drawn the mewling blood-slimed pup from her torn belly.

He stroked the dog's heaving flanks. Once he could have run fifteen miles behind a horse without effort: those great crushing

371

jaws could have killed a man with ease. Soon he would be blind; crippled, chivvied from corner to corner by the younger dogs, a useless bulk of decaying flesh. He shivered. He'd never let it come to that. He'd set his own blade to the dog's throat before he'd let it come to that.

He walked on down the river bank. The sun was up now, an aura of pale light behind Warkworth that showed the turrets black and formless above the walls. The wind rose with it, stirring the clumps of oak and beech on the far bank, shivering the tall reeds at the water's edge where a wild swan cleaned its plumage. It carried the smell of decay on its breath, the smell of burnt and rotting fields of sterile earth and death. He should have been used to it by now. Familiarity blunted sensitivity but each time it was a fresh horror to him, each time he railed and wept and vowed his vengeance. Even now it still pained him to see the desolate fields and the ragged bairns queueing for dole at his door. It would be worse this year. What little harvest the Scots had left them had been swept away by summer storms. There had been plague at Durham, a festering sickness that had slaughtered man and beast alike. He had ordered the tainted cattle to be burnt and it had seemed a dreadful irony to see ravenous children weeping over the smell of roasting meat that they could not eat. Some had eaten and died from it. At least they had not died hungry.

The mist was rising from the river on shafts of sunlight, lifting the sombre ochre of the dead trees to flaming gold. It would be winter soon. At Candlemas he would have to face Douglas again at the Marcher Court. He held out little hope of peace, though God knew they needed it. It would be a repetition of the last futile wrangling, with Douglas demanding terms that he knew full well Hal could not meet, and he buying time with flimsy truces that he knew would not be kept.

It was Bolingbroke who had weakened them. To the Scots, as France, he was 'usurper', and the war had gone beyond their own differences and become a crusade for Richard. And what Henry had hoped to gain from that pompous little foray up to the walls of Edinburgh to demand his rights as overlord, God himself only knew. It had achieved nothing save the humiliation of a hurried retreat at the news of Glen Dwr's rising; worse, it had given the Scots a heaven-sent chance of retaliation.

And then there was George Dunbar. Henry had taken in the Scots refugee Earl as if he were a long lost kinsman. It was an uncomfortable alliance for the north. The man who had been their enemy for the last ten years was now their ally. And privileged: the gifts of the castle of Somerton and a manor in Nottingham, annuities for both Dunbar and his son—more than many a loyal Englishman had received. It had lost Henry more than a few loyalties in the north and soured any hopes of peace. It was not their quarrel. Dunbar's grievance was with the Douglas himself over the marriage of Elizabeth Douglas to the Scots heir, Rothesay. But it would soon become their quarrel. Douglas would yield them nothing while they harboured Dunbar.

He called Ceolwulf back from where he snuffled uselessly at the long abandoned lair of a fox. Across the shining water the dark cave of the hermitage beckoned. He came here often but never ventured further. He was too fond of looking back as it was. The small boat stood unused, locked to the shore by the tangle of reeds that grew over its hull. On the far bank the path was overgrown, a white thread beneath long seeding grass that led up to the clifftop and the wasted patch that had been the priest's little orchard and pasture for his few goats. The old hermit had been dead these last two years. He had never replaced him. It added to the heaviness of his heart to be always looking back. There was only grief and loss to see. Life was now: the sun, the sky, the smell of earth and new growth. Harry was life. His only life since Richard had died. His own was null and void, smothered beneath an unutterable weight of guilt and regret. He was content to live through Harry now.

He turned back toward Warkworth and paused to watch the sun break over the tip of the Grey Mare. He still loved to see the play of light upon the golden stone. It had its own life. Past, present, future, the memories absorbed and mellowed and returned to him soft and glowing in the constant beauty of stone. His eye caught a flash of colour. A figure leant from a window. Her arms gleamed white, her fiery hair blew out in a cloud from her pale pointed face. It was Elizabeth.

The dog came and whimpered beneath his hand. Behind him the wild swan rose from the water and filled his ears with its mournful whooping call.

The first distant flame gnawed minutely at the vast blanket of darkness. The bored and dozing sentry posted on the roof of Ford Castle saw it on the periphery of his vision, a dull unseen candle amid the brightness of his other thoughts. He had drunk well that night, too well to be sitting here sweltering out the hot August night. He could have had that plump little Flemish wench in his bed by now if that sour-faced bastard Nolle had been willing to take his duty. She'd been willing enough; by Christ had she been willing, sitting on his lap half the night, chafing his manhood with her buttocks. He closed his eyes and wiped the beading of sweat from his lip with the back of his hand. It was not so bad if there were two to the watch. There was company then, and dice and perhaps a tale or two to be told and embellished. He thought of the big-breasted tavern girl again. Christ, would he have had a tale to tell of her in the morning!

He settled his back more comfortably against the wall and unlaced the neck of his jerkin. He consoled himself. She'd still be there tomorrow and he had money: his pay from the Scots rout at Nesbitt Moor last month, though he still owed the armourer half of that. He'd had another ten marks for booty and there was still the Scots fighting axe to be disposed of. The sword and the harness he would keep. They were better than the ones he had.

He stretched his legs and belched up a mouthful of sour wine. Jesu, but it was bloody hot and his throat was as parched as sand. He'd have willingly traded both sword and harness for a mouthful of cool ale. He opened his eyes and closed them again, squeezing them shut till the blood danced redly behind his lids. He was dreaming, he was drunk—Holy Mother of God, let him be drunk! He opened them cautiously. Oh God, they were still there, gobbets of red flame growing larger as they moved toward him; diminishing into tiny pinpoints in the far distance, thousands of them, like the candles in a funeral procession. As he watched, spurts of fire detached themselves and whirled like

374

comets through the air to burst into roaring sheets of flame. He hauled himself up onto his knees. The fields, the harvest—they were firing the harvest. He could see them now. The banners, the pennons, the swift shaggy ponies of the pikemen, the gaudy fluttering housings of a noble's horse, and everywhere the burnished sheen of armour glowing with reflected flame. Ten, fifteen, twenty thousand? He did not know. His stunned mind could not conceive of numbers.

He ran then, doubled up with fear and shock; shouting, cursing, stumbling, his voice roused to a womanly shriek. He fell headlong down the turret stairs and landed painfully on his knees. A hand grabbed him and hauled him up.

'The Scots!' he gabbled. 'Thousands of them! And Frenchies too—I saw the Oriflamme.' The hand released him abruptly and he sank back to his knees and fetched his supper up onto the floor. He stayed crouched and trembling while feet tramped around him and sleepy voices groaned and then grew sharp with alarm. Someone kicked him and thrust a sword into his hand. His numb fingers closed round the hilt and he used the point to lever himself to his feet. The dark figure of the lord's chaplain brushed past him. He heard the rattle of the rosary beads at his waist and the whispered prayers: 'Christ have mercy on us.'

He staggered drunkenly out onto the bailey. Two of his fellow guards were dragging a brazier toward him with iron clamps. They shouted to him but he did not hear. The heat from the burning made him feel sick. Spitting the bitterness from his mouth he looked down on the little town with red and streaming eyes. The tower roof was already ablaze and, ridiculously, he thought of the Flemish girl. He crossed himself. She'd not warm any man's bed now save the Devil's.

The outriders of the army were abreast of the castle now. He could see their faces, black as nubians with smoke and soot. He closed his eyes, began to pray, his voice halting and stumbling on the seldom spoken words. His eyes were still closed when the arrow struck him full in the throat.

The smoke darkened Hal's eyes and his mouth was full of the black whirling dust that was worse than the smoke. He could see nothing, hear nothing. There was nothing to see. The fire had choked and smothered all life.

He rode blind, with nothing to guide him but the glowing hulks of towns and villages. Ford, Chillingham, Alnham, down to Thropton where the enemy had crossed the Coquet. There they had turned aside and laid Elsdon waste. From then on they had had a clear run down to the Tyne. At Powburn he turned back toward Alnwick. The road through the village threw out an almost radiant heat. The church was still burning; the stone shell with its tall lancet windows glowed suddenly like a lantern as the roof fell. A women with her hair singed clean to the scalp sat by the roadside weeping dementedly. In the church porch what was left of the priest hung obscenely naked. His flesh was split and blistered like a roasting pig. They had nailed him to the door before they fired the church.

He rode on, sick with rage and full of nightmare—the woman at Cornhill, staked out in the market square and trampled to death by horsemen, the horror of the decapitated corpses in the church with their heads grotesquely interchanged: the young girl top-heavy with the bearded jowls of a soldier, the fat greasy merchant with the small perfect head of a child. He leant from the saddle and retched.

So much for truce, so much for friendship. Had he really deluded himself that that was what there was between him and Douglas? He would never have believed that Douglas could be so small and mean in his vengeance. The holocaust made his own victory at Nesbitt pall into insignificance. And was it such a victory now? A thousand of the enemy dead, a hundred prisoners; not so very much to set against all this. He understood now. It had been a diversion, a ruse to draw him west so the main army under Douglas could cross the Border unhindered. He had picked his moment well, with all the northern lords save Clifford and himself in Wales with the King. He had been marching his battle-weary army back through the high August heat when the news came. He had seen the flames from twenty miles away.

He smiled grimly, remembering Otterburn. He would not make that mistake again. The Douglas had slipped through his fingers then but this time his enemy would not so much as change his shirt but that he would know of it. There were relays of scouts on every road south and west, every ford and crossing-place was watched, every peel tower manned. This time he would have him. The Black Douglas would not see Scotland again unless he saw him first.

Once he reached Whittingham the air was cleaner, though the smoke still blew seawards in great drifting clouds. Alnwick itself was still untouched. Was Douglas saving that for the return march?

Dunbar was there: tense, anxious, eager to please and divorce himself from Scotland. Feelings already ran high and the presence of the Scottish earl did little to ease the tension. Harry especially was his antagonist. He had been riding the Border since dawn and had seen all that his father had seen and more. He had already called Dunbar a traitor to his face and as the Scots earl entered the hall where they were gathered after supper to discuss stratagems, the last of his self-control fled.

'Do we have to suffer him?' he shouted. 'He's turned his coat once. What's to stop him doing it again?'

Dunbar flushed but he answered steadily. 'No turncoat, sir; merely an exile, as your own lord was in France before the Percys raised him up.'

Hal laid his hand in restraint upon his son's arm and stared at Dunbar with dislike. He did not trust the Scotsman any further than he could spit, but he was prepared to concede that they had a cause in common. Both would give much to trap the Douglas. 'We might as well make use of him while we can Harry,' he said loudly. 'He has cost us dear enough.'

Dunbar inclined his head. 'You are gracious, Northumberland,' he said cynically. 'More, I fear than can be said for your son.'

Harry's face grew white with rage and he would have struck Dunbar if Hal had not stepped between them. He motioned Harry abruptly to his place. 'There will be no quarrelling,' he said evenly, 'between any. We'll save our anger for the enemy. There are more than enough of them.'

'How many?' Dunbar asked.

Hal sat down in the high-backed chair between Harry and Tom Clifford. 'Twenty thousand,' he said. 'Perhaps more.'

'There'll be Frenchmen then,' Dunbar said. 'Albany has been brewing an alliance for a while now.'

Hal nodded. 'The Oriflamme has been seen,' he agreed. He took the small parchment map from its ivory case and weighted it. 'But which way, my lord? Which way will they come home?'

The Scotsman moved from his place and came to stand behind him. 'With those numbers there's not too much choice. If they have plunder as well they dare not risk too rough a terrain.'

'Then there are only three choices. The west route through Harbottle and over Windy Gyle; the way they came, down the Till Valley; or the east road along the coast.'

'They'll not march back the way they came,' said Clifford.

'They might,' Dunbar said. 'They say that lightning never strikes twice but it could with a man like Archie Douglas.' He tapped his finger thoughtfully on the map. 'I'm surprised that he gave you such early warning. In the past he always forbade burning until we were on the homeward run. And the killing—' He frowned. 'It's not like Douglas somehow.' He smiled unpleasantly. 'He is usually so gentle with you English.'

'He's an old man,' young Clifford said. 'Old men lose their judgement.'

Not so much older than I, thought Hal. He said to Dunbar, 'Think, man. You know the Douglas. How will he think?'

Dunbar tugged at his small beard and smiled. 'If I were so apt at predicting the Douglas I should not be here now,' he said. 'All I can tell you is that wherever he thinks you are not, he will come that way. You are the only man that the Douglas is afraid of, my lord.'

Hal stared down at the little parchment map. 'And with cause, my lord,' he said grimly. 'With great cause.'

He did not sleep that night though his bones ached with weariness. His thoughts ran back over the years, from that day at Berwick when they had conceived the foolish unattainable ideal. There had been bloodshed and destruction since but in his heart he had always felt that so far as it lay within their control they had kept the essence of it. Without malice. There had been no real malice between them till now. He recalled their last meeting at Candlemas. It was the first time they had ever parted in anger;

and all because he would not deliver Dunbar to him. No, perhaps not all. There had been other reasons, other shadows between them. Bolingbroke, his own desertion of Richard. Douglas had not asked him why. He could not have told him if he had. But the essential trust had gone between them and they had parted as near enemies as they had ever been. He remembered that soft eloquent voice: *'What else could Percy and Douglas ever be?'*

Now the long postponed reckoning was due. He realized that in forty years he had never met Douglas face to face on a battlefield. Was that by chance or design? It would be the final confrontation. No more parleys or truces, no more chasing a faceless enemy through their hills. He had him now. Through the eyes of his scouts he saw every destructive step that Douglas took. Tynedale was laid to waste though for some reason Newcastle itself had been spared. Wark had been burnt as he sat down to supper; they had recrossed the Wansbeck as he had spoken with Dunbar. Now they were camped in a little dip in the hills five miles north of Morpeth. Tomorrow they would make the final run for home, toward Scotland, toward him. He would be waiting. There was much to be paid for.

From the top of Hedgehope he could see almost all of his earldom. At his back, across the ridge of Comb Fell, the Cheviot rose into mist then dropped to the rounded cone of Yeavering Bell and the valley of the Till. Beyond that there was the Tweed and Scotland; the sullen green of Ettrick Forest, the slate blue of the Lammermuirs. To the west the distant peak of Skiddaw rose from hills and shining lakes and to the east he could see as far as the sea and Bamburgh. The line of the Scots march ran south, a black disfiguring scar through the summer greenness. Tynedale was still hidden from him by a pall of smoke and Belsay still burnt, a pallid torch that belched a black plume across the smiling summer sky.

His eyes were fixed nearer home, on the bright undulating serpent that crawled toward him through the Breamish valley. The gaudy bannered head of the vanguard antennaed with lances, the body bristled with pikes and scaled with armour plate. The tail was a long sluggish column of laden carts trailing streams of outriders. For all their conjecture and prediction the Scots were coming home by Cheviot. He had been watching them for over an hour. Time enough to count their numbers: not so many as he had feared but more than he had hoped. Twelve thousand at least, and he had only half that.

He looked down to where his own men were massed, insect—small on the flanks of the low hills. His David to Douglas's Goliath. He could see the scarlet plume in Harry's helm, bright and virulent as a streak of blood, and the distinct yellow jackets of Musgrave's bowmen like clumps of marsh flower. Dunbar was there, his colours flaunting and shameful among the English. There were some of Westmorland's knights too. He forced a grim smile. Ralph Neville would not like that, his men riding under Northumberland.

He turned his horse for the descent and the wind beat hard into his face. It still blew from the south and filled his throat with a harsh acrid taste of smoke. In the cleft of the valley his army awaited him. The mounted knights stood in quiet grey ranks with the arrowheads of the foot soldiers between them. On either side the wedges of bowmen sloped back in swallow curves and he knew that if there was to be any victory it would be theirs. All his strength lay there.

It was the waiting that was the worst. There was time for doubt then. Would the element of surprise be enough to take Douglas off his guard? Would his archers be able to hold the Scots chivalry long enough? He fixed his eyes on the gap in the hills where the Scots would appear. They could be heard quite clearly now, a thousand sounds merged into a dull continuous roar. He glanced up at the summit of Hedgehope and the speck against the sky that was his scurrier. Now. It must be now.

Then he saw it. The flaunting scarlet streak of the Oriflamme and beside it, on a ripple of azure silk, the bleeding heart of Douglas.

'I'll make your heart bleed, Douglas,' he whispered. 'I'll make it bleed until it breaks.'

They came on into the neck of the valley. He could see they rode at ease, full of confidence, glutted with slaughter. He raised his hand and saw that it was trembling. '*Avaunt en baner!*' he cried. '*Esperance, esperance en Dieu! For God and Northumberland!*'

They poured down from the silent hills, two molten waves of steel and horseflesh that merged on the valley floor into an impenetrable barrier across the line of the Scots march. They were close enough to see faces, white and startled but still indistinguishable. The van was wheeling in confusion, being carried forward by the impetus of the rolling column at its back. He heard frenzied shouts from the rear and saw the desperate attempts to turn the horses. But there was nowhere to go. The hills hemmed them in on either side and their retreat was blocked by their own baggage train. Hal smiled grimly. He had him. Douglas had walked into his trap.

At this signal the archers streamed forward, the sun and wind at their back. The Scots had barely reached the lower slopes of Homildon before the first shafts ploughed into their flank. The bowmen went forward with smooth concerted movements, like the pattern of a dance. Pull, aim, loose. Pull, aim, loose. Six shafts a minute, then three paces back to replenish their quivers while the second division took its place.

The Scots bowmen made a futile attempt at reply from the confusion of their own ranks. Horses were wheeling and plunging, bolting pell-mell down the slope with broken shafts in their bellies. The Scots captains rode desperately through the chaos trying to bring the disordered footmen to order and saw them scattered as soon as they were assembled by the English arrows. The steady steel-tipped rain of arrows was undiminishing and the hiss and whine of flown shafts filled the valley like a wind. In the centre of the enemy, where the standards were, the ranks were steadier. The whole Scots army was shrinking in towards its heart. They were forming for a charge despite the continuing onslaught of bowshot that harried and nipped their flanks.

Harry rode up and grabbed his arm. 'For God's sake, call the bowmen in. They'll be trampled to death if the Scots charge.'

Hal did not answer him and stared at the broad-muscled backs of the bowmen. There was the slightest flaw in the pattern now as the archers sensed the enemy's intent but they did not cease firing. They would not stop until he gave the word. He turned to look at

381

the enemy and imagine the speed at which they would come down the hill. He rode forward and called Musgrave from the fray. He jerked his head toward the archers.

'Will they stand if the enemy charge?' he asked quietly.

'They'll stand,' said Musgrave grimly. 'Or I'll know the reason why.'

'Then one last volley,' Hal said. 'Every man firing together at will. When the Scots reach that little belt of trees I want every shaft you've got pumped into their front line. If we can bring them down the others will follow.'

He watched, his flesh steaming within the steel oven of his armour, as the bowmen ceased firing and fanned out at the foot of the hill. Three deep, stepped behind the kneeling front rank that waited as the Scots began to pour down the hill. He could feel the earth shudder with the weight of steel and horseflesh. Harry's voice close to him went unheard, a mere vibration of air against his cheek as two thousand bows were drawn tight against grim and angry mouths.

'*Loose!*' Musgrave's command was almost drowned by the sudden roar of torn and ruptured air. For a brief moment Hal could not even see the enemy for the black rain of arrows. He heard the dull metallic clang of steel against steel as the shafts gouged their way through armour plate and impaled rider and horse together. He heard the high naked screams of the horses as they fell, spitted through to the bone. Then men were screaming, hauling at rein and bit to turn their mounts from the tangle of dying men and horses that rose up like a wall before them. The Scots were going down in their thousands, an avalanche of broken and bleeding flesh that carried all before it. Those who could were turning in flight, streaming up the hillside. He glanced up the hill to where Douglas's standard had been. It was down. He saw its bright colours fluttering feebly in the dust like a trampled butterfly.

In the small low-roofed hall of Etal Castle, Northumberland sat quietly, chilled to the bone despite the summer night. He still trembled with disbelief. He had won—against all the odds, he had won and without the loss of a single man. He raised his head from the cradle of his hands. It must be almost dawn but the tramp of feet past the door was undiminishing; they were still bringing the prisoners in. He listened, picking up the heavy tread of mailed feet, the jerking defiant step of a captive, the dragging walk of a wounded man and softer, almost unheard, the quiet briskness of the monks who had come from Hulne to tend the wounded. There were enough of those. They filled the small timbered hall with their groans and there was not room to stand in the chapel for the dying. There were more dead, scattered the length of the Breamish road, drowned beneath the flood of Tweed with his pursuing archers still at their heels. The cream of Scottish chivalry was in his hands: the lords Montgomery, Erskine and Graham; the earls of Moray and Orkney; Albany's son, Murdac of Fife. And the prize, the glittering jewelled prize of his revenge: he had the Douglas.

He rose stiffly and heard the crack of his bones. To the guard who stood by his door he said quietly, 'Bring me the Earl of Douglas.'

He did not look up immediately. He listened while the heavy limping tread crossed the room and stopped an arm's length away from him. A trickle of blood splashed onto the point of his shoe. He watched it spread and blacken the leather before he raised his eyes. One brilliant rabid eye stared at him. The other was hidden behind a swathe of bandages, a red empty socket gouged out by the shaft that had ploughed a furrow down his cheek from brow to lip. Hal sprang to his feet in shock. It was as if time had snatched at him and dragged him back forty years; torn and bleeding, distorted by blood and dirt, this was the Douglas of the time at Berwick. Then his mind cleared. No, not Douglas. No, of course not Douglas. This was Archie Douglas his son.

'I asked for the dog,' he snapped. 'And you bring me the whelp.'

Archie Douglas swayed against the guards who held him upright. 'I *am* the dog now,' he said viciously. 'My father is dead. He died a month ago of the fever at Douglas.'

His image blurred through sudden tears. So it was finished. The Black Douglas was dead and all those long years of near friendship with him. There was gladness too. That this last had not been the Douglas's work, that after all he had kept faith to the end. He gave a wry twisted smile. He might have known that the old dog would cheat him at the last. What use was victory now without the Douglas there to see it? He turned away from the reminder of Archie Douglas's torn and bloody face and spoke over his shoulder to his guard.

'See that my lord of Douglas is well cared for,' he said, 'and treated with all honour.'

He did not know why he cared so much, except that perhaps it seemed to bring death a little closer to him. All the old men were dying. Only he seemed to be indestructible.

'I'll *not* give them up!' Harry yelled. 'He has no right to demand it. Both Douglas and Mar gave their parole on my word that they would be ransomed, not shut up in the Tower for the rest of their lives.'

Hal sat hunched in his chair staring down at the scarlet splash of Bolingbroke's seal on the writ. At his feet Ceolwulf lay scarcely breathing, his eyes glazed with pain. He dropped his hand gently to the dog's massive head. At this moment he cared more about Ceolwulf than King Henry Bolingbroke and his demands.

Harry continued to pace, beating his fists against the flat of his hand. 'Christ—to think I once loved that man!' He whirled round to face his father. 'Are you going to let him get away with it?' he said bitterly. 'He's had us fighting his battles for nothing, now he wants the ransom money as well.'

'Let him have it,' Hal said slowly. 'Give the Scots prisoners up. All of them—except Douglas,' he added softly.

Harry turned white with anger. 'Give them up? After all this you say give them up?' His eyes hardened to pale steel. 'It's as well that Douglas did not think likewise after Otterburn or you'd not have seen me again.'

Hal sighed. 'Can you not see it, Harry?' he said wearily. 'He's driving you deliberately into a corner. He's a frightened man, afraid of shadows and ghosts and old memories. In his way he is afraid of you. He loved you once, before he was King, when you could only do him good. Now you can harm him. Your wife is a

Mortimer; your nephew was once heir to England—and still is, in the minds of some. It might even have crossed his mind that your own son is closer in blood to the crown than he.' He smiled wickedly. 'You put him there, Harry. Perhaps he is afraid you will pluck him down again. Edmund Mortimer will not be a boy for ever, neither can Henry keep him confined for ever. One day he'll be a man and that is what Henry is afraid of.'

All that Elizabeth had said and more. 'If Henry lets him live that long,' Harry said.

'Henry will not do anything rash. He is not that kind of man. The most audacious thing he ever did was to set sail from France with only a dozen men at his back. But you, Harry—you can be rash, hot-tempered, wilful. You can be provoked to the wildest things. Henry knows this and will use it against you if he can.' He stared gravely at his son's handsome face. 'Unless you are prepared to defy Henry openly and I don't think you are. Then we must yield the prisoners up. All of them, except the Earl of Douglas. Honour forbides that we yield Douglas. Henry will see that.'

'I'll not do it,' Harry muttered. 'You know what he means to do with them—keep them immured for years in his dungeons while he extorts a crippling ransom.'

'Henry thinks to keep the peace that way,' Hal said mildly. 'Perhaps it is we who are the fools, playing games of chivalry, letting our enemies go so that they can come back and fight us again the next year.' He rose from his chair. 'Let me take them Harry. Let me talk with Henry and show him we are still loyal.'

'*Are* we?' said Harry venomously.

'What other choice is there? Rebellion? D you see yourself a king-maker Harry?' He smiled sadly. 'It's not so easy to make a king—or unmake one either for that matter.'

'It's not only I who think this. I could name you a hundred men of rank who would put Richard back on the throne if he were still alive. Glen Dwr of Wales for one.'

Hal laughed. 'Would you put your trust in a man who thinks he's a magician, Harry?' he said. 'Men are always wise after the event. Henry is King now and any man with any sense would leave it so.'

385

'King, yes—but also liar, cheat, usurper and murderer!' Harry shouted. It was as if Elizabeth spoke through him. 'When he first came back he was in the right. We supported him because he was in the right and he swore to us at Doncaster that he came for naught else but his rights. Even when he claimed the crown it seemed right and just. But I did not bargain for Richard's death. Does it mean nothing to you that he murdered King Richard?'

Hal did not answer at once. Yes, it meant something; loss of conscience, loss of pride and honour, all left behind at Conway four years ago.

'The guilt is not all Henry's,' he said at last. 'We murdered Richard too when we allowed Henry to become King.'

'Is that why you still protect him? Why not purge your conscience clean if it troubles you so much?'

'Because I am old and tired, Harry, and I've had my fill of Kings. I'm like old Ceolwulf here, old and passive and obedient, content to warm myself at any man's fire now.'

'Well I am not!' Harry flung at him. 'Take the prisoners then, and grovel to Bolingbroke if it pleases you. I will not. He'll not see me again unless he asks it.'

Hal let him go. Harry would cool as he always did, when commonsense had doused the angry flame that always burned inside him. Hal knelt by the still, almost lifeless dog. He was almost finished, his hind legs had gone and he could barely walk now. He lifted the great head into his lap and soothed the dog's whimpering with his hands. The golden eyes watched him, the pupils shrunk to needles of pain.

'It's time, old friend,' he said softly. 'You've waited long enough.' He drew the misericord from his belt. Its blade was thin and sharp and pliable enough to slide between the joints of a man's armour. He had killed enough men with it. It would serve as well for Ceolwulf.

He laid down beside the dog and cradled his head against his arm. He felt the great heart thudding against the fleshless ribs. 'Quick and clean, Ceolwulf,' he whispered. 'A noble death.' It was the way he would have wanted to die himself, not left a rotting pain-filled hulk dragging out the last of his days in misery. He laid the point of the knife to the dog's heart. 'Forgive me, old friend,' he said and slid it home. He heard the rattling growl of its last breath, its great body jerked once then lay still. He stayed for a long time beside him, the warm trickle of the dog's blood against his hand. Then he rose and covered the body with his cloak. He wished that he had some kind hand to put him from his pain.

From the narrow window of the Grey Mare's Tail, Elizabeth watched her children. All she could see of Bess was the silk-shod feet and the glint of her hair through the low sweeping branches. She was fifteen now and old enough to hide the burning dislike that was still between them, behind the douce little smile that irritated Elizabeth so much. The girl's true feelings showed to none but her mother. All save Elizabeth herself thought that little Bess was perfect.

Young Hal was hauling inexpertly at the fletch of a miniature bow. He loosed too soon and the blunted shaft fell harmlessly at his feet. She heard the warm rich sound of the Earl's laughter and looked on jealously as he knelt beside the boy, his broad arm round the slim shoulders as he showed him how to fit the shaft. He had the look of her brother Roger when he had been young, the same thick curling yellow hair, the bright speedwell eyes. She turned abruptly from the window. Roger was dead and Edmund Glen Dwr's prisoner since his crushing defeat at Bryn Glas when his Welsh tenantry had deserted to Glen Dwr.

'Does Bolingbroke know what the Welshwomen did to the English prisoners?' she said to Harry. 'That they castrated them with their bare hands?'

Harry nodded. 'He knows. There is not much that he doesn't know.'

'And still he refuses to agree to my brother Edmund's ransom. He ransomed Grey of Ruthin speedily enough last year.' She turned back to the window. 'So Bolingbroke has nothing to fear from the Mortimers now.' Her voice was brittle and hard as ice. 'Roger's sons are mewed up at Windsor still and Edmund is prisoner to the Welsh with no hope of release.' She whirled to face him. 'How much more, Harry? Must he cast his eyes on your own son before you will move against him?'

387

Harry turned from the intoxication of her eyes. It was the truth. Bolingbroke had treated Mortimer shamefully, he had treated them all shamefully. His father had fared no better for all his loyalty. Hal had gone to Westminster in June and taken all the Scots prisoners save Douglas with him. If he had thought Henry would be satisfied with that he was disappointed. The King was not to be cheated. He had demanded Douglas and he had demanded that Harry himself bring him to Westminster by the end of September.

'And now he commands *you*, Harry.' Elizabeth's inexorable voice fanned the flame of his resentment. 'Will you go, Harry? Will you go cap in hand and yield Douglas to the Usurper? Will you grovel before the man who by rights should grovel before you?'

He looked up into her face and felt all the force of her will. 'Yes, I'll go,' he said. 'But I'll not yield Douglas. I shall be a dead man before I give up Archie Douglas.'

King Henry the Fourth of England fingered the great ruby on his hand as Northumberland's son came toward him. There were few men he was deeply afraid of, but this was one. This and the arrogant unpredictable old man who had sired him. No, that was a lie. Henry was afraid of all men these days, even those nearest to him bound by ties closer than blood. He saw treachery everywhere, in the whisper quickly stifled as he entered a room, in the furtive aversion of men's eyes. He could not eat but his food was tasted; he could not sleep till the royal bed had been stripped cover by cover and the mattress turned, and even then sometimes he lay wakeful till dawn. And then there were those fears against which he had no defence, shadows that came by night and leant over him, whispering, accusing: Salisbury, Wiltshire, and always Richard. Richard, martyr, King—God's anointed, and foully murdered by him. He felt the sweat break out on his lip. He had never meant it to come to that. Yet how else could he have held England, how else could he have been safe?

Beneath the heavy silk doublet he felt his skin begin to crawl with the irritation that had plagued his body of late. It had all been for nothing. He was still not safe. Oh, he knew; he knew the ones who plotted behind his back, those who secretly wore

Richard's badge of the White Hart. And Harry. He looked at last into the face that was so close now. His beloved Harry, his valiant Hotspur who had always been so much a part of the coveted dream. Was Harry traitor? That evil bitch of a wife of his was a Mortimer, close kin to the two little knaves he had shut up at Windsor and who grew more of a threat to him each day. Her brother Edmund was her tool. Glen Dwr's also? He had heard it said that his capture by the Welshman had been no accident. A rumour, hearsay, false report, the deadliest of weapons against an uneasy conscience. And he was prey to them all.

Yet when Henry looked into the steady grey eyes, some of his fear left him. Harry was still loyal. He had not the temperament for dissembling and treachery. It was why he had always loved him so well.

'Welcome,' he said softly. 'Welcome, my dearest lord.'

Harry looked hard into the King's face. 'Am I welcome my liege?' he said stiffly. 'It is not what I heard from my father. I heard that I was commanded to your presence under the threat of arrest.'

'Temperament, Harry. Only temperament.' The King smiled. 'All is well now. You came, Harry. That is all that matters. I thought for a while that you would not.' He looked past Harry to the throng of lords who crowded discreetly at the far end of the hall. 'I do not see the Earl of Douglas,' he said and smiled again.

'That is because he is not here,' Harry answered him. 'I have not brought him.' He saw the dull flush creep above the ermine collar of Henry's robe.

'Perhaps my lord of Northumberland did not explain himself to you clearly, Harry. I asked that the Earl of Douglas be brought.'

'I heard, Your Grace. I heard him then and I hear you now.' Harry paused and drew a long breath. 'I will not yield up the Earl of Douglas,' he said flatly. 'And moreover—' better to say all now while he was still at liberty to do so, 'I am informed that you have denied my brother-in-law Edmund Mortimer ransom and that you have confiscated his chattels without just cause.'

'You were informed rightly, my lord,' Henry said tightly. 'The State does not ransom traitors.'

'How is he traitor, my lord?' Harry demanded furiously. 'Because he is Mortimer, or is there more?'

'Careful, my lord, or I'll think you traitor with him.'

'Think what you please,' Harry shouted. 'I ask you again. Will you ransom Edmund Mortimer or not?'

'I will not.'

Then Harry smiled, a dangerous cold little smile that renewed the fear in Bolingbroke. Harry turned to the lords and knights who strained their ears from the back of the hall. 'Did you hear?' he cried. 'The heir to the realm is robbed of his right and the robber will not redeem him with his own!'

In the ensuing silence only the sound of the King's enraged breathing was loud. He leapt from his chair.

'Traitor!' he yelled. 'False and bloody traitor!' He had drawn the small jewelled dagger from his belt and it was halfway to Harry's throat before his wrist was caught and held. They stared at each other for a long time; a lifetime of friendship and shared triumphs remembered and destroyed in that long cold look.

Then Harry said quietly, 'Not here.' He loosed the King's wrist and heard the dagger clatter at his feet. 'Not here, but in the field.'

Hal awoke sweating and terrified. He could not remember the dream, only the horror of it. He crawled slowly from the bed. He was shivering, his skin tight and pricked with cold beneath the film of sweat. There had been blood, he could remember that, blood and pain and death. But not his. He was not afraid of death. He was too close to it for the thought to fill him with more than a vague unease. He was past sixty now, an old man, though his body had always struggled to deny it. Now, when he needed his strength most, it seemed that all those years were coming on him with a vengeance. He had been sick with the fever for almost four days. This was the first day that he had been able to rise from his bed.

He stared from the high window. It must have been long past midnight but it was never really dark in the north at this time of year. He could see as far south as Holy Island and the tiny scattered pebbles of the Farne Islands. Behind him, rising like a mirage through a mist of dusky summer heat, were the hills of

Scotland. Not enemy hills now—half the men camped within Berwick's sprawling walls were Scots.

He drew his cloak around him and clenched his teeth against the feverish trembling of his limbs. It would be dawn in a few hours. Too late to turn back then. At dawn the vast army would march out of Berwick, the spearhead of rebellion that would join with Glen Dwr of Wales and with Harry, already on his way to Chester.

Bolingbroke would know by now. Harry's cartel of defiance renouncing their allegiance and proclaiming Roger Mortimer as King would have reached Henry. He must have known before that, perhaps from the minute Harry had stormed from his presence that day at Westminster six months ago. If Henry had known, he had been afraid enough to try and make amends in his mean, penny-pinching way. The grant to Northumberland of the earldom of Douglas was a subtle insult, perhaps more subtle than they had first thought: to give the lands of the captive they refused to yield to the captors—and then to deny them the means to conquer it even if they had had a mind to. The gift had cost Henry nothing and perhaps he had hoped it might persuade them to give Douglas up. Hal smiled grimly. Bolingbroke had not known his man very well if he had thought that Harry would be turned from his course with such an empty bribe.

He remembered the last time he had seen Henry. He had gone to Westminster willing to concede all but his pride and Douglas. The King had refused to let him keep either. They had quarrelled mildly but he was not the quarry that the King was after. It was Harry he wanted, a yielding humble Harry ready to give all because he, the King, demanded it. Hal had foreseen the outcome of it then. Harry would rather have died than yield an inch of his pride, and the King had pushed him to the limit. Hal had not needed to hear Harry's furious account of what had passed between them; he had known what was in Henry's heart since he had come back from Wales with the image of Elizabeth burning in his eyes.

And there was the heart of it. Elizabeth was the link that drew them all together; Elizabeth with her pale pointed face and other-world smile. Since the King's refusal to ransom Edmund

Mortimer her brother had married Glen Dwr's daughter Cathryn; Glen Dwr was their ally now, as was Douglas. That rankled more than anything else but Harry said that the means justified the end. Did he believe all that Harry said? Perhaps only because he wanted to. But he knew Owain Glen Dwr well enough; no Welsh savage out of Snowdon but a shrewd clever man who had been schooled in law at Westminster and who had been squire to both Arundel and Bolingbroke once. Glen Dwr was a strange mingling of hard logic and ancient superstition, fanatically proud of his Welsh blood and his descent from the princes of Powys. All the Welsh thought themselves sons of Merlin. And to Glen Dwr the fall of Bolingbroke was predestined.

Hal smiled, remembering the prophesy: '*And there shall come out of the north a Dragon and a Wolf which shall be the help of the Lion, and bring the realm great rest with peace and glory. These three shall rise up against the Moldewarpe which is accursed of God and shall thrust him forth from the realm....*' The meaning was quite clear, Glen Dwr had told him gravely. Mortimer was the Lion, the Dragon was Percy and the Wolf Douglas. Bolingbroke was the Moldewarpe, accursed of God. ... Hal had smiled with polite disbelief. He had never found the pattern of his own life so predictable, but then he had never thought that he would ever have to put his trust in a man who claimed he was a magician. There was nothing magical about the terms Glen Dwr had demanded for his support: all of Wales, without tie or fealty to the English. That had been a hard indigestible fact stuck in the throats of all them—but it was only one of many now. It did not seem to matter so much now. Nothing was ever gained without some loss. There was always grief, regret, the subtle torture of hindsight, knowing that the pattern might have fallen out differently if this or that had been done, or not been done. If he had not sworn to Richard at Conway. ... If he had not sworn to Lancaster. ... Perhaps he had too high an opinion of himself to think it had all come about because of him. The burden would not have been so heavy if there had been others to share the guilt. But who could he blame for Conway? Bolingbroke because he had deceived him? Harry because he had wanted Bolingbroke to be king? His mind had chased through the labyrinth of excuse and vindication a thousand times but it always came back to the same impasse. It was he who had brought Richard out of Conway, it was he who had handed him over to Bolingbroke and death.

Perhaps now his conscience was a little eased. There was some relief in the prospect of revenge. Richard would be avenged. Nothing would bring him back but at least they would not have to suffer the constant reminder of his murder. That was the only reason he had allowed it to happen. Rebellion did not mean the same to him as it did to Harry. He was past all thought of gain or glory now. He'd had all that he'd ever wanted. He still had the north, perhaps that was all he had ever really wanted. All else was transient. Nothing endured or ever stayed the same. Except the land; Northumberland would always be there long after he was gone.

He blinked his eyes. They had grown dry and painful with staring. Slowly he went back to the bed and pulled the furs over him. It was the middle of July but he was still cold. He looked round at the walls of the high stone chamber, a bare impersonal room that said nothing of all the men who had once governed Berwick in his name. He remembered most of them: old Ralph Neville had been governor once in his father's time and then there had been that drunken fool Boynton. Young Ralph Neville had had it briefly before he had become Westmorland. He smiled a cold tight little smile. That would be the settling of another old score. Of all the lords who had lent their name to the rebellion, Neville had not been one of them. He was the King's man still; he was wise enough to know when he was well off. They had lost George Dunbar, to the relief of all. The continued presence of young Douglas had sent him quickly south to join the King. Hal had given Douglas an easier choice. This was not his fight, he had nothing to gain from their victory and everything to gain from their defeat. He had offered Douglas his freedom and it had been one of the brighter moments of the last few months when he had refused it.

'I'll stay and fight with you,' Archie Douglas had said. 'My father would have wished it.'

He was with Harry now en route for Chester. Hal wondered, if the Douglas had been alive, would he have seen the irony of it? Percy and Douglas together (what else could Percy and Douglas ever be?). He closed his eyes and lay back on the hard bolster. Where was Harry now? The last he had heard he was nearing Bolton. He should have reached Shrewsbury at least by tomorrow. His brother Tom was with him as a curb on his rashness. Tom's desertion of Bolingbroke had been both joy and surprise—and he with his nest so well feathered. All those years of assiduous attendance given up for no better reason than that he could not bring himself to fight against his own brother. To Hal it was the best of reasons. The loyalty of blood was still the strongest. It was a good omen too. Tom was always on the winning side.

His eyes flew open as a spasm of pain lanced through his chest. The corners of the chamber were still plunged in shadow but there was light showing at the high windows. It was almost dawn.

They rode out at first light and took the road south to Newcastle. Hal sat his horse stiffly, his mind and body numb from the potion that his physician had given him to dull the terrible ache in his chest. He watched the great column roll out from Berwick, narrowing to almost single file as they crossed the bridge over the Tweed, then fanning out again to block the wide Roman road. He saw the myriad colours of the banners merge into a rainbow haze, the azure lion of Northumberland, the gold of Scotland, the white hart emblem of Richard on every breast and sleeve. This was Richard's army, instrument of his revenge, and his was the hand that wielded it. That would have pleased Richard, to see Northumberland eating his words and riding as hard for him as once he had done against him. He could imagine that red mouth curving in its smug malicious smile. He smiled himself. He did not grudge Richard that. It was no more than he deserved.

The pace was slow, slower still as they reached Bamburgh and waited for the thousand men crammed inside its walls to join the great unwieldy column. He found it hard to keep his mind clear. The movement of his horse lulled him into a wakeful sleep. He thought of Margaret and of the fair at Elsdon, the day that his brother had brought him the news of Thomas's death. He glanced at the young boy who rode beside him, Thomas's son, with the poignant look of his father in the grave, steady eyes. Henry was seventeen now—the same age as he had been when he had fought his first battle at Poitiers.

They reached Warkworth by sunset. There was barely room for a third of his army within the town; the rest spilled out into the meadows and flat haughs along the river bank, and by nightfall the smoke from their cooking fires hung like a great cloud over the castle. He watched their tiny darting flames from the hill above the river. He had buried Ceolwulf down by the water's edge and he could see the mound of his grave overgrown with choking weeds and meadowsweet. It was strange how he missed that joyful whine of greeting, the feel of that great head thrust beneath his hand to wake him in the morning. Another part of his life dead and buried. His world grew smaller, narrowing to the last point of light that was Harry. He thought again of Ceolwulf, the old blind dog following desperately the last dim shadow of remembered warmth, terrified lest he should be left alone in the darkness.

He paced the narrow rounded edge of the hillside where it fell away to the darkness of the river. He'd had no news of Harry for three days though he'd sent messengers to Chester a week since. He pushed down the sudden sparking of fear. What was there to be afraid of? It had all been planned too well to go wrong now. Harry was to wait at Chester for Glen Dwr and himself. The insidious little voice of doubt whispered louder: like he had waited at Otterburn? But no. Harry had learnt his lesson from that. There was too much at stake to take risks like that. All that they had, lands, title, property, life. And Tom was there to keep him in check. He could trust Tom to see that no harm came to Harry or their cause. It was a just cause, Richard's cause. They had the promised allegiance of almost all the greater magnates; more than Bolingbroke had had when he landed at Ravenspur. With patience and caution they would be invincible. The fear came back, a physical pain across his heart. Had he forgotten that Harry possessed neither?

By nightfall the next day they had reached and passed Newcastle and were camped on the flat open ground by Tyneside. From inside the thin silk walls of his pavilion Hal listened to the sleeping drone of his army. They were almost ten thousand strong now and would be more than twice that by the time they reached the West. He felt almost jubilant. The dreadful pain had abated and he'd had no need of the physic tonight. For the first time in a week he had eaten more than wine-soaked bread. He could almost feel the strength returning and with it came confidence and optimism.

He smiled across the rim of his cup at his grandson. He had never really noticed before what fine eyes Henry had: blue, like his father's, and with the same wistful gravity. He said little but there was a comforting solidarity about him, the kind of man that you would have trusted with your life. Hal suddenly wondered how much he had lost by loving Harry so well. He allowed the boy to fill his cup again, then Henry went and smoothed the piled furs on the truckle bed.

'Will you sleep now, my lord?' he asked in his quiet emotionless voice.

Hal nodded and lay down on the low bed. Yes, he'd sleep, sleep as he'd not slept for over a week. Henry pulled the rug up over his knees. The solicitous hand brushed his in passing and he was suddenly irritated by it, as if he were an old man who needed coddling. But then to Henry he supposed he was. He smiled into the quiet blue eyes before he closed his own. Had he such a wealth of affection that he could afford to turn it away?

It seemed only minutes before the same hand shook him awake. He heard Henry's voice, the quiet even pitch disturbed by fear.

'My lord, my lord! Oh for pity's sake wake up, Grandfather!'

He opened his eyes but it was not Henry's face he saw. Thomas of Bardolf leant over him. His face was white beneath a crust of dirt and blood. He was crying.

'It's finished Hal. Oh sweet Jesus Christ, it's finished. The King was there at Shrewsbury, waiting for us. God knows how he did it. He must have marched his men till they were dead on their feet. But he was there. Oh God—' he dragged his great hand across his face, smearing the dust into grotesque streaks: 'There was no help for it. We had to fight or yield. Believe me, Hal. There was nothing else to do.' He began to cry again, his long thin mouth dragged down like a child's. 'Oh my lord, my dearest lord!' He lifted his dirty tear-streaked face. 'He's dead, my lord,' he sobbed. 'Hotspur is dead.'

Hal did not move or speak. He felt Henry's arm slide round him and cradle him like a child.

Only by keeping perfectly still could she keep the horror and grief at bay. If she closed her eyes she could still see his face, the blood springing like small red flowers round the shaft that was buried in his brow. He was dead. Her beloved Harry was dead.

She had watched him die. She had felt the wind of the flying arrow on her cheek, felt the explosion of pain in her head that had momentarily stopped her heart. She had lived every moment of that dreadful day with him. *She* still lived, God help her.

She heard the dull toneless chiming of the monastery bell; eleven o'clock. He had been dead for almost four hours. So little time to have seen so much. She wondered how many years it would take her to forget. It had been just after noon when the first vision had assailed her. Bess had brought her wine; she'd had no stomach for food these past three days. This was to be her triumph, the culmination of years of bitter scheming and set-backs. It was almost accomplished; before the year was out there would be a Mortimer on the throne of England.

She had raised the cup smilingly to her lips. She had caught sight of her mouth reflected in the dark wine-red surface. But not hers, these lips were trembling and drawn down in grief, they sobbed and wailed and cried out nameless blasphemies. She had laid down the cup sharply and spilt the wine over her hand. She had watched it trickle through her clenched fingers. In her mind it had become blood.

She had closed her eyes and seen the swan rise up from the marsh and circle the turrets of Shrewsbury. She heard the steady beat of its wings like the echo of her own heart. Below, on the Whitchurch road, the two armies were drawn up in battle order. She saw the furtive scurryings of envoys between the camps.

What was there to parley about now? More of Bolingbroke's trickery? Would Harry be fool enough to let himself be bought off now? One of them passed quite close to her. She had seen his face quite clearly. It was Northumberland's brother, Thomas.

She had strained her mind beyond the ranks of silent waiting men for Harry. She found him, faceless and anonymous in glittering steel, but she had known him. The man by his side with the great two-headed axe resting on his knees was Archie Douglas. Then the scream of the trumpets had sent a flock of nesting starlings skywards with a frantic roar of wings. Harry had raised his visor and glanced up at the sun. The roar of his voice had seemed to drown all sound except the thud of her heart. *'Avaunt en baner! Esperance en Dieu, esperance Percy!'*

She saw the banners rake the azure sky, the lions of Northumberland and Scotland and her own white lion of March. Then her mind had checked and frozen like a wounded horse. Where was Glen Dwr? Where was the dragon of Wales? Surely Harry was not fool enough to give battle without him? Then she was swept along on a surging tide of noise and movement. The thud of ironshod hooves, the clank of armour, the chafing creak of boiled and hardened leather and louder than all of them the chant of Harry's name—*'Hotspur, Hotspur!'*—louder, faster, gaining in momentum as the horses broke into a gallop.

Then there was silence as her mind shrank and retreated. She was flying above them. She saw them spread beneath her, pinpoint-small and insignificant, with nothing to tell of the pain and death she only felt in her soul. She was among them again, part of the screaming anguish, the torn and bleeding flesh and broken bone. Douglas was advancing towards her, the red silk eyepatch glaring at her like some fearsome eye. She saw Prince Harry and the Douglas hack their way to the royal standard; three from an arrow wound in his cheek. Three times she watched Harry and the Douglas hack her way to the royal standard; three times the man in the crown and gilded helm fell—but not Bolingbroke. God damn his cowardly craven soul! Bolingbroke had never risked himself. He was safe from Harry, safe and as far out of his reach as he could put himself, at the far end of the field beside Dunbar. She cursed him softly in an ancient unintelligible tongue.

She stayed close by him. He was growing tired. They had been fighting for nigh on five hours without respite. She could feel the stretched agony of his muscles, the drag of steel armour on his limbs. He was bare-headed now, his hair plastered in black serpentine coils around his face. She breathed all her strength into him, whispering endearments and encouragement into his mind. Once she heard him cry her name: *'Elizabeth! Elizabeth! Help me, Elizabeth!'*

For another hour he fought on. He had lost his horse and fought on foot beside the Douglas and his uncle Thomas. Men fell, others rose in their place, some had begun to desert, sneaking off into the marshland. She saw the arrow long before it reached him, the sharp steel barb rotating in a blur of light, the feathers at its tail quivering with vibrating air. His body had jerked only once as it plunged into his brow. There was hardly any blood.

It was growing dark. The sun had lodged in a great red ball behind the distant peaks of Wales. The swan glided slowly into her vision, the long white wings tipped with blood. She had heard its mournful anguished cry echoed a thousand times: *'Hotspur is fallen! Hotspur is dead!'*

She had not moved or spoken since.

He came down to York of his own free will, riding the tall Spanish horse that made him look so formidable. The people watched him with a kind of breathless reverence; he looked so proud, so unassailable, yet in his heart he was like a child.

He knew it all now. The long bloody hours of Shrewsbury, Harry's death. His army had broken and fallen away after Harry had died. He knew the numbers of the dead, the names, the faces, edged in fire in that inexorable memory of his. They said that Bolingbroke had wept over Harry's body. If he had, then his grief had been short-lived. The next morning he had torn Harry's body out of the simple grave in the chapel at Whitchurch where Neville's youngest son Thomas had buried him. He'd had the bruised and bleeding body rubbed in salt and exposed between two millstones in the marketplace at Shrewsbury. His Harry, his beloved Harry, made a spectacle for scum to come and gawp at! A week later the head had been hacked off and the body quartered, the mutilated limbs distributed between Newcastle, London, Bristol and Chester. The head had been sent to York. It watched him now from the bar above Micklegate.

His brother Thomas was dead—taken and beheaded on the field. Douglas was barely alive and Henry's prisoner. Bardolf had told him that before Shrewsbury the King had asked for peace and Tom had refused it, unbeknown to Harry. He could understand that. It would have been too late for Tom to turn back then. He doubted if it would have made any difference even if Harry had known. Elizabeth and Bess and little Hal were Bolingbroke's prisoners, dragged from sanctuary and taken to Westminster a week ago. Only he was left—and there was the dreadful irony of it. Of all of them he should have been the one to die. But perhaps there was more justice in his staying alive than he knew. There would be no quick easy death for him. His suffering would be a dreadful lingering thing. The candles were doused now. He was alone in the darkness.

It was a miracle that he was still free. After Shrewsbury he had given up all hope. Even the news that Neville and the royal army were advancing on him had not been able to stir him from the paralysis of grief. Bardolf and young Henry had been all his strength on that long ride back to Newcastle, then on to Warkworth where Bolingbroke's summons to yield himself up had come. He had torn it into shreds. He would sooner have died. Then he had heard that Bolingbroke held young Hal hostage— Harry's son, all that was left of him. There had been a glimmer of light in the darkness. It was why he was here now.

He dismounted a little way off from the gates. He could see the King framed in the arch of the gateway, enthroned on a gilded chair and crowned. 'Still King!' the pose shouted at him. 'Still King—despite you!' He walked on through the crowds that pressed so close to him. He could feel their avid breath like a warm wind on his face. A woman was weeping and several of the men whispered a furtive 'God bless you my lord!' Deliberately he paused before the gate and forced himself to look up. He knew what he would see. He had seen it a thousand times in his dreams, but the reality still slowed his heart and dragged the breath from his body. The eyes had gone. Margaret's eyes, pecked clean and red by the crows who shrieked and flapped round the walls. A trickle of blood had dried and hardened on the rotted cheek—tears of blood, yet there were none left to weep for now. Only him and Elizabeth and the boy. The wind blew softly and stirred the dark curls and he felt the tears well up inside him. Sweet Jesu, how he had loved him.

He dropped his eyes slowly and looked to where the King sat. He saw that the brow beneath the circlet of gold was beaded with sweat. Yes—sweat, you foul, murdering bastard, he thought; I'll see you sweat blood before I forgive you for this. He smiled and began to walk slowly towards him.

Henry's hands clenched on the arms of the velvet chair as he watched Northumberland advance. Tall and erect as a man half his age, it was only when he came close that he could see how the grief had marked him. There was hardly an ounce of flesh on him. The high arrogant bones of his face showed white beneath the taut bronzed skin—a death's head, in which only the eyes were alive. He met them steadily and prayed that the sickly lurching of his heart did not betray him to those eyes, the cold pitiless yellow eyes of a hawk.

The death's head stooped and he felt the hard mouth brush his hand.

'My liege,' Northumberland said softly.

Who else could have put such a wealth of hatred and loathing into just two words?

Henry snatched his hand away sooner than he had meant to and beckoned to the clerk who stood behind his chair. In its way this was defeat for him too. He had wanted Northumberland dead and had been denied it by a council who had more sympathy with Northumberland than they would admit. Traitors, they were all traitors. Even his own son Prince Harry was casting speculative eyes on his crown. Then he smiled up into the hated arrogant face. This would do as well, to see him stripped of all he had and his pride trampled in the dust. He wanted to see Northumberland squirm. He lowered his eyes as the clerk began to read the list of forfeiture. He was to be kept under close guard until Parliament had named a day for his trial, all his lands to be yielded up to the King's government, all his castles to be governed by Henry's officers. He was to be stripped of his office as Constable and Warden of the Marches. The east was to go to the King's son Prince John, the west to go to Ralph Neville.

'All the lands of his son, the late Henry Percy, and his brother, Thomas Percy Earl of Worcester, to be sequestered to the Crown. . . .' The clerk paused. 'By order of the most blessed prince, Henry, King of England and France, Duke of Lancaster and Aquitaine, Lord of Ireland.'

The King kept his eyes cast down a moment longer then he raised them in triumph. He opened his mouth to speak but the words stuck in his throat.

Northumberland was smiling at Henry's hesitation. 'Is there more, Your Grace?' he asked. Then he leant close and spoke so softly that only Henry heard him. 'Has Your Grace looked under the beds?'

Henry drew back as if he had been struck. 'Take him,' he said, and saw Northumberland's smile widen at the tremor in his voice. Beneath his robe the raw itching skin burned beneath a film of sweat. He was still not safe. He would never be safe while Northumberland was alive.

1403–1409

'The raven wys, the crow with vois of care'

—Chaucer

The river mist had cleared enough for him to see across to Coldstream. He could see the low huddle of roofs and the sharp intrusion of the church spire; the high crag of moorland with the road to Branxton and Ford curling at its feet. Beyond that all was shadow and mist—he had known for a long time now that he was going blind.

Not that he needed eyes. He knew every stone and blade of grass, every ridge and curve of hills. His memory went far beyond the field of his vision—Alnwick, Bamburgh, Warkworth—all forbidden to him now. He was no longer Northumberland. He was Henry Percy, rebel, fugitive and outlaw and had been these past three years since that last futile rebellion that had cost Archbishop Scrope his life and him Northumberland. Three years of running and hiding, three years that had not even touched the edge of his grief and heartache. It was nearly five since Harry had died. Was it so long? Sometimes it only seemed like yesterday, sometimes it seemed a lifetime ago.

They had taken him to Pontefract after his submission at York where he had been formally deprived of his castles and lands. The shrewd little queen, Joanna of Navarre, whom Bolingbroke had married for a fabulous dowry that had never materialized, had had the lion's share. The King's son John of Bedford had had Northumberland but Ralph Neville had not been forgotten.

Bolingbroke had seemed to take a particular pleasure in bestowing Harry's lands on him. Perhaps they had thought that he still cared.

After Pontefract he had been imprisoned at Baginton for almost a year. Even that in its way had been welcome. It had given him time for the wounds to heal, outwardly at least. Inside he had been as raw and bleeding as ever. When they had torn Harry out of his grave they had torn Hal's heart out with him. He still slept and woke with the terrible image of his son's severed head before him. It had been six months before Bolingbroke had given consent for it to be taken down, and all through the time of his confinement he had tortured himself, almost pleasurably, with a vision of its decay. Was the flesh gone yet? Did the once sleek curls still move in the wind; did those red weeping sockets still stare unseeingly north? Mercifully he had never known. By the time he was released Elizabeth had taken what was left of him to be buried in York Minster.

Poor Elizabeth. Poor defeated Elizabeth. If he had felt pity for any it was her. He knew her pain and grief. It was the only thing that they had ever held in common, that and the boy Hal. He'd had news of neither during his imprisonment. When he had come to Westminster to stand trial in September she was already wed to Bolingbroke's henchman, Thomas Camoys. What agony that must have been for her after Harry. He had seen her only once, a pale wraithlike creature who moved with the slow, dragging tread of a sleepwalker. She might have been dead herself if it had not been for the madness of her eyes. Elizabeth would not forget. Harry might be dead and scattered to the four corners of England but he still held all their hearts. Neither Hal nor Elizabeth would ever forgive or forget. He had not even contemplated revenge then, not while Bolingbroke held the boy. Revenge had seemed so futile, an indulgence of his tortured heart, and he had not even been a free man then.

His trial had lasted a week. He had come prepared for the worst. He was not afraid of death; in some ways he had longed for it. The body was only a shell; it was the heart and soul that gave a man life, and he was already dead, his heart and soul buried in York Minster. But he had still been enough alive to feel

404

pride in the love of the people. They had turned out in their thousands to watch him enter London. To see him fall? He had thought so till he had seen their faces and heard the roar of their voices: '*Northumberland, Northumberland, Northumberland!*' He had forgotten that the memory of the man they had loved so well was incarnate in himself.

'Northumberland.' He breathed the name to himself, his voice hoarse with memory. He was not Northumberland now. But he had been then. He had ridden back the same way, a free man. Despite King Henry Bolingbroke, despite the bribes and threats put out to ensure his death, Parliament had judged him not guilty of treason. He had still led his charmed and seemingly immortal life. Death was not ready for him yet.

He had spent that first night of freedom in the house in Aldersgate Street. The Queen's men had already stripped it bare of valuables, the rats and thieves had done the rest. He had walked from empty room to empty room. Not empty for him, his mind had filled the rooms with memories: Margaret, Harry, Thomas and Ralph, little Meg and the baby who had died; Maud and his brother Tom; his father; the cold, barely remembered beauty of his mother. All dead now, all together in paradise. He had wept like a child at being left behind.

The next day he had left for the north. Bardolf and his grandson Henry had been waiting for him at St Albans and had ridden the rest of the way with him. He had hardly been able to believe it. He was free and, more important, Parliament had granted him custody of Harry's son.

He smiled and drew his cloak a little closer against the wind. Had Bolingbroke really believed that he would go home to die so quietly? He remembered the multitude of oaths he had had to swear. Bolingbroke of all men should have known how easily they could be broken; he should have known that Hal would have sworn away his very soul to get Harry's son back. He should have known that Hal would not keep the peace for long.

He stood for a little while longer, watching the last of the winter day drain out of the sky. He was tempted to cross by the ford and climb Yeavering Bell. He could see all of Northumberland from there. Once before, a long time ago, he had ridden down as far as Alnwick and almost been captured by John of Bedford's men. He sometimes forgot that there was a price on his head: *Dead or alive—Henry Percy, late Earl of Northumberland.* He turned back towards Scotland. It would be dark soon. He smiled wryly to himself; he would have to get used to the dark.

He rode at a leisurely pace. He was in no hurry to get back to Albany's grudging charity. That he suffered it at all was only for young Hal's sake. Then there was always the uncomfortable thought that Albany might be tempted to exchange both him and the boy for his own son who was still Bolingbroke's prisoner in England. He'd had to grow used to charity—Scots, French, Welsh, it did not matter whose now; the erosion of his pride had been so gradual that he had hardly noticed it. Three years was a long time to be a fugitive.

Looking back, it was hard to believe that they had failed. All had been so right, so carefully planned. Bolingbroke had been at his weakest; Glen Dwr had never ceased to harry the Marches and, with Edmund Mortimer, was virtual master of Wales. The Duke of York's and his sister's attempt to release the young Earl of March and his brother from their captivity at Windsor had failed, but it had been enough to stir old memories, to remind men that there was another choice to Henry Bolingbroke for king. They had even had the blessing of the Church in Archbishop Scrope. Poor martyred Scrope. It was said that after Scrope's death Bolingbroke had been struck with leprosy. Glen Dwr had made the first move. It had been July—two years, all but a day, since Harry had died. The pain was always worse then, the old hatred and grief come dangerously near to the surface. He had been ripe for revenge.

He had met with Glen Dwr at Sychart. The old magician had not changed. He still kept the wild primitive state of an old Viking chieftain, surrounded by his bards and his harps and his magical Welsh music. He still believed that he could turn water into wine, defeat into victory. Edmund had been there, a changed, harder Edmund since his marriage to Cathryn Glen Dwr. Hal was reminded vividly of Elizabeth again. Edmund had asked after her and he had been surprised that her brother had not had word from her. He could tell him little; he had not seen her since the day of his trial. He had not wanted to see her. All he knew was that she was still kept closely on Camoys's Sussex manor, alone now, since Bess had married young John Clifford. There had been a few brief impassioned letters asking after her son. He had answered them carefully and formally: the boy was well, growing strong, learning his letters. They had never spoken of Harry.

And so for the third time Hal had lent his name to rebellion. They had timed it well: Bolingbroke was at his lowest ebb, Parliament grumbling and unco-operative at crippling taxes and a still empty treasury, the lords casting jaundiced eyes on his Welsh defeats and penny-pinching Court. But it was in the north that the real discontent seethed. The north had not forgotten Hotspur; they had not forgotten him. It still held. In the north there was no king but a Percy.

It had been a holy cause, blessed by God. He had needed something more than the cold hard fact of his revenge, and Archbishop Scrope had given it the semblance of a crusade. Hal had listened to him preach outside York Minster, against Henry's usurpation, against his misgovernment and the terrible burdens he laid on the people, against his oppression of the clergy. He had been a wonderful sight, in full gleaming armour beneath the banner of Five Wounds, his army of priests and dalesmen armoured with swords and staves at his back. Eight thousand men in all. He'd listened and felt nothing but an awful gnawing ache in his belly. He wondered what Scrope would have said if he'd told him that he could not care twopence for Henry's oppression and misgovernment. He only cared about Harry and the pitiful shattered body that lay behind him in York Minster.

He had prayed all night over his grave. Harry, Harry, dear beloved Harry. Did you die swiftly, did you feel pain? Believe me, Harry, the pain of living is worse. Did you know that you had lost, that we had all lost? That would have been a worse agony for you wouldn't it? But soon, Harry, soon you'll be avenged. We'll all be avenged. You and I and Elizabeth. He closed his eyes against the hot bitter tears. Sweet Mary, Mother of Christ! Give him strength. Let him have the victory this time, for Harry's sake, for the boy Hal's sake—for Richard. Dear God, don't let it all have been for nothing.

But it *had* been for nothing and he'd not even had the satisfaction of honourable defeat in battle. There had been no blood shed save Scrope's and he'd almost envied him that terrible pain of death.

They were to have mustered at his castle of Topcliffe on St William's Day. Scrope had gone on ahead with his priestly army and camped at Shipton Moor, six miles from York. He had been sixty miles away at Durham when Ralph Neville and the King's son Bedford had reached York. And that was the pity of it, the terrible wasteful pity of it: Scrope could have won; Neville had only a quarter of his strength. He could have routed him without effort and carried the day. But he had forgotten that Scrope was essentially a gentle man. His cause had been good governance, not revenge.

For three days the armies had faced each other; Neville unwilling to attack and knowing defeat to be certain if he did; Scrope allowing the priest in him to be swayed by Neville's promises of justice and redress. They had met and taken wine together in amity. Hal could imagine Neville; jovial, conciliatory, smiling his courteous smile till he had persuaded Scrope to disband his army. And poor Scrope: how jubilant he must have been to think that he had brought all to rights without bloodshed. He would not have been so joyful if he had known that within the hour Neville would have arrested him, that within the week Bolingbroke would have condemned him to death.

Hal had not seen Scrope die but he had heard. It had become a legend, told over and over to the pilgrims who flocked to his tomb in the Minster. He was called Saint Richard Scrope now—the martyr of Christ, the glory of York. He had died bravely. At dawn he had been led from his palace at Bishopsthorpe, cloaked and hooded in scarlet, mounted on the bare-backed collier's horse that they had forced him to ride. He had sung the '*Exaudi*' as they led him to the block; he had even jested with the King's physician that at least he would not have to suffer his vile potions any longer. He had asked the headsman to sever his neck in five blows in honour of the five sacred wounds of Christ. Only at the last fall of the axe did he cry out. Hal had wept when he had heard—for Scrope, for Harry, for all his fallen dreams, for the end of hope. He had wept easily in those days.

The King's summons had come a week later, demanding his submission at York. Hal had stared at Bolingbroke's seal, as he had stared at it two years before; the same brief wording, the same uniform clerkly script, even the same stripling courier standing watching him with smug complacence. He had remembered that long solitary ride two years before; Harry's head upon Micklegate, Bolingbroke in a sweat of fear and triumph, and himself smiling above the pain and anguish of his heart. This time he had not gone. With Bardolf and his grandson Henry and the boy Hal he had fled to Scotland. Since then he had known neither peace nor rest. From Scotland he and Bardolf had fled to Wales and Glen Dwr. As at Shrewsbury the promised Welsh army had failed to appear. He had listened to the Welshman's excuses with grim humour; as the Welsh awaited the coming of Arthur, so he had waited for Glen Dwr. Then on to France and the squalid court of the mad King Charles, then back again to Wales—always running, hiding, the price on his head great enough to tempt all but the very wealthy and even they were not above betrayal. There was always a hostage kinsman held somewhere who could be exchanged for him. The King would have emptied the Tower to have him captive.

The King. It was a long time since Hal had thought of Henry Bolingbroke as king, yet it seemed useless to deny it to him now. Richard was just a memory, a ghost that only lived in the minds of old men like him. There were a few who still believed he was alive, living as a fugitive in Scotland. But he knew that Richard was dead. There was no Richard of Bordeaux here. He had come back to Scotland at the beginning of this last year, the old blind hound come home to die, or as near home as he could get to it. He was sixty-five years old now.

Bardolf was waiting for him, standing in the doorway of the small hunting lodge that Albany had graciously loaned them.

'For God's sake, my lord.' Bardolf's huge face was puckered with anxiety. 'Where have you been? We've had all but the scullions out looking for you.'

409

Hal smiled. Bardolf sometimes treated him like a wayward child and though he rarely showed it he was grateful for the rough affection. Bardolf and young Hal were all he had left now. He'd sent Henry and his young wife home a long time ago. There were too many already who had suffered because of him.

The boy was sitting by the fire, whittling a length of wood. He was twelve years old now, tall for his age, with pale silver-gilt hair. Sometimes Hal would search his face for a look of Harry and find none—till he smiled. It was in the smile, the easy charm, the quick volatile temper. It was even harder for the boy to bear captivity and poverty.

They ate the simple meal in silence, fresh meat and bread, a wedge of cheese and a pitcher of the bitter Scottish ale. It satisfied Hal well enough. He had eaten worse in the last three years: pigswill and turnips, and sometimes he and Bardolf had had nothing for days. The boy never went without, Hal saw to that. If he starved himself he saw that Harry's son never had a hungry day.

He was watching him now with green expectant eyes. Hal glanced at Bardolf, who was picking crumbs of cheese absently from his plate. Then Bardolf said, 'Rokeby came today.'

'Thomas Rokeby, Sheriff of York?' He knew Rokeby well enough. He had fought under Hal in the old days in France and with Harry at Shrewsbury. 'What did he want?' he added cautiously.

'There's to be a rising at York. They want you to lead it.'

Hal looked down at his hands holding the jug of ale to cover the thudding of his heart. 'And who are "they"?'

'Clifford, Henry Scrope, most of the northern lords. Rokeby says that some will not declare themselves till they have your support.'

'And what use have they for me, a broken, beaten old man?'

'You are still Northumberland. You could still bring out the north,' Bardolf answered him quietly.

Hal rose stiffly from the table. Yes, he was still Northumberland. In his heart he would always be Northumberland.

Then Bardolf caught at his arm. 'What have we got to lose, Hal? This—' He swept his arm round the small bare hall. 'This and the rest of our lives living on handouts? We might be able to bear it Hal, but the boy can't. He can't live all his life like this. For his sake we should at least try.'

Hal shook his head. He was tired of trying, tired of failing, tired of even living. 'I don't know,' he said abruptly. 'I must think, I must think. I'm tired now.'

He lay staring up at the low smoke-stained ceiling. His eyes grew worse at night and all he could see were shadows and the hazy burst of light on the wall that was the cresset's flame. His ears had grown sharper. He could hear the scratching of rats in the walls despite Bardolf's lusty snore, the shifting of dead wood in the smouldering fire, the flurry of scattered ash. He heard the boy's soft footsteps as soon as he left the bed. Not until he was close enough to touch did he become more than a blur of light and shadow. Hal stretched out a hand and touched his cheek.

'What is it?'

'Will you go, Grandfather?'

'Do you want me to?'

The boy lowered his bright gaze. 'I don't want you to leave me.'

Hal pulled him down onto the bed. 'If I stayed it would only be for a while,' he said gently. 'I shall have to leave you one day. I am an old man now.' He stared with his tired eyes at the young handsome face. It could have been himself fifty years ago except there had never been that quiet sadness in his eyes, that desperate look of uncertainty. Hal had been Mary Plantagenet's indulged and pampered son; he had never known the meaning of the word uncertainty until now.

'If you do go, will you take me with you?' the boy said gravely.

'I cannot.' He ruffled the pale soft hair. 'I dare not.'

'Why not? My father fought at Berwick when he was fifteen. I am not that much younger.'

'But your father was not a fugitive. He had only the sharp edge of a Scotsman's blade to fear. There are other things for you to be afraid of.'

'I am not afraid,' the boy said.

'Then you should be,' Hal said sharply. 'Only halfwits and martyrs are never afraid. Fear will keep you alive.'

'My father was never afraid.'

'Oh he was, Hal, he was. That is the difference between cowards and heroes. A coward is afraid and knows it. A hero is

411

afraid and never knows it. Your father was not like other men only in that if he was afraid he never knew it, and if he did he never showed it. That's the secret. Never show it, Hal. Whatever you feel inside, never show it, not to all the world anyway.' He took the boy's hand; the fingers were long and well shaped, the palms soft and uncalloused. He remembered Harry's hands at that age, hard and sinewed from hours in the tilt yard. But then Harry had never done anything by halves; he had always had to excel in everything.

Hal looked up into the quiet eyes. He'd never really thought of the boy as anything but an extension of Harry. Harry's son—never Elizabeth's son or his grandson, only Harry's son. He was more than that; he was half a Mortimer and first cousin to the rightful heir to the throne. He was heir to Northumberland. Would a child with that heritage be content to be an exile all his life? But that was all he'd ever be while Hal was alive; he himself was the stumbling block. There would be no pardon or forgiveness for the boy while he lived. Bolingbroke could not last forever any more than he could; there might be hope for the boy then, whether it was Mortimer's son or Bolingbroke's who was king after him. But in the meantime Bardolf was right. He would have to try. He held out little hope of victory. Bolingbroke was too deeply entrenched to be brought down now. But—win or lose—for the boy's sake, he had to try.

'You must go to the Bishop at St Andrews,' he told him. 'He is a good man and will care for you better than I can.'

'He'll turn me into a priest.'

Hal laughed. 'No, you'll never make a priest, Hal. The Percys are not known for celibacy.' Then, more gravely, he said, 'You will be Earl of Northumberland one day, Hal. Always think that, however badly it goes. Never forget that Northumberland is yours. Take it if it is offered to you, whoever gives it.'

'Even if it is Bolingbroke, the man who killed my father?'

Hal raised his hand to his cheek. 'You must not make his quarrel yours, nor mine. What's done is done. Accept what you cannot change.'

'Then why are you going to York?'

'I have not said yet that I will, but if I do it's because I have to,

Hal. Because my life is almost finished and yours is only beginning. It is the only way I know.'

Hal suddenly flung himself against him. 'Don't go, Grandfather, don't go! Stay with me. I don't want to be alone.'

Hal straightened the soft, curling hair. 'In the end we are always alone, Hal,' he said quietly. 'Others come and go and perhaps for a while they warm the cold out of our lives. But in the end we are always alone. The one person in all the world you can never escape from is yourself.'

He held the boy tightly against him, all that part of him that was Margaret, that was Harry, that was himself. All his life and love come down to this one small boy.

He crossed the Border at midnight with no more than five hundred men at his back. The wind was cold and sharp, and snow still lingered on the high ground and capped the peak of the Cheviot. There was a new moon, a luminous silver crescent riding high in a cloudless sky. A good omen, Bardolf said. Hal had given him a grim smile. They would need all the luck they could get.

They kept to the open country, riding the spine of moorland that ran unbroken to the Tyne. The hills passed in a blur of shadow and sound; the sudden flurry of grazing cattle veering from their path, the startled flight of night creatures in the woods. He heard the harsh baying call of a wolf from Redesdale forest. He thought of old Umfraville. Ralph Neville had Redesdale now. They passed within five miles of Alnwick and he could not resist a last look. From the brow of the hill it looked small and unreal. He saw it only as a shadow among shadows, but memory served him better than his eyes; the unique half-moon towers of the keep rising clear above the walls, the town crouching on the flat ground at its back. It was unchanged, save that John of Bedford's banner flew the keep instead of his.

He rode on, self-contained within his own world, an old man's world of memory. That was all there was left now. There was no future; the present was a meaningless empty void, only the past was bearable. There were no shocks or surprises in what had gone.

Once past Durham they halted. It was almost dawn, though in

the forest the darkness covered them a little longer. He lay down on the cloak that Bardolf had spread for him and closed his eyes. He thought of young Hal. He had sent him to the Bishop a week before. He had cried, the angry unwilling tears of a boy who had thought he was a man. Hal smiled quietly to himself. By the time he was it would all be finished. He turned on his back and looked up. The tall skeletal trees engulfed him in twilight but here and there he could see a patch of pale sky. It would be spring soon, the beginning of new life—the end of his? The thought did not disturb him. He did not believe in death now. He would live on in the boy Hal as Harry did. While there were Percies he would never die. He closed his eyes. He would sleep a while. He was tired now.

They reached the outskirts of York the next day. The five hundred had become a thousand and they were still coming in—and the joy of it was that it was because of him. Not the glittering army that Rokeby had promised, but ordinary men, men who had once tilled his fields and gathered his corn, old gnarled bowmen who had fought with him in the French wars. They came to stare at him, as if they needed the affirmation of the sight of him. He felt tears burn his eyes as he saw their stubborn loyalty. Did they know he was leading them to their deaths? If they did, they did not seem to care; it was enough that he was among them again.

He slept in open moorland three miles from York. It was still bitterly cold but he did not feel it so much now. It was a clear night and the slick of moonlight that crept up from the Ouse showed the spires of the Minster sharp and defined. It was good to be close to Harry again.

At first light they rode to Tadcaster and the edge of the Bramham Moor. There was nothing to see but an endless stretch of dark barren waste.

Bardolf grabbed Hal's arm. 'Where's that bastard Rokeby? He should have been here by now.'

'Oh, he'll come,' Hal said, and suddenly gave his twisted, mirthless smile. 'He'll come all right.' He turned and looked at Bardolf. 'Can't you see?' he said. 'It's a trap. How else do you think we could have ridden as far as York unchallenged?' He waited out the next few minutes in silence, straining his ears to catch the distant drumming hoofbeats that only he could hear. Then he looked up and smiled again. The first of the horsemen were coming over the hill. He saw Ralph Neville's banner, brilliant as blood against the metallic February sky.

'You see,' he said softly, 'I knew he would come.'

Then sharply he said, 'Turn the men, tell them to go home. It's me they've come for. There is no need for us all to die.'

Bardolf stared at the oncoming army and then at him. '*You* tell them,' he said and grinned. 'We'll go down together, Hal. There's nowhere else for me to go either.'

Hal turned to the men who stood ranked behind him. 'Go home!' he shouted. 'There is no hope. Rokeby has betrayed us. These are the King's men.'

He saw the ranks break into disorder. He could not even make himself heard above the noise. A few horsemen broke away, a few ran towards the cover of the sparse woodland, but unbelievably the rest came together and held. Silent and stubborn, they stared up at him. Then one of them came forward, a squat and wizened little man in a torn and patched jerkin.

'While you stay, we will stay, my lord.'

What better accolade could he have had, Hal thought, turning back to the sight of the advancing royal army. They were barely a bowshot's length away but all he could see was a blur of bright steel. He nodded to Bardolf. 'For the last time,' he whispered. Then he raised his voice so that it rang like a clarion across the field. '*For God, for Hotspur, for Northumberland!*'

He felt no pain when he was wounded in the first few minutes of the assault. He saw and heard nothing but his own inner voice—it is good, it is well done, both pain and guilt expiated in blood. There were faces mirrored in the heaving steel-clad bodies, Harry's, the boy Hal's, but more often Elizabeth's; Elizabeth smiling, urging him on. 'For Harry,' she whispered. 'For Harry and our son.'

He brought his sword down hard across the upturned face of the fallen horseman. He heard her soft laugh and almost turned his head to see if she stood beside him. It was then that the axe struck him full in the chest. He fell, limp as a doll, and was caught and tossed beneath the hooves of his own horse. He felt a great hand fasten in his belt and haul him clear.

'Up, up, my lord!' Bardolf yelled. 'The toll is not completed yet.'

He fought on, oblivious to the pain and shock of his bruised and bleeding body. Bardolf was still beside him, swinging his great two-handed axe like a reaper, laughing grimly as he sliced a man in half like a cheese. He had felled another ten men before he died. There was not time to mourn even for Bardolf. The shadows were closing in on him. He could hardly raise his sword arm now. Then he was on his knees, his fingers clawing at the soft bloody earth as he tried to push himself to his feet. Blood pumped from the wounds in his chest and back, his left arm was almost severed. He was only half a man now, but still he lived. Sweet Jesus Christ—where was the kind hand to put him from his pain? Then he saw the prancing hooves come close. He saw the dangling sword dripping with blood. Slowly he lifted his eyes. He would not die like a dog with his head down.

The curtained litter paused before London Bridge and a slim black figure emerged for an instant and looked up. There was nothing left of him now, only the stark splendour of bone, the faint remembrance of that proud and splendid head—all that was left of Northumberland.

Elizabeth looked away and smiled the evil little smile that made her husband Thomas's flesh crawl. She had wept when she heard that Northumberland was dead, not out of pity or grief but because the last of her hope had died with him. Edmund was dead too, starved to death in the victorious English siege of Harlech. Only she was left, alone, solitary, but still alive. She had learnt to live again since then. Her son was alive, too, and safe in Scotland; he would soon be a man. She would be able to begin again then.

She looked once more at the bleached white skull. 'Rest easy, old man,' she whispered. 'It's not finished yet.'

She climbed back into the litter and told the groom to move on. The flight of sleek crows that had watched her in sinister silence from the bridge rose suddenly and screeched above her head.